Ashley
& Jen

Ashley
& Jen

JACK WEYLAND

BOOKCRAFT

Library of Congress Catalog Card Number: 00-056425

ISBN 1-57345-803-1

Printed in the United States of America   42316-6691

10   9   8   7   6   5   4   3   2   1

*In grateful acknowledgment
to the three young women who assisted me
with this book, as well as to Dr. Michael Berrett
for helping me understand the role of therapy in
eating disorder recovery.*

1

Even as Ashley Bailey threw the smoldering pan of burned stew at Jennifer Hobbs, she thought, *This is crazy–I don't do things like this.* Then, because she felt bad for losing her temper, she began to plan how she'd apologize. Maybe a flower-bordered note to Sister Ross, the girls camp director. The note would begin, *I'm so sorry. I just don't know what got into me.*

It was no mystery to anyone else though what had set Ashley off. Jennifer, or Jen, as she now demanded everyone call her, had been horrible to everyone. She verbally abused the younger girls, grumbled whenever she was asked to help, and often talked back to the leaders.

Not that Ashley's throwing the pan did any real damage; it missed Jen by at least two feet. And besides, the stew was burned anyway, so that was no great loss, either.

The entire incident might have been forgotten, except for the fact that everyone had seen it. And, also, because, just minutes before, Sister Ross had given another of her "Let's all try to get along with each other" pep talks. With it had come a warning to those who couldn't get along– they would spend the night separated from the rest of the girls at an isolated campsite about a quarter-mile away.

Even though Sister Ross sympathized with Ashley, she couldn't let what she'd done go unpunished. She did feel bad, though, that Ashley was the one who had finally cracked under Jen's reign of terror.

Ashley had never been in trouble before. With her bouncy, blonde hair, blue eyes, perky smile, and cooperative attitude, she was every adult's ideal youth.

Jen was another story. For the previous two years, she had been less than enthusiastic about church, but now her attitude was really bad. She seldom came to Young Women activities anymore, and almost never to church. The girls reported that at school she was running with a group of renegades known as the cowboys.

In the two days they'd been at camp, Jen had made more enemies than friends. She seemed to take delight in hurting the other girls' feelings.

How can I put Ashley alone with Jen overnight? Sister Ross thought, followed by an equally disturbing thought. *But if I don't and lose control, who knows where it will end? I have to act now.*

"All right, that's it!" Sister Ross announced. "We can't have this kind of dissension in camp. I'm sending the two of you to the Lone Wolf campsite. Maybe you can learn how to get along together up there all by yourselves."

"Go ahead and do it, but don't be surprised if you find her in the morning lying in a pool of blood," Jen warned.

Sister Ross felt the eyes of all the girls in camp on her. She took a deep breath. "Let me talk to each of you separately," she said.

Sister Ross and Ashley took a walk out of camp. "Ashley, tell me what happened."

Ashley was still upset—on the verge of tears. "Jen burned the stew on purpose," she said, her voice trembling.

"Are you sure?"

"I'm sure. I kept telling her to take it out of the fire, but she wouldn't do it."

"Why would she burn the stew?"

"To pay us back for telling her we were tired of doing all the work while she sat around and did nothing." Ashley was thinking more about how badly she had behaved than she was about Jen's problems.

"Is she friends with anyone in camp?" Sister Ross asked.

"No. Everyone here hates her."

"Well, can you stand to be with her for one night?"

"Do I have to?"

"I would appreciate it so much if you'd try—for the sake of girls camp . . . and as a personal favor to me." Sister Ross knew it was unfair to ask it that way, but she was desperate.

Ashley didn't want to do it. Feeling the way she did, the thought of being alone with Jen was almost more than she could stand. She walked in silence for almost a minute before finally shrugging her shoulders, sighing, taking a deep breath, and saying, "All right."

Sister Ross patted her on the back. "I knew I could count on you."

"Yes, of course," Ashley said quietly.

A short time later Sister Ross walked the same path with Jen. "You're not very happy here, are you?"

"Duh, what was your first clue?" Jen shot back.

"You don't have to take that tone of voice with me."

"It's the only tone of voice I've got, Lady."

"How unfortunate." Sister Ross was struggling to control her temper. As much as she hated to admit it, Jen's attitude had also gotten under her skin.

Jen was a remarkably pretty girl. Her dark, thick eyebrows could have added to her beauty but now only served to accentuate her perpetual scowl. Since March, she had worn her dark brown hair cut razor short along the sides. It was what the rebel girls at school did. Her hair was long enough on top that she could cover over the sides, and the way she wore it was a barometer of how rebellious she was feeling. Since coming to camp, she had kept the longer hair pulled back to show off the sides.

She has everything a girl could want except a good attitude, Sister Ross thought. *I wonder what she looks like when she's sleeping, without the scowl, without the muttered disapproval of what anyone in authority says, and without the cruel jokes at others' expense.*

"What happened back there?" Sister Ross asked, trying not to sound too judgmental.

"You saw it."

"Ashley's usually not the type that blows up like that."

"Oh, so you're saying it's all my fault, right?" Jen challenged.

"I didn't say that."

"No, but you were thinking it."

"You're completely blameless in all this?"

Jen smirked. "That's right. Completely."

"Ashley says you burned the stew on purpose."

Jen snickered. "Oh, that. Well, sure. I did that. So what? I mean, it's not like it's *real* food, right?"

"It's the only food we have here."

"So what are you going to do, send me to stew prison?"

Sister Ross fought off the urge to grab Jen and shake her. She took a few deep breaths. "What can we do to make you happier at camp?"

"Nothing. The only reason I came was because my mom bribed me. She promised me a shopping trip if I'd go to girls camp. I can hardly wait to get me some new halter tops and tight jeans."

Sister Ross sighed. "Sometimes you say things to shock people, don't you? That's why you mentioned the halter tops and tight jeans, isn't it? Because you knew I wouldn't approve."

"No, I said it so you'd know I couldn't care less what you think. I've had it with church and with people like you. I won't be coming to church anymore. As soon as my mom picks me up on Saturday, you won't ever see me again."

"What have we done to you here that has made you so bitter?"

"I don't belong here—we both know that. Look, let's just get this over with, okay? Send me home, okay? It was totally my fault. The truth is I was trying to get Ashley mad at me. It's not that easy though. Usually she acts like it's her fault if I'm mad. She's such a doormat. I was surprised as anyone when she hauled off and threw the pan at me."

"Jen, I need your cooperation. I told everyone what I'd do if there was any more conflict. I need to have both of you go to the Lone Wolf camp. I have to send you both."

"Put me with anyone else but her. She's such a phony. She's been like that ever since grade school. She puts up this big front like she's so much better than anybody else. I really can't stand that."

Jen and Ashley had known each other since they were little girls, living in the same neighborhood, and starting kindergarten together. When they were kids, they had played dolls and house together and had sleepovers, but when they got into middle school, they had made new friends and gone their separate ways.

"Maybe you could help her."

"Yeah, right. Like I could cut her hair so it's like mine."

Even Sister Ross smiled at the thought of Ashley with shaved sides. "I need your help, Jen. Please go along with this. It's only one night."

Jen thought about it then shrugged her shoulders. "Sure, no problem. But when I get home I'm telling everyone you're the reason I quit going to church. I got to blame somebody, right? So it might as well be you. But don't sweat it, okay? Because I was going to quit anyway. The truth is, I don't belong in church."

"I hope you'll change your mind."

"Forget it. That's not going to happen."

An hour later Ashley and Jen walked out of camp, hauling their equipment up the hill to the remote campsite. Everyone watched them go. Officially, at least for the night, they were outcasts. By the time they made it to the campsite, it was six-thirty.

"You planning on getting any sleep tonight?" Jen asked.

"Yes, why?"

"If I were you, I'd try to stay awake."

"Why?" Ashley asked.

"Because it'd be a shame to fall asleep and wake up with all your hair cut off."

"You wouldn't do that."

"Wouldn't I? Don't count on it." Jen sat with her back up against a tree, her head down, playing a video game on her Gameboy.

Ashley emptied the canvas tent bag unto the dirt. The aluminum poles clattered as they hit the ground. She was hoping that would be enough of a hint for Jen to get up and help.

"We need to set up the tent," Ashley said.

"What for?" Jen answered, not even looking up from her game.

"In case it rains."

"It's not going to rain."

"Well, then, for privacy."

"Who you worried about seeing us here? Chipmunks?"

Ashley unfolded the tent. "You're not going to help at all, are you?"

"Why should I? You're the one who wants to set up the tent, not me."

Ashley turned away and mumbled something.

Jen stood up and came at her. "Excuse me, what did you just say?"

"Nothing."

"No, you said something. Was it about me? Because if you got a problem with me, then say it to my face."

"Why? So you can get mad at me? What good would that do?"

"Let me put it this way, if you don't tell me what you said, I'm going to beat you up."

"Beat me up?"

"You heard me."

Ashley cleared her throat nervously. "This is a church camp."

"So? I can still beat you up. Tell me what you said."

"No."

Using both hands, Jen gave Ashley a shove. Although Jen wasn't any bigger than Ashley, she had a reputation as a fighter. At the beginning of the school year, Jen had gotten into a knock-down, drag-out fight with another girl in back of the school with a crowd of boys cheering them on. The fight ended with Jen tearing the girl's clothes and giving her a bloody nose. Ashley hadn't seen the fight, but everyone said the other girl ran away in tears.

Jen gave Ashley another shove. "If you know what's good for you, you'll tell me what you said. I can't stand people talking about me behind my back. If you got something to say, say it to my face."

"All I said was I can see why people talk about you at school."

"You think I care about what people say? Besides, you should hear what people say about you."

Ashley was stunned. "What do they say?" she asked.

"That the only reason you get good grades is because you're all . . . " Jen began a mean-spirited imitation of Ashley: "Oh, gosh, Mr. Anderson, you're such a good teacher. I just can't believe how much I'm learning in this class. Is there any extra credit reports I can do?" Jen glared at

Ashley and said in her own voice, "How can you do that day after day and even respect yourself?"

"I know this will be a new thought to you," Ashley replied, "but some people like to learn."

"Yeah, right," Jen scoffed, "and others just like to cozy up to their teachers."

Ashley didn't like to fight. It upset her when people got angry, and at home she was always the peacemaker. "Look," she said, "I really don't want to talk about this anymore." She turned away from Jen and reached for the tent poles. "Besides, we need to get everything set up."

"I got a flash for you, Ashley. I'm not helping you set up the tent."

"Fine, but don't blame me if it rains and you end up getting all wet," Ashley said. She pulled her journal out of her pack and sat down on the folded tent to write while Jen went back to playing her video game.

After a couple of minutes, Jen asked, "What are we going to do about food?"

"I'm not hungry," Ashley said.

"How come you're not hungry?"

"I don't know. I'm just not, that's all."

"Well, I am."

Ashley snorted. "If you hadn't burned the stew, we'd have eaten by now."

"I know that, okay?" Jen said nastily. Then after a few moments, she said more sweetly, "Why don't you cook me something to eat?"

"What! Why should I do anything for you?"

"Because you threw the pot of hot stew at me," she came back at Ashley. "If it'd hit me, I'd probably be on my way to the hospital by now."

"But you burned the stew."

"That was no reason to throw the pan at me. The way I see it, you owe me supper."

"You really think that's fair?" Ashley asked.

"I do. I tell you what—if you'll cook me something to eat, I'll forget the whole thing. I mean, I'm a reasonable person. Compare a little burnt stew with the fact that you could've killed me, and then ask yourself what the more serious offense was."

"But the pan didn't come anywhere near you."

"But it could've hit me in the head, and then where would we both be now? I'd be in the hospital in a coma, and you'd be in jail for attempted murder. I think what you did at least rates you cooking my supper."

Ashley thought about it for a moment, then nodded her head. "All right, I'll cook you supper."

Jen suppressed a smile. "I knew you'd do the right thing."

Ashley stood up. "I'm going to get some kindling now."

"Yeah, you do that," Jen said with a smirk.

"What?" Ashley asked.

"Everybody else in the world would say, 'I'm going to get some sticks to start a fire.' Not you, though, right?"

"Kindling isn't just sticks. Kindling can be dried pine needles. So if I said I was going to get sticks and ended up bringing back pine needles, then you'd probably tell me that pine needles are not sticks. Well, I know that. I know what a stick is, and I also know what kindling is, and I'm going to get some kindling now, which can be either sticks or pine needles."

Jen rolled her eyes. "Whatever. Just hurry, okay? Because I'm starving."

A few minutes later, Ashley returned, lugging an armful of wood in her arms. "I'm back."

Jen glanced up momentarily. "You were gone so long I thought maybe a bear got you. I was trying to decide what to put on your head-stone. I finally came up with: *She went out for kindling, but she never came back.*"

"Very funny."

"Thanks. I thought so, too."

While Jen lay down on her sleeping bag and took a nap, Ashley started a fire, opened a can of beans, poured them into a pan, and set the pan on the fire. She took great care to keep stirring so it wouldn't burn. She even picked out each tiny piece of ash that fell in.

When it was ready, she spooned the beans into a bowl, got some crackers, arranged them around the bowl, then called out quietly, "Jen, it's ready now."

Jen sat up and stretched, then reached for the bowl and started to eat. She ate hunched over, not talking, finished one bowl, then asked for another.

Ashley dished up another bowl for Jen, who continued eating. "How come you're not having any?"

"I'm not hungry."

Jen shrugged her shoulders. "Just leaves more for me, right?" A short time later she finished off the second bowl. "Not bad. You got any dessert?"

"No." She paused. "Well, I do have a Snickers®."

"Sounds good."

7

"I was saving it," Ashley said.

"If I was back with everyone else, I'd get dessert. Since it's all your fault we're up here, I figure you owe me dessert."

Ashley nodded, retrieved the candy bar from her backpack, and gave it to Jen.

"You want a part of this?" Jen asked. "I'd be willing to share."

"No, that's okay."

"Sure, no problem." Jen polished off the candy bar. "You did so good on supper, I was wondering, if you're not too busy, if you could wash my sweatshirt. I got it dirty yesterday when I got into a food fight. I got most of it out, but it's still pretty dirty, and the thing is, it's my favorite sweatshirt."

"Where would I wash it?" Ashley asked.

"Down at the lake."

"The lake?"

"Yeah, just dump it in the water, get it wet, then take some bar soap and rub it over the worst places and scrub it real good until it's clean. Then wring out as much water as you can, beat it against a rock to get more of the water out. Then bring it back here and put it near the fire. Of course, not too near, because you don't want to set it on fire. But not too far away because I'll need it dry by the morning. Just turn it over about every ten minutes. Could you do that for me? I'd really appreciate it."

"But it's getting dark. I don't want to go down to the lake and then have to make my way back here in the dark."

"When you're ready to come back, call me and I'll put some more wood on the fire. So then you'll be able to make it back to camp."

Ashley sighed. "Where's the sweatshirt?"

Jen shook her head and began laughing.

"What?"

"What is wrong with you, anyway? You would've washed my sweatshirt in the lake—in the dark? I can't believe how you let people walk all over you. Don't you have any self-respect? For once in your life why don't you stick up for yourself? No wonder people at school don't respect you."

Ashley was shocked. "People don't respect me?"

"Not the people I run around with. They make fun of you all the time."

"Why?"

"All school year you let Chelsea copy your homework all the time."

"Once in a while."

"Don't give me that," Jen scoffed. "You let her copy it every day. She makes a copy and gives it to Chad. From there it goes to the girls' and

8

boys' basketball teams and then to the cheerleaders and then to anyone else who wants it. As far as I can tell, you're the only one in school who actually does any homework. So now you're like the school joke. That's why people break out into big grins when you walk by. You probably thought it was because you were popular, right?"

Ashley's chin began to quiver. "Chelsea's taking advantage of me?"

"Yeah, she is—big time. Haven't you ever wondered why she ends up in all your classes? Sorry I had to be the one to tell you. Well, come to think of it, I'm not sorry. Actually, I enjoyed it."

Ashley sat down and pouted.

* * * * *

Sister Ross tried to eat something at dinner, but she wasn't hungry. She was too worried about Ashley being with Jen overnight with no adult supervision. Her mind ran wild. What if Jen went after Ashley with a knife? Or decided to do a prank that ended in tragedy? She knew she'd gone way beyond what anyone would say was reasonable. *It's going to be a long night,* she thought. *If I have to, I'll stay up there all night to make sure nothing happens to Ashley. What a dumb idea. I should never have said I'd send troublemakers to Lone Wolf campsite. What if some psychopath comes along and finds the two girls all alone? Or if a bear gets them? It could happen. And if it does, whose fault will it be? Mine. I've really messed up this time.*

She felt a comforting hand on her shoulder. It was one of the other adult leaders. They'd both been going to girls camp for ten years.

"They'll be okay," she said.

"Sure they will," Sister Ross said, not really believing it. She decided that after it turned dark, she'd sneak up and see how the two girls were doing.

* * * * *

As the darkness closed in, Ashley decided to get ready for bed. Her sleeping bag had been in the family for a long time. A few rips had been patched, and the drawstrings that used to go around it had long since pulled out. Now it was held together by two black bungee cords. Because Ashley didn't want to risk losing them, she had neatly written her name on them in white ink at one end. She undid the bungee cords. "Where should we sleep?"

"Anywhere you want," Jen said. She was sitting next to the fire, stirring the coals with a stick and then blowing out the flame when it caught fire.

"If we set up the tent, then I'd know, but the way it is now, I could put my sleeping bag in any direction."

"It doesn't matter."

"I know, but where are you going to put yours? We ought to lay them parallel."

"Sleeping bags don't have to be parallel."

"I know, but that's the way people usually have them."

"So? For once in your life, live wild and free."

"Put yours down first, okay? Please?"

"I can't believe this," Jen fumed, standing up. She grabbed her sleeping bag from next to the tree, unrolled it, and flung it to the ground. She then returned to playing in the fire with her stick.

Ashley put her bag down parallel to Jen's. "It's better if they're parallel. That way we can talk."

"We can still talk if our sleeping bags aren't parallel."

"I know, but it's better if they're parallel."

"Why?"

"I don't know. It just is. It's more like we're together."

"Parallel sleeping bags—let me guess—you did well in geometry, right?"

Ashley nodded her head. "I did all the proofs."

"The entire school thanks you for doing 'em too. We owe all our grades to you."

"But I'm the one who learned," Ashley said.

"Yeah, right—like anyone cares about that." Jen was shielding her face with her hand, probing the coals of the fire with her ever-shortening stick.

"I care about it, and my teachers do, too."

"Oh, right. And you got to make your teachers proud of you, don't you? And your folks. And your church leaders. That's what your life is all about, isn't it? Making people proud of you."

"Well, no one could accuse you of that, that's for sure," Ashley said.

"That's right, I'm my own person."

They fell silent for a few moments.

"I really think we should set up the tent," Ashley said.

Jen threw the stick into the fire and stood up. "Look, let's get a few things straight. I'm not going to help you set up the tent. Also, I don't want to tell ghost stories around the campfire, or sing songs. I especially do not want to look up at the stars and have you point out all the constellations. There, does that pretty much cover it? So just leave me alone. Or is that asking too much?"

"The way you're acting, leaving you alone will be a pleasure."

"Fine, do it then. I think I'll just relax a little." Jen pulled a cigarette out of her backpack and lit it with a glowing stick, took a drag on it, then slowly blew the smoke in Ashley's direction.

"I hope you know that isn't good for you."

"You're wrong. It's very good for me. It helps me relax." She held out the pack. "You want one?"

"No, I think it's disgusting."

"That's just because you haven't tried it."

"Excuse me. I've got work to do." Ashley spent the next half hour gathering firewood. Once she got it into the campsite, she arranged everything into three neat piles: one pile for kindling, one pile for medium-sized pieces, and one pile for larger chunks from downed trees.

Jen was the first to break the silence. "Is there any pork and beans left?"

"Yes."

"Are you going to eat it?"

"No, I'm not hungry."

"I guess I'll finish it, then."

Ashley picked up the pan. "Not after all the terrible things you said about me. There's another unopened can. So if you want more, then go get some firewood, start a fire, open the can, put it in the fire, stir it constantly, and cook it yourself."

"Why should I go to so much work? Give me the pan."

"No." Ashley picked up the pan and stepped back.

"Don't make me take it away from you. I'm a lot meaner than you are. I can easily take that pan away from you."

"Not this time." With an uncharacteristically wicked chuckle, Ashley turned and lobbed the pan high into the darkness of the night. A short time later they heard it hit the ground and clatter down the hillside.

Jen was in her face. "Are you crazy? What did you do that for?"

"Am I letting people walk all over me now, huh, am I?"

"You idiot! You just threw away our only pan!"

Ashley pursed her lips. "Oh, yeah, right." She sighed. "Well, we'll look for it in the morning."

"In the morning? What if I want to cook something now?"

"That's the least of your worries. You don't even have a fire to cook over. This is my fire." Ashley walked over to her stash of wood and started pointing to the various piles on the ground. "This is my kindling pile, and this is my medium-sized wood pile, and this is my big-sized wood pile. So if you want to make a fire, get your own kindling. Oh, excuse me, get your own *sticks*."

"Don't make me beat you up." Jen advanced, but this time Ashley didn't back away.

They stood there, toe-to-toe, glaring at each other.

"Like you could," Ashley said softly after clearing her voice nervously.

Jen blinked. "What did you say?"

"I said, like you could."

"Oh, I can. Don't worry about that. How many fights you ever been in?"

"Plenty," Ashley lied.

"You liar. You never even get angry."

"I do, too."

"When?"

"Well, one time my cousin pushed me in the lake, and when I got out I was real mad because I had an ear infection and wasn't supposed to go in the water. So I really let him have it."

"What'd you do?"

"I yelled at him."

"You *yelled* at him?"

"Yes, so his mother could hear me. I practically shouted in his ear."

"You call *that* letting somebody have it?"

"He could tell I was mad by the tone of my voice," Ashley said.

"You don't have a tone of voice. You go from sweet to sickeningly sweet."

"That's not true."

"Oh, no? Try saying something mean to me," Jen dared.

"No."

Ashley held her hands out and gave a *let me have it* gesture. "C'mon, give me your best shot."

"I don't want to say something I'll regret later on," Ashley said.

"Say something to get back at me, something really mean."

"All right! You asked for it!" She paused. "You really could spend a lot more time on personal hygiene! Like would it kill you to brush your teeth once in a while? And how come you have your hair shaved like that? What's that all about anyway?"

Jen laughed and shook her head in disgust. "That's the best you can do?"

"Yes, and now I'm sorry I said it."

Jen shoved Ashley again. "Say something to make me really mad so I can beat you up."

"You think every disagreement has to be settled with a fight? I bet you learned about fighting from those degenerates you hang around with."

"That's right," Jen said. "At least they let you know what they're thinking, so they're a lot better off than you." She shoved Ashley again.

"You can't push me around like that," Ashley said.

"Why can't I?"

"Because you just can't."

Jen pushed her again. "There, I just did it again. What are you going to do about it?"

"Why are you so mean? You never used to be like this. What happened?"

"It's none of your business what happened. Are you going to fight me or not? Because if you don't stand up for yourself, you'll get hurt a lot worse."

"There are ways we can settle this without fighting."

"Like what?"

"Well . . . we could . . . arm wrestle," Ashley said. "I can easily beat you at that."

"There's nothing you can beat me at."

"Except arm wrestling," Ashley said confidently. She poured a little water on her hands, then used her fingers to try to sweep her hair on the side back to look like Jen's shaved sides.

"What's that all about?"

"You'll find out."

Jen shrugged. "Fine, then, we'll arm wrestle."

Ashley offered to make all the arrangements. She found the stump of a tree that someone had cut down. If they knelt on the ground and faced each other, it would be perfect for arm wrestling. She cleared the ground around the stump and brushed away most of the ants that called the stump their home.

Jen, still at the campsite, screamed.

"You okay?" Ashley called out.

"I just stepped on a snake!"

"Where?"

"Over there."

Ashley went over to investigate.

"How come you're not afraid?" Jen asked.

"I've taken every life science course at school, that's why. Besides, this is the problem." She bent down and picked up one of the bungee cords from her sleeping bag. "You call this a snake?"

"You put that down there on purpose, didn't you?" Jen accused.

Ashley shook her head. "Oh, sure, it was all part of a big conspiracy." She returned to the tree stump. "Look, I've got everything ready now. We should probably bring our sleeping bags so we'll have something to kneel on."

"What for? It's not like it's going to last that long. It'll all be over in a couple of seconds."

"Don't be so sure of that. Remember one thing, I used to play the violin, so my right arm is pretty strong."

Jen went over to the tree stump. "This place is crawling with ants."

"So? I didn't see you trying to find a place."

"All right, let's just get this over with."

Ashley carefully folded her sleeping bag into thirds, placed it on the other side of the stump, and then, still standing, began to blow out air and then suck it in again with a *kaa*-sound.

"Now what are you doing?"

"Breathing exercises. Mr. Foster taught it to us in choir. Proper breathing is important for any activity—even arm wrestling."

Jen threw up her hands. "Why can't we just fight like normal people? Why does everything you do have to be such a big production?"

"I'm ready now." Ashley kneeled down. She put her right elbow on the stump.

"Finally," Jen grumbled, kneeling down and getting into position.

"Okay, now," Ashley explained, "how this works is on the count of three . . . one . . . two . . . th—" Just before she finished saying *three,* Ashley slammed Jen's arm down on the stump and jumped up to celebrate. "I won! I won!"

"You cheated! You started too early!" Jen complained.

"I started on three."

"You started on *th*!"

"The *ree* was silent. You're just a sore loser."

"Let's do it again, and this time I'll be the one who counts!"

"Sorry, but that's it. You had your chance, and you blew it. We're done fighting for the night. Face it, you lost."

Jen brought her face within inches of Ashley's face. "I'm only going to say this once. I want a rematch, and I want it *now!*"

"I know you do, but you're not going to get it because, well, to tell you the truth, I kind of hurt my arm, so I'd better not do it again."

"Something else, then."

"Well, all right, I suppose we could try leg wrestling. Have you ever done that? I used to do it with my cousin when we were kids. I was good at it, but that might be because he let me win. You want to try it?"

"Anything, as long as it will end up making you hurt all over."

"You ought to work on that attitude of yours."

Ashley and Jen returned to their camp. Ashley laid her sleeping bag so that it was parallel to Jen's. "Okay, what we do is lie down on our backs, side by side, and we go 'one, two, three,' and then we put up one leg up in the air, and we lock legs and try to dump each other over. Okay?"

"You don't have to explain every little thing to me. I'm not dumb, you know."

"I know you're not dumb. It's just that the things you do are stupid."

It was dark by now, but the fire gave them enough light to see. They both lay down, side by side. "Oops, this isn't going to work, I can see that now," Ashley said, getting up again.

"Why not?"

"Because when I dump you, you'll end up rolling into the fire. Let me just move the sleeping bags a little."

Ashley chose another location, and then lay down to test it. "Nope, this isn't good either. I've got a rock digging into my shoulder. I'll just move it again."

Ashley ended up moving the sleeping bags two more times before she was satisfied.

"All I wanted to do was fight you, but no, with you in charge, we'll end up putting on the Summer Olympics," Jen complained as she got in position for the match.

"Okay, you ready?" Ashley asked. "One . . ."

"Stop right there!" Jen interrupted. "I'll do the counting this time."

Ashley shrugged. "If you want to count, go ahead. It won't make any difference."

"One . . . two . . ."

"Look, a shooting star!" Ashley called out.

Jen wasn't buying it. With one lunge, she flipped Ashley over and then crawled over to gloat in her face. "You thought you could fool me with, *Oh look, a shooting star*, didn't you?"

"I wasn't trying to trick you. There really *was* a shooting star. And because I was distracted, it wasn't fair. I know I can beat you. Let's do it again."

They agreed to the best out of seven. By the fourth time, though, they were both laughing too hard to continue.

As their laughter subsided, they lay on their backs, staring up at the sky through the canopy of trees. Ashley finally said, "What happened to us? We used to be such good friends."

"I don't know. We just lost track of each other, I guess."

They were quiet for awhile, looking up.

There's a lot of stars out tonight," Ashley said.

"I was just thinking the same thing."

After a time, Ashley asked, "Do you ever think about God?"

"Not much." Jen paused, then said, "Well, once in a while I guess. What do you think God is like?"

"I think he wants us to always do our best," Ashley said. "What do you think he's like?"

"I think he's pretty much written me off."

"How come?"

"Because I've messed up big-time. I mean . . . big-time."

"Well, I think he's pretty disappointed in me, too," Ashley said.

"Why would he be disappointed in you?" Jen asked.

"Because we're supposed to always do our best, and my best is never good enough."

"Everyone else thinks it is."

"I know, but he's God, and so he's got higher standards."

"So we both think God doesn't like us?" Jen asked.

"Yeah, pretty much," Ashley said. "I guess we have something in common, after all."

"I guess so."

"Jen, can I ask you something? You used to be really nice. What happened to make you change?"

* * * * *

Sister Ross moved up the trail, but it was slow going in the dark. She used her flashlight until the last turn heading up to where the girls were camping, then turned it off so they wouldn't see her coming.

These girls meant more to her than she ever let on. She and her husband had five boys. They were wonderful, but she missed not having a daughter, so every year these girls became her daughters. She loved them all. Even Jen.

She stumbled over a tree root in the trail and banged her shin on a rock as she landed. She stayed on the ground, rubbing her leg to try to take away the pain. *This is insane,* she thought. *I'm getting too old for this. I don't have good judgment anymore. If Ashley or Jen's parents find out what*

I did, they're going to be furious with me. I don't blame them, either. Sending them up here by themselves was a bad idea.

Still rubbing her shin, she looked up the trail. She could see the light from the girls' fire now. Just a few more steps, and she'd find out how they were doing. If things were out of hand, she'd bring them down for the night.

As she drew closer, she saw Ashley and Jen sitting next to the fire, talking.

She watched them for a while. *I can't believe this,* she thought, amazed at seeing the two former enemies talking to each other like old friends.

I might as well go back, she thought.

* * * * *

"So after my dad walked out on us, I figured what difference does anything make? That's when I started going out on weekends and drinking." Jen shook her head. "It doesn't sound that bad, but the thing is, it's never just drinking, you know what I mean?"

"Not exactly."

"Drinking changes who you run around with, what you talk about, who your friends are. It changes everything."

"Like what?"

"Everything. Like guys coming on to me. It's like a game with them. Guys I don't even like, that I wouldn't have anything to do with any other time. And they come up and they're all, 'Hey, how's it going?' like they're nice and friendly and just want to talk, and they keep wanting me to have a little more to drink, and I know what they're up to, but I still keep talking to them, so it's like this big game, but it's okay, I can take care of myself."

"Sure."

"Except one time, it didn't work out the way I wanted it to, because I'd had too much to drink. Do you even know what I'm talking about?"

"I think so."

"So after that, everyone at school was talking about me behind my back, and there wasn't any place to go except down. And that's where I am now." Jen fell silent for a few moments. "You're the only person I've ever talked about this with." She shook her head. "I don't even know why I told you. It was a stupid idea to think you'd understand any of this."

"No, it wasn't. I appreciate you telling me."

Jen got up and stretched. "All this exercise has made me hungry again. Maybe I'll cook up that other can of beans."

"I can help if you want."

"No, I can do it. Just help me open this can, will you? I'm not used to this kind of can opener."

"Sure, it can be a little tricky." Ashley opened the can and handed it back to Jen.

"Thanks." As Jen took the can from Ashley, they made eye contact. "I know you probably always thought I didn't like you," Jen said, "but the truth is, sometimes I wish I could be more like you."

Ashley turned away. "You need to keep stirring the beans or they'll get burned on the bottom of the can."

"Yeah, okay, thanks."

Ashley dropped one of the large pieces of wood on the fire. It landed with a thud, and sparks rose up into the black sky. She looked upward and watched them, every one eventually losing its red glow. "The truth is, I'm not always the way I'd like to be, either," she admitted.

"I guess nobody is."

"I guess not," Ashley said. She watched Jen stir the beans. "How come you never come to Young Women anymore?"

"I've got such a bad reputation now that when I do end up going, the other girls look at me like 'what is she doing here?' And at school they never even say hello. To tell you the truth, I don't think I'm ever going to go back."

"I say hello when you come to church."

"I know, but I figure you do it just because you're supposed to. And you don't talk to me at school, either."

"That's because you're always with your friends," Ashley said.

"You could still say hello."

"Well, maybe so, but your friends scare me."

"They're not so bad. They just look a little weird."

"Why don't you go with me to Young Women? I could pick you up. We could hang around at school, too."

"I don't think so."

"Why not?"

"You don't really want to go out in back and smoke with me and my friends during lunch, do you?"

"No."

"I didn't think so. In school, if people even saw us eating together, they'd say you were really going downhill."

"I wouldn't care what they said," Ashley said.

"The way I see it, that's all you do care about."

Ashley paused. "Maybe with your help, I could change."

"It might not hurt me to spend some time with you," Jen said. "Maybe some of your perfectness would rub off on me."

Ashley shook her head. "I really don't think you'd want that to happen."

"Why not?"

Ashley moved away from Jen and wiped her eyes.

"Is something wrong?" Jen asked.

Ashley turned around. "No, I'm fine. I just got some smoke in my eyes."

"Something is wrong, isn't it?"

"No."

"Don't lie to me. I didn't lie to you," Jen said.

"Okay, I won't." Ashley ran the sleeve of her sweatshirt across her cheek to wipe up a tear. "The fact is that sometimes I'm scared."

"What are you scared of?"

"Me."

"Why?"

"Because everything has to be perfect—everything—my grades—my makeup—my hair—my homework—everything. I have to be nice all the time. And I can't get mad because that wouldn't be perfect. Sometimes I feel like a rubber band that keeps getting stretched tighter and tighter until it's almost ready to break." She paused, then said bitterly, "But, hey, other than that, everything's just great as long as everyone thinks I'm perfect."

"Why do you think you have to be perfect all the time?"

"That's what we do in my family. Anything else is unacceptable."

"Weird."

"You have no idea. Dinnertime at our house is the worst."

"Why?"

"Because that's when we're all together as a family. And my dad has us go over how our day went. One time a couple of years ago I got a B+ on an English paper and he told me he was sure I could do better than that. So that's what I've been doing since then. Doing better."

"So things are better then, right?"

"No, it never gets better. They just keep raising the bar they want me to jump over."

"So quit playing their stupid game."

"I don't know how. And it's not just my family I have to be perfect for. It's everyone . . . at school . . . at church . . . all the time."

"I can show you how to be normal."

Ashley nodded. "That'd be nice."

"Hold still for a minute," Jen said, picking up a stick that had been in the fire but had cooled off. She got some charcoal from the charred end on her finger and slowly and carefully made two marks resembling a streak of lightning on each of Ashley's cheeks.

"You having fun?" Ashley asked.

"Yeah, I am."

"Do you mind if I ask what this is all about?"

"Not at all." Jen leaned back to examine her work. "Not bad. I just made you an official member of the Warrior Women of America." She paused. "Actually, you're the first member."

"You're not a member?"

"I will be, if you do me." Jen ceremoniously handed over the stick.

Ashley smiled. "My pleasure."

"Make 'em look like lightning, okay?" Jen said.

It took Ashley about twice as long to do one as Jen had taken to do both.

"Look, this doesn't have to be a work of art, okay?"

"I know. I'm done. Now I'll do your other side. Can you turn toward the fire a little so I can see better?"

Jen repositioned herself.

"What do warrior women do?" Ashley asked, resuming her work.

"They always say what's on their mind, and they don't let people run all over 'em. And they help each other. Like if one of them is having a hard time, all she has to do is yell 'WWA!' those are the initials, and before she knows it, she's got all the help she needs."

"Sounds good."

"It is good."

Ashley finished. "Did you bring a camera? I'd like to get a picture of us like this."

"Sorry. I didn't bring one. I wasn't expecting anything to happen here I'd want to capture on film."

"I brought one, but I used up all the film on the first day taking pictures of a squirrel."

"It doesn't really matter. I mean, who would you show it to? Your folks? 'Look, Mom, here's a picture of me with the school tramp.'" Jen shook her head. "I don't think they'd be too thrilled with that. Do you?"

"No, they wouldn't," Ashley said, setting the stick back in the fire. "But I really did do a good job on you."

"I'll take your word for it."

"Now that we're official, what do we do?" Ashley asked.

Jen smiled. "We do girls camp pranks."

A few minutes later they stood in the trees on the edge of camp. It was late enough that everyone was sleeping.

"What are we going to do?" Ashley whispered.

"Run Sister Ross's pants up the flagpole."

"Oh, we couldn't do that," Ashley said.

"Why not?"

"She'd wake up."

"Not if we're careful. Follow me. I'll show you how it's done."

They stopped a few feet from the leaders' tent. "The trick is to listen to their breathing," Jen whispered. "That's how you can tell if they're really asleep."

They crawled until they were next to the tent, then stopped to listen. They could hear the slow, even breathing of Sister Ross combined with the soft snoring of Sister Everett.

Jen found the zipper to the tent and slowly moved it a few inches, then waited. The breathing of the two women continued as before. She slipped her hand through the opening and began to feel around.

It was slow work, but finally she found a pair of jeans. She pulled them out through the opening in the tent door. Then the two girls retreated to a safe distance away from camp.

"I can't believe we got away with that!" Ashley said, giggling. "You are so cool. If it were me, I'd start laughing and wake everybody up."

Jen shrugged. "What can I say, it's a gift." Jen went through the two front pockets of the jeans they'd taken, and got a big grin on her face. "But, hey, right now I'm hungry. Let's break into the commissary."

"We can't. It's locked."

Jen held up a set of keys. "That's okay. We've got the key." She waved it in Ashley's face.

The commissary was a small cement-block building with just one window.

Jen used the key to unlock the door and they stepped inside. "Let me have your flashlight," she said.

Ashley handed it over. Jen removed the contents of one box, turned it over, turned on the flashlight, and placed it underneath the box. Light escaping through the flaps gave them enough light to see, but not enough to alert any of the adult leaders who might be getting up to go to the bathroom.

Boxes of food planned for the camp lay neatly on shelves.

"You hungry yet?" Jen asked.

"Maybe a little."

"Let's see what they got." Jen rummaged through the supplies. "Here's cookies . . . not much else that's good. You want some cookies?"

"Maybe one or two."

"One or two packages, you mean." Jen reached into the box and tossed a package of cookies at Ashley.

"I can't eat this much," Ashley said.

"Save some for breakfast then."

They each opened a package of cookies and started eating.

"You and me, Bailey and Hobbs, partners in crime. Who'd ever believe it?" Jen asked.

"Nobody."

"That's right, nobody."

"I never would have broken in here by myself," Ashley said.

"Me either, actually. And this is just the beginning of what we're going to do."

"What else are we going to do?"

Jen located some bottles of maple syrup. "Let's put some of this on the toilet seats."

Ashley grimaced. "That would be too messy in the morning."

"Hey, that's why they call it a prank."

"I just think about how I'd feel if that happened to me."

"Sticky?" Jen joked.

Ashley started laughing. "This is so much fun!"

"It is, isn't it? Let's go. Oh, take your cookies with you. We probably won't be back again tonight."

"Okay, but I've really had plenty already."

"Take 'em with you, anyway."

"Okay."

"And let's each take one of these squirt bottles of syrup, too."

Before they left, they undid the latch of the window and opened the window a crack so they could break in any time they wanted.

Doing the toilet seats took ten minutes, and then they put the empty syrup bottles in the pockets of Sister Ross's pants and ran the Levis up the flagpole. Struggling to quiet their laughter, they returned to their campsite and climbed into their sleeping bags.

After she thought Jen was asleep, Ashley sat up in her sleeping bag and quickly wolfed down the rest of the cookies. Then she got up quietly and walked into the darkness and threw up.

When she returned, Jen was waiting for her.

"You okay, Girl?" Jen asked.

"Oh, yeah. Too many cookies, I guess."

They didn't say anything for a few minutes.

"You sleepy?" Jen asked.

"No."

"Me, either. You want to do something?"

"Like what?" Ashley asked.

"I don't know. Let me think about it for a while."

Ashley was nearly asleep when Jen tugged on her sleeping bag. "I've got it! I know what we can do!"

"What?"

"The girls camp prank of the century, that's what!"

2

At six-thirty in the morning, Ashley poked her head into the leaders' tent. "Sister Ross, there's something important we really need to talk to you about," she said, sounding as though she were about to break into tears.

Jen stood nearby with her head lowered.

"What's wrong?"

"Well, Jen and I got talking, and we decided to do some girls camp pranks last night, and I was so excited because I'd never done any before. We started by taking your pants and raising them up the flagpole."

Sister Ross suppressed a smile. As a girl she'd done the same thing at girls camp. "That doesn't sound so bad."

"And then we put syrup on all the toilet seats."

"Ashley? You did that?" Sister Ross asked.

"Yes, but don't worry, because during the night I woke up and felt so bad about it that I got Jen up, and we've already cleaned it up."

Sister Ross relaxed and lay back in bed. "That's fine then. I'm glad you told me about it."

Ashley cleared her throat. "Well, actually, there's one more prank."

"There is?"

"Yes, and this one I really feel bad about because, well, it kind of got out of hand," Ashley said.

"What did you do?"

"Well, we thought it would be fun to put a snake in one of the shower stalls. You know, to scare the girls. So we caught a water snake this morning, and we put it in the shower, but . . . well, now this is the part we didn't think about . . . the snake went down the drain. Not only that, but it's still down there. We both feel really bad about it."

"But don't worry," Jen added. "We're pretty sure we can catch it if it comes out."

Sister Ross, now fully awake, sat up.

Ashley continued "The thing is, we're kind of afraid it might come out when the girls are taking showers. You know, because of all the water."

"Don't worry though," Jen said. "We've already gone to every tent and told all the girls to be on the lookout for a snake when they're taking a shower."

"Which shower stall did you put the snake in?" Sister Ross asked.

"That's just it," Ashley answered. "We can't remember. It was still kind of dark, and we were in a hurry."

"And all the drains are connected to one big pipe," Jen said. "So there's no telling which drain the snake will decide to come out of."

"But don't worry," Ashley said. "It was our fault this happened, so Jen and I are willing to do whatever it takes to fix the problem. We'll stand guard while the girls are taking their showers. So whatever drain it comes out of, we'll rush in and catch it before it goes back down again."

By ten o'clock nobody in camp had even tried to take a shower. With a friend to stand guard, a few of the braver ones had used the small washbasin to wash their faces, but nobody wanted to spend much time in a building infested with what Jen and Ashley said was a very large snake.

"This is ridiculous," Sister Ross announced to the girls during lunch. "A little water snake isn't going to hurt you."

"Then how come none of the adults have had a shower, either?" one of the girls asked.

Sister Ross smiled weakly but didn't answer the question. She was scared to death of snakes.

Nobody took a shower that whole day. It gave Ashley and Jen plenty of time to fasten one end of Ashley's bungee cord inside the drain of one of the showers. They tied the other end to some fishing line, so when they tugged on the fishing line, the bungee cord would wriggle out of the drain. When they let it go, it would snap back inside the drain. During a shower with the water running, to someone paranoid about snakes, they were certain it would be convincing.

It also gave them both time to take long showers themselves without being concerned about running out of hot water. As Jen was taking a shower, Ashley stood near an open window and, for the benefit of the other girls, shouted, "There it is! I'll get it! Oh no, it got away! Wow, it's huge!"

Jen did the same thing while Ashley took her shower.

At noon Ashley made an announcement to all the girls. "We're going back to our campsite, so, if you're going to take a shower over lunch, we'll leave you a shovel so you can hit the snake over the head. It's a pretty big snake, so I'm not sure that'll kill it, but it might stun it enough so you can get away before it comes after you."

"I'm not going to take a shower until I go home," one of the girls said.

"That's probably for the best," Ashley said. "We'd feel awful if someone ended up in the hospital over this."

"Or dead," Jen added ominously.

As they headed back to their campsite, they kept a straight face until they were out of sight and then they laughed hysterically all the way to their campsite.

"This is *so* much fun!" Ashley cried out.

"It is pretty good, isn't it?"

"It's awesome. Have you been around Tiffany? She smells like a horse."

"She always did sweat a lot."

"And Erin? Her hair looks like a rat's nest. This is so much fun! You think they'll ever find out?"

"No reason for them to," Jen said. "Nobody's going to want to go in and look in the drains for a snake, so we'll probably get away with it."

"I have you to thank for all this. I never would've done this if it weren't for you."

"That's 'cause I have nothing to lose. But what about you? You're everyone's ideal girl. That could end with this."

Ashley took a deep breath. "I just want to be me, that's all." She paused. "Whatever that is."

Jen mimicked a TV reporter: "The notorious Bailey and Hobbs Gang has struck again! Will they ever be caught? Details at ten."

Lunch that day was to be sandwiches. They'd taken their share with them to their campsite.

"You going to eat?" Jen asked, sitting on her sleeping bag, making herself a sandwich.

"Yeah, I am," Ashley said. She'd decided to set up the tent, so they'd have a place to put their things during the day other than just under a tree. They had agreed to stay together for the rest of girls camp.

Jen was on her second sandwich when she noticed Ashley still hadn't begun to eat. "You have to eat something, okay?"

"I know."

"It's just a sandwich, for crying out loud. What's the problem?"

"Nothing. Maybe I'll just have some of the lunch meat."

"Good grief, Girl, what's so scary about a simple sandwich?"

"Nothing, it's just that . . ."

"What?"

Ashley cleared her throat nervously. "The bread."

"The bread? Are you crazy? What is wrong with you? It's just bread."

"I know, but it might make me . . . fat."

"I promise it won't make you fat."

Ashley sighed. "Maybe one sandwich then."

"You've got to eat. We're going to be busy all day, so you have to eat so you'll be able to keep up with me."

Ashley thought about it, then nodded her head. "You're right. I have to eat."

After making a sandwich, Ashley ate it slowly.

"I need a cigarette," Jen said, reaching into her backpack for one.

"It's okay, I guess, if you have to," Ashley said.

"What are you saying, that I have to ask your permission? I don't need that," Jen grumbled. "I pretty much do whatever I want." But before lighting up, she took a long look at the cigarette in her hand, then crushed it with her fingers and tossed it on the now cold ashes of the fire of the night before.

"What did you do that for?" Ashley asked.

"I just felt like it, that's all. It's no big deal."

"You trying to quit?"

"Leave it alone, okay?" Jen got up and walked out of camp.

With no one to watch her, Ashley finished her second sandwich and then went off into the woods and threw up.

Ten minutes later Jen returned to camp. "Nobody in school respects me, do they?" Jen asked.

"I don't know."

"You know, but you just don't want to say."

"Well, people do talk about things you've done."

"Like what?"

"Lots of things."

"What's the worst you've heard?"

Ashley hesitated to answer, but finally said softly, "That one time at a party you went swimming without your clothes on. And there were guys there and they saw you dive into the water."

Jen cleared her throat. "I've heard that story, too."

"Is it true?"

"To tell you the truth, I don't know. I drank a little too much that night." She paused. "I can't remember what I did."

27

Ashley shook her head in disgust. "And the fact you can't remember, is that supposed to make it okay?"

"I didn't say that, did I?"

"So, in other words, you *might* have done it?" Ashley asked.

"It's possible."

"It's not right to do that."

"You think I don't know that?"

"Then why did you do it?"

"Like I said, because I drank too much."

"That's no excuse, and you know it."

"I know it isn't."

"You've got to quit drinking and going to parties before something really bad happens."

Jen sighed. "You're right. I've got to stop."

Jen and Ashley spent the afternoon standing guard at the entrance to the showers with a camp shovel in their hands, trying to scare off anyone even thinking of taking a shower.

At three-thirty, Sister Ross showed up to see how they were doing. "Have you caught the snake yet?"

"No, not yet, but we saw it coming out of the drain," Ashley said.

"Which drain?"

"Actually, the truth is, we saw two snakes," Jen said.

"Two? But you told me you only put one down the drain."

"Well, that's true," Ashley said. "We were wondering if the one snake somehow told his friends about what a great place it is. That's the only explanation we can come up with. But there are definitely two snakes in there now."

"At least two," Jen added. "Of course, there could be more than two."

"But we're making sure no more go in," Ashley said.

"And we'll clobber 'em if they come out," Jen added.

"That's for sure."

During lunch Sister Ross looked at the girls. They all looked awful. Their hair was stringy and matted down, their faces smudged with dirt. She couldn't let this go on any longer. "I want everyone to take a shower this afternoon."

"What about the snakes in the shower?" one girl asked.

"I'm sure that they've left long ago. Snakes do not live in drainpipes. To prove it to you girls, all the adult leaders will take their showers first. After we're done, the rest of you will follow."

Ashley and Jen waited until all the adult leaders were in the showers, then they went to the shower building. Ashley pulled the fishing line until the bungee cord popped out of one of the shower drains.

A woman's scream could be heard throughout the camp.

Ashley let the bungee cord snap back into place.

The women cleared out of the building, and no more showers were taken that day.

"Have you caught the snakes yet?" one of the girls asked as Jen and Ashley, clean and radiant and mysteriously happy, walked through camp.

Jen let out a frustrated sigh. "You know, I wish it was just a few snakes."

"What are you saying?"

"Nothing, nothing at all. But if I were you, I wouldn't even wash my face in that place."

"It's that bad?"

"It's pretty bad."

"How bad is it?"

"There are so many snakes that the rats that usually live there are being pushed out of their dens into the shower area."

The girl gasped. "Rats?"

Ashley sighed. "Yes, I'm afraid so. But don't tell anybody, okay?" Ashley pleaded. "We wouldn't want to worry any of the girls."

That night there was a talent show. Jen and Ashley asked to be excused so they could try to get the snake problem cleared up so the girls could take showers in the morning.

Halfway through the program, the girls heard yelling from the shower building.

"It's getting away!"

"I got it!" They heard the sound of shovels being whacked again and again.

"That's the biggest one yet!" Ashley yelled.

"Go ahead with your program," Ashley called out. "We're getting things under control here."

"But if you need to go to the bathroom, it might be best to use the outhouse," Jen said.

"Just for tonight, and then we'll have everything fixed for you."

To make sure nobody would go in there, the girls wrote a hasty "Closed for Snake Removal" sign on the door to the shower room.

They stayed there until eleven o'clock and then returned to their campsite. It looked like rain, so they moved all their stuff inside their tent. Jen used some cord to rig a flashlight from the top of the tent so they'd have light.

"I'm not sleepy," Ashley said as she was changing into the sweats she used as pajamas. "I'm still too excited. This has been so much fun."

"It has been good, hasn't it?"

"The girls look like those old-time pictures of pioneer women."

"Right, and they smell like either bad cheese or three-day-old roadkill, I can't tell which," Jen said with a chuckle. She high-fived Ashley. "I think we've made a real difference in this year's girls camp."

"Yeah, I'd say so. Except they're going to kill us when they find out."

Jen rolled up her pants to use them as a pillow. "No reason for them to find out, is there?"

"I just thought we'd tell 'em, that's all."

"No reason to." Jen set the makeshift pillow at the top of her sleeping bag.

"You're right. You know what? I'm hungry. You want to have a snack?"

"Sure, why not?"

Ashley rummaged through her pack for a box of cookies. "I can't believe how much I ate today. Every time I turned around, I was eating. But I didn't even think about it."

"How come?"

"I was having too much fun."

"That's great. I had fun, too. I mean, I really did."

"We're like friends now, aren't we?"

"We are, pretty much." Jen said. "I'm just not sure how it's going to be for us after girls camp, you know what I mean?"

"I know." Ashley put her hand on Jen's forearm. "Jen, you have to quit partying."

"I know."

"You have to, that's all there is to it."

"There's nothing else to do," Jen said.

"There're lots of things to do."

"Name one."

"We could go roller blading at the rink," Ashley said.

"At the rink? Good grief. I'm not ten anymore."

"Well, we could go to a movie together every Friday night."

"Woo, woo! Girls night out!" Jen mimicked, then shook her head. "Do you know any actual guys we can hang out with?" she asked.

"Guys? I don't know. I'd have to think about it."

"I'm not spending my Friday nights watching you do extra credit."

There was a long pause. "I've got to tell you something," Ashley said. "I never know what to say when I'm around a boy."

"That's easy. I can help you with that. No problem. I'll tell you my secret."

"What's your secret?"

"Most guys have something they do that they're proud of. Find out what it is and then just ask a lot of questions, like you're totally interested."

"Show me."

"Okay, I'll be the guy. Let's say I'm on the basketball team." Jen reached for her baseball cap, plopped it on her head backwards, then turned to Ashley and grunted in her version of a low, manly voice, "Hey, Woman, wassup?"

"So, I understand you enjoy basketball, is that right?" Ashley asked.

"Yeah, Man, it's my life," Jen answered in her low voice.

There was a long pause.

"You going to say something?" Jen asked in her regular voice.

"I don't know what to say. I never know what to say. That's the way it is for me. I spend all my time trying to figure out what to say to people. Not just boys, but everyone."

"When are you the happiest?"

"When I've done everything I'm supposed to do."

"Does that happen much?"

"Not much. When are you happiest?" Ashley asked.

There was no answer. Ashley thought that maybe Jen had fallen asleep.

But then quietly, Jen said, "When I'm at a party and I've just met a guy, and he's obviously interested in me, and we're talking, and he's had a few drinks so he thinks he's cool, and I've had enough to drink to pretend that he is too. I always think that we'll still be friends the next day, although we never are. But for that one brief moment, I'm happy."

"And then what happens?"

Jen sat up in bed. "Not what you're thinking of. That does not happen. Believe me, I know how to take care of myself."

"I wasn't thinking of that."

"Don't lie. You were too."

"Well, maybe I was wondering."

"Well, you don't need to wonder anymore. I'm not that dumb."

Ashley paused. "Boys are never going to want to have anything to do with me."

"Why do you say that?"

"Because I'm boring, and I never know what to say."

"You know your problem? You go around trying to fit into other people's idea of what you should be . . . what kind of grades you should

31

get . . . how you should dress . . . what you should say. Is there anything about you that's your own idea? You're just this perfect little girl, aren't you?"

"Well, obviously, you don't worry about that."

"Maybe we could help each other," Jen said.

"Everything will change once camp is over. We both know that." Ashley said bitterly,

"I suppose you're right," Jen said.

"Of course I am. The moment I walk in my house, everything will be the same, and all this will seem like just a dream."

"And I'll go out and party."

"We're both stuck where we've been," Ashley said. "I'm going to go to sleep now."

"Okay."

"You want to have prayers?" Ashley asked.

"No. Forget it."

"It wouldn't kill you."

"It wouldn't do me any good, either. What good are your prayers doing you? You're at least as messed up as I am."

"That is so not true."

"Oh, no? The only creatures in these woods without a backbone are snakes . . . and you."

"That does it!" Ashley declared. "I don't have to stay here and listen to you criticize me all the time." She put on her boots, grabbed her sleeping bag and her flashlight, and crawled out of the tent.

"Where are you going?" Jen asked.

"Anywhere but here."

Ashley took five steps before Jen called out, "Are you going back to the others?"

Ashley stopped. "Probably." She took two more steps.

"Please don't."

It was the *please* that stopped Ashley in her tracks. She'd never heard Jen use that word. "Why not?"

"Because then I won't have any friends in the church. Look, I don't know where my partying is going to take me, but sometimes it scares me. I'm only going to say this once." She paused. "Please stay."

Ashley let out a big sigh, returned to the tent and plopped her things down, then crawled back into her sleeping bag. She fussed with her zipper and fluffed her pillow and wriggled around, trying to get comfortable. "I'm here. Now what?"

"I don't know. I guess we just see how it goes."

"Warrior Women of America, right?" Ashley said.

Jen sighed. "Maybe so."

After a long pause, Ashley sat up. "You don't have to go along with this, but I'm going to say a prayer and thank God for bringing us together."

Silence.

"Heavenly Father—"

"Wait for me," Jen said.

The two girls got out of their sleeping bags and knelt in prayer as it started to rain.

When they were done praying, they crawled back into their sleeping bags.

"It's raining," Ashley said.

"Yeah, I know."

"It's a good thing we set up the tent," Ashley said.

"Yeah, it is. It was a real good idea of yours."

"We'll be okay here," Ashley said.

"I know."

"Good night."

"Good night."

It continued to rain.

3

The next morning Jen and Ashley toured the camp. All the other girls, with their greasy, matted-down hair and smudged faces, looked like they'd spent their lives in a coal mine.

Jen and Ashley ran into the trees and laughed until their sides ached.

"Bailey and Hobbs strike again!" Ashley shouted with her fist raised high.

Jen shook her head. "Oh my gosh. I think I've created a monster."

By five o'clock, the parents of the girls began to arrive for the traditional girls camp program. Jen and Ashley were the only ones who looked halfway decent because they'd taken a shower that afternoon. Even during the shower, one or the other kept yelling about seeing a snake to discourage the others.

After supper and halfway through the talent show, one of the fathers, who happened to be a plumber, returned to the group. Sister Ross had asked him to check out the shower drains.

Between skits, Sister Ross, in front of everybody, asked the plumber, "Did you find anything?"

"Yeah, I found this in the drain." He held up the bungee cord. "It says here it belongs to Ashley Bailey."

"Oh, you found my bungee cord!" Ashley, sweet-faced, called out. "Thanks a lot! I was wondering where it'd gone."

"Nice try," Jen whispered under her breath.

It was then that Sister Ross knew they'd been had. "Ashley and Jen, is this the snake you were telling us about? Was this whole thing just a prank?"

Ashley was hardly able to control her pride. "Yes! We did it!" she blurted out. "Can you believe it? My very first prank! It was a good one, too, wasn't it? I mean, it kept all of you from taking a shower. My gosh, I hate to say anything, but you all look *so* awful!"

Sister Ross felt the eyes of all the parents on her. How would she react? Would she be dignified? Would she be fair? Would she show the proper decorum?

No, not really. This very well might be her last girls camp. If she was going out, she was going out in style. She pointed at the two culprits. "Get them!" she shouted. "Let's throw them both in the shower!"

Ashley and Jen tried to get away, but there were too many. They both ended up in the shower, their clothes sopping with water.

"Boy, you sure got us!" Jen said as she and Ashley returned to the campfire after going back to camp to change into dry clothes.

"Not as bad as you did to us," one of the older girls said.

"And we're not done yet, either," another girl threatened.

Because it was their last night at camp, Ashley and Jen asked if they could spend it together at their campsite up the hill. Sister Ross reluctantly agreed. She could see that some good was coming out of this, after all. "All right, but no tricks."

"I can't believe we got away with it for so long," Ashley said as they arrived back at their campsite.

"I knew we would," Jen said. She enjoyed being street-smart for Ashley. "Some of the girls will be coming to pay us back tonight. So we'll need to be ready for them."

They left the tent where it was but moved their sleeping bags behind a boulder.

"When they get to the tent, we'll be waiting here for them . . . with water balloons," Jen said.

"Where are we going to get water balloons?"

"I don't know. That's the one part I haven't figured out yet. I thought you could help me with that. Maybe come up with some ideas."

"I think there's some plastic bags in the food shack."

"Okay, let's get going. It's going to be a long night."

They went into the food storage building through the window they'd left unlatched the first night. They found some plastic bags, filled them with water, and hauled them back to their campsite, and then waited for the invasion.

"When do you think they'll come?" Ashley whispered.

"Anytime now."

"This is fun!"

"Yeah, it is. It's been great." Jen stopped and listened. "Quiet, I think someone's coming."

They peered out from the boulder. In the dim light they could see four girls tiptoeing toward the tent.

35

"Wait until they get closer," Jen whispered.

The phantom raiders quietly pulled out the tent stakes one by one.

"Now!" Jen whispered.

Jen and Ashley stood up and began throwing the water-filled plastic bags at the invaders. They hit one of the girls. The other missed and hit the ground.

"Get out of our camp!" Jen yelled, lobbing another water bag.

The girls ran away.

"I guess we showed them, didn't we?" Ashley said.

"We sure did. But they'll be back."

The battle went back and forth until Sister Ross caught them all and demanded that it stop before someone got hurt. She sat in the main camp, keeping an eagle eye on the girls until nearly two in the morning. And then, with everyone asleep, she returned to her tent.

Ashley and Jen ended up back in their tent. They slept until eight in the morning when Sister Ross came and told them it was time to break camp and head home.

"I'll miss this place," Ashley said, after they'd rolled up their sleeping bags and taken down the tent.

"Yeah, me too."

On the way home, riding in Sister Ross's car, the closer they got to town, the more Jen returned to her old self.

When Sister Ross pulled in front of Jen's house, Ashley asked Jen, "Are we going to do something together tonight?"

"Not tonight. I have plans."

"Oh," Ashley said. "I thought we were—"

"Not tonight. Sorry."

"Here you are, Jen," Sister Ross said.

"Thanks."

Sister Ross opened the trunk and Jen grabbed her gear.

Ashley stepped out of the car and approached Jen. "I just thought we'd do something tonight."

"I have other friends, you know. Can't I spend some time with them?"

"You mean the people you get drunk with?"

The girls still in the car were watching.

"What I do is my business."

"But we had an agreement."

"I don't remember agreeing to let you smother me for the rest of my life."

"But we were going to help each other."

Jen shrugged her shoulders. "What can I say? Girls camp is over. Deal with it."

Ashley watched her go and then got back into the car.

"It's just as well," another girl in the car said. "I mean, you know what kind of a reputation she has, right?"

"She told me she wanted to change."

"Oh, people like that never change. Don't you know that?"

"What do you know about anything?" Ashley grumbled.

Her parents weren't home but even being in the house brought a feeling of oppression. She wasn't sure why that was, but it was real, something she could almost reach out and taste.

When she first entered the house, she was the girls camp rebel, but somehow just being in the house, it all seemed to slip away, and she became, once again, the dutiful child—washing the clothes she'd brought from girls camp, taking a shower, spraying the shower curtain with a cleaner so there'd be no hard water buildup, running an old towel over the floor to dry up any water she might have tracked out of the shower, then hanging up that towel in its special place, far from the towels that were used as towels.

Ashley thought of calling her older sister, Alauna. She was certain that Alauna, a sophomore at BYU, would appreciate their girls camp prank.

Ashley had grown up watching the fireworks between Alauna and her parents. In her frequent disagreements with her parents, Alauna never backed down. She specialized in walking out of the house and slamming the door, or getting up in the middle of supper and storming out of the house.

After one of these arguments, Ashley would either be ignored, or else she would be told, "We're so glad you're willing to live by family rules."

At first it made Ashley glad to be told that because it meant that she was the favored child in the family. And that made Ashley try even harder to please her parents, to never do anything that would destroy the trust they had in her.

Ashley's room was the master bedroom, complete with its own bathroom. It had not always been that way. There were three bedrooms on the main floor of the house. Up until two years before, Ashley's room had been the first room, followed by Alauna's, with the master bedroom at the end of the hall. But when Alauna began sneaking out at night to be with her friends, her parents had decided they needed to sleep where they could hear Alauna if she tried to leave, so they traded bedrooms with Ashley.

Having the big room was a privilege that could easily be taken away, especially with Alauna now away attending BYU. Ashley loved the spaciousness and having her very own bathroom and did everything she could to be allowed to stay there. She spent five to ten minutes after every shower, on her hands and knees, wiping the floor and drying down the tub and fixtures to keep them shining brightly, worried that her mother might find a reason to make her move back to her old room.

Now that she'd started throwing up after big meals, it was even more convenient to have her own bathroom, and even more important to keep it clean so her mother wouldn't find out. To hide any evidence, she took particular care to clean the toilet nearly every day.

After her shower, she weighed herself. She did that every day. In a way it was like report card time, to see how well she'd done. She was happy she hadn't gained any weight at girls camp. In fact, she'd lost a pound. That was even better. She was well on her way to being down fifteen pounds by the end of the summer and to meeting her goal, which was to be the same weight she'd been just before she started ninth grade. And she was almost there—just another ten pounds.

She got dressed in an oversized T-shirt and jeans. She liked wearing baggy clothes because they hid her body. Even though her mother was constantly on her for being too skinny, Ashley felt fat. She especially hated her thighs, which she saw as being huge. It was discouraging, because no matter how hard she tried, she hadn't been able to reduce their size.

As soon as the washing machine finished with her load from girls camp, she lifted the still-soggy clothes out, put them in the dryer, and started it. Her goal was to have everything cleaned up and put away before her parents came home, so that they wouldn't be able to tell she'd even been to camp.

She unzipped her sleeping bag and laid it out on the trampoline to air out. And then she went through her backpack and cleaned it out, then put it back on the shelf in the garage where they kept camping equipment.

Finally, she did a walk-through, looking for any dirt she might have brought in. She found a few small clods that she had tracked into the house on the treads of her sneakers. *I should have taken my shoes off,* she thought, reaching for the broom to sweep up.

Finally she was done with everything.

Until then she'd avoided the kitchen. She thought about what she had eaten that day and decided that, so far, she'd done well. All she'd had to eat was a granola bar and some orange juice. She was happy about that.

She opened the fridge, trying to decide what to have—something that wouldn't take much preparation. She found part of a cake in the refrigerator. She needed to be careful not to arouse her mother's suspicions and told herself she wasn't going to eat the whole thing. She hated it when her mother would ask, "Ashley, what happened to the cake? Did you have some friends over?" At first she took only a little to avoid raising any concern.

This will make me feel better, she thought. *It's too hard to go the whole day without eating anything.*

A few bites quickly turned into several, and then she was out of control. Soon she had eaten almost all the cake. The little bit left on the plate looked stupid, and she quickly polished it off, then experienced the familiar wave of guilt. She hadn't planned on throwing up, but by doing so she could get rid of the calories.

With nothing to fear now, she continued to eat. She found a donut and picked it apart, eating the frosting first, and then quickly consuming the rest.

Then she hurried to the bathroom, closed the door, turned on the water in the washbasin, knelt down in front of the toilet, put one arm on the seat, and stuck her finger down her throat until she gagged, then heaved the food into the toilet.

Vomiting always made her face perspire. She rested there a minute, grateful to be done with it before her parents got home.

And then she stood up, went to the faucet and doused her face with water and carefully washed her hands and face. *There,* she thought, *I feel a lot better now.*

Having taken care of that, she went in the living room. Now that her stomach was empty, she started to think about food again.

To get her mind off eating, she sat down and played the piano.

And that is what her parents heard when they first entered the house—the sound of music from their beautiful, gifted daughter.

* * * * *

Her parents waited until supper before they brought it up. "We've been told that you were somewhat of a terror at girls camp," her father said.

"Who told you that?" Ashley asked.

"Someone we saw while we were shopping. What do you have to say for yourself?"

"It was just a girls camp prank, that's all."

"I must say I was surprised at such behavior from you," her mother said.

"We understand that you made it so nobody could even wash their hands for several days."

"We didn't stop anybody from doing anything."

"I'm told that some girls refused to even enter the shower building for fear of snakes."

Ashley made the mistake of giving an honest reaction: she smiled.

Her father caught it. "Maybe this is humorous to you, but I wonder if you ever stopped to consider the risk you placed on this family by such irresponsible behavior."

"There was no risk."

"Really? Is that what you think? What if one of these girls were to come down with dysentery as a result of this so-called prank of yours?"

"David, I really think you're exaggerating the possible danger here," her mother said.

"These days it doesn't take much for someone to come up with a reason to sue someone."

"I doubt that will happen," her mother said. "What I am concerned about is that I heard you pulled these pranks with Jennifer Hobbs? Is that correct?"

"She goes by Jen now. Yes, that's right."

"Well, I can understand you might have wanted to make her feel welcome at girls camp," her mother began. "And a certain amount of fellowshipping is good in these circumstances, but I would hope you won't be seeing her now that girls camp is over."

"Why do you say that?"

"Well, I'm not sure you know this, but she has a reputation."

"In what way?"

"I've been told she drinks beer and smokes cigarettes and goes to wild parties," her mother said.

"She's not going to do that anymore. Besides, that won't affect me."

"Well, that remains to be seen," her mother said.

"Jen and I are friends now," Ashley said softly.

"We need to choose our friends carefully," her father said.

"We don't want you to see her anymore," her mother said.

"But I can help her stop doing those things."

"If she's going to be helped, she'll have to help herself."

"I'm sure that what she needs is counseling from a trained professional," her father said. "What are your qualifications for that?"

"I just want to be her friend."

"If she comes to church, then, certainly, you should say hello," her mother said. "But as far as doing things with her, I think that would be very unwise."

"May I be excused?" Ashley asked.

"What for?"

"I need to write in my journal."

Ashley went to her room, closed the door, went into her private bathroom, locked the door and knelt down in front of the toilet. She stuck her finger down her throat and gagged herself. Her stomach convulsed, and the food, some of it still recognizable, pulsed out of her mouth and into the toilet. There was a terrible taste in her mouth and some of it had gotten into her nose. She was perspiring all over, and her face was wet with sweat. She was also trembling and felt weak. It was always a struggle to get back up on her feet. She took one fleeting look at the food and flushed the toilet.

Even though she felt drained, there was a sense of euphoria that she had cheated nature. She had eaten but would not have to pay the price of getting fat.

She cleaned up the bathroom so there would be no sign of what she had done, and then she sat at her desk and pulled out her journal. The excuse of writing in her journal was one she used often. It gave her a justifiable reason to leave the table after supper so she could purge.

She did write in her journal, though. It would be the gift she would leave to her parents if she should die young. She sat down at her desk and opened the journal. She devoted one page for each day. She looked at the calendar and picked up the expensive pen her mother had given her, along with the leather-bound journal. She wrote in her best handwriting:

July 10. Nothing much happened.

And then she closed the journal.

She knew that if her parents ever wanted to know her inner thoughts, they might sneak in her room to read her journal. This was all they would find, each page numbered with the date, and the words: *Nothing much happened.*

It's for the better, she thought. *They would be totally shocked if they had any idea of what I'm really like.*

In a way it was better when Alauna was home. It wasn't that Alauna was all that wild, just that she wasn't afraid of sticking up for herself. Slamming doors, storming out of the room, coming back a few minutes later for another round.

The more Alauna raged, the more their parents appreciated Ashley. But now that Alauna was gone, that appreciation had all but vanished, and they took her good grades and her trying to get along with them for granted.

And then came more expectations.

At eleven-thirty the phone rang. Her parents had gone to bed by then, so Ashley got it.

"Hello."

It was Jen. "I need you to come get me."

"Where are you?"

"Just a minute." She could hear Jen ask someone, "What's the name of this place?"

Ashley heard a muffled man's voice say something she couldn't make out.

"B and L Truck Stop," Jen said.

"Where's that?"

Jen gave directions for getting there, then added, "It's about ten miles. You can't miss it."

"What's happening? What are you doing there?"

"I'll explain when you get here. I'm counting on you, Bailey, so don't let me down, okay?"

"Okay."

"And hurry. This place is full of jerks. I don't like the way they're looking at me."

"Okay, I'll be there in a minute."

Ashley grabbed the keys on her dresser and started out the door, and then stopped, trying to decide whether or not to tell her parents where she was going. She was afraid that if she told them, they'd forbid her to go, and she'd be in for another lecture from her mom about how she didn't want her spending time with Jen, and what was a girl her age doing at a truck stop at this time of night, anyway.

She wondered what Alauna would do. That was easy to figure out. Alauna would just go and explain later.

That's what I'll do, Ashley thought as she went out the front door.

Ashley got in the car, released the emergency brake, let the car roll slowly back down the driveway, turned, and then coasted halfway down the block before starting it up. She'd learned all that from hearing her parents get after Alauna.

I wonder how much trouble I'll get in for doing this, Ashley thought as she entered the highway on her way to the truck stop.

I suppose I could get grounded, but I never go out anyway, so what difference does it make?

The best part of my summer will probably end up being girls camp.

That's strange in a way because I wasn't really looking forward to it all that much. Jen made it fun.

A few minutes later she pulled into the brightly lit truck stop and parked at the curb. She got out of the car and looked around. Four big semis were parked off to the side of the store, fifty yards away, their diesel engines still running. The air had a strange smell—a mixture of diesel smoke and freshly cut alfalfa from a nearby field.

Ashley stepped inside and knew immediately this was male territory. A dozen men turned to watch her as she entered the café. They were men who drove until they couldn't stand it any longer, then stopped for greasy food and stale conversation before heading on down the road.

Jen left two of the men at the counter and came over to meet her. "Those two want to know if we've ever ridden in a semi before. They'd like to take us for a little ride."

Ashley looked at the two, one wearing a black sleeveless sweatshirt that revealed a set of large tattoos on his muscular arms, the other in a dirty white T-shirt with a catsup spill on it and a big part of his belly showing.

"You've got to be kidding," Ashley said under her breath.

Jen turned to the men, who were leering at them both. "Hank, Ace? Not this time. Catch you guys later, okay?"

The two men waved, then returned to their coffee.

Once outside, Jen gave a sigh of relief. "Thanks for getting me out of there. I was starting to get worried. Hank started talking about going to take a shower and shave. I guess he wanted to impress me that he knew the words."

"I can't believe you'd even talk to any of them."

"I figured it was better to be friends with the most harmless ones."

"How did you end up here?" Ashley asked.

"Well, I was at a party up in the hills. This guy kept trying to get me drunk. A girl there told me he'd made a bet with his friend about how far he could get with me tonight. I decided I didn't want to play that game. So I slipped into the woods, hiked down to the truck stop, then called you. I'm glad you came. What did your folks say?"

"I didn't ask them."

"How come?"

"They'd have told me no."

"You'll get in trouble for this, won't you?"

Ashley shrugged her shoulders. "I suppose. It doesn't matter, though."

"Of course it matters. I'll talk to your folks."

"No. Don't do that."

"Why not?"

Ashley didn't want to say that her parents didn't trust Jen. "It won't do any good," was all she said.

A short time later they pulled into town.

"You want to go home now?" Ashley said.

"Not really. I'm not even tired. How about you?"

"I'm not tired either."

"Let's drive by the school and swing on the swings."

It was their grade school, where they'd first met.

"I've decided I don't want to party anymore," Jen said.

"I'm glad."

"It's not doing me any good, that's for sure."

"No, it isn't. Not really."

"I want to quit smoking, too. I mean, for good."

"That'd be great."

"And start going back to church."

"Good for you."

"You think it's possible for someone like me . . . you know . . . to turn my life around?"

"Sure it is."

"I'll need your help."

"Whatever I can do. You know that."

Jen looked over at Ashley. "You mean it?"

"Absolutely."

"Well, okay, here goes." Jen took a pack of cigarettes out of her pocket and stared at it. She took a deep breath, then ripped open the pack, dumped all the cigarettes onto the ground, and ground them into the dirt with her shoe. She turned to face Ashley. "This isn't going to be easy. It feels really good, but it also scares me. I'm going to need your help. Then maybe I'll be able to do it."

"Of course I'll help you. I mean, after all, we're Warrior Women of America, right?"

"Yeah, right, that's what we are."

They were sitting side by side in the swings, but without swinging.

"Can I stay over at your place tonight?" Jen finally asked.

"I guess so," Ashley said.

"Maybe we could drop by my house, and I'll tell my mom and get my things for church in the morning. It's going to be weird to be going to church again. It'll be good to have you with me."

Jen's mom wasn't home. Jen left a note, picked up a few things, and then came back to the car.

44

"My mom's on a date," Jen said.

"Weird," Ashley said.

"You have no idea. But I don't blame her. It's been a year since my dad walked out on us."

When they entered Ashley's house, Mrs. Bailey was waiting for them. She was wearing a long purple satin nightgown that Ashley's father had given her a long time ago as a Valentine's gift. It had been elegant then, but now it was just old. She was also wearing an angry look. "Ashley, where on earth have you been!" she demanded, barely able to control her emotions.

"Jen called me and asked me to come get her, so I did."

"What for?"

"I was trying to get myself out of a bad situation," Jen said.

"You should have at least let us know what you were doing," her mother said to Ashley.

"Sorry."

"After Alauna left, I thought we were done with this sort of thing," her mother said.

"I said I was sorry."

"We'll talk some more about this tomorrow. Your father is as disturbed as I am."

"If he's so disturbed, where is he?"

"He has a seven o'clock high council meeting in the morning, so he needs his sleep."

"Oh."

"Where did you go in the car without even asking for permission?" her mother asked.

"I can answer that question," Jen said. "I got stranded at a truck stop just outside town. Ashley picked me up and then we came home."

"I heard you leave, and it's been nearly two hours since then. What have you been doing all this time?"

"We went to the grade school and sat on the swings and talked," Ashley said.

"She's right. That's what we did," Jen added.

"If you're going out in the middle of the night, you need to tell us where you're going."

"If I told you, you wouldn't have let me go."

"Why do you have to be the one to come to Jen's rescue? What about her mother?"

Ashley didn't think it would help things to explain that Jen's mother was out on a date. "She called me, Mother, and she needed my help. So what was I supposed to do, tell her to forget it?"

"We'll talk more about this after church."

"Jen is coming to church with me tomorrow. Also, I asked her to stay the night."

Her mother fumed. "I see," she said, tight-jawed.

"Is that all right?"

Her mother let out a pained sigh. "I suppose it's fine for tonight, but in the future we'd like you to have a good night's sleep so you're rested for church."

"We'll go right to bed."

Her mother nodded. "All right, then. Good night. Turn out all the lights before you go to bed."

Jen and Ashley washed up in Ashley's bathroom. They decided to sleep on the trampoline, and Ashley went to the garage and got the sleeping bag she'd taken to girls camp. She would let Jen use Alauna's sleeping bag.

A few minutes later they were situated on the trampoline, looking up at the stars. "How you doing?" Jen asked.

"I feel bad."

"How come?"

"I don't like it when my mom and dad are mad at me."

"They'll get over it."

"I used to picture myself growing up doing everything my folks wanted me to. I wanted to be a good girl, perfect in every way. But now, I don't know. But I am glad we're going to be friends."

"Why?"

"Because, with you, I don't have to pretend I'm better than I really am. I can just be me, whatever that is. I'm still not sure."

"Who is?"

"I know."

"Are you hungry at all?" Jen asked.

"I don't know."

"You don't know? I am."

Ashley sighed. "I suppose we could go and see what's in the fridge. But if we make too much noise, my mom will get really mad."

"We'll be real quiet. Do you have any ice cream?"

There was a long pause.

"You still awake?" Jen asked.

"We have ice cream," Ashley said in a dull monotone.

"We could eat it out here on the tramp. That way we wouldn't wake your mom up."

Ashley sighed. "All right, we'll have some ice cream."

"You okay?"

"Yes, why?"

"You're acting so weird. Look, if it's a problem, I'll pay for what I eat."

"No, it's not that," Ashley said.

"What is it then?"

"Nothing. I'll go get it. You stay here."

A few minutes later Ashley brought out two bowls of ice cream, spoons, and a jar of hot fudge sundae topping. She handed the bowls to Jen, then rolled up onto the trampoline.

"I heated the topping in the microwave."

Jen put a big spoonful of topping on the ice cream and took a taste. "Wow, this is so good!"

"Yeah, it is." Ashley scooped out three big spoonfuls of the topping on her ice cream.

"Don't hog it all, okay?" Jen said. "I might want some more."

"There's plenty."

They eagerly finished the ice cream.

"You want any more?" Ashley asked.

"No, that was plenty. I'm ready to get some sleep now."

"Me too," Ashley said. "I think I'd better go rinse out the bowls and put 'em away so my mom doesn't get mad at me for not cleaning up." She got off the trampoline and grabbed the empty bowls.

"You need any help?"

"No, I can do it."

"I think I'll just go to sleep then."

"Sure. I'll be back in a minute."

While Jen was crawling into her sleeping bag, Ashley went inside, washed and dried what they'd used, and put the topping back in the refrigerator.

And then, without turning on the lights, she made her way down the hall, past her parents' bedroom, to her room at the end of the hall, closed the door, then in the darkness made her way to her bathroom. She entered, turned on the fan, then, in the dark, knelt down in front of the toilet.

She had just finished purging when Jen opened the door.

"Don't come in," Ashley said.

"I have to go to the bathroom. How come the light's off?"

"Don't turn it on."

"Why not?" Jen turned on the light and saw Ashley just getting up. "What were you doing down there?"

Ashley wiped away the perspiration from her forehead. "Nothing."

Jen leaned over and looked into the toilet. "What's that?"

"I must've eaten too much. It made me sick."

Jen glared at her for a long moment. "You think I'm really that stupid not to know what's going on?"

"Keep the noise down, okay?"

"Don't tell me what to do! I'll make as much noise as I want. In fact, I think I'll go wake up your folks and tell them what a lying hypocrite they've got for a daughter."

Ashley flushed the toilet. "Don't do that. Please. It'll only make things worse."

Jen came back. "How could it be possibly get worse than it is now?"

"It's not that bad."

"You are *so* pathetic. Well, that's it. I'm out of here." She took one last disappointed look at Ashley then shook her head. "Oh, one other thing."

"What?" Ashley asked, hopefully.

"You owe me a pack of cigarettes."

Then she was gone.

4

Ashley hurriedly rinsed the acid taste out of her mouth, then ran out the back door of the house to try to patch things up with Jen.

Jen was just finishing tying her shoes in the backyard.

"We need to talk," Ashley said.

"There's nothing to say, Bailey, not anymore. Good-bye. Have a nice life."

Once Jen got on the street where there were street lights, she started to jog.

Ashley tried to catch up with her, but she was slowed down because she was barefoot—and because she felt weak.

At first she didn't dare call after Jen for fear her parents would hear, but after a block, seeing the distance between them steadily increase, and with her bare feet hurting, she did call out. "Jen, wait up!"

Jen kept going.

"Please!" she pleaded.

Jen stopped, put her hands on her hips, and stood facing away from Ashley.

Ashley caught up. She stopped when they were about twenty feet from each other. "I'll quit."

"No, you won't," Jen said, turning to face her.

"I will."

"Why should I believe anything you say?"

"I don't know. I just know that you're the only friend I've got."

"What makes you think I'm your friend?"

"We were friends at camp."

"Friends don't lie to each other."

"I know that."

"You do this all the time, don't you?"

"Yes."

"I don't want to be friends with a hypocrite like you." Jen turned and started walking away again.

"So what will you do now? Go get drunk with some sleazebag guy that only has one thing on his mind?"

Jen turned around and came back. "Don't you ever talk to me like that." Her jaw was nearly clamped shut as she said it. She shoved Ashley backward, then took off again.

"You want to arm wrestle?" Ashley called out after her.

Jen stopped again but didn't turn around.

"It looks to me like we're both pretty much messed up," Ashley said.

"So what if we are?"

"Maybe we could help each other," Ashley said.

Jen shook her head. "I don't think so."

"Well, you're probably right, but couldn't we at least try?"

Jen turned around. "I used to look up to you."

"I know. I'm sorry."

The light from a nearby street light gave a bluish-gray tint to their faces.

Jen ran her fingers through her hair. "If we did this, you couldn't ever lie to me again."

"I know. I won't. I promise."

"Because the first time you do, I'll be gone."

"I know. I won't ever lie to you again. If you won't lie to me."

"I've never lied to you."

"I know. I'll do the same with you from now on."

Jen pursed her lips. "Well, I guess we could try it and see how it works."

"That'd be great."

"All right then. Let's go back and get some sleep."

"Thanks."

Jen shook her head. "It's way too early for thanks."

A short time later they lay in their sleeping bags looking up at the stars. Jen asked one embarrassing question after another, partly from curiosity and partly to see if she could get Ashley to lie.

Ashley, her face red from embarrassment, answered every question.

This went on for another hour until finally Jen said, "I guess we'd better get some sleep now."

"Good night, Jen."

"Yeah, right," Jen mumbled, turning on her side away from Ashley.

* * * * *

Morning came sooner than either one of them was prepared for.

"Ashley, it's eight-fifteen," her dad said to the lump inside the sleeping bag. "We have to all go together this morning because there's practically no gas in the car you used last night. I nearly ran out of gas on my way to high council meeting."

Ashley stretched.

"You should have told us you decided to sleep out here. I've been knocking on your door for five minutes. Finally, I opened the door and you weren't there. Can you get ready real fast?"

Ashley, still confused, sat up. "What?"

"Get up now and get dressed. Church starts in forty-five minutes."

Ashley yawned. "What time is it?"

"Eight-fifteen. Hurry up or you'll be late." He left and returned to the house.

Ashley poked Jen. "We have to hurry so we won't be late."

Jen's voice was muffled inside her sleeping bag. "I'm too tired to go to church. You kept me up too late last night."

"Don't do this to me, Jen." Ashley pulled the sleeping bag away from Jen's face.

"Do what to you?"

"You've got to go to church with me."

"Why?"

"If we don't go, then for the rest of the week I'll be hearing what a bad influence you are on me."

"It's true. I am a bad influence on you. Now let me go back to sleep." She rolled away and pulled the sleeping bag back over her head.

"No, you're good for me. Please, you have to get up. Do it for me."

Jen moaned, then sat up and yawned. "I'm going back to partying."

"How come?"

"It's a lot easier than this." Jen unzipped her sleeping bag. "Well, you coming or not?"

The girls were doing their hair when Ashley's father knocked on the bathroom door. "Are you two about done?"

"We're not ready yet," Ashley said.

"Church starts in fifteen minutes."

"We're hurrying as fast as we can."

"Well, hurry up even more then."

They could hear Ashley's parents discussing the situation. "Did you tell them we need to go?" Ashley's mother asked.

"I told them. They said they're hurrying."

51

"I knew it would be like this. We should have a policy, no sleep-overs on a Saturday night."

"I think they're nearly ready," her father said.

"I feel like we're being held hostage," her mother complained.

"What do you want me to do?" her father said. "I told them to hurry. What else can I do?"

"Why is it that Ashley has to pair up with the one rebel girl at camp?"

"Maybe she'll help the girl."

"I'm not sure who'll end up where at this point. It sometimes goes the other way, you know. Look at what they did at girls camp. I think we need to monitor this very carefully—very carefully indeed."

Ashley and Jen could hear everything. Ashley had quit fixing her hair and was holding her right hand on her side where she was having stomach pains.

"You okay?" Jen asked.

"I don't feel very good."

"How come?"

"It'll go away," Ashley said.

"You can't please everyone. Whatever you do, somebody's going to be mad at you. That's just the way it is."

"So what should I do?"

"Do what you think is best for you."

"That's hard for me to do."

"I know. That's where I come in."

There was a knock on the door.

"Yes?" Ashley asked.

"We'll be in the car waiting," her mother said sternly.

Ashley closed her eyes and shook her head.

"What's wrong?"

"I hate it when my mom does that."

"Does what?"

"Says she'll be in the car waiting for me."

"They've got to wait somewhere, so why not in the car?"

"Because when we get in the car, my mom will say something about how long she was kept waiting in a hot car."

"Then you say, 'Wait inside next time.'"

"I could never say that."

"Why not?"

"I don't know. I just can't."

"But why?"

"Because it's what Alauna would say."

"And you're better than her, right?"

"Alauna put my mom and dad through a hard time."

"A hard time? How bad can Alauna be? She made it into BYU, didn't she? And she stuck up for herself. That's more than you're doing."

"I can't do what she did."

"Why not?"

"Because my stomach gets tied up in knots when there's tension. I'd rather just go along with what my folks say."

"So you play the part of the perfect little daughter, but then you go in your bathroom and puke your guts out. That's not right, either."

"I know that."

"Then quit being so perfect all the time."

"I can't."

"Fine, then don't, but at least stand up for yourself once in a while."

"I will."

"You promise?"

"I promise."

"Today?"

"I don't know."

"Just one time today. How hard could that be?"

"Maybe."

They hurried out to the car and climbed into the backseat.

"Do you realize how long you kept us waiting?" her mother asked.

"Sorry."

"And we're going to be late. You know how I hate to be late all the time."

"I said I was sorry, didn't I?" Ashley snapped.

"Yes!" Jen mouthed, making a fist.

By the time they got to sacrament meeting, it was in the middle of sacrament. The doors were closed, and so they waited in the foyer.

A deacon opened the door and brought over a tray of bread. They each took a piece. He looked around to make sure nobody else was in the hall, then went back inside the chapel.

They stood there in silence. Her mother refused to look at Ashley.

Ashley and Jen went over to look at the pictures of the missionaries from the ward. There were eight.

Jen pointed to one of the missionaries. "He is *so* hot," she said in a whisper.

"Girls," Ashley's mother said.

They quit talking.

A few minutes later the same deacon brought out a tray of water. They each took a cup, drank it, then returned the cup to the tray.

After standing quietly for a few minutes, one of the teachers opened the door to the chapel, and the four of them walked in. The seats near the back were full, but there was a small pew on the side near the front still open. Ashley's father led the way. He went in first, and then Ashley's mother, then Ashley and then Jen.

Ashley was still sleepy. She ended up resting her head on the back of the pew in front of her.

Her mother touched her shoulder. "Sit up and pay attention."

Ashley sat up. She was, once again, bored at church.

There was a youth talk, a deacon who took all of two minutes. And then the ward choir sang.

One of the bishopric introduced the high councilor speaker, who got up to the pulpit and set down four large books.

"I'm happy to be here today. Uh . . . there are many people here today that I know, but of course there are many people here that I don't know. I hope that I will get to know those that . . . uh . . . I don't know . . ."

Ashley looked over at Jen. She was asleep.

She glanced at her parents. They appeared to actually be listening.

Ashley nudged Jen with her elbow. No response.

She did it again, this time a little harder.

Jen opened her eyes. "What?"

"You were sleeping."

"What else is there to do?"

"Listen to the talk."

"What's he said so far?" Jen asked.

"He's happy to be here."

"Well, he's the only one."

Ashley covered up her giggling by putting her hand to her mouth as if she was clearing her throat.

Her mother gave her a disapproving scowl.

The speaker had a habit of filling in between sentences with *uhs*. On the back of the program, Jen started making a mark with a pencil for each one. It made it easier for them to stay awake to count the *uhs*.

Ashley wondered what she would do about lunch. So far she was perfect for the day. She hadn't had anything to eat. Except for the sacrament. The question was how long she could keep it up.

Jen might get me to quit bingeing and purging, but that doesn't mean I'm going to quit losing weight. I can always just not eat.

She didn't like Sundays because all the meals were at home where her folks could see what she was eating. It was better when she was gone all day.

She didn't know what she'd do about lunch.

Ashley glanced at the score sheet. The speaker was up to 78 'uhs'. She didn't like to sit this close to the front because she couldn't look at everyone else.

Jen leaned over. "Do you know what I'm going to say if anyone asks me what this talk is about?"

"What?"

"Uh . . ."

Ashley started to giggle, but her mother turned to her and gave her The Stare.

Jen stopped counting uhs when she got to 100. She turned the program over and made a list of boys their age in the ward, drew a column, put a heading on it, "Hot or Not?"

The first name on the list was Nathan Billingsley.

Ashley shook her head, and wrote "Not."

Nathan was their same age, the youngest child in a large family. Ashley had always felt sorry for Nathan because of his parents, who looked old enough to be his grandparents. He had been born long after all the other children, and it had been like he had grown up without any brothers and sisters.

Nathan had gone through middle school and high school being made fun of by others. It wasn't totally his fault. His mother set him up for it. In seventh grade, she was told by a choir teacher that Nathan could sing better than any boy his age. Thinking he had the potential to be an opera singer, she poured her energies into helping him achieve her goal. In eighth and ninth grade he took private lessons from a professor at the University of Utah; he learned art songs in Italian and French. He spent summers listening to recordings of famous operas.

Because his mother pushed it, he had often sung in sacrament meeting and ward talent shows. At that time his speaking voice had not yet caught up with his singing voice, and so it was a source of constant amusement among the youth in the ward to hear Nathan, in a high and squeaky voice, announce the next song he would sing, followed by a resonant singing voice.

Nathan's downfall took place when he was in the ninth grade. Because of his outstanding singing voice, Nathan made the high school choir that year. The choir drew a diverse group of students: mostly girls and a few boys like Nathan, who were in choir because they loved to sing; and guys who had little or no interest in singing, but just wanted an easy credit.

In the class, Nathan found himself sandwiched between two defensive linemen for the football team. They outweighed him by thirty pounds each, and when Mr. Montenegro, the choir leader, would turn his back, the football players often had a contest seeing who could slug each other the hardest, reaching over or around Nathan to do so.

Nathan endured them stoically, occasionally even talking to them. Not that they cared. Whenever he did say anything to them, they mostly ignored him.

The incident for which Nathan became known throughout the school happened in November of that year.

Mr. Montenegro was not happy with the way the sopranos were sounding their high notes, and knowing Nathan's talent, he happened to say, "Why, I bet Nathan can sing that passage better than you sopranos."

The two hulks on either side of Nathan punched him on the shoulder and began chanting "Na-than . . . Na-than . . . Na-than . . ."

"Nathan, you try singing the soprano part."

Unfortunately, Nathan did it.

That afternoon, as Nathan was walking to class, one of the boys who stood next to him in choir, called out in a high falsetto voice, "Oh, Nathan!"

By the next day, the entire school, or so it seemed to Nathan, called out to him in a high-pitched voice every time they saw him.

Nathan couldn't handle the ridicule. He quit choir, and, as much as he could, tried to disappear into the drab hallways of school, never to be noticed again. People continued to say his name with a high voice, and, in fact, Ashley did that to remind Jen of his past.

"He's not as weird now, is he?" Jen asked.

"No, he's still the same," Ashley said.

"Girls, that's enough," Ashley's mother warned.

When sacrament meeting ended, Ashley's father looked over at the two girls. "Ashley, did you notice how Jen took notes on the last talk?"

Ashley suppressed a smile. "Yes, I did notice that."

"I think she was setting a good example for you."

"I guess she was. Excuse us. We need to go to class."

Once they were out of the chapel, Ashley asked, "You want to go to Sunday School?"

"Will Nathan be there?"

"I suppose."

They got a drink of water first. When they walked into the class-room, five or six girls who'd been to girls camp were there.

"You all look so pretty today," Jen said sweetly to the girls. "I bet you all took showers, didn't you? That's what does it, all right. Lots of hot water. I imagine it'd be awful to have to go a few days without a shower."

None of the girls were smiling.

"Can't you girls take a little camp prank?" Ashley asked.

"Why are you still hanging around with her?" one of the girls asked Ashley.

"She's my friend," Ashley answered.

"She'll corrupt you. In fact, I think she already has."

None of the girls would sit with Ashley and Jen, which turned out to be good because Nathan came in late. "Is this seat taken?" he asked.

"No, I was reserving it for you," Jen said with a big smile.

Nathan seemed delighted. "Really? How come?"

"In case you need help answering some of the questions."

Nathan laughed and sat down next to Jen. "I might need that."

"I'm at your service," Jen said.

"Really? What about when school starts? I'll be taking calculus. Could you help me with that, too?"

"Sure, no problem," Jen said.

"Chemistry?"

"You bet."

"You're amazing."

"That's true. I am."

Nathan leaned forward to look around Jen and greet Ashley. "Hi, Ashley."

"Hi, Nathan."

"You still going to take calculus in the fall?" he asked.

"Still am."

"You worried?"

"A little."

"Me too. Good thing we'll have Jen to help us, right?"

"Yeah, good thing."

Brother Brisbane, the teacher for the class, entered the room. During the class, he played an audio tape of a talk given in general conference. Nathan leaned forward, his elbows on his knees, and listened to the tape.

Jen put her hand on Nathan's back and began to write on it with her thumb and forefinger.

Nathan looked around at her and smiled. He didn't sit up, so Jen continued.

She leaned forward and whispered into his ear, "Can you tell what I'm writing?"

"I'll try. Do it some more."

Hardly anyone in the class was paying any attention to the audio tape. Jen wrote, "I love you," on his back. The girls behind them read it as it was being written.

Jen leaned forward. "Did you get that one?"

"I love you?" he asked quietly.

"Really, Nathan! Gosh, this is so sudden," Jen said out loud.

Nathan smiled and whispered, "What I meant was that you wrote, 'I love you.'"

"Sorry, that wasn't it."

"What was it then?"

"It was actually the Twelfth Article of Faith."

"Really?"

"Oh, yes. Why would I write 'I love you'? I mean, we hardly know each other."

By this time Brother Brisbane realized nobody was listening to the tape. He didn't know Jen by name because she hadn't come to Sunday School since he'd been teaching. He turned off the tape. "Nathan, could you please sit up and pay attention."

"Okay, sorry. We were just having a lover's quarrel," Nathan said, glancing at Jen.

That made her laugh.

Brother Brisbane didn't seem to hear. "We need to finish the lesson," he said, opening his manual.

After class, Jen and Ashley walked into the hall. "Are we going to Young Women?" Jen asked.

"I think we should, but we probably won't be real welcome."

Jen smiled. "Let's go then."

They went and sat on the front row, which nobody ever did.

Sister Ross came over to welcome Jen. "I'm so glad you came today!"

"Ashley's the one who made it happen."

"Good for you, Ashley."

There was still some time before the meeting began, so they had a chance to talk. "What do you usually do on Sunday afternoon after church?" Jen asked.

"Go home, change clothes, eat—"

"After you eat, what do you do?"

"Go to my room and write in my journal."

"Do you usually hurl right after you eat?"

Ashley looked around, concerned the others had heard, but they were involved in their own conversations.

"Yes."

"You can't do that anymore."

"It's hard not to."

"That's because you're in a rut. We got to get you out of it."

"Like how?"

Jen smiled. "Leave that to me. Can I eat lunch with you?"

"I don't know. If I ask my mom, she'll say she would have liked to have known a little earlier."

"I promise I won't eat that much. So what do you want to do?" Jen asked.

"I don't know."

"You want to eat at my place?" Jen asked.

"If I tell my mom I'm going to eat at your place, she'll say she's fixed a nice meal for me."

"So either way, she's mad at you, right?"

"That's true."

"So what do we do?" Jen asked.

"I don't know."

"We need a little mental toughness here, girl."

"I can't decide. I'm kind of tired."

"That's why we eat. To give us energy to think. You should try it sometime."

"Maybe we should just split up after church," Ashley said.

"No way."

"Why not?"

"Because you'll throw up and spend all your time in your room. And . . ."

"What?"

"Well, the truth is I'm dying for a cigarette, but I do want to stop smoking."

"So we need to stay together today, don't we?" Ashley asked.

"Looks that way."

Sister Ross started the lesson. It was about making choices. Unfortunately, Jen and Ashley talked through most of it.

5

On the way home from church, Ashley's mother said, "Jennifer, do you need us to take you home?"

Jen looked over at Ashley for some direction.

"I invited Jen to eat with us, if that's okay," Ashley said.

"Really? How nice." Her mother's voice had just a hint of an edge to it.

I'll hear about this, Ashley thought.

"Did you girls enjoy church today?" her father asked.

"Yes, we did," Ashley said.

As they pulled into the driveway, Ashley's mother said, "Jennifer, in our family, we usually don't change a tire after church." At least that's how it sounded to Jen.

Jen laughed. "I'm not sure I'd even know how, although I did watch a guy do it once, but, of course, that was at night out on the highway."

There was a prolonged, awkward silence.

Ashley turned to Jen and spoke softly. "She means change clothes. You know, clothes, attire, same thing."

"Oh, my gosh! I guess I didn't understand. Boy, Mrs. Bailey, you got me there, didn't you?"

"Apparently so, although not intentionally, of course," Ashley's mother said.

Once they got home, Jen and Ashley went to Ashley's bedroom and closed the door.

"Your mother hates me," Jen said.

"I wouldn't say that."

"What would you say then?"

"It's not personal. She doesn't like anyone our age very much."

"I can't stay in these clothes all day. Let's go over to my place after we eat. We can change a tire there. You can wear some of my things. To tell you the truth, I don't think I can stand to be here much longer."

They sat on the bed and talked until Ashley's mother knocked on the door and told them dinner was ready.

They ate in the formal dining room, on good plates, using cloth napkins.

"Everything looks so nice," Jen said.

"Thank you," Mrs. Bailey said, then added, "Ashley, I could have used some help."

"Sorry. I forgot."

"It should be no surprise that I could use some help every Sunday. Please try to remember that from now on."

"Yes, of course," she said quietly.

Jen looked at Ashley for any sign of stress, but there was none.

"Ashley, will you say the blessing on the food?" her father asked.

Everyone bowed their heads, and Ashley said a short prayer. Afterwards, Ashley's mother said, "You can all get started on your salad while I bring out the hot food. Jennifer, we usually have roast beef, mashed potatoes, and a vegetable on Sundays. I hope that's okay with you."

"Sure it is. We usually just have McDonald's on Sundays."

"Really?" Ashley's mother said.

"You're not supposed to buy things on Sunday," Ashley whispered.

"Sorry."

"That's quite all right. Not every family is the same."

"It's just that my mom works all week, so when it comes to Sundays, she likes to take it easy."

"Of course. And your father?"

"Oh, he's out of the picture . . . totally."

"Oh, I see."

"But my mom is dating a guy. So that might work out."

"Is he a member of the Church?"

"Well, not exactly. But he had a friend in the army who was a member."

"Well, that sounds promising," Ashley's mother said.

Instead of eating, Ashley was busy using her fork to separate the tiny marshmallows from the Jell-O.

"You probably think I'm corrupting Ashley, don't you?" Jen asked.

"No, not at all," her mother said.

"Good, because we might end up being really good friends," Jen said.

"How nice," Ashley's mother said with a forced smile.

Ashley was sitting erect, her back not even touching the back of the chair. She put down her fork and stared at her plate.

61

"Finish your salad, Ashley," her mother said.

"Yes, of course," Ashley said.

"Hand me your plates, and I'll go dish up the food," Ashley's mother said. She went into the kitchen, loaded each plate, and brought them in two at a time. As Ashley's plate was set before her, Ashley looked at the heaping plate as if it were an obstacle to be overcome.

"I'm not sure I can eat this much," Ashley said softly.

"Oh, nonsense, there's not that much there. The mashed potatoes are mostly air anyway."

"You know what?" Jen said. "Could I be excused to use the bathroom?"

"Yes, of course."

"Ashley, I might need you to come with me."

Silently Ashley and Jen left the table and went down the hall to Ashley's room. Jen closed the door so they could talk without fear of being heard.

"How you doing, Girl?" she asked.

"The same as usual," Ashley said in a dull monotone.

"What's your plan?"

"The same as always."

Jen placed her index finger under Ashley's chin and lifted it until they made eye contact. "It can't be the same as always. Not anymore. Not now that I'm in the picture. We're Warrior Women of America, remember? The WWA."

Ashley shrugged. "That's not going to change anything."

"It's got to. Look, it's not easy for me either. I need a cigarette in the worst way."

"Maybe we should just end this now."

"Is that what you want?" Jen asked.

Ashley was near tears. "I can't fight this."

"I'll help you."

"Sometimes I just want to die," Ashley said.

"I know, me too."

Ashley seemed surprised. "Really?"

"Sure, not every day of course. It comes and goes. So, what do we do now?"

"If we go back there, I'll have to eat everything on my plate. And if I do that, then I'll throw it all up, and then you'll be mad at me."

Just then the doorbell rang. "Who's that?" Jen asked.

"I don't know."

A minute later there was a knock on the door. It was her father. "Ashley, the home teachers are here."

"We'll be out in a minute," Ashley said.

They waited a couple of minutes and then went into the living room.

Ashley didn't know the names of their home teachers. It seemed to her they changed every few months. They were men she'd seen in church. One of them was a ward clerk, the other had something to do with family history.

"Ashley, you know Brother Jones and Brother Gardner, don't you?"

"Oh, sure," she said, smiling politely. "This is my friend Jen."

Brother Gardner glanced at his watch. "Brother Jones is going to give the lesson today."

The lesson took forever. Ashley's parents seemed compelled to expand on it by reciting everything they'd ever learned about the topic.

"Well, that's our lesson. How's everything going with you folks?" Brother Gardner asked.

"Just fine," Ashley's father said. "Things seem to be going along good for us."

"Tell them about your work," Ashley's mother suggested.

"They don't want to hear about that," her father said.

"Of course we do."

Ashley's mother took the lead. "Well, the place where David works was bought out a few months ago. The new people don't know anything about the business. They don't care one bit about customer satisfaction. All they care about is cutting costs."

"It's not that bad," Ashley's father said.

"It is that bad. You come home every day complaining about what they're doing." She turned to the home teachers. "David worked so hard to build up the business, and these new people seem intent on tearing down everything he's worked so hard to achieve."

"Isn't that something the way things are these days? Anything we can do to help?"

"No, not really," Ashley's mother said. "It's just a constant source of frustration to David, that's all."

"We'll get by," Ashley's father said.

"Fine then, well if you can think of anything we can do, let us know. I guess we'll be going now."

"I have something you might be able to help us with, though," Ashley's mother said. "Do you know anything about aphids?"

"As a matter of fact, I do."

"Well, I'd like you to look at my roses and tell me what you think."

"Sure, no problem."

The four adults went into the backyard.

"This is our chance," Jen said. "Let's get rid of the food on our plates. I'll eat mine real fast, and you eat what you feel safe with and then dump the rest in the toilet."

"In the toilet?"

"Sure, that's where it'd end up anyway, right? Hurry up, we don't have much time."

Jen quickly ate the meat and about half of the mashed potatoes while Ashley had mostly mashed potatoes. And then they both ran to the toilet. Ashley dumped what she hadn't eaten and flushed.

"Now let's get out of here. Leave a note saying we're going over to my place."

Ashley scribbled a note and laid it on the dining room table. Jen added a note of her own, thanking Ashley's mother for dinner, ending with, "It tasted real good."

And then the two of them hurried out the front door and walked over to Jen's place. Jen's mom was taking a nap.

"First thing we need to do is change a tire," Jen said. "I've got some stuff you can wear. Follow me."

They walked into a bedroom strewn with clothes. "Sorry about the mess. I'm going to clean it up today."

"It smells like a bonfire in here."

"That's 'cause I still haven't taken care of my stuff from girls camp."

Jen opened a drawer and began pulling things out for Ashley to pick from.

They changed clothes and then went outside. Jen got a basketball from the garage and tossed it to Ashley.

"I usually don't play basketball on Sunday," Ashley said.

"Oh, right, I forgot, you're Miss Perfect. Well, just stand there then and I'll practice fouling." She dribbled the ball next to Ashley and gave her a gentle shove with her hip.

"Don't."

"Then play me a game."

"It's been a while since I've played," Ashley said.

"Good. I might win then." Jen brushed past Ashley for a layup. "Two-zip."

"What?"

Jen looked back with a big smile. "I'm ahead of you by two points."

"We didn't start."

"I did. You're now two points behind."

"Oh, I see. It's going to be like that, is it?" Ashley asked.

Jen stole the ball and went in for another layup. "Four-zip."

"I wasn't ready."

64

"And that's my fault?"

"Don't get me riled, Jen."

Jen laughed. "Yeah, right, like I'm scared to death."

A car pulled into the driveway, and Jen looked up. "I'll be right back," she said.

As Jen walked away, Ashley dribbled up near the basket and shot. "That's two for me."

"I called a time-out."

"There is no time-out in this game."

Ashley took another shot. "Four-up."

A boy got out of the car. He had long black hair and was wearing a black sport shirt, but had not buttoned any of the buttons, revealing what even Ashley had to admit was a great chest and good abs.

He leaned against the car while they talked. He spoke very few words.

A few minutes later he got back in his car to wait.

"That's Boone," Jen said, walking back to where Ashley was standing.

"Boom?" Ashley asked.

"Not like an explosion. Like Daniel Boone. He wants me to go with him."

"Where?"

"Just for a ride."

"Are you going with him?"

"Yeah, actually, I think I will."

"Why?"

"I don't know. Just for something to do. I'm going to change." Jen started for the house.

Ashley followed her inside. "Is this really what you want to do?"

"What else is there to do around here?"

Ashley followed Jen into her room where she changed into shorts and a black T-shirt.

"Don't go with him," Ashley said.

"He's not that bad. You want to meet him?"

"No."

Jen shrugged. "Suit yourself."

"What happened to Warrior Women of America?" Ashley asked.

"That was then, this is now."

Ashley followed Jen back outside where Jen approached the car and got in.

I can't let her go with him, Ashley thought. She ran to catch up with them as they pulled out of the driveway. "Hey, you guys, wait. I've decided to come with you!"

Boone braked to a stop. He looked irritated. "You're coming with us?" Jen asked.

"Sure, why not?" She leaned down to look at Boone. "Hi, there! I'm Ashley." She put out her hand to shake. He looked at her like she was crazy.

"How about I just get in the back," Ashley said, opening the back door and climbing in.

As they drove off, Jen moved over close to Boone, who put his arm around her shoulder, pulling her close. He didn't say anything but had kind of a smirk on his face. Ashley tried to think of something to say.

After about a block, she said, "Boy, I bet you can hardly wait to hear Jen and me sing songs we learned at girls camp, right? We've got about a hundred of 'em, so we'd better get started. If you want to join in, hey, be our guest."

Boone grumbled something.

"What'd you say?"

"He said he doesn't sing," Jen answered for him.

"Well, great, Boone, 'cause we don't, either, at least not good. But we'll sing our hearts out for you. Okay, let's start." She started to sing as loud and off-tune as she could: "'If you're happy, and you know it, clap your hands!' Come on Boone, join in! Sing your heart out! We've got a hundred songs just like this."

Five minutes later, Boone pulled up back in front of Jen's house and waited for the girls to get out of the car. As soon as the doors slammed, he spun the tires and pulled away.

With a big smile on her face, Ashley said, "I didn't even get to "Michael, Row the Boat Ashore.""

"You should register that singing voice of yours as a dangerous weapon."

"I know, like if we're surrounded by thugs with guns and knives, and I go, 'I'm warning you, don't make me sing.'"

They walked back toward the garage, and Jen threw Ashley the ball. "I guess I'm stuck with you for the rest of the day."

"How could you even think about spending time with him? I mean, just the way he looks."

"He's not that bad."

"He's pretty bad."

"After a couple of beers, he looks a lot better."

"What do you two talk about?" Ashley asked.

"Not much. Boone prides himself on not speaking more than fifty words a week. He prefers to let his macho qualities speak for him."

"You mean, like his abs?"

"Yeah, sure. And what about his chest? He has good definition there, too. And his arms. He has very good arms."

"Okay, but is there an actual brain in that head?" Ashley asked.

Jen shrugged her shoulders. "I'm not sure, but that's why it's good he doesn't talk much. I mean, I can always hope, right?"

"Jen, c'mon, you can do better than him. I'll find you a nice guy."

"What makes you think you can?"

"I know lots of guys."

"Do any of them ever phone you?"

"Sure they do, all the time."

"I don't mean because they want help on their homework."

Ashley paused. "Well, not as often as for that, of course."

Jen shot and made it. She pumped her fist in the air. "I'm on a roll. I can't be beat." She turned around to face Ashley. "Whataya say we go see our old buddy Nathan."

"Why? What would we say to him?"

Jen smiled. "You leave that to me."

They started for Nathan's house.

He lived in an old two-story house with shake siding that had once been brown, but, because of weathering, had turned gray. Someone had planted a pine tree in the front yard. The tree had been planted too close to the house, and over the years it had grown so big that it filled most of the front yard. The house was barely visible from the street.

"Is this place haunted?" Jen asked as they made their way to the front door.

Nathan's mother answered their knock. She had dull gray hair rigidly held in place, and when she opened the door, they could hear classical music coming from inside the house.

"Is Nathan here?" Ashley asked.

"He's taking a nap."

"Could you wake him up? It's kind of important," Jen said.

"All right, just a minute."

Nathan came to the door a few minutes later, yawning and running his fingers through his hair, trying to smooth it.

It had been a long time since Ashley had paid any attention to Nathan, and she looked at him as if for the first time. Appearance-wise, he was like a puzzle—not quite put together, with several missing pieces.

He was no longer tall for his age, as he'd been in junior high school. Or as awkward. He had naturally curly dark brown hair and brown eyes. The clothes he usually wore looked like they'd been put in a time capsule twenty years before and then suddenly appeared in his closet. Ashley decided they must be hand-me-downs from his much-older brothers.

The house had high ceilings and too many decorations cluttered on shelves on the wall, and it smelled musty and stale, as if nobody had opened a window in years.

"Hi, Nathan," Jen said.

"Hi," he said, yawning again.

"We came to visit you," Jen said.

"How come?"

"Well, we think it'd be nice if we could . . . well . . . be friends," Jen said.

"What would we do as friends?" Nathan asked.

"Do?" Jen asked.

"We need to do something," Nathan said.

"Like what?"

"I don't know."

"How about if we start a club at school?" Ashley asked.

"What kind of a club?"

"We'll let you decide, Nathan," Jen said. "What do you like to do?"

"I'm learning Italian on my own."

"Good. We could start an Italian club," Jen said.

"Oh, and I still like to listen to operas."

"Great! Now we're rolling! We'll start an Italian opera club."

"And I've always wanted to be a soccer coach."

"Okay! We'll start an Italian opera girls soccer club. And you can be our coach and speak Italian. Let's make plans, okay?"

"Okay, I guess." Nathan seemed surprised that any girl, much less two, would pay him any attention. After being ridiculed so much in ninth grade, he had made it his goal to never be noticed. And he had mostly succeeded.

Jen reached over and took Nathan's eyeglasses from him.

"What are you doing?" he asked.

"I just want to see something," Jen said, staring at Nathan.

"What?"

"How come you don't wear contacts?"

"I don't know. I just never thought about it."

"You should think about it."

"Why?"

"You'd look a lot better without glasses. Ashley, what do you think?"

68

She took a good look at Nathan. "Without glasses, you remind me of Superman."

He seemed flattered.

"What would you do if you were Superman?" Jen asked.

"Oh, you know, just the usual . . . save the world from destruction."

"Tough job," Ashley said.

He smiled modestly. "Somebody's got to do it."

"After a while, you'd probably need a vacation," Ashley said.

"Superman on vacation—what would that be like?" Jen asked.

The idea captured Nathan's imagination. He stood up and began to act it out. "If I were Superman on vacation, I'd go to Yellowstone National Park and rent a rowboat, and go maybe a mile above Yellowstone Falls and start fishing down the river. And when people started yelling to me about the falls, I'd pretend I couldn't hear them and show off the fish I'd caught and smile and wave at everyone on the bank. And they'd be trying to warn me about the falls, and then, just before I went over, I'd turn and see them, and go, 'Why didn't someone tell me?' And then I'd go over the falls, then come up, swim over to the bank, and wave to everyone that I was all right. That's what I'd do if I were Superman on vacation."

"You're too much, Nathan! That was really good!" Jen called out.

"Really?"

"Absolutely."

Nathan flashed a broad smile, the kind not seen coming from him since ninth grade.

They had a great time together, sitting in the living room, planning how they would start an Italian soccer club in the fall.

Nathan asked if they'd like some herb tea. Jen said yes right away, so Nathan left to go prepare it.

"Herb tea?" Ashley asked.

Jen nodded. "I know, but I didn't want to hurt his feelings. We need to work with him, Ashley. I mean, if we don't, who will?"

Ashley looked around the living room. It seemed to her like a museum for cheesy vacation souvenirs.

Nathan's mother was working at the kitchen table on family history. She insisted they have some English cookies with their tea, and transferred the hot water from the everyday cups Nathan had chosen to fancy cups reserved for company.

To Ashley, the tea tasted like the whole house smelled—musty like an attic filled with old clothes. "What kind of tea is this?" she asked.

"Chamomile," Nathan said.

Ashley couldn't decide whether the tea had taken on the smell of the house, or if they'd spilled some of the dry tea and the whole house had taken on the smell.

In either case, it was like drinking the essence of a stuffy room.

Nathan asked if they'd like to hear his favorite song. They, politely, said yes.

"It's called *Adagio for Strings*. It's by Samuel Barber."

As Nathan hunted for the CD, Ashley glanced at Jen, expecting her to give her a *let's get out of here* look. But she didn't.

"Why do you like it, Nathan?" Jen asked when he returned with the CD.

"Because it speaks to my soul," he said.

"I've never had anything speak to my soul," Jen said.

"This will," he said confidently.

Jen smiled weakly. "I'm not even sure I have a soul."

"We'll soon find out," Nathan said with a superior grin.

Nathan put in the CD and sat down across from the two girls.

The moment the music began, Ashley felt herself relax; the music was like a down comforter on a cold night. It soothed her and made her feel at peace.

Jen closed her eyes and listened attentively. And when it was over, she said softly, "That was *so* beautiful."

"Samuel Barber wrote it one summer when he was still a student. Most people love it more than anything else he wrote."

"I can see why. Thanks for sharing it with us," Jen said. "I'd forgotten that guys can be interested in ideas and culture and music. The guys I run around with never talk about Samuel the Barber."

Nathan suppressed a smile but didn't correct Jen.

"Nathan, you must be one of the last decent guys in the world. I'm glad we came over today," Jen said.

"Me, too." He let out a big sigh. "I've never been friends with girls before."

"Well, it's about time you were then, don't you think?" Jen asked.

"That'd be nice."

Jen sighed. "I know you've heard things about, you know, me."

Nathan nodded. "Yeah."

"Well, most of it isn't true, but some of it is. I want you to know, from now on, I'm going to try to be a good girl."

"Good for you," Nathan said.

"And I'm trying to change, too," Ashley said.

"There's nothing you need to change," Nathan said.

"Actually, there is," Jen said.

Ashley braced herself for the worse.

"Ashley needs to quit being Miss Perfect," Jen explained.

Ashley breathed a sigh of relief. She didn't want Nathan to know about her eating problem.

"Nathan, can I ask you a question?" Ashley said.

"Sure."

"Was it hard for you when people in school, you know, made fun of you?"

He lowered his gaze. "Yeah, it was."

"You just sort of disappeared after that, didn't you?" Ashley asked.

"I guess so."

"I'm sorry people were so cruel."

"Thanks."

"You used to sing a lot, didn't you?" Ashley asked.

"Yes, but I quit."

"How come?"

"I just didn't feel like it anymore."

"You mean anything that would put you in front of people, where they could make fun of you, right?" Jen asked.

"Yeah."

"I know a little of what you've gone through, Nathan," Jen said.

Nathan nodded his head. "I know. This is good, isn't it? I mean, that we can just be ourselves. I like that."

Nathan's folks invited Ashley and Jen to stay for supper. They had tuna sandwiches and tomato soup.

About ten that night, Nathan drove them home. He dropped Ashley off first.

When she walked into her house, her mother was at the dining room table, her father on the phone.

"Where on earth have you been all this time?" her mother asked.

"I was over at Jen's house, and then we went over to see Nathan Billingsley."

"I would have appreciated knowing where you were."

"Sorry," Ashley said.

"I hope you're not planning on spending much more time with that girl. While you've been gone, I've done some checking on her. Would you like to know what I found out?"

"No, I don't want to know."

"I think you should."

"I'm going to bed, Mother." Ashley turned and headed for her bedroom.

Her mother followed her.

Ashley entered her room and closed the door.

Her mother walked in. "You're going to listen to this, whether you want to or not. I found out that Jennifer—"

"It's *Jen*. She goes by Jen."

"She has a very bad reputation. Drinking, smoking, getting drunk, running around with any boy who will buy her beer."

"She's quitting all that."

"People can say they're going to do something and never do it."

"She will. I'm sure of it."

"I shudder to think what will happen to you if you keep seeing her."

"Do you know what will happen to me if I *don't* see her?"

"No, what?"

"I'll go on like before."

"And that's so bad?"

"Yes, it is. It's very bad."

"I don't understand you anymore."

"You never have, Mother. You just never knew it because I was trying so hard to be your perfect little daughter. Well, I can't do that anymore."

"I think we need to get your father in here."

"Oh, yes, let's be sure and do that. He'll come in. You'll tell him the problem, and thirty seconds later, he'll back you up, and then walk out with the matter cleared up in his mind. He's basically your puppet, isn't he?"

"How can you say that about your own father?"

"It's a little hard at first, but I'm sure it'll get easier with practice."

"Your father is under a lot of strain now at work."

"So what else is new?"

"I'm going to get him."

It was just as Ashley predicted. Her mother presented her case. Her father listened, then told Ashley she was grounded and that she was not to see Jen anymore, and that she was to come right home from school every day and work on her homework. And then he glanced at his watch and left.

Five minutes, Ashley thought. *That's ten times as long as I thought it would take.*

Her mother looked at the clock. "Well, it's late, and you need to get some sleep."

"So I can do well and make you proud?"

Her mother shook her head. "I can't talk to you when you're this way."

Her mother left and Ashley was, once again, alone in her room.

She felt like her head was going to burst. She knew she wouldn't be able to sleep. Her stomach was hurting, like it did whenever she was stressed, like in school before a test, or when she came home from school.

She was so hungry she could hardly stand it. She decided to wait until her parents were in bed and then go raid the refrigerator and grab something to eat.

She began thinking about her sister, Alauna, and the struggles she'd had her senior year in high school. At the time, Ashley had been very critical of Alauna for putting her parents through so much grief, but now she saw it in a new light.

Ashley grabbed her cordless phone, went into the bathroom, closed the door, turned on the exhaust fan, and phoned Alauna.

After realizing it was Ashley on the phone, Alauna's first words were, "Is anything wrong?"

"No, not really."

"Mom and dad are okay?"

"Yeah, they're fine."

"Good. You had me worried there for a moment."

"Why?"

"Because you've never called me before."

"I should have. I mean, you *are* my sister."

"I wasn't much good to you when I was home. Especially right there at the end of my senior year."

"I didn't understand then what was happening. I guess I blamed you for being such a . . ."

"Troublemaker?"

"Yes, I guess that's right." Ashley paused. "But now I can see how it was for you."

"Are you the bad guy now?"

"I'm starting to be."

"Is that okay with you?"

"I don't know. It's hard either way."

"Tell me about it," Alauna said.

"Do you and I come from, well, a normal family?"

"It seems pretty normal to outsiders, doesn't it?"

"Yeah, it does, but is it?"

"Are you trying to figure out who's crazy, you or Mom and Dad?"

"Something like that."

"You might not be asking the right person for this, you know."

"But, at BYU, do you fit in?"

"Yeah, pretty much."

"So how bad can you be, right?"

73

"Getting away from home has helped me settle down quite a bit."

"Because you don't need to deal with Mom and Dad?"

Alauna laughed. "That's part of it."

"The same thing is happening with me that happened to you. I have a friend. Her name is Jen. Do you remember her?"

"Yeah."

"She's been kind of wild, but we got to be good friends at girls camp. We made an agreement that I'd try to help her quit drinking and partying, and she'd help me with my problem."

"What is your problem?"

Ashley paused. "I'd rather not say."

"You don't have to tell me, but by any chance is it something that makes you hold everything inside and pretend nothing's wrong, but inside you're hurting all the time?"

"How did you know?"

"I could see that in you when I was home. You hold all your feelings inside, don't you, and make everyone think you're this perfect girl with no problems. That's not good, Ashley."

"I know that."

"Don't do it then."

"But when I try to break out, Mom gets on my case."

"Find a friend you can confide in."

"I have, but that's the problem. Mom and Dad said I can't see her anymore."

"Is she that bad an influence?"

"No. She's good for me."

"You'd better find someone who can take your side with Mom and Dad."

"Who?"

"Somebody in the church, someone Mom and Dad respect."

"Like the bishop?"

"Sure, like him, or one of the Young Women leaders. Just someone who can see both sides."

By the time Ashley got off the phone, she felt much better, and a short time later, she went to bed.

She wanted to go to sleep, but she was so hungry that all she could think about was eating. *This time I'll stay in control and not eat too much. I'll just go in the kitchen and say I'm hungry and I want a snack. And Mother will say, At this time of night? And I'll say yes. And she'll go, you wouldn't be hungry if you'd eat the meals I prepare. And I'll go, I know but I'm still hungry. And she'll go, I suppose you want me to fix it for you? And I'll say, no, I can fix it myself. And she'll go, Well, make sure you clean up*

74

after yourself. And I'll say I will. And she'll tell me about the time I left some turkey out overnight and how she had to throw it away and what a waste of money that was. And I'll go, I'll clean up. And she'll go, make sure you do.

Ashley got up, turned on the light, went into the bathroom, and weighed herself. She was down half a pound.

If I don't eat, then that will be good. I'll have lost weight for the day. But if I don't eat something now and keep it down, then I'll get up in the middle of the night and binge and purge. And then when Jen asks me, I'll have to admit what I did.

I've got to eat something now. And I've got to keep it down. Even if it does mean having to deal with Mother.

She went to the door and opened it and walked quickly down the hall to the kitchen.

Her mother and father were sitting at the dining room table. They seemed preoccupied.

Ashley said, "I'm hungry. I'm going to make myself a little snack."

"That's fine, dear," her mother said.

"I'll clean up after I'm done."

"I appreciate that."

She made herself a roast beef sandwich and sat in the kitchen to eat it. While she was eating, she heard her mother say, "We don't know for sure that's what they have in mind."

"What else could it be?"

"I don't know. We'll just have to see, that's all."

Something's wrong, Ashley thought.

She went to the door leading into the dining room. "What's happening?"

"Oh, nothing," her father said. "Nothing at all."

Ashley nodded and went back to her sandwich. She ate slowly, telling herself with each bite that what she was eating was not going to make her fat. *I didn't use butter and I didn't use mayonnaise, so it's just a little bit of meat and some bread. It'll be okay this time.*

After she finished, she washed up the plate and knife she'd used and returned to her room.

She got ready for bed, spending as little time as possible in the bathroom, so she wouldn't be tempted to throw up her sandwich. She was sure that Jen would ask her the next day. She didn't want to get in the habit of lying to Jen because if she started that, then she'd have nobody to be truthful with. Besides, if she started to lie to Jen, then maybe Jen would start lying to her about her smoking and drinking and being with her low-life friends.

She lay in bed and thought about Jen and Nathan and about the time they'd spent together that day. She felt bad that Nathan had been made fun of all these years for no reason, and about how cruel people in school were. The boys who made fun of Nathan were the ones who spread stories about Jen and, also, the ones who ridiculed girls they said were fat. It wasn't fair that the boys with the least intelligence were the ones who got to decide who was acceptable and who wasn't.

Well, they won't make fun of me. I won't let them. I'll keep my weight down so they won't tear me down behind my back.

She was excited for school to start in the fall, excited to see what it would be like to be in an Italian soccer club with Nathan as the coach.

6

It was a hot, unusually humid Sunday night in August. Jen hadn't been able to sleep because of the heat, so she was awake when a car pulled into the driveway. She knew it was her mother and Billy James Dean, the man her mom had been seeing for the past six months.

Billy James Dean liked to be called by his full name. He ran a pawn shop in the part of Salt Lake City that the tour buses avoided. He was a thin, wiry man with a mustache, which he was always smoothing.

Jen sat up in bed to watch her mother and Billy James in the car. *If I see them kissing, I'm not sure I can handle it. I might be like Ashley and end up running for the bathroom.*

How can she stand being with him? He's such a creep, with his shirt open to the navel, and his greasy mustache, and all the time giving presents to us. Like we don't know where they came from—cheap trinkets from his store. If something doesn't sell, he gives it to us.

And the lies he tells. Like "This used to belong to Queen Victoria." Yeah, right, like she couldn't make her payment on the castle, so she pawned her necklace. Sure, Billy James Dean, I believe that. Whatever you say.

I hate it when he tries to be friendly to me and asks dumb questions, like what grade in school I'm going to be. I don't know how many times he's asked me that.

What am I going to do if Mom ever actually marries the loser? She might, too, if he asks her. She's desperate enough. She probably thinks nobody better is going to come along.

Jen got out of bed and stepped to the window and closed the blinds. Then she turned on her bedside lamp and made her way to her closet. There, from a box on the top shelf of her closet, she took out a pack of cigarettes, pulled one out, and sat cross-legged on the floor. She held the cigarette in her hand, looking at it. It was like meeting up with an old friend she hadn't seen for a long time.

Once or twice a week, she went through this ritual. Once she'd even lit a match and brought it to the cigarette, and then blew it out.

I can't let Ashley down. She's trying so hard to be good. And she's doing a lot better now. So that's good.

I'm doing better, too. Except sometimes I miss smoking and drinking and partying.

Not all the time. Just sometimes. Like now. Mostly late at night, when I can't sleep.

A car door slammed shut. Jen quickly reached to turn off her lamp, then peeked through the blinds to watch her mom and Billy James Dean come up the walk. She could hear them through the open window.

"Thanks," her mom said.

"I'm the one who should thank you," Billy James Dean said with his raspy voice.

"Good night."

"Oh, wait, I almost forgot. I got you a gift. Didn't have time to wrap it, but here it is."

"It's real nice, Billy," her mother said with only a hint of enthusiasm.

"It's solid gold."

"Billy . . . are you sure about that?"

"Well, maybe not *solid* gold, but pretty close to that."

"Thank you. I'll put it with the others."

"I treat you real good, don't I?" Billy James Dean asked.

"I guess so."

"So why don't we get hitched?"

"Jen has already gone through so much already. I can't put her through any more."

"Why, I'd be a stabilizing influence on the girl, a real father figure."

"I got to be honest with you, Billy James. She's not that fond of you."

"That's 'cause she don't know me very well. I could take her huntin' with me this fall. I bet that'd help. Especially after she shot her first buck. That's always a thrill, let me tell you."

"Well, I'm not sure she'd go for that, but I'll talk to her about it and see what she says. I really need to go now."

"Sure, me too. I got a big day tomorrow. Big sale on handguns. Wish me luck."

"Yeah, sure, good night, Billy James."

Jen climbed into bed, pulled up the covers, and pretended to be asleep. Her mother always checked her room when she came in from a date. Sometimes, if she didn't have to work the next morning, she'd even stay awake for Jen to come home. But if she had to work, she just went to bed but always left a note on Jen's pillow, asking her to wake her up and tell her when she got home.

Her mother came inside, turned on the hall light, and walked quietly to Jen's room, looked in, then went to her own room and closed the door.

Jen sat up in bed, still holding the cigarette in her hand as if she were smoking it, listening to the sounds of her mother getting ready for bed.

In twenty minutes the house was quiet again.

Jen waited another half an hour, then grabbed her sleeping bag from the bottom of her closet, and went out to the trampoline in the backyard.

A minute later she was staring up at the night sky.

I'm the same age my mother was when she got pregnant with me. After that she didn't have that many choices.

She could have aborted me. I'm glad she didn't.

She could have given me away.

She did what she thought was the right thing to do. She married my dad.

But that didn't last.

And now, if she marries Billy James Dean, she'll go from one bad choice to another.

I'm so critical of her, but I very nearly made the same mistake. If I'd have kept going the same way I was going, I'd probably be pregnant now.

And the whole cycle would repeat itself over again.

A shooting star flashed its way across the sky. It reminded her of girls camp. She brought the fabric of the sleeping bag to her nose. It still smelled of smoke from campfires.

She'd been to church every Sunday since girls camp. Always with Ashley. And she always sat with Ashley's family.

She wasn't sure if she believed everything that was taught, but she did believe in what she saw. Like a young-married couple in the ward with a three-month-old baby. During each sacrament meeting, Jen watched them.

Jason and Natalie Rudd: Jason, twenty-six, an accountant who worked in Salt Lake City, studious looking, sometimes unaware of his surroundings, especially when he was reading. Natalie, long blonde hair that she kept threatening to cut short, still nursing her baby boy. They came to church like they were going to war—loaded down with infant seat and burp bibs and bags and bottles and diapers. They were still new enough parents that when their baby cried, Natalie turned red with embarrassment. Jen liked the way Jason didn't just let Natalie handle the problems with the baby. He was often the one who took little Andrew out when he cried, and he was always holding him, making faces at the baby and kissing and playing with him.

Jen had asked Natalie how old they'd been when they got married. "I was twenty, but Jason was twenty-three. He was just finishing up at the university."

Jen watched them every week at church. And the more she watched them, the more she wanted to someday have what they had.

She looked up at the stars and made a wish. *I want to be married in the temple some day. Not because I know what goes on there. Or even that I know that the Church is true. It's more because I can see that getting married in the temple has worked for Jason and Natalie. Maybe it will work for me.*

I want to be married to a returned missionary, like Jason. Not because I believe so much in the teachings of the Church but because of the tenderness I see in Jason's eyes when he looks at Natalie and at Andrew.

And when I get married, I want it to be because of respect and friendship, and maybe even love—not because I'm pregnant and can't think of anything else to do.

I want to be a "good" girl, not because I believe there's some grand reward in the hereafter if I am, but because I want a Jason in my life, someone who'll think first about me and our baby.

From now on, I don't want to settle for less, like my mom has done all her life.

So I'll wait.

And wait.

And wait.

And wait.

Until the time is right.

She smiled, closed her eyes, and soon drifted off to sleep.

7

Ashley thought it was a miracle that they were able to get official school recognition for the Italian Soccer Team for girls, especially since there was already a school sponsored boys and girls soccer team.

Nathan, wearing his father's dark brown button-down sweater and with his hair neatly combed, played the part of the inquiring student to perfection. Ashley and Jen let him do the talking.

"We are interested in exploring Italian culture as it is reflected in soccer," Nathan explained to Miss Fairchild, the newly hired activities director for the school. "As they say in Italian, *Avete qualcosa di diverso.*"

"I'm sorry. I don't speak Italian. What does that mean?"

"It means 'Soccer is the heartbeat of Italy.'"

"I see. Well, I'll be interested in seeing how this goes."

"So we're officially a school organization?" Ashley asked.

"Yes, of course."

"Thank you very much," Nathan said politely.

"Yeah, thanks," Jen added.

The three retreated to the hall. "I didn't know you knew Italian that well," Ashley said.

"I don't. I got this paperback book for people going to Italy. I just memorize phrases from it."

"What did you actually say?" Jen asked.

"In Italian it means, 'Have you got something different?'"

"Close enough, I'd say," Ashley said with a big grin on her face.

The next thing they needed to do was recruit players. "We don't plan on actually winning any games," Ashley said to a girl in her calculus class. "We just thought it'd be fun to get out there and have a good time. Also, for people like me and you who just mainly worry about grades, this is going to look *so* good on our applications for college."

"It will? How?"

"The Italian part will set you apart as a person of culture and sophistication. The soccer part will show that not only are you smart, you're also well-rounded in other areas of life."

"But I don't know anything about soccer," the girl said.

"So much the better. We're just in this to have fun."

They had eight other girls at their first meeting. After reading the constitution for the club, Ashley said, "Our coach should be arriving any minute now. He's a foreign exchange student from Italy."

When Nathan showed up, Jen and Ashley had a hard time not bursting out laughing. Wearing a long trench coat, a yellow bike racing cap, and dark glasses, he spoke only Italian phrases from his tourist book.

They met in a classroom and then after the meeting walked down to the track-football field.

"Can I have a bag, please!" Nathan shouted to the girls in Italian. In his tourist book it was a question, but he barked it out as if it were a command.

"What does he want?" one of the girls asked.

"Do any of you speak Italian?" Jen asked.

Nobody did.

"He wants us to run around the track," Ashley said.

They ran laps around the track. Every time they came by, Nathan, holding a stopwatch and a clipboard, would shout another phrase from his book.

"Where is the toilet!" Nathan shouted in Italian.

"What is he saying?" one of the girls asked.

"Run faster."

After four laps around the track, Nathan, using gestures and unrelated Italian phrases, got the girls into two lines so they could kick the ball back and forth.

"Very good!" Nathan shouted in Italian. "Is the train on time!"

"What does he want us to do now?" one of the girls asked.

"He wants us to kick the ball to each other as we're running toward the goal."

"How do you know?" one of the girls asked Jen.

"I grew up listening to my grandparents speaking Italian," she lied. "They came to the United States from Italy just after they were married."

After an hour, Nathan shouted, "Where is the hotel!"

"That means our practice is over. You can all come back tomorrow, unless you want to quit," Ashley said.

"I'm not quitting," one of the girls said.

"Me, either. I want to play Italian soccer."

Pulling Jen aside, one of the girls said, "Can I ask a question?"

Nathan was still out on the field, waving his arms, shouting one Italian phrase after another, trying to run off two seventh-grade boys who wanted to use the field to throw a football back and forth.

"Sure," Jen said.

"That's Nathan from calculus class, isn't it?"

"Yes, it is."

"Why's he acting like he's Italian?"

"Good question. Let's ask him. I'll go get him."

Jen walked out on the field, put her arm around Nathan's shoulder, and spoke confidentially to him, then brought him back to where the girls were resting.

"Girls, this is Nathan. He's going to explain why, as our coach, he's going to be Italian."

Nathan's face was red and he kept his eyes down.

"It's okay, Nathan. You can tell us. We're all friends here."

"I can't be myself in public," he said softly.

"Why not?"

"Because when I am, people make fun of me."

"You mean like from ninth grade?" one of the girls asked.

Nathan nodded.

"That doesn't matter now, Nathan," the girl said.

Nathan, his head still down, nodded.

"I think we're all in agreement here, Nathan. You can either be yourself or be from Italy," Jen said.

He nodded again, lifted his gaze slightly, wiped his eyes, then flashed a shy grin. "I want to be from Italy."

"Then it's settled!" Jen said. "Girls, I'd like you to meet Giovanni Gabriella, our soccer coach."

"*Buon giorno,*" Nathan said tentatively.

"*Buon giorno,*" the girls enthusiastically called back.

Two weeks later, on a Friday afternoon, they played their first game. They played the girls soccer team from their own school, who had team jerseys while Nathan's team wore white shirts with a number magic-marked on the back.

After twenty minutes the score was 10–0. Nathan made a substitution and took Ashley out of the game. As he escorted her away from the other girls, he put his hand on her back and said out loud, in Italian, "I do not wish to buy anything today."

Privately he whispered, "Ashley, you are the most polite soccer player I've ever seen."

"Thank you."

"Actually, it's not a compliment."

"It isn't?"

"No. You need to toughen up—get more aggressive."

"Why? We're losing so bad now, what's the point in even trying?"

He spoke in her ear. "Life is like a tournament, Ashley. Even though we lose, we get better with each game."

"You're starting to sound like a real coach, Nathan."

"I *am* a real coach."

"Why are you taking this so serious?"

"Pride in my Italian heritage."

"You don't have any Italian heritage."

"I could have, though. Look, you're way too polite. I want you to go out there and kick a girl in the shins."

"Why?"

"Don't ask questions, just do it."

Ashley did as she was asked. Unfortunately it was during a time out. The official saw it and carded Ashley.

"I do not like my room!" Nathan shouted at Ashley, taking her out of the game.

On the sidelines, as they walked away from the other team members, Nathan quietly said, "When you kick someone, it should be while going for the ball."

"You didn't say that."

"Anyone would know that's what I meant."

"I didn't."

"You should have."

"Don't talk down to me, Nathan. I can learn—but not when you're being mean."

"I'm not being mean. You think I'm being mean?"

"You are being mean."

"I'll show you mean," he smiled. "All right, Ashley, we're going to do some play acting here. I want you to throw a fit now, okay? Follow my lead." He stepped back and threw his hands up in the air. "I need the bus for Florence!" he shouted in Italian.

Ashley, suppressing a smile, yelled back at him, "That does it! You don't talk to me like that!"

He followed after her, yelling in Italian, "How much does it cost to take the bus!"

She came over to him and together they walked away from everyone else. "What now?" she asked.

"I want you to go ballistic on me right here and now."

"Why?"

"Just do it. Turn the bench over and yell and say you won't stand for this anymore. Say you're going to play soccer the way it was made to be played—rough and dirty. Then demand I send you in."

Ashley did as she was told with the bench and the yelling. "Send me in!" she shouted.

Nathan shook his head vigorously.

"Send me in, or I'll rip your tongue out!"

Nathan threw up his hands in resignation and, in Italian, said, "*Ho mal di cuore.*" (I have a heart condition.) He feebly waved her back into the game.

Ashley turned away from everyone and smiled. *I love this,* she thought.

Once in the game, she found that her temper flare-up had been noticed by the other team, and now they seemed reluctant to tangle with her.

For the rest of the game she growled under her breath and bared her teeth at anyone who got in her way. Not that it did that much good. They ended up losing 16-0.

On the way home, after the game, Ashley felt great. She'd had a great time. She'd kicked a girl in the shins, she'd knocked a bench over, she'd growled at a girl on the other team, and, in Italian, she'd yelled, "Is there breakfast included with my room!" She felt liberated and free, as if she could express any emotion, step into any conflict, overcome any obstacle.

She felt that way until she got home.

Nathan let her off. She said good-bye to Nathan and Jen and then jogged up the sidewalk, threw open the door, and marched in, full of hope for the future, ready to take on the world.

"Ashley, is that you?" her mother called out.

"Yeah, it's me."

Her mother came out from the kitchen. "Where have you been all this time?"

"Playing soccer. I told you last night."

"Well, yes, I know, but I had no idea it would take so long. I expected you home an hour and a half ago. Are you going to do this very often?"

"I am. We have a couple of games every week. And then, of course, we have practices the rest of the time."

"I would think you could use your time more wisely than that."

"This is a wise use of my time," Ashley said, her mood already darkening.

"Well, that's up to you, but don't blame me if you don't get into BYU."

It was a threat she'd heard since seventh grade—that if her grades weren't perfect, she wouldn't get accepted into BYU.

"Don't you even want to know how the game went?"

"Well, yes, of course. How did it go?"

"We lost 16 to zero."

"Oh, my."

"But they didn't score as many points during the second half. So we got better as the game went on."

"That's nice, dear."

She was going to tell about turning over the bench and about Nathan spreading the rumor that she was a hothead, and how she told off a girl in Italian and got her to back down, but she knew her mother wouldn't understand why that was the best part of the day for her.

While she was taking a shower, she turned on the fan and practiced yelling in Italian, "Can you direct me to the museum!"

There was a knock on the door. "Ashley, are you all right?"

"I'm practicing my Italian."

"You're not taking Italian in school, are you?"

"No, Nathan is teaching it to us in soccer."

"Well, it's very disruptive."

"Then go somewhere in the house where you can't hear it." She ended with calling out in Italian, "Where is the bottled water!"

"We'll talk after you get out of the shower," her mother said.

Ashley bristled at the thought of sitting down with her mother. *She doesn't care what I do as long as it's quiet and doesn't cause any waves. Like throwing up my food. That's quiet. And it keeps me quiet, and no problem because I have no energy left to fight her. But let me keep my food down, and get mentally tough, and she's threatened. No wonder Alauna was so much trouble. It was the only way she could survive in this place. Well, I'm not going to quit soccer, and I'm not going to quit being friends with Jen and Nathan. They're good for me. I feel like a different person when I'm with them.*

She felt her stomach knot up as she dried and got dressed. Her mother always came out on top of every discussion. Except with Alauna. And Alauna would argue every point until finally she would start shouting and run out of the house. Once Alauna had been gone for two days. She stayed with a friend but wouldn't call and tell where she was. And now Ashley knew why.

I have to stick up for myself, she thought. *I can't cave in like I usually do. I have to stay strong.*

On her way out of the room, she picked up her soccer T-shirt. She brought it to her face. There was a faint smell of sweat on it from the game. *That's from me,* she thought proudly. *It's my smell, and I like it because it means I can fight back. I like that about me now.*

She brought the shirt with her as she sought out her mother. She went in the kitchen. Her mother was fixing a favorite of her parents, baked fish, coleslaw, and cornbread. The smell of the fish was almost too much for Ashley.

"I'm here to talk," she announced.

"Now? When I'm fixing supper?"

"Yes, now."

"Well, okay, if it must be now . . ."

Ashley knew her mother was waiting for her to say, "That's okay. It can be after supper." But she didn't.

"Let's talk in the dining room," her mother said wearily. They sat down. "To be perfectly honest, Ashley, I'm worried about you," her mother said.

"There's no reason to be."

"Well, maybe not. It's just that since you've been running around with that Hobbs girl, things are not the same."

"I know. They're better."

"Taking the car out in the middle of the night without permission is not better, Ashley. Practically ruining girls camp for other girls is not better. Wasting your time kicking a ball instead of studying is not better. And yelling at the top of your voice in Italian while you're taking a shower is not better. I'm seeing behavior I thought I would never see in you. Alauna, maybe, but not you."

"I'm on a soccer team. We play games. That's what teams do. They play games."

"Well, it's not like this is an official school team. I don't think you should see these people anymore. How are you going to get into BYU if you don't settle down and apply yourself?"

"I'm not going to BYU. There, did that take care of it? I feel better now that that's all settled. Can I go now?"

"Of course you want to go to BYU. Your father and I both went there. Alauna is there, and even she is enjoying it."

"Sorry, not interested."

"You see what I mean? This is exactly the kind of attitude that worries me, and you're picking it up from those so-called friends of yours."

"They are my friends. They're the best friends I've ever had. They help me be me."

"That's not true. This is not the real you."

Ashley brought the shirt to her face and took in the smell. "This *is*

87

the real me, Mother." She thrust it in her mother's direction. "Want to take a whiff?"

Her mother turned up her nose. "You should put that in the washing machine right away."

"No, that would be bad luck. I think I won't wash it until after our season is finished."

"Don't be silly, of course you want it washed. I'll take care of it." Her mother reached for the shirt.

Ashley backed away. "Leave it alone! If I want it washed, I'll wash it myself."

"I want you to quit seeing that girl Jen. She's not a good influence on you."

"Sorry, but I won't do that."

"I've heard some more things about her that are really quite disturbing."

"She's going to church now. And she's not partying anymore. I know that for sure."

"For the most part, Ashley, people don't change."

"Not alone, maybe, but with a friend they can."

"If you insist on spending time with her, you're the one who will change, and you'll become just like Jen. Is that what you want?"

"You don't know anything about me, Mother, and even less about Jen. Why can't you just trust me to do the right thing?"

"I will not stand by and watch you throw away your opportunities. I want you to quit soccer and stop seeing Jen."

"I will never do that, Mother. Excuse me, I have to go now."

"We'll talk about this some more after supper."

"No, we won't. I'm done talking. As they say in Italian, *Penso che questo sia sbagliato.*" (I think this is wrong.)

"What does it mean?"

"You wouldn't understand, Mother. All you have to know is I'm not eating here."

"Why not?"

"Because if I stay here and eat supper, I'll get sick."

"You've had fish before."

"I mean it, Mother. I have to go now."

"I haven't given my permission for you to leave."

"Then I'll do it without your permission. I'll be home by midnight."

"Ashley, come here . . ."

She ran out the door and over to Jen's house. It took her ten minutes.

"What's happening?" Jen said when she opened the door.

"Can I stay here for a while?"

"Sure, what's up? Problems at home?"

"My mom wants me to quit soccer and quit seeing you."

"How come?"

"Because of my bad attitude."

"I like your attitude."

"She doesn't."

"Does she know about your eating . . . problem?"

"No."

"Maybe you should tell her."

"No, she'd overreact and send me to a hospital for who knows how long."

"You're doing better now, aren't you?"

"Yes."

"Maybe that'd make a difference to her—if she knew soccer is good for you."

"It's not just soccer. It's you and Nathan," Ashley said.

"I know. It's good for me, too."

"It's the best."

"We've got to keep it going," Jen said.

"I know."

"No matter what happens." Jen looked worried as she said it.

"What could happen?"

Jen said softly, "Nathan asked me to go to a movie with him tonight."

"Oh." Ashley tried not to show how hurt she felt. "What did you tell him?"

"I said yes, but I'll call him back and tell him you're coming with us."

"No, don't do that."

"The three of us have to stay together. I can see that now. I'll call and tell him."

"I don't want to be in the way."

Jen draped her arm around Ashley's neck. "Look, it's just Nathan, okay?"

Ashley looked into Jen's eyes for confirmation, saw it, then said, "Okay."

"All right, I'll call him and tell him of the change in plans."

She was halfway to the phone when Ashley called after her. "Jen?"

"Yes?"

"If I'm ever in the way, just tell me, okay?"

"That'll never happen."

Even though they had a trampoline at home, Ashley never jumped on it. But while Jen talked to Nathan on the phone, Ashley went outside and started to jump on Jen's trampoline, at first making tiny little hops into the air and then gradually gaining confidence. She got high enough to do a seat drop. She knew that most people her age could do so much more, but for her it was a triumph.

She felt a connection between her body, her mind, and her spirit, as if every part of her was enjoying the experience, momentarily freed from the bonds of earth, her arms out to maintain her balance, reaching the top and then starting down, her hair shifting slightly as she gained in speed, her knees bent to absorb the shock, and then pushing down to propel her once again into the air, growing closer to tree tops and the birds that perched on branches to watch this new flying creature. She felt pride that her body could perform even this simple feat, and she took joy in being at a friend's house, a friend who genuinely liked her and could see through her weaknesses and still be her friend.

She jumped higher and higher.

She felt so happy, just being there, savoring the moment.

This is the way life should be, she thought.

Jen came out of the house and saw how high Ashley was jumping. "What happened? And what have you done with the real Ashley?"

"I *am* the real Ashley! Look at this!"

She did one magnificent seat drop.

"You go, girl!"

Ashley burst into a giggle. She loved it when Jen talked to her like that.

"I just talked to Nathan. He's actually glad we're all going together. But the more we got talking, the more we decided to really have some fun with this. So he's going as a famous Italian movie director and we're going as his bimbo girlfriends, one on each arm. You okay with that?"

"I guess so. It depends on what I have to wear."

"It'll be okay, maybe a little weird, but still okay. Tell me what you think. We'll dress up for the occasion. And the only thing we'll say all night is, "Oh, Antonio, Antonio!" And then we'll giggle a lot, like he's the funniest guy in the world. Oh, also, we have to each kiss him on the cheek at the same time."

"Why do we both have to kiss him at the same time?" Ashley asked.

"Because it adds to the image of our being ditsy."

"And this is a goal of ours?" Ashley asked.

"No, but it's like being in a play, though. I mean what else can we do around here for some excitement?"

"What if someone sees us?"

"Anyone from school will know it's not for real."

"What if my parents see me?"

"How many movies have your folks gone to in the last year?"

"One or two maybe."

"What are the chances they're going tonight?"

"Zero."

"Exactly. Relax, it'll be fine."

They ended up in Jen's mom's room, in the far reaches of her closet, trying on dresses her mother had worn years ago, working to get the most outrageous look they could manage. It had been clear back to grade school years since they had played dress-up, but this brought back the same feelings of excitement and intrigue.

By six-thirty they'd both decided on what they were going to wear: long dresses with high heels and fake pearl necklaces. This, combined with tousled hair, over-made-up eyes, dark gray lipstick, and too much blush on their cheeks added to the overall effect. After they finished getting ready, they stood in front of the mirror together and looked at themselves.

"We look like Cinderella's wicked stepsisters!" Ashley said before bursting out laughing.

"You're right. We do," Jen said, reaching out and putting her arm around Ashley's waist for what would have been a photo-op if there'd been a camera nearby. "What were the wicked stepsisters' names?"

"I don't know."

"Me either. You hungry?" Jen asked.

"I'm starving."

"For real?"

"For real."

"Good for you. Let's change clothes, then go see what's in the kitchen."

They found some ground beef and potatoes.

"I can cook us up some fried potatoes. Can you make us some hamburgers?" Jen said.

Ashley gulped. "I guess so. I've never done it before though."

"You're kidding?"

"My mom doesn't like people to mess up her kitchen."

"Well, look around, we don't have that problem here." And it was true. The kitchen looked like it was in need of a thorough cleaning. Jen's mother was out on a date with Billy James Dean.

Ashley painstakingly worked to form a couple of hamburger patties. Jen peeled four large potatoes, then cut them up into little pieces.

91

"How you coming on the patties there, Chef?"

"I'm almost done."

"Whoa, look at that, perfect circles," Jen said.

"Yeah, pretty much."

"We're going to eat them, gal, not frame 'em. Next time we do this, you get one minute to turn out ten patties."

"Impossible."

"Not if you don't care what they look like."

Jen set the frying pan on the stove, covered the bottom of the cast-iron skillet with oil, turned on the heat, and waited for the oil to get hot, then dumped the potatoes she'd cut into the skillet.

"Right about now I should be smelling hamburgers cooking," Jen said.

"I'm almost finished."

"You better get going."

"I need another frying pan."

"Open that cupboard door. There should be one in there."

Ashley pulled out an identical cast-iron frying pan and set it on the counter. "This is so heavy!"

"You get strong when you cook in this house."

"How much oil do I add to the hamburger?"

"Don't add anything. They make their own grease."

"They do?"

"There's so much you've got to learn," Jen said.

"I know. There really is."

Ashley carefully positioned each hamburger patty on the frying pan, then set the pan on the stove's other large burner. "This is so much fun," she said.

"What?"

"Cooking."

"Cooking's not fun."

"Cooking together then."

Jen thought about it. "Yeah, you're right, it is fun."

"You want to know something? When I was jumping on the trampoline while you were talking to Nathan, for just a minute or two, I felt so good. I don't know how to explain it. It was like I really liked my body and my mind and everything about me, like I was standing outside my body, and I could see what a magnificent creature I am."

"Really? That must've been great to feel that way."

"It did. It felt great. See, the thing is, most of the time I hate my body."

"I'm that way, too, a lot of the time."

"Do you think guys hate their bodies?" Ashley asked.

Jen shook her head. "Guys don't have to be any particular way. However they turn out is just fine."

"Some guys who are short get teased, though."

"Yeah, but it doesn't seem to get to them. Well, maybe it does, but maybe not as much."

"I wish I could like who I am, and not keep beating up on myself all the time."

"You know what? I think I know why girls can be so mean to each other."

"Why?"

"Because we feel so bad about ourselves." Jen turned the potatoes over with a spatula. "Look at that, golden brown. You can't get any better looking or tasting potatoes than this. Years from now, when you're old and gray, you'll look back on your life, and you'll say, 'Boy, those sure were good fried potatoes. After that, my life pretty much went downhill.'"

"They look good, but how do they taste?" Ashley took a spoon and dished up some of the fried potatoes.

"Hey, none of that," Jen warned lightheartedly.

"They are good!"

"And it's going to stay down after you eat it?"

"It is."

"That's my good girl."

"It's easier when I'm with you. It's at home that I have the most trouble."

"And at school?"

"There's nothing I care to eat at school."

"The reason we eat is so we have the energy to do fun stuff. Make sense so far?"

"Sure, no problem."

"Good."

Ashley ceremoniously tapped Jen on the shoulder. "I challenge you to a duel with spatulas."

Jen picked up another spatula. "Don't start something you can't finish."

"Oh, I can finish it—don't you worry about that—no problem."

Ashley held out the spatula like a sword. "Anytime you're ready."

"Let me turn down the heat on the hamburgers first," Jen said, reaching over to turn the control to simmer. She then backed away, held out her spatula, and said, "Give me your best shot!"

They did a sword-fight into the living room and from there to the back door, and then outside. Laughing, giggling, threatening each other with awful fates unless the other surrendered.

From spatulas it went to glasses of water to buckets of water, until they ended up both soaked, both on the lawn, lying on their backs, laughing, giggling,

"I feel so . . . so normal," Ashley said.

"No kidding?"

"It's a great way to feel. I mean, you know, about eating . . . and about my life."

"Good for you. Normal is good."

"I don't have to be perfect, either, do I?"

"Not here, you don't."

"That feels so good just to know that."

"Let's eat and then get ready."

They went inside, and Jen cleaned off a place on the kitchen table. "Sorry about the mess. We don't usually eat here, at least not as a family."

"Where do you eat?"

"I usually eat in front of the TV 'cause my mom's working most every night at supper time. But that might end if she gets married to the guy she's dating. His name is Billy James Dean. It's so weird to have your mother going out on dates."

"What's he like?"

"Look up the word *sleaze* in the dictionary, and his picture's there."

"It can't be that bad."

"It is. It's worse. He runs a pawn shop, and whatever junk he can't sell, he gives to my mom and me. And he lies about what he's given us. Like the other day he gave my Mom a watch he said belonged to the Queen of Egypt. Yeah, sure, whatever you say, Billy James."

Later that night, the bizarre nature of what they were doing hit Ashley as they waited in line for tickets outside the theater.

Nathan looked like the villain in a western melodrama. He was dressed in a black cape he'd borrowed from a drama-type friend of his. His hair was slicked down with oil and combed back, and he had glued on a large black mustache. He was wearing pegged trousers, a pair of black and white spats on his feet, and a black bow tie. To complete the look, he had Ashley clinging to him on the left and Jen on his right

As the two girls leaned to lightly kiss Nathan on his cheeks, Ashley caught their image in the reflection from the glass enclosing one of the posters. She was captivated by the image. *Jen and I both look good in a brainless kind of way. That's a new look for me.*

Nathan spoke Italian phrases borrowed from his tourist guidebook.

After each phrase, Jen and Ashley would burst out laughing, crying out, "Oh, Antonio!" And then they'd each stand on their tip-toes and kiss him on the cheek.

The people ahead of them in line were polite enough not to turn around and stare, but it was clear they were very much aware of what was going on. They would sneak quick glances, then speak in hushed tones to whoever they were going to the movie with.

"Please show me to a table!" Nathan called out merrily in Italian.

"Oh, Antonio!" Jen and Ashley, cried out. And then they burst out laughing and each kissed him on the cheek.

They reached the ticket counter. Nathan put down way too much money. "I'm so sorry," he said, shrugging. American money, . . . you know?" He gestured broadly with his hands.

The ticket seller nodded, made correct change, then slid the tickets and his change out to him.

"*Grazie*," he said, grinning. Then, putting an arm around Jen and Ashley, he hugged them, and said in English with an Italian accent, "My little turtle doves, hey?"

"I hope you enjoy the movie," the ticket seller said.

"American movies . . . not so good, hey?" he said with a big smile, then still holding Ashley and Jen close to him, the three entered the theater.

They sat near the front so that everyone could see them. Ashley on the left, Jen on the right, leaning into him, hanging on his every word, which always brought peals of laughter from the girls.

"Laugh in the wrong places," Nathan said quietly just as the movie started.

It was a comedy, but they made it a point never to laugh when everyone else was laughing.

Nathan grabbed each girl's hand and when he squeezed their hands, they all laughed. The harder he squeezed, the louder they laughed. "Oh, Antonio!" each cried out.

In time the movie captured their attention and they did as everyone else was doing, just watched the movie.

After the movie, they went to Dairy Queen and ordered one milkshake and three straws and huddled around it, taking turns and laughing and playing, "Oh, Antonio!"

And then it was time to go home.

Because she was wearing Jen's mother's clothes, Ashley needed to go to Jen's house. Jen said goodnight to Nathan, and together the two girls went in so Ashley could change. Nathan said he'd wait for Ashley.

A few minutes later Ashley got back in Nathan's car so she could get a ride home.

"Did you have a good time tonight?" he asked.

"I did, Nathan. I think it was the most fun I've ever had."

"Me, too. Thanks for being such a good sport."

"No problem. I've never been happier than I am now."

"That's good. I'm glad."

He walked her to her door and then, quite unexpectedly, he kissed her on the lips. It happened so fast and was so unanticipated, she wasn't sure if she even liked it.

"Well," she said, "I'd better go inside."

He nodded and said, as Antonio, "*Arrivederci.*"

She went inside, troubled about what had just happened, and feeling that in some way she had betrayed Jen.

She was so bewildered at being kissed by Nathan that she forgot that she might be in trouble with her parents. It was dark inside except for a light down the hall that gave some light in the living room. She walked in, hoping her parents would be asleep. She took two steps and heard her mother's voice. "Do you have any idea what you've put me through tonight?"

Ashley turned to face her mother, who was wearing a robe and slippers, sitting in a rocking chair.

Ashley still wasn't sure what the problem was. "It's only eleven-thirty. I'm not supposed to be home for another half hour."

"But you walked out without even telling me what your plans were. For all I knew, you could have been dead alongside some road."

"I went to the movie with Nathan and Jen."

"And you couldn't call and tell me that?"

"If I would have called, you would have told me to come home."

"So you didn't call because of that?"

"That's right."

"You don't care how much I worry about you, do you? That doesn't even matter to you, does it?"

"Have I ever done anything that would cause you not to trust me?"

"I don't know what you do when you're not here."

"Mother, you don't know what I do when I *am* here." It was the closest she had ever come to admitting the struggles she had when it came to food.

"What's that supposed to mean?"

"Nothing. Can I go to bed now?"

"No, we need to talk."

"I don't want to talk."

"Have you been drinking?"

"No."

"Come here and let me smell your breath."

"I said I haven't been drinking."

Her mother came over to her. "Open your mouth and breathe out."

"This is ridiculous. You know I don't drink."

"How do I know what Jen is exposing you to? Just let me smell your breath and then you can go to bed."

Ashley took a deep breath and blew it in her mother's face. "There, are you satisfied?"

"You smell of cigarette smoke."

"There's no way that could happen."

"Have you been smoking?"

"No."

"Have you been with someone who smokes?"

"No."

"You were with Jen, though, weren't you?"

"I was."

"She smokes, doesn't she?"

"She's quitting. She didn't smoke around me all night."

"Then why do you smell of cigarette smoke?"

"I don't know, Mother."

"You went to a movie?"

"Yes."

"What movie?"

"Why do you care what movie we saw? Are you trying to trip me up? We saw a movie."

"Just tell me what movie you saw. Is that asking too much?"

"Yes, it is. Good night, Mother. I'm going to bed." She started down the hall toward her bedroom.

"A friend of mine called tonight. She said she saw you and another girl and a boy outside the movie theater, and that you the other girl were dressed like hussies, and that the two of you were clinging to the same boy and kissing him."

"That was just Nathan. We were pretending like we were bimbos and—"

"So it's true, then?"

"Yes, but it was just a joke."

"I do not approve of you spending time with Jen and that boy. They're corrupting you."

"No, that's where you're wrong. They're saving my life."

"You can't be with them anymore."

"I will continue to spend time with them, Mother."

"Maybe we should wake up your father and see what he says."

"It doesn't matter what he says. I will still continue to play soccer, and hang out with Nathan and Jen."

"You're just like Alauna now, aren't you?"

"Thank you for the compliment, Mother. Good night."

"I'm not through talking to you, young lady."

"I'm through talking to you, Mother. Good night." She went into her room and slammed the door shut and locked it.

She got into the sweats she wore as pajamas, then brushed her teeth.

She tried to sleep but she couldn't. She thought about going to Jen's, but she felt guilty Nathan had kissed her. Had she done anything to encourage him? She wasn't sure. Maybe she had but she didn't think so.

She felt that in some way she'd betrayed Jen, but she didn't know what to do about it.

Nathan was the first boy who'd ever kissed her. She wished she could say it had been nice, but it hadn't. Not really. It was too much of a shock, too unexpected for it to mean much of anything.

I just wish I knew why he'd done it, she thought. *I'll ask him the next time we're together, when Jen isn't around.*

She sighed. *Being normal is way more complicated than I ever thought it would be.*

8

On Monday morning, Christine Bailey, Ashley's mother, woke up just before five o'clock, five minutes before her alarm was set to go off. She reached over, turned off the alarm, and quietly slipped out of bed so as not to wake her husband, David.

She liked the solitude early mornings gave her and the time it provided for her to prepare for the day. She had a routine that she had developed over the years. First she ran on the treadmill for two miles while watching morning news, and then she showered, got dressed, read the scriptures, and then wrote in her journal. And then she'd straighten up the house, or, in the summer, spend some quiet time in her garden.

At seven she'd begin to prepare David's breakfast, which was not much work, since he usually just had some cereal and toast, but she liked to do it anyway. It gave her a chance to be with him a few minutes before he went to work.

But on this particular morning, she couldn't seem to get started. She went downstairs to run on the treadmill. She actually got on the treadmill and started walking but then she shut it off and plopped down on the sofa and pulled a blanket up to her chin and sat there, staring at the ceiling.

Everything seems to be unraveling, she thought. *First David with his job and now Ashley is pals with the wildest girl in school. What's next?*

David's problems had begun six months before, when the locally owned landscaping company he'd worked for all these years had been bought out by a corporation based in Atlanta, Georgia.

David had started working part-time in high school, when the company first started up. After a mission and their temple wedding and one year at BYU, when Christine was pregnant with Alauna, he'd quit college to work there full-time. Over the years he became an expert in

99

designing and sales. In fact, it was David's personal integrity and resourcefulness that had helped make the company a success.

And now new directives and policies from the headquarters in Atlanta were tearing the company apart.

It was David's feeling from the very first, that the company should do landscaping for homeowners as well as handle the big jobs for companies. Quite often in the twenty years he'd worked there, the big jobs had come from someone who'd first been impressed by the quality of work they'd done on his house.

With the new chain of command, David had at first tried to be diplomatic by suggesting that what worked in Atlanta, Georgia, would not necessarily work in Utah. But he'd lost far more battles than he won, and he knew he'd become a source of irritation to his new bosses. He'd grown used to the old way of doing things, and their strict new policies and procedures made it difficult to provide the kind of personalized service people had come to appreciate under David's leadership. And so when they hired Andrew McPherson as an assistant for David, it was clear what the new owners intended to do.

"I'm not sure how much longer they'll keep me," he had told Christine two weeks earlier.

"Of course they'll keep you. You're the main reason the company has done so well."

"Why do you suppose they want me to teach McPherson everything I know? Of course they'll let me go. It's only a matter of time."

"You can always get another job."

"What else can I do?"

"Plenty of things."

"I should've stayed in school," he said.

"We've done all right for ourselves."

"But who's going to hire someone without a degree?" he asked.

"You're the best in the business."

"I used to be. I'm not so sure anymore."

"You are. I'm sure of it."

"We might end up losing the house."

"It's just a house. If we do, then we do. It's not going to change anything."

She wasn't sure how convincing she sounded when she said it. The truth was that she was scared. Losing their house would be a tremendous personal loss because this was the house of her dreams. She'd come with nothing to her name when she'd first enrolled at BYU—just barely the clothes on her back and enough money to pay the first semester's tuition and books. For everything else she'd had to work, sometimes two jobs a day just to be able to bring in enough to keep up with the monthly expenses.

Because she'd come from such poverty, she'd promised herself her own children would have it easier. And she'd kept that promise, although her children didn't seem as grateful as she would have expected.

Alauna had been a handful from the very beginning, a naturally rebellious child, never satisfied.

I don't care for Ashley's new friend, Jen. She looks like a real troublemaker to me. And for some reason she seems to have some kind of power over Ashley.

The two of them together seem to feed off each other. Ashley looks more attractive and Jen seems more intelligent when they're together. At a party I could imagine the two of them together could get the attention of every boy in the place. Jen will attract the rebels while Ashley will bring in the boys with intelligence.

I don't want Ashley to be popular. That's what I was. From ninth grade on. Just because I got a figure sooner than my friends. And what did it get me? Having to learn to keep away from boys with only one thing on their minds.

I've always wished that Ashley would be ignored by boys in high school and only become attractive her senior year at BYU. And then she could marry a returned missionary in his last year of school. They'd both have degrees and a future that couldn't be taken from them just because the company her husband works for is sold out from under them.

I wish Ashley would eat supper with us more often. She could stand to gain a little weight, too. But I guess she's just like I was when I was her age. Too busy to eat.

She eats, though, often late at night after David and I have gone to bed. I notice things missing from the fridge in the morning. I used to do that, too, so I can't blame her too much. She just likes to keep herself busy, that's all.

I seem to be destined to be disappointed by my children. Alauna was such a handful. Especially in high school. She fought every decision we made. I know I shouldn't feel this way, but right now I'm glad she's gone. If it weren't for us, she'd have never made it to BYU. But does she ever thank us for insisting she take math and science courses and that she keep her grades up and that she graduate from seminary? No, not her. She thinks she got there on her own, without any help from us. Someday, though, when she gets older, she'll thank us for pushing her to do better.

And now it's Ashley's turn to give us grief. We almost made it with her. Just the end of the school year and then she'll graduate. But who knows what will happen now that Jen is in the picture?

All I've ever wanted is for Ashley to stay sweet and obedient, for David to be happy, and for us to stay in this house. And now all of those things are being threatened, and I'm not sure what to do about any of it.

If David loses his job, then I might need to get a job myself. But what kind of a job will I be able to get without a college education? I'm too old to work at Burger King.

I should have insisted David finish school, even if it meant postponing getting married. I've gone my whole life being embarrassed when my friends ask me where I went to college. I usually just say BYU and leave it at that, even though I only went two semesters before David and I got married and I got pregnant and we gave up on the idea of ever finishing.

David is taking this so hard. Every day he comes home depressed, and he wants to talk about his day with me. He needs me now more than he ever has. I try to be supportive, and I think I am. When he leaves for work, then I walk through the house wondering how much longer we'll be able to afford it, and what we're going to do if they let him go after all these years.

We haven't told Alauna or Ashley about any of this. We don't want them to worry. Maybe we should though, sometime. It just doesn't seem fair. I wasn't able to finish college, and now it's possible that Alauna and Ashley won't, either, or at least, if they do, they'll have to work their way through, just like I was going to do twenty years ago, before I met David and became so certain I couldn't stand to live without him.

Not that I'm complaining. We've been happy, I suppose. Happier than some, that's for sure. But what will we do if we end up in an apartment like when we first started out?

She sat with the comforter wrapped around her watching TV.

I should be on the treadmill now, getting in my two miles. Not that it does much good. I remember when I could exercise a little and watch the pounds roll off, but not anymore. It's all I can do to keep from gaining. I guess that's what happens when you get old. But David doesn't seem to mind. I'm not sure I could do anything about it if he did. There are too many other things to worry about. Like Ashley, and David's job, and how long we'll be able to keep this house.

She looked at the clock and realized she needed to get up to make David's breakfast, but, more important than that, to be upbeat and encouraging for him, until he left for work, and then she could go back to worrying about their future.

Welcome to the new day, she thought wearily as she stood up and went upstairs to make David some breakfast.

9

Ashley waited nearly a week before she had a chance to talk to Nathan alone, and that was during their next soccer game, when Nathan took her out of the game and put his hand on her shoulder and walked her away from everyone else.

"You're getting polite on me again," he said confidentially.

"Why did you kiss me the other night?"

His face turned red, and he looked around to make sure nobody could hear them.

"Actually, this is probably not a real good time to talk about it."

"I can't talk to you about it when Jen is around. I don't want to hurt her feelings. Do you like me, Nathan?"

"Of course I do. You know that."

"Do you like me more than Jen?"

"No, pretty much the same, I'd say. I like you both."

"Have you ever kissed her?"

"No. Just you."

"Have you thought about kissing her?"

"Well, sure, once in a while, I guess."

"You can't be kissing us both."

"Why not?"

"Because that would be just too weird, that's why."

Nathan sighed. "I suppose you're right."

"Jen is very important to me, Nathan. I'd never do anything to hurt her. So, if it comes to choosing between you and her, I'll choose her. She's the best friend I've ever had."

"I know she is."

"So I guess what I'm saying is . . . I'd rather not be kissed by you anymore, unless you're really in love with me."

He thought about it. "I'm not in love with you. I just like to be with you, that's all. And I like the way you look. I enjoyed kissing you, too, if you want to know the truth."

"You can't kiss someone just because you like the way they look."

"You're right. Don't worry. You won't have to worry about me anymore."

"Okay."

"Now go kick someone in the shin . . . once play resumes, of course."

"Sure, Nathan, whatever you say."

After the game, Ashley went home to change. "Will you be eating here tonight?" her mother asked.

"No, I'm going over to Nathan's house. He's going to cook us spaghetti."

"You never eat here anymore."

"Sorry."

But it's okay because I'm doing so good with my eating, she thought. And it was true. She'd nearly quit throwing up since she'd started soccer. She couldn't afford to. She needed all the energy she could get during a game, running up and down the field. She stoked up on spaghetti at Nathan's house at least once a week, sometimes twice a week. And she kept it down.

She still had trouble with desserts, though. Once when she was at Nathan's house and they had a rich dessert, she took two bites and then began to feel fat, and guilty, and she hurried into the bathroom to throw up.

Jen walked in on her in the bathroom while Ashley was bent over the toilet throwing up.

"You can't do this anymore, Ashley."

Ashley got up and rinsed off her face. "I haven't done it for a long time."

"Why do it now, then?"

"I had too much dessert."

"I had a lot more than you."

"It made me feel fat," Ashley said.

"You'll burn it off at our next game."

"I don't like the feeling."

"Then don't eat any dessert," Jen said.

"I like the way it tastes."

"We won't have dessert then, ever again, so you won't have to worry about it."

"You don't need to do that."

"The team needs you healthy and strong. Okay?" She searched Ashley's eyes for an answer.

Ashley nodded. "Okay."

"All right then, let's go back."

After that Ashley didn't throw up again when she was with Jen and Nathan.

They spent the evening in Nathan's basement, watching Italian language video tapes. The basement was unfinished, but the summer before Nathan was born, his father had turned one of the rooms into a TV room.

Since then, clutter had begun its slow assault on the room. Along the sides were stacks of boxes, some filled with old copies of the *National Geographic,* going back ten years, others filled with clothes that had belonged to brothers and sisters who had long since left home and never come back to reclaim their things.

An old sofa sat in front of the TV. The room was always cold when they entered it, but there was a gas fireplace that quickly warmed it up.

Nathan stopped the tape every once in a while so they could practice words and phrases.

Nathan's father came downstairs, something he very seldom did. "Nathan, we're going grocery shopping. Anything you need?"

"Some salsa and chips maybe."

"All right. We'll get some. Any special brand?"

"Not really."

"They have so many kinds these days. When I was your age . . ."

Ashley didn't pay much attention after that, but she did study Nathan's father as he gave a long and boring account of how chips had evolved in his lifetime.

Most of the time Nathan's father looked like someone who was lost in a big city. At home he usually wore a cardigan, button-down sweater, usually brown. He always buttoned his shirts to the top, even when he wasn't wearing a tie. He read constantly when he was home and didn't say much, but he did smile at Ashley when she and Jen came to visit Nathan, as if he were grateful for the attention they were paying to his son.

Mr. Billingsley didn't like the quality of the picture they were getting on the TV and so went and adjusted the tint. Ashley smiled at this attention to detail, especially since the room was so chaotic because of the boxes stacked two-high along one wall.

Finally his father was satisfied and stood up. "I think this will work better for you," he said quietly. "Well, we'll be going now."

"Thanks, Dad," Nathan said.

His dad smiled. "No problem."

"Aren't you going to tell us to behave ourselves?" Nathan asked as his father started up the stairs.

"Oh, I have no worries about that. We'll be back in about an hour." He went up the stairs. A minute later they heard the front door close.

"I'm tired of watching videos," Nathan said. "I know. Why don't I teach you guys about opera? Let's listen to something from *Tales of Hoffmann*." Nathan ran upstairs and came back with a CD. "Okay, first I have to tell you the plot."

"How boring is this going to be?" Jen asked.

"Not boring at all."

"Not to you, but what about to us?" Jen asked.

"Ten minutes, max."

"I guess I can stand it then," Jen said.

"Okay, here's how it goes. There's this girl. Her name is Antonia."

"Oh, Antonio, Antonio!" Jen called out, kissing Nathan on the cheek.

"No, it's *Antonia,* and she's a girl, but she has this rare disease. If she sings, she'll die."

"You're kidding, right?" Jen asked.

"Nope, afraid not."

"Why is she in an opera then?"

"I don't know."

"How long is the opera?" Jen asked.

"Four hours."

"If I was in the audience, I'd yell out, 'Sing, Girl! Maybe we can both get out of here a little early.' "

"Do you mind?" Nathan asked with a smile.

"You go right ahead."

"Well, anyway, she's been seeing this guy, and his name is Hoffmann. He asks her to sing. Well, she wants to make him happy, so she sings and that makes her faint. Her dad comes in and tells her never to sing again. Next the evil doctor, Dr. Miracle, shows up."

"He's an evil doctor and his name is Miracle?"

"That's right."

"This is so weird," Jen said.

"Dr. Miracle treated Antonia's mother years ago, and she died. In fact everyone he treats, dies."

"How does a doctor like that get any new patients?" Jen asked.

"Referrals?" Ashley joked.

"Dr. Miracle does his magic, and the picture of her dead mother comes alive and sings a duet with her daughter. Dr. Miracle picks up the tempo and Antonia sings up a storm, and that kills her. Hoffmann rushes in and finds her dead. That's the story."

"That can't be the story," Jen said.

"Why not?"

"Because it's so stupid."

"Well, maybe so, but the music is nice. Let me play some music from the opera."

Ashley excused herself to go upstairs to use the bathroom. When she came down, one of the songs from the opera was on, so Nathan and Jen couldn't hear her come down the stairs. Jen was sitting on the couch, just as before, but now Nathan was standing behind her, massaging her shoulders. Jen's eyes were closed and she was rolling her head back, as if she were very much enjoying the experience.

Ashley froze on the stairs, not sure what to do—whether to go back up the stairs and wait for the CD to be done so they could hear her come down the stairs, or to walk in on them.

She couldn't understand what was happening. *Why is he doing that? I thought we had an agreement.*

She quietly went back up the stairs and into the bathroom. She closed the door and knelt down in front of the toilet, but nothing would come.

Why did I come here? she thought. *Why do I always end up here?*

She stood up and looked at herself in the mirror. She thought she looked fat.

She left the bathroom and walked through the house. She decided she could go anywhere because Nathan's parents were gone.

She ended up at Nathan's room. At first she stood at the door and looked inside. The bed wasn't made, and there were dirty clothes lying on the floor. On the wall was a picture of a beach in Italy, and on another wall a poster for an Italian sports car, and on another wall a poster of a great Italian soccer player. She entered the room and opened Nathan's closet. The bottom was filled with boxes.

I wonder when the last time someone in this family threw out anything, she thought.

Nathan had a CD player and a storage tower to store them in, but he had more than the tower would hold, so the albums were stacked on top and to the side, and a few had fallen to the floor. She knelt down, picked them up and returned them to his desk.

Nathan wouldn't last ten minutes in my family, she thought.

She wondered what the name of the soccer player on the poster was, so she went over to look more closely. She heard a door shut.

Nathan's mother caught her leaving Nathan's room.

"Hi, I was just curious who the soccer player was, so I went in to read his name," she said quickly.

"Where's Nathan?"

"He's downstairs with Jen. I just came up to use the bathroom. And then I saw the poster and I . . . I'm on my way downstairs now. We're listening to *Tales of Hoffmann*."

She opened the door and made a clunking noise with her shoes as she made her way down the stairs.

By the time she made it to the bottom of the stairs, Nathan had jumped up and hurried to the CD player to remove the CD and put another one in. Jen was sitting erect. It seemed innocent enough, except they were both blushing.

He kissed her while I was gone, she thought.

"Nathan, your folks are home from grocery shopping," Ashley said.

"Oh, good."

"So they probably have the salsa and chips, so we could have that now."

"Oh, sure, I'll go get it."

He went upstairs.

"You okay?" Ashley asked.

"Yeah, sure, why wouldn't I be?" Jen said quickly.

"No reason. Just wondering. Your face is all red."

"Oh, is it? I didn't notice."

"You'd tell me if anything was wrong, wouldn't you?" Ashley asked.

"Yes, of course, you know I would."

"Okay, then . . ."

Nathan came down with a tray of salsa, chips, and some drinks. They watched an Italian movie without English subtitles. With their limited skills, they tried to figure out what each person was saying. It ended up being very funny as each one came up with a more ridiculous explanation of what the actors were saying.

After a few minutes the three of them were laughing so hard they couldn't stop.

After the movie was over, Nathan drove the girls home. He dropped Ashley off first. That was no surprise to Ashley. In fact, she expected it.

When she walked into her house, her mother was there, in the semi-dark in an antique rocking chair.

"Hello, Mother," Ashley said.

"What time is it?"

Ashley looked at the clock. "Eleven-thirty." She was glad she was half an hour early. Maybe that would please her mother.

"What did you do tonight?"

"We watched movies at Nathan's house."

"Were his parents there?"

"Yes, of course."

A few minutes later Ashley went to bed, but she couldn't sleep. She tossed and turned for a long time, trying to figure out what was going on.

In some ways she didn't mind Nathan kissing Jen. *He kissed me and it didn't change anything, so that means it probably didn't mean anything to Jen either. For me it was like when a dentist checks my teeth. I mean, it wasn't like I was even a part of it. Like he could have been kissing a statue.*

So what does it matter if he kisses Jen? If he's got to kiss somebody, I'd rather it be Jen.

The worst thing, though, would be if he takes Jen away from me. I don't know what I'd do if I lost her as a friend. She's been so good for me. I'm hardly ever at home anymore, and that's good.

Nathan kissed me, and that was the end of it. Maybe it will be the same with Jen. Even if Nathan moves on to someone else, and leaves us, I won't care that much. As long as Jen and I stay friends. That's the most important thing.

I'm doing so good right now. I'm learning to stand up to my mother. And the people we play in soccer think I have a bad temper, and I pretend to blow up on the sidelines of a soccer game, and I don't do my homework on scratch paper and then recopy it again so it will be neat, and I don't sit in my room and think about food until I can't stand it and then go raid the fridge and stuff myself and then come back here and get rid of it all. And then have the whole thing start over again.

All my progress would disappear if I quit spending time with Jen.

She's the best friend I've ever had.

By twelve-thirty Ashley still wasn't asleep. She needed a release, something that would get rid of her pent-up emotions. Instead of going to the kitchen, she pulled on some sweats and socks and her soccer shoes and grabbed her soccer ball and went in the backyard.

She needed a goal to kick to. She opened the garage door, stepped back to the beginning of the driveway, and kicked the ball into the garage. It hit one of the cars and careened up to the ceiling and then onto a work bench, hitting a bottle, which fell to the floor and shattered.

The lights in her parents' bedroom turned on. A short time later her mother was at the back door.

"Ashley, is that you?" her mother asked.

"Yes, it's me."

"What on earth are you doing?"

"I couldn't sleep, so I thought I'd practice kicking."

"What broke?"

"I kicked a ball into the garage. I guess it knocked over a bottle."

"You can't be making so much noise at this time of night. Just go back to bed."

"I can't, Mother."

"Why not?"

"I just can't, that's all."

"Well, you can't be making so much noise. Your father has to go to work in the morning."

"I'll be quiet."

"Why can't you just go to bed, like everyone else does?"

"I can't sleep."

"Don't stay up much longer."

"I know. I won't. Just a few more minutes."

Her mother closed the door and went back to bed.

Ashley stood in the driveway trying to decide what to do. What she wanted to do was to kick the ball as hard as she could, over and over again, until she was exhausted and spent and so tired she'd fall asleep and not think about Jen and Nathan and all the leftover food in the kitchen.

She jogged two blocks to her old grade school. They had soccer goals made out of stiff wire. She stood in the light of a streetlamp and kicked the ball as hard as she could into the goal over and over.

She knew her mother would not be happy having her out alone so late at night, but she wasn't worried. Her greatest fear, her greatest challenge, her greatest obstacle was at home.

She loved the feeling when she hit the ball just right, when it seemed to leap from her foot as if it had a life of its own, darting in the darkness into the net of the goal.

A carload of boys passed by slowly, checking her out. "She's not that bad," one of them said.

They'll be back, she thought. *It's time to go now.*

As soon as the car turned a corner, she took off, running as fast as she could, not down the street, which would be easy for a car to follow, but through people's yards, keeping away from streetlights.

They're no match for me, she thought proudly. *Nobody can run as fast as I can, not when I'm in a zone. Nobody can stand in my way.*

By the time she walked into her house, she was sweating and panting from her run. She felt tired but happy. Happy and proud that she'd done what she wanted to do. She'd run and she'd kicked the ball and she'd outrun a carload of boys.

She took a long hot shower, and a few minutes later, happy and exhausted, she fell into bed and went to sleep.

* * * * *

As the days passed, it became clear that things had changed. Now whenever the three of them went some place, Jen always sat in the front seat, with Ashley always in the back.

"Let's go to another movie," Ashley said one Friday afternoon after soccer practice. "We can play 'Oh, Antonio, Antonio.' "

"I'm not in the mood," Jen said.

"C'mon, it'll be fun. We'll dress up again, like we did before, and we'll be ridiculous, and we'll laugh, just like the first time."

"I have other plans, too," Nathan said. "Maybe some other time."

"Sure, maybe," Ashley said. *They've made plans to do something without me,* she thought.

She didn't say anything for fear it would ruin what little they had left as a threesome.

And yet she couldn't leave it alone.

She wanted things to be the way they had been, but, every day, there were more and more indications that was impossible. She kept catching Jen and Nathan gazing into each other's eyes. Or, in passing by, one of them touching the other on the shoulder. Or Nathan lingering at Jen's locker even though he was about to be late for class.

October 17th would be Ashley's birthday. She decided to have a party and to invite the girls from her soccer team and their dates. She couldn't think of anyone else to invite. The girls from her ward were still resentful of her and Jen.

Her mother agreed to host the party, and took care of most of the arrangements: the invitations, planning the refreshments. The plan was they would watch a homemade video of their soccer games, which had been taken by a father of one of the girls. And then they would have pizza and soda, then maybe watch a movie.

Ashley had high hopes for the party, hoping Nathan and Jen would realize how much better it was for them to stay friends and do things as a threesome.

Ashley felt like the distance between her and her mother was lessening because of the time they spent working on plans for the party. They had even laughed and been silly in planning the event. And that made Ashley feel closer to her mom.

They had hoped for a nice day so they could eat out on the patio. To add a festive touch to the party, Ashley's father had even come home early from work the day before to spruce up the yard and hang some lights around the patio.

The day started out nice, but then a cold front caught up with the pleasant fall they had been enjoying, and it began to snow.

Snow in itself could have made it nice. It was the first snow of the season, and during her history class, Ashley imagined herself and her friends making a large snowman in the backyard.

The temperature hovered around freezing all day, so the snow alternated with a freezing rain, leaving the streets covered with ice that made traveling nearly impossible. Even walking up a sidewalk became a treacherous activity.

It's happening to me again, Ashley thought. *It always happens to me. All my dreams end this way, and this one will, too.*

At lunchtime she was feeling depressed. She had decided not to eat lunch but go to the library and work on a term paper that was due in four weeks. *Might as well get it finished,* she thought, *so I can move on to something else.*

But Jen and Nathan were waiting at her locker. "Let's go to lunch," Jen said.

"Oh, I don't know. I was thinking of just going to the library."

"No way, not on your birthday!" Jen said, tugging at Ashley's sleeve.

"We're going to take you to lunch!" Nathan said.

"To an Italian restaurant so we can talk Italian? You like?" he teased.

"I like very much."

And so they took off.

"We've already ordered. They promised they'd have it ready for us so it won't take that long. I know you've got math after lunch. And you have to be there in case the teacher gets stuck."

It was not always true, but one time the teacher had been unable to work one of the problems in the book, and, after he had fumbled on the board for what seemed like an eternity, Ashley had raised her hand and offered to do the problem for the class. After that, Ashley had a reputation of being smarter than the teacher and everyone kidded that she went to class only to help him out in the event he had trouble.

Lunch was silly and fun, just like it had been between them. Nathan spoke in loud, outrageous Italian, most of which was a recitation of his favorite phrases from the tourist guidebook.

By the time they left to go back to school, the streets were glare-iced. The drive back took them twenty-five minutes, even though, half an hour earlier, the trip to the restaurant had only taken ten minutes.

They got to the school just in time to learn that afternoon classes had been canceled in order to allow the buses plenty of time to deliver students before conditions worsened.

"Nobody will come," Ashley said as Nathan took her home.

"It's not that bad," Jen said. "See, there's a truck putting sand on the streets. By the time your party starts, it'll be okay. Won't it, Nathan?"

"I guarantee it," he said.

"You see? You can always take Nathan's word, right?" Jen asked.

"Can I? I'm not sure anymore."

Nathan dropped her off, then left with Jen. But they promised to be there at seven, when the party officially was scheduled to start.

Ashley found out from her mother that three girls had called, saying their parents were refusing to let them go out on a night like this.

One of the girls who couldn't come was the one whose father had videotaped all their soccer games. She lived on a steep hill and the roads were impossible now. So the girl and the videotape would not be at the party.

"This is going to be a disaster," Ashley said to her mother.

"Not everyone has called saying they can't come."

"But the reason people were coming was to watch the video."

"That's not the only thing you can do at a party. Do what we used to do when we were young."

"What's that?"

"Play party games."

Ashley groaned and rolled her eyes and went to her bed and lay down. She would have let herself be more discouraged about the prospects for her birthday party except for one thing that cheered her up. And that was that Jen and Nathan would be there. *Today it was like it used to be. Maybe it will stay that way from now on,* she thought.

Four girls showed up along with Nathan and Jen. Two of the girls could only stay a few minutes because they had other plans and quickly excused themselves.

After they ate, the other two girls left. Ashley and Jen and Nathan decided to watch a video.

"You going to get us something to eat while we're watching?" Nathan asked.

You're just trying to get me out of the room so you can kiss Jen, Ashley thought.

"We just ate," Ashley said.

"How about some popcorn?" Jen asked.

She wants me to leave, too. Why can't they just let things be the way they were?

"Fine, if that's what you want, I'll go make popcorn."

113

She left the door open so they could hear the popcorn popping and wouldn't suspect she'd be spying on them. Once the popcorn was popping, she went to the door so she could see what was happening.

Just as she suspected, they were kissing.

She felt betrayed.

When the popcorn was done, she dumped it into a big bowl and then marched into the TV room. "Looks like I forgot our drinks. Jen, why don't you take care of that while Nathan and I make out."

Jen turned and stared at Ashley. "What?" Jen asked.

"Nathan kissed me before he kissed you. I don't think it matters to him which one of us it is as long as he gets his daily quota. Isn't that right, Nathan? Why don't you tell Jen about the time you kissed me?"

"I don't know what she's talking about," Nathan said.

"That is such a lie, Nathan, and you know it. Tell the truth."

Nathan stood up. "Let's go," he said to Jen.

Jen nodded. They both stood up, slipped past Ashley, and left.

Ashley was left with a just-cooked batch of popcorn and a movie. She made the most of it.

* * * * *

"I'm so glad you're not running around with those people any-more," her mother said a week later. It was a Friday night, a night Ashley had set aside to do homework, since there was nothing else to do, and nobody to do it with.

Even though she was no longer friends with Nathan and Jen, it bothered her that her mother would not call them by their names. It was true, generally, of anyone she did not approve of—they remained nameless.

"I know that, Mother. Excuse me now. I'm going to study."

"I'm proud of you for standing up for what you've been taught."

What have I been taught? she thought as she made her way to her room to study. *Nothing that I can remember.*

She worked hard until ten-thirty, when her parents called her for family prayer. They knelt down in the living room with the drapes open. She wondered if anyone walking by ever saw them praying. And what they would think if they did.

She never really thought much about prayer. She knew to close her eyes and lower her head. And, when she was asked, she knew some stock phrases, which seemed to be satisfactory to those who heard her. She had a prayer for family prayer, and one for seminary and Sunday School and Young Women. That seemed to be enough to get by with.

Her mother offered the prayer. Ashley did not pay much attention to it. And when it was over, she politely hugged her parents and then started for her room.

"Ashley, do you have much homework left?"

"Yes, quite a bit still."

"Well, don't stay up too late. You can always finish it tomorrow."

"All right. Good night, Mother."

"Good night, Ashley. I love you."

Of course you do, because I'm doing everything you want me to do. You love me when I'm good, but don't even like me when I step away from what you want. If that's love, I don't want any part of it. You don't love me, Mother. You only use that word to control me. As far as I can tell, nobody in the world loves me, or ever will.

She stepped into her room and closed the door.

In an hour her parents would be asleep. There was cake left over from supper. She hadn't had any then, but she would have some in an hour.

After all the work I've done tonight, I deserve some reward, she decided.

She thought about Jen and Nathan and wondered what they were doing. Maybe a movie but without costumes. They were a couple now. They didn't need to call attention to themselves. They were each enough for the other.

She missed Jen because she was so much fun and so easy to talk to. Jen knew about her eating disorder, and still liked her, and tried to help her get over it. There was nobody in her life like that now. *Maybe there never will be,* she thought. *Maybe things will always be like this.*

Well, why not? The only thing I really want now is to graduate and leave home so I can be on my own.

10

Six months later, in mid-May, David Bailey went to his pickup to get an ice chest filled with ice and soft drinks for his crew. He had been working with them all morning, beginning at six-thirty. Not that they needed his help. They were one of the best landscaping crews in Utah. He'd hired and trained each of them.

After all these years, I still enjoy this, he thought. There was a mountain of paperwork at the office that needed to be done, but he had decided to spend the day with his crew. They were finishing up the landscaping on a luxurious new home owned by the CEO of a company that built and managed professional buildings used by attorneys, doctors, and dentists. David had done the landscaping for ten such buildings in Utah, and so when the CEO had asked David to do the landscaping on his new home, David gladly agreed to do the work and promised to be personally involved in the project.

The only problem was that it violated company policy. The people from Georgia who bought the company had decided not to do private homes anymore.

Because he viewed it as a way to ensure they would be asked to do additional landscaping jobs on the CEO's other projects, David had taken on the job anyway.

David still enjoyed getting into the soil, making a paper design turn into an actual landscape of trees, shrubs, sod, and decorative boulders. He'd never gotten over the feeling of satisfaction that came when everything was in place, and the sprinklers were turned on for the first time. But the real reason he'd worked with the crew was to try to finish up the job before it became too much of a sore point with his supervisor, Roger Turner. Roger was a slow-talking Southerner, fond of bad-mouthing Utah's dry climate and its people. He didn't know much about landscaping in a western desert, but he did know how to please his boss and father-in-law in Atlanta. His rule was to follow company policy, even if it made no sense.

David lugged the ice chest into the backyard where the house provided some shade from the hot sun.

"Who's thirsty?" David asked, opening up the ice chest. The crew of five gathered under a canopy built over the patio.

"Oh, you didn't need to go to so much trouble," Bill, the oldest on the crew, said. "We could get by fine with just water."

"I know, but I don't get out here every day. I just wanted you guys to know how much I appreciate your hard work, day in and day out."

"That's real nice. Yes sir, real nice," Bill said. "And much appreciated."

The younger men came and got their can of soda pop without a word.

"I said, much appreciated," Bill said sternly.

The others took their cue and also thanked David for the soda.

As David sat down next to Bill, he let out a small groan.

"You're not used to this anymore, are you?" Bill asked.

"Is it that obvious?"

"No, you did your share. I just noticed you kind of slowed down a little toward the end."

David smiled. "That's right. I did . . . but just a little . . . but at least I was working. I mean, I wasn't standing around like you were, seeing who was getting tired." The banter was part of the fun, and David enjoyed it.

Bill laughed. "This is just like old times, right? You and me, getting after each other all the time."

"I've missed that. I'll tell you what, it's not as much fun being in the office."

"Especially now, right?" Bill asked privately.

"Don't get me started," David said quietly.

"I bet for you, going to work every day is like fighting the war between the North and the South all over again."

David didn't want to bad-mouth the new management. "It's not that bad."

"Don't give me that. I know better."

David nodded. "I don't know what's worse, that Roger doesn't know anything, or that he thinks he does."

"He asked me once what I thought about putting in a magnolia tree in his backyard."

"What'd you say?"

"I said that'd be fine, if his backyard was in Georgia."

"What'd he say?"

"He said, some people say certain things can't be done, but others look for reasons why they can. What's that got to do with a magnolia tree?"

"He thinks of himself as a visionary."

"I think of him as a fool, if he thinks he can get a magnolia tree to make it in this climate."

Just after Bill said that, Roger came around the corner of the house. David couldn't be sure whether or not Roger had heard Bill's comment about magnolia trees.

Roger didn't even smile. "David, may I have a word with you in private?"

They went out to Roger's company pickup, which Roger had left running with the air-conditioning on high.

As soon as they were both inside the pickup, Roger said, "Is this what I'm paying you and your people for? To sit around, doing nothing?"

"We've been working since six-thirty. We needed a break. And, it's a hot day."

"That's what lunch breaks are for. We can't have crews stopping every five minutes just because it's hot out."

"They've worked nonstop since they got here."

"Well, they should be working now."

"I'll get right on it, Roger," David said, opening the door to get out.

"Don't think I don't know what you're doing here," Roger shot back.

"What are you talking about?"

"Undermining me in front of the crews. Trying to take advantage of your popularity with them."

"I'm just trying to do my job, that's all."

"You know our policy now is we don't take private landscaping jobs anymore. But yet you went ahead, without my permission, with this one. Would you mind explaining yourself?"

"We've done ten jobs in the past year for the man who owns this house. Big jobs. Through all that, he and I have become friends. I was not about to turn him down when he asked me to do his house."

"You should have turned it over to me. I'd have told him what our new policy is."

"And that would be the end of any more jobs from him."

"You have to look at the big picture, Son."

David bristled at being called son. He was a year older and a lot more experienced in landscaping than Roger.

"Well, you can go now, but let me tell you something. We don't pay

118

you to lay sod. We need you in the office. McPherson has had a lot of questions today already. I need you to bring him up to speed."

"And then you'll fire me, right?"

"We'll evaluate your performance on a semiannual basis, as provided by company policy. And you can be sure this little incident will be noted in full for your performance evaluation. Now finish up and get back to the office as soon as you can. And let's try to be a little more professional from now on."

"Are you finished?" David asked, barely able to contain his anger.

"Don't play high and mighty with me. And another thing, this is not just about you, okay? If you go, your crew goes with you. Every last one of them. So if you want to keep them working, you'd better knuckle down, or you'll be out of here faster than a flea off a dead dog."

David got out of the truck and watched as Roger sped away.

He walked slowly back to the backyard. Bill saw him and joined him.

"I got a couple of questions about where to put the fruit trees," Bill said. "Let's take a walk."

They walked away from the rest of the crew.

"Are you in the doghouse?" Bill asked.

"No, nothing like that."

"Don't give me that."

David nodded.

"The man is a complete idiot," Bill said.

"He's our boss now."

"He's still an idiot."

David put his hand on Bill's weather-tanned arm. "I don't want this infecting the rest of the crew, so I'd appreciate it if you'd keep your comments about the new management to yourself."

Bill nodded. "I don't say much, anyway, so that's no problem."

"I've got to get back to the office."

"To see how bad McPherson, the Boy Wonder, has messed things up?"

"Something like that."

"I'll get 'em up and working. We ought to be done by tomorrow around noon."

"Thanks, Bill. See you around, okay?"

"Yeah, sure."

David fully intended on heading back to the office, but he found himself an hour later at Liberty Park in Salt Lake City, parked in the shade with his windows open.

This is where I learned about the magic of trees and flowers, he thought.

He'd grown up less than a block from the park. As a boy, in the summer, he came nearly every day with his friends to play, and to drink in the beauty of the place. It was his refuge, no matter how bad things got at home.

His dad had been a traveling man, a salesman, and an alcoholic. He was gone most of the time. And even when he was home, he wasn't around much. His mother had been the anchor for the family. She took her kids to church every week and tried to teach them the gospel.

David's older brother had followed the example of his dad, but David let his mother be his guide. And that had made all the difference in his life.

How long is it going to be before I lose my job? David thought. *And what will I do when it happens, with no college degree? How can I compete with college graduates? Who's going to hire me? What will I do? Go back to school? At my age?*

I could probably get a job working for other landscape companies, but they're not going to pay me what I need to cover all our expenses, what with Alauna in college and Ashley about to go. We might not even be able to keep the house. That'd be hard on Christine.

Of course, if I were to be fired, Christine's mother would offer to help with college for Alauna and Ashley. The only problem is, she'll throw it in my face, like she always has.

For all the time David had known him, Christine's father had refused to do much of anything except farm on land he'd inherited from his father. Every year it was the same—either the crop was good but the prices were down, or else bad weather wiped out what profit he could have made. When David first met Christine, she was dirt-poor, and was only in college because of money she made by working summers and after school.

After David and Christine were married, they had frequently been called on to help out her family. David said he didn't mind when Christine forwarded each request from her mother, but privately he resented having to send money to bail out her dad time and time again.

Although Christine's father had been a failure in his lifetime, five years after he died, the family fortunes changed dramatically. An up-and-coming software company approached Christine's mother and offered to buy the farm. They had it in mind to build an office complex and manufacturing facility on the property. At first Christine's mother had refused to sell, out of respect for her husband's wishes, but over the next six months, with each more generous offer, she gradually gave in and finally sold the farm for a huge sum of money.

And now Christine's mother had become the champion for her grandchildren's education, providing them with tuition and living expenses, and, in Ashley's case, even a car for her to have when she went to Ricks.

But there was a price to this generosity—it made David feel even more unimportant in his daughters' lives.

She never wanted Christine to marry me in the first place. And now that she has money, and I'm about to lose my job, she's going to throw it in my face what a failure I've always been. So her helping my girls will be done with a price, and the price is my dignity.

Life used to be so simple once. But that was long ago.

He decided to take a walk along a line of trees that had been planted way before when he'd been born. He'd played among them as a boy, but now they were gnarled and old.

I've made such a mess of things, he thought. *The only trouble is, I can't pinpoint exactly where I went wrong. I've always worked hard and tried to do a good job. What could I have done to make it different than it is now?*

He thought back to the first time he saw Christine. It was just after his mission. He'd been released only six weeks earlier, and was now a freshman. She was a sophomore, and they met at an opening social at one of the BYU wards.

The first time he saw her, he quickly turned away. It was a reflex from his mission—that a beautiful girl was something to avoid. And she was indeed beautiful—sexy is how he would have described her before his mission, but in time he learned other ways to say the same thing. Over the last ten years he had finally come up with a word he could use to describe her physical charm—and the word was voluptuous. He'd even looked it up once and memorized the definition—*voluptuous—sexually attractive because of a full, shapely figure.*

The first time we met she seemed as embarrassed by her beauty as I was. I couldn't look directly at her. And I kept thinking, this can't be happening to me. I'm not the kind of guy who gets a girl like her to want to spend time with me.

He smiled. *I think by the end of that first conversation we were both well on our way to being in love. After that it was like a freight train rolling down a steep hill. It was all we could do to keep things in check. We were goners.*

Now that he had daughters, he wasn't particularly happy that they knew he and Christine had gotten married just ten weeks after they'd first met. He was afraid Alauna or Ashley might use that as an excuse

121

to justify their getting married too young or too quickly after meeting some guy.

He stopped to examine one of the trees he'd played around as a boy. It was being attacked by bores. *This tree needs to be sprayed. I wonder who I call to tell them that. If they don't spray soon, it'll spread to the other trees and in time this whole group will have to be pulled up and destroyed.*

He decided to inspect each tree along the line of trees bordering the park. *Maybe it's too late. Maybe they're all infected now anyway.*

He walked to the next tree. *I wouldn't change anything about meeting Christine—falling in love, and getting married when we did. Maybe I should have stayed in school though. But the reason I quit school was because she got pregnant right away. Would I change that? I don't know. It was like once she got pregnant, we weren't kids anymore. We were adults, with adult responsibilities, not quite ready for what we were being called upon to face.*

The next tree was also infected.

These two trees still look healthy from a distance, but it's just a matter of time before they start showing the damage. If it's not corrected, it could spread to all the trees in the park. I'll call the parks department and let them know what I found out.

He looked at his watch. He had stayed too long.

Roger will want a detailed explanation of where I've been. And then the Boy Wonder will whine about me not being around to give McPherson the training he needs. And we both know that as soon as he's trained, I'll lose my job.

He walked quickly back to where his pickup was parked.

Too bad about the trees, he thought. *Of course, for all I know, maybe they've been infected since when I was a boy, but I was too naive to notice that.*

He put his hand to the back of his head and massaged his neck muscles. *My work headache is back, right on schedule. And it will only get worse because I have to go in and face Roger for three more hours, and then I'll go home and Christine will tell me I need to be more involved with the family. And I'll say how can I do that when Ashley is never home. And when she is home, she doesn't seem to want to do anything with me. And then Christine will tell me I should have spent more time with her when she was younger. She'll say, "You never even took her to the zoo." The zoo? And I'll tell her we went to the zoo plenty of times. And she'll say, "but never with just the two of you."*

So this is what it's like to be my age. I'm inadequate at work, and I'm inadequate at home. Welcome to the golden years, right?

He took one last look at his beloved park. *I was so full of hope when I was a boy. And now what have I got?*

Once inside his pickup, he ignored the flashing light on the company cell phone, indicating he had three messages, most likely all from Roger.

He slowly drove back to his office.

11

Ashley was done with classes for the day at Ricks College. She'd started classes the first week in June, just a few weeks after graduating from high school. The fast-track plan at Ricks enabled students to finish two years of school in a little over a year, by going to school over two summers.

Ashley liked summer school. Classes were small. She had three roommates, but one of them was engaged to be married in August to a local boy, so she spent most of her time at her future in-laws' house planning the wedding reception, working on invitations, and hanging out.

Ashley had a perfect schedule—classes every morning until noon, and then she was free for the rest of the day.

She was also fortunate to have a car, a graduation present from her grandmother on her mother's side as a reward for doing so well in school, and also, she suspected, for being so little trouble to her mom and dad after she quit hanging around with Jen and Nathan. The car was ten years old and pretty beat-up, but at least it was dependable.

Nathan would be going to BYU in the fall. Jen wasn't accepted there because her grades hadn't been good enough, but she did get into UVSC. She wanted to be close to Nathan before he went on his mission.

Before they graduated from high school, Jen had tried to patch things up between her and Ashley, but, even though Ashley said she wanted to be friends again, she made up excuses whenever Jen called to set up a time they could get together.

Ashley had developed a daily routine at Ricks that seemed to work well for her. After her morning classes, she would walk back to her dorm, drop off her books, then drive to a grocery store to pick up a few things. Then she would drive out into the country, to one of several places she had found off back roads where she could be alone.

She would stay in the car, take out the groceries, open each package, and begin to eat. Today it was Hostess Twinkies and a bag of sweet rolls.

She ate fast but didn't bolt the food down. The trick was to eat fast so the food didn't have a chance to be digested.

On this day she ate her way through four packages of Twinkies and a half-dozen big sweet rolls, then, getting out of the car, she hurried down a hill to some tall weeds. It was better when there was a boulder on the ground because then she could rest her chest on the boulder and lean out. She had progressed to the point where she didn't need to stick her finger in her mouth anymore. The gag response was automatic now.

She purged and then walked slowly back to the car, feeling a little weak because she'd skipped breakfast and had thrown up her supper the night before, but feeling victorious that she'd enjoyed forbidden treats but wouldn't have to pay the consequences of getting fat.

I'm doing so good, she thought. *Except for this, I haven't had anything to eat all day.*

She smiled. *It's so great not to have to worry about my mother catching me. I'm on my own now. And I'm doing so good.*

She drove back to town.

There had been one troubling thing that had happened when she bought the food earlier in the day. The store clerk, a girl not much older than her, looked at all the junk food she'd bought and then studied her face. The girl hadn't said anything, but Ashley was certain she suspected that Ashley might have an eating disorder.

From now on, I'll go to two or three different stores, so nobody will get any ideas.

On the way into town, she stopped at a park and put the boxes and trash into a trash can, so it would be taken care of before she got back to campus. She liked things neat and orderly.

She felt cheerful that things were working out so well for her. *I'm totally in control of my life now,* she thought. *Now that I've taken care of that, I'll start studying.*

She picked up her books and headed for the library, passing by a girl in her ward talking to a boy, also in her ward. She didn't know either one of their names. Nor did they know her. In fact, she hardly knew anyone on campus, but that was okay. She didn't mind. She kept herself plenty busy as it was.

She'd been at the library half an hour when she felt the urge to go binge again.

No, once a day is enough, she reasoned.

Just one more time.

She thought she'd made it very clear to herself, but, even so, she left the library, walked to her car, drove to three stores, bought more junk food, drove out in the country once again, bolted down the food, hurried into a field of weeds, and vomited it all away. And then drove back to town, dumped the trash in a dumpster, and drove back to campus and went to the library.

She studied frantically now because she didn't know when the urge would come back. When it came, it was almost more than she could manage.

She made it for two hours before the urge came back. She was hungry, which meant she had to do it again.

I'm not going to do it this time, she thought. *Once or twice a day is all right, but not more than that because that would mean that I am out of control, and that's not true. I'm totally in control now, more than I've ever been in my life, mostly because I'm away from home.*

She stood up to leave but forced herself to sit down. *Not before I read my assignment in English,* she thought.

You know you're going to give in, don't you? a voice within her said. *You know you're going to do it, so why not just do it now and get it over with? Then you won't have to worry about it anymore.*

No. Three times a day is too much, she thought.

Don't think about that. Just do it. You know you want to do it.

She was trying to study, but all her energy was going into the private war raging inside her.

A boy from her ward came up to her. She couldn't remember his name.

"Studying hard?" he asked with a smile. He wore small wire-frame glasses. His short hair was the color of ripe wheat. His soft voice might have put her at ease, but the way he looked intently into her eyes made her feel very uncomfortable.

Even if I don't do it again, I still need to go to the store and pick up a few things, she thought.

"I guess so," she said.

"Mind if I sit down here and study with you?" he asked.

If you go to the store to pick up a few things, you know what'll happen.

"I guess not," she said.

He sat down across from her.

I can go to the store and buy groceries for the week without ending up out in the country.

No, you can't, and you know it.

"My name's Troy. We're in the same ward."

There was so much going on in her head that trying to talk to Troy was like trying to carry on a conversation with someone at a noisy football game.

"And you're Ashley, right?" he asked.

"That's right."

Don't waste time with him. You need to go grocery shopping and pick up a few things.

"We're in the same home evening group," he said.

"Oh, sure, I knew I'd seen you somewhere."

"That was where, all right."

"Oh, sure."

"You and I were the only ones not eating ice cream at family home evening last week."

"Oh."

"Are you lactose intolerant like me?"

"No."

"Must be on a diet then, right?"

If he thinks I'm on a diet, he must think I'm fat. And he's right. I am. But I'm getting it under control. Like today. I haven't really eaten anything all day, at least not to keep down.

"Not really. I just don't like it."

"I like it, but it doesn't agree with me."

Why is he wasting his time talking to me? I might want to talk to him after I get my weight down, but not now, not like this, not with my arms the way they are, and my calves, and my stomach. There's fat all over me. Anyone can see that.

And right now I'm so hungry. I need to go shopping and pick up a few things.

"This is your first semester here, isn't it?" he asked.

"Yes."

He nodded. "I could tell."

"How could you tell?"

"My sister was the same way last year."

"How do you mean?"

"Homesick, but don't worry, you'll get over it. I noticed it at family home evening. You didn't say much, and you looked kind of like you felt out of place, like you didn't really belong. My sister was the same way. I helped her, so maybe I can help you."

I really don't need this. I wish he'd just go away so I can get in some studying.

No, you have to go to the store and pick up a few things.

"I'm okay, really."

"I could drop by once in a while and see how you're doing."

126

"Well, you're probably really busy."

"Not too busy to help someone in my home evening group."

"I'm fine, really."

"I could show you around campus if you want."

"I don't think so, but thanks, anyway."

He tapped his forehead. "Oh, my gosh, you probably think I'm coming on to you, right?" He held up his hands. "I didn't mean it that way. I just meant we could be friends, that's all."

"Oh."

When I go to the store to pick up a few things, what if I pick up one package of glazed donuts? And then I can have one a day, and not purge. That wouldn't be too bad.

You can't eat one donut, the voice in her head raged. *You know that. It's either nothing or a dozen or more.*

I've got to go to the store to pick up a few things. That's all there is to it.

"I just got off my mission."

"Oh?"

"Don't you want to know where I served?"

"Okay. Where?"

"Italy."

"*Avete dei picchetti da tenda?*" she said.

He broke out laughing. "I can't believe it! You speak Italian?"

"Very little."

"Do you know what you just said?"

"Not exactly."

"You said, 'Do you have any tent pegs?'"

"Well, do you?"

"How do you know Italian?"

"I used to be on a soccer team, and our coach wore European clothes and pretended to be Italian. I guess some of his phrases stuck with me."

"That is amazing. Say, would you like to get a bagel and a drink?"

You can't do that and you know it. Because you'll have to excuse yourself to use the rest room, and who knows how many people will be in the rest room, and it's better not to have people listening to you puking.

"Well, actually, this isn't a good time. I need to run some errands downtown."

"Maybe some other time then. Okay?"

"Sure, maybe so."

"I'm really looking forward to hearing more of your Italian."

"Well, I don't know much."

"Before you go, give me one more in Italian."

"*Ha un documento di reconoscimento, per favore?*"

He pursed his lips as he translated. "Have you an identity document, please? Is that right?"

"I think so. I need to go now."

"I just have one more question. How did that come up in a soccer game?"

"It's a long story."

"You are a woman of mystery, aren't you? You're probably an undercover agent for the CIA, and you're off to some foreign country to save the world from destruction. And you speak like, what, twenty languages, and you have a black belt in karate. Am I right so far?"

She turned and said, "*Vorrei cambiare questi soldi in lire italiane.*"

He broke out into a belly laugh, his voice loud enough to distract anyone else on that floor of the library. "You are too much, Lady!"

She smiled for the first time in months and hurried out of the library.

He likes me. We could become good friends.

She walked back to the dorm, basking in the warmth of his attention and obvious delight with her.

He seems like a nice guy. I like the way he laughs. He's not at all like my dad. Wouldn't it be something if I ended up marrying him someday? Just because I know a few phrases of Italian. That would be something. I wish I could talk to Jen. I miss her so much. She's the only friend I've ever had I could talk to about anything. Well, not anything. We couldn't talk about Nathan kissing us. I wonder if she knew I was telling the truth but couldn't face losing him. I guess I'll never know.

I don't want to get married though. Not for a long time. I wouldn't want my husband seeing me the way I am now. Maybe someday though, after I lose ten pounds. I'm doing so good now. If I just keep this up, it'll be really good. Maybe I should lose more than ten pounds just for a cushion. That would be so good. Then I wouldn't have any fat anywhere.

I'm doing so good now. I haven't eaten anything all day, at least not to keep down, so that's really good.

If I was married, I wouldn't want my husband to see me. And I wouldn't want him to know about what I do after I eat. I'd keep it a secret. Maybe only eat when he was gone.

I'm doing so good now.

She paused at the stairway leading up to her apartment in the dorm. She felt dizzy and light-headed and wasn't sure if she could make it up the stairs without fainting. She wished her apartment was on the first floor. It was hard enough walking from class to class without having to climb stairs to get to her apartment.

I should eat something and let it stay down. I feel so weak.

No, you can't eat, you know that. If you eat anything and keep it down, you'll get fatter. You know that. Don't spoil your perfect record. You're doing so good today.

If I don't eat and if I exercise, then I'll lose some of my fat, so I have to force myself to keep going. That's all there is to it.

She had to stop halfway up the stairs to rest. She steadied herself on the railing to keep herself from falling down the stairs. But then, after a little rest, she made it to the second floor.

I'm doing so good, she thought.

* * * * *

On Sunday she went with her roommates to their campus ward. They sat together, Ashley in the middle.

She liked her roommates, or at least she didn't dislike them. They seemed to be more involved with things than she was. They knew many of the names of the boys in the ward and always had news about the girls who lived in the ward.

Ashley was known as a shy girl, but that was okay with her. It helped her save her energy. Being friendly and outgoing took more energy than she had. It was hard enough to get up in the morning and make it to class.

During the opening song, she touched her stomach reassuringly. She felt skinny today, and that made her happy.

I'm doing so good today, she thought. She hadn't eaten anything yet today and already it was eleven o'clock. Church didn't get out until two o'clock, so she wouldn't have anything to eat until at least three o'clock. And if she took a nap it might be five or six before she had anything to eat.

They were singing the sacrament hymn, but she didn't sing. She didn't feel like singing because she didn't like the sound of her own voice.

I'm doing so good, she thought. She closed her eyes for the sacrament prayer.

"'O God, the Eternal Father, we ask thee in the name of thy Son, Jesus Christ, to bless and sanctify this bread to the souls of all those who partake of it, that they may eat in remembrance of the body of thy Son, and witness unto thee, O God, the Eternal Father, that they are willing to take upon them the name of thy Son, and always remember him and keep his commandments which he has given them; that they may always have his Spirit to be with them. Amen.'"

She said "amen" along with her roommates and then continued her train of thought. *What will I do after church? I'll be so hungry by then. And the girls will want me to eat with them.*

It was a request from their bishop that they eat at least one meal a week together. And that presented a problem because she couldn't eat a big meal now without purging. It was almost automatic now, and she didn't seem to have any control over it.

But with their dorm apartment being so small, she was sure they'd hear her in the bathroom throwing up. And then they'd know. And who knows where that might end? They might turn her in, either to the bishop or to the counseling center.

She didn't want anyone knowing about this. She was doing so good, and she didn't want anyone trying to change that.

What am I going to do about eating after church? I could pretend like I was taking a nap, but they might wake me up when it was time to eat, but I could say I was too tired to eat then. That might do it. And then I could wait until everyone's gone and then I could drive out in the country and have the brownies I put in the trunk yesterday.

That's what I'll do. She smiled. *I'm doing so good.*

The bread came to her. She put a tiny piece in her mouth, but a short time later she brought a tissue to her nose with both hands and got rid of the bread into the tissue. *I'm doing so good,* she thought.

After church she begged off eating with her roommates by saying she was too tired and had to take a nap. She lay on her bed with a blanket over her and listened to her roommates talking and preparing food.

She was famished, and the smells coming from the kitchen were tempting. She could hardly wait until she could sneak out to her car and drive out into the country and devour the two packages of brownies she'd bought the day before at half price. She would, of course, throw it all up, but it would taste good, even though afterward she'd be even more hungry.

I'll have to eat something today, she thought. *Maybe a piece of toast. That wouldn't make me too fat. But I need to eat something because my legs are so weak, and it's so hard to climb stairs anymore. So maybe a piece of toast. If I can keep it down. It used to be so hard to make myself throw up, but now what's hard is to make myself keep the food down. Anything I eat now comes up without me even thinking about it. That's not good. I have to eat something, even if I am still fat.*

To measure her progress, she began to examine her body. When she relaxed the muscles on her calves, and pinched the skin, there was nearly an inch of fat. That was something she had to get rid of.

And then there was her stomach. She didn't like the fact that her stomach bulged when she breathed in. She wanted it to stay the same, but she wasn't there yet.

Next she checked her arms. If she held them out and didn't flex her muscles, it was like fat hanging down from her arm. Even as hard as she'd worked, it was still there. So it had to go, too.

I have to do better, she thought. *I'm still fat.*

She got out of bed and pulled her bathroom scale from underneath her bed and stood on it. She weighed twelve pounds less than she'd weighed a year ago.

Just ten pounds to go, she thought. *Or maybe even a little more. It would be great to weigh the same as what I weighed in seventh grade. That would be great. I wasn't a bit fat in seventh grade.*

She felt a little light-headed from standing up, so she lay back down on the bed.

I'm doing so good, she thought.

Her plan for the afternoon was ruined when she heard a knock on the door, and then one of her roommates opened the door and whispered, "Ashley, it's Troy, from our home evening group. He wants to see you."

"Tell him I'm too sleepy."

"I did. He said that's okay, he'll wait for you to wake up. He brought his guitar. He's going to sing Italian songs for us. You'd better come and listen."

Ashley scowled. If she didn't go in right away, then he might wait there for her until she did, and that would delay her driving out into the country and enjoying the brownies, so she might as well get up, listen to his songs, and then send him on his way.

She stood up too quickly and had to sit back down to keep from fainting, then stood up more slowly, then entered the kitchen, where Troy, surrounded by her roommates, was playing the guitar and singing.

He's been on a mission. Maybe that's what makes him so comfortable with people. He's not the world's greatest singer or guitar player, but that doesn't seem to bother him. I like his smile, too, that is, the smile he has for everyone he meets, not that it's just for me. No way. I'm nothing special in his eyes, just one of the girls in his home evening group. That's good, too. I have too much to do these days.

When he finished his song, they all clapped and told him how good it was. Ashley checked the clock, wondering how long he'd be there. She felt like she might pass out if she didn't sit down, but all the kitchen chairs were taken.

"Ashley, come sit next to me and I'll sing a special song just for you," Troy said.

"I know, sit on his lap," one of her roommates suggested.

"Oh, no, I'd crush him."

"I bet you hardly weigh a thing."

"That's 'cause she never eats," a roommate said.

"I eat," she said.

"Sure, after everyone is asleep," another said.

She wanted to change the subject. "Sing another song, Troy," she said, sitting on the armrest of the sofa. She didn't like to be so close to him. She was worried he'd touch her on the arm or hand. She always felt cold, and when anyone touched her hand or arm, they always remarked how cold she felt.

Troy sang another song.

She looked at him as if she were enjoying it, but the whole time she was thinking, *I wish he'd leave so I can go have my brownies in the country.*

He finished another song. Again, everyone told him how good it was. As a feeble afterthought Ashley added, "Yeah, right, it was real good." She tried to sound as enthusiastic as her roommates, but it was hard to do because being enthusiastic took more energy than she had.

I should eat something for real, she thought.

No, that would ruin everything, the other voice in her head answered. *You have a perfect record so far today. Don't ruin it. Just go eat the brownies, all of them, then you'll feel better.*

But they won't stay down, she answered.

No, of course not, if they stayed down, you'd get even fatter than you are now.

Why can't I just eat something and let it stay down?

You know the answer. You're already fat. If you let it stay down, then you'd get gross and people would make fun of you behind your back. Is that what you want?

But I feel like I'm going to pass out.

That will go away with time. Just keep on like you're doing until you're not fat anymore.

When will that be?

When you weigh the same as you did in sixth grade.

But I'm taller now than I was then.

What difference does that make?

I was a little girl then, now I'm a woman almost.

Well, do you want to be fat like your mother? Is that what you want?

Something's definitely wrong, though. When I stand up, I feel like I'm going to pass out. That can't be right.

It's just until you lose another twenty pounds. And then you can eat all you want anytime.

Twenty pounds? I thought it was ten pounds.

Twenty pounds to be on the safe side. That's all. Just another twenty pounds.

I don't think this is good for me.

It doesn't matter what you think.

Why doesn't it matter?

Because I'm in charge now.

Ashley, frightened for her life, staggered to her feet and hurried into the bathroom and closed the door. She looked at herself in the mirror, trying to see if she looked any different. Who was this other person who had just spoken to her in her mind, who now seemed to have control over her, who had such power over her to be able to tell her what she was going to do?

I can stop this anytime. It's not like it's something I have no control over. I have perfect control over it. If I want I can go in there and eat a regular meal and keep it down just like my roommates.

Maybe I should stop doing this for a while.

Sure, back off next week. But as far as today, you might as well have the brownies in the trunk.

She saw nothing wrong with that.

She returned to Troy, who was entertaining her roommates with another song.

When he finished the song, the others thanked him and left to go next door, leaving her alone with Troy.

"You want to take a walk?" he asked. "It's a nice day."

"A walk?" she asked, panicking that she might faint.

"Sure, why not? It'd give us a chance to talk."

"Well, the truth is, I've been fasting today."

"How come? It's not fast Sunday."

"Well, no, it isn't. It's . . . you know . . . personal."

"I understand. When are you breaking your fast?"

"Uh . . . in a couple of hours."

"Okay . . . so you'd rather not walk until after you eat, is that right?"

"Yes, that's right."

"No problem. We can talk, though, can't we?" he asked.

"Sure, that'd be fine."

"What do you want to talk about?"

"Tell me about your mission."

It worked out well to have him talk about his mission. All she had to do was nod appreciatively once in a while, and he did the rest. She prided herself that she could get him to open up without revealing any of her inner thoughts. *Appearing to be perky and upbeat is the way to go, all right. I don't want anyone to know what I'm really feeling.*

As he talked about the people he'd taught and baptized, her thoughts kept going back to the tray of brownies in the trunk of her car. *How long is this going to take?* she thought.

"You had a lot of wonderful experiences on your mission," she said enthusiastically. "Thanks for telling me."

"Oh, I'm not done yet," he said.

"I would be disappointed if you were," she said. At the same time thinking, *Just ten more minutes and he'll be gone. And then I can go have some brownies. I can hardly wait.*

Why am I encouraging him? Why don't I just tell him I'm not interested in being his friend? That would be the most honest thing I could do. I'm not interested in him. I mean, not really. I'm busy enough as it is with school work and everything else.

Do I even like him? I must not because I never think about him. Today I've thought more about the brownies in the trunk than I have about him.

I could tell him not to come by anymore. And I would, except for the other girls. It's sort of like a trophy to have a guy coming around to see me. Especially an R.M. So maybe I'll keep him just for the status of having him come around.

I should feel some sort of attraction for him; after all, he's a guy. But I don't, and I don't think I ever will for him, but that's okay. Maybe that's not even necessary. Maybe I could even be married and never open myself up to my husband. Maybe he'd never even know what I was doing.

He continued his story. "So I asked them if they'd fast as a couple, and I told them we'd fast with them. It was hard for them to see how that would help them know the Church was true, but finally they agreed. We started our fast about ten minutes later. The four of us knelt down and I asked the father to say a prayer. He said he thought it would be better if I said the prayer, but I told him it was his duty as the head of the family. So finally he agreed."

Ashley glanced at the clock. *It's three-thirty and I haven't eaten anything all day. I'm doing so good.*

While Troy continued his story, she reached down and touched the calf of her right leg. She tried to flex her muscle. It was still flabby, but she thought it was just a tiny bit smaller. That made her feel good. She was doing so good.

Troy finished.

"That was real good," she said.

"I've gone on too long. Now it's your turn. Tell me more about yourself."

"Oh, there's not much to tell."

"Do you ever open up to anyone?"

"Not very often." She paused. "I did open up once to a friend of mine. Her name was Jen. We were best friends in high school. We could talk about anything. I've never had a friend like her since then. She knew everything about me, and it was the same way with me."

"You said her name was Jen. Did she die?"

"Oh, no, she's still alive. She's in Provo, going to UVSC."

"Are you two still close?"

"No, not really."

"What happened?"

"A guy got in the way of our friendship. That happens, you know, with girls. It happens all the time. She started spending all her time with him, so that left me out. It's all right, though. I mean, it was bound to happen sooner or later, right?"

"But you're still friends, though, right?"

"Well, not exactly, not anymore."

"What happened?"

"There were some hard feelings."

"Oh. Do you want to talk about it?"

"Not really."

"Good friends are hard to come by."

"That's true."

"Are you sure you don't want to take a walk?"

"Well, no, not today. I'm kind of weak from fasting."

"Some other day?"

"I guess so."

He stood up. "Well, I'll be going then. It's been nice talking to you."

"Sure, you, too."

She walked him to the door, said one more good-bye, then closed the door.

She didn't want him to see her driving away, so she decided to wait before she left to drive out into the country where she could enjoy her brownies.

Just as she was about to leave, her roommates returned, excited to find out about Troy.

"So, what happened?"

"Nothing. We just talked."

"What's he like?"

"He's okay."

"Just okay?"

"He's nice."

"Do you like him?"

"I don't know. I guess so."

"When are you going to see him again?"

"I don't know."

"You don't sound too excited."

"Should I?"

"He could turn out to be the guy you get married to."

"I'm not ready to get married."

"But maybe you should start thinking about it."

She again denied any interest, then left to drive into the country so she could enjoy her brownies.

12

I'm doing so good, Ashley thought a few minutes later as she pulled into the secluded spot she often used. *I haven't eaten anything all day. And this won't even count.*

She turned off the motor and looked around to make sure she was alone and then opened the door and stepped out. She felt a little dizzy, so she put one hand on the car for balance as she made her way to the trunk of the car.

She stopped to catch her breath for a minute, then opened the trunk. There, in all its glory, were three packages of brownies. They looked so inviting.

She reached down, picked them up, and passed out.

When she opened her eyes, she was on the ground, surrounded by three men with rifles in their hands. Fearing the worst, she wanted to run away, but she was so weak she couldn't move. She stared at them and they stared back.

"She's awake," one of them said.

His voice betrayed him, and she realized he was not much older than fifteen. Looking around, she saw the others were about the same age.

"You okay?" one of them asked.

It was then she realized they meant her no harm. She sat up and tried to get up but it was almost more than she could do.

One of the boys helped her up.

"I'm okay. I just must have passed out for a minute, that's all."

"You got a lot of brownies," one of the boys said.

"Oh, yes," she said. "It's for my roommate. It's her birthday today, and we're going to have a surprise party for her, and I was just looking for a place to have it. I decided this was a good place, and so I was getting the brownies out of my car . . . for the party."

She realized the story didn't make much sense, but hoped the boys wouldn't ask a lot of questions.

She was right. "Well, okay then, do you need any help?"

"No, not now. I'm fine. I'll just head to a phone and call my roommates and tell them to come out here for the surprise party."

"Well, I guess we'll be going then. We're doing some shooting."

"I see. Well, I appreciate your thoughtfulness."

She watched them as they headed across a field. She got in her car and drove away.

Once in town, she pulled into the Wal-Mart parking lot, parked the car, and broke down crying, reliving again the feeling of panic when she saw the boys standing over her, not knowing their intentions, and having no energy to do anything to protect herself.

This has gone too far. If I keep on this way, it's going to kill me. I don't want to die now. I'm too young.

After a few minutes, she wiped the tears away and drove back to her apartment. She went inside and went to her room and lay down and pretended to sleep. Even though she was weak from not eating, she didn't want her roommates to see her this way, so she would wait until ward prayer at eight before she got up to have something to eat.

It was more complicated than just eating. The hard part would be to trick her body into keeping the food down so it would do her some good.

A little before eight, the girls had all left the apartment for ward prayer.

Ashley sat up and tried to muster enough strength to walk into the kitchen.

After a few minutes, she stood up. She felt the same dizziness that she'd felt just before she passed out in the country. She sat down on the floor and waited for the feeling to pass.

Not trusting herself to walk, she crawled into the kitchen, over to the kitchen table and pulled herself up. She sat down on one of the chairs and rested her head on the table.

A few minutes later, she opened the fridge and looked in at the food left over from their big meal that day. She spotted a large baked potato, a hamburger patty, and some leftover corn. Even imagining herself eating all that brought a gag response, and she knew that in spite of her intense hunger, her body had been so conditioned that she would throw it all up. And then she'd be worse off.

I feel so weak, she though. *I need something to eat that I'll keep down. I need to eat something fast or I'll pass out again.*

Everything in the fridge made her feel queasy, so she closed the door.

Toast, she thought. *I can keep toast down.*

She put two slices of bread in the toaster and tried to decide what to put on it.

I need to put something on the toast, she thought. She opened the cupboard and looked at what was available.

Not peanut butter, she thought. *That has fat in it. And that would make me throw up. Not butter because that has fat in it too. Not jelly because that has sugar in it. And not honey because bees make honey.*

After going through what she could see on the shelf, she rejected everything.

Just plain toast then, she thought. *It's better than nothing.*

She took two bites and then stopped.

That's enough, she thought. *If I eat any more, I'll get fat. Bread has carbohydrates.*

She was going to get up from the table, but she felt too weak to stand up.

She wanted to eat more but was afraid she was so conditioned to throw up, she wouldn't be able to stop herself.

She closed her eyes as tears began to roll down her cheek. *If I can't eat more than this in a day, it's going to kill me. I've got to eat more.*

She took another bite of dry unbuttered toast. It was too much. She staggered into the bathroom, and, through her tears, threw up the only food she had wanted to keep down that day.

The voice inside mocked her. *You're doing so good.*

She lay down on the bed and fell asleep.

A few minutes later her roommate Ruth Ellen sat down on Ashley's bed and said softly, "Ashley, can you wake up? We need to talk."

Ruth Ellen, a doe-eyed elementary education major from a small farming community near St. Anthony, always spoke slowly and distinctly, as if she were talking to a Sunbeam class in Primary. Her goal in life was to some day start a daycare center back in her hometown.

Ashley didn't respect Ruth Ellen mainly because she had a pear-shaped body, and because, even at eighteen, she came across as the designated mother of the apartment. Ruth Ellen might have been a real hindrance to Ashley's weekend bingeing, but she usually went home for the weekend.

Ashley sat up. "What is it? I'm really tired."

"I want to show you something in the bathroom."

I cleaned up after the last time. It can't be about that, Ashley thought as she followed Ruth Ellen into the bathroom.

"It's not my week to clean the bathroom," Ashley complained.

"I know. It's not about that."

Ruth Ellen opened the shower curtain. "Look."

"Look at what?"

"Look at all the hair."

The bottom of the tub was strewn with hair, as if someone had cut their hair while taking a bath.

"How do you suppose it got there?" Ruth Ellen asked quietly.

"You woke me up for this?" Ashley complained. "Look, girls live here, they take showers, a few hairs come out with each shower, and before long, it adds up."

"That's what I thought too," Ruth Ellen said. "So I completely cleaned the tub, and this is what it looks like after two days."

"So?"

"My hair is so dark that it's easy to spot. And there were a few strands that came from me. You're the only one in the apartment with really light-colored hair like this."

"How can you tell what color it is?"

"Well, that's true. You can't tell that much just looking at it from here, can you? But if you gather some of it up, and put it on a white piece of paper, you can get a better idea. If you want, we can do that."

That can't all be my hair, she thought, *because if it is, then that would mean I was losing my hair. But that can't be happening. There must be another explanation.*

Ruth Ellen went and got a sheet of typing paper, brushed a damp washcloth across the bottom of the bathtub, set the paper on the counter, and gently shook the washcloth over the paper. "Look, you can see it better this way. I think that one is mine, and this one I think is Jordan's, but look at all these others. They're all the same color, and it's pretty close to the color of your hair."

I can't deal with this, she thought. *The most important thing is to keep Ruth Ellen from ruining everything that I'm achieving right now. I'm doing so good. Once I get down to my goal-weight, I can stop doing what I'm doing and then my hair will come back and things will be okay again. This is just temporary. But I'd better hurry up and lose some weight, so I can get back to normal, so I don't lose all my hair.*

"It is your hair, isn't it?" Ruth Ellen said.

"That's not the only explanation, Ruth Ellen."

"What would be another explanation?"

"Well, maybe next door they had some problems with the plumbing and so the girls next door came in and used our shower."

"If that happened, wouldn't you and I know about it?"

"We're not here all the time."

"But somebody would have had to let them in."

"The manager might have let them in when nobody was here."

"I think we would have been notified," Ruth Ellen said slowly. "I have another explanation. Would you like to hear it?"

"Not really. I'm really very tired right now." Ashley brushed past Ruth Ellen and returned to her room, lay down on her bed, and pulled up the covers because she was cold.

Ruth Ellen came in the room and sat down on the bed and put her hand on Ashley's shoulder. "I'm worried about you, Ashley."

Ashley turned to escape Ruth Ellen's touch. "Leave me alone. I'm really tired."

"You're not eating right."

Ashley sat up. "Who made you my mother, anyway?"

Ruth Ellen's sad eyes got moist. "I'm only trying to help."

"I don't need any help."

"I think you do. Your problem is lack of nutrition, Ashley. And I can help you with that."

Ashley needed time to think. "You can?"

Ruth Ellen's expression brightened. "Yes, I really can."

"Maybe we should talk then."

"There's nothing I'd rather do more than that. I care about you, Ashley, you know that."

"That is so kind of you, Ruth Ellen. You're just about the best room-mate a girl could ever have."

Ruth Ellen beamed.

"Let me make a quick trip to the bathroom, okay? And then we'll talk."

"Yes, of course."

Ashley went in the bathroom mainly to collect her thoughts. Ruth Ellen was leaving at the end of second summer term, just two weeks away. *If I deny everything, Ruth Ellen will take it to somebody in authority and then who knows what will happen? All I have to do is say I'll work with her and then she'll relax and I'll pretend that things are getting better, and then she'll leave, and I'll continue on as before.*

She cleaned out her hair brush and passed the brush through her hair. The brush picked up a wad of hair. *This can't be happening to me. It just can't. If I lose all my hair, then what am I going to do? Nobody will want to have anything to do with me.*

She closed her eyes. *Heavenly Father, please don't let me lose all my hair. Not now. Not when I'm doing so good. Amen.*

Ruth Ellen gently knocked on the door. "Are you okay?"

"I'm fine. I'll be right out."

A few minutes later they sat on their beds and talked. Ruth Ellen suggested she eat more vegetables and offered to cut up a big bag of carrots, celery, and green peppers. "And maybe if you had a little cheese every day, that might help."

"That sounds real good, Ruth Ellen. I'll do whatever you say. I mean, the thought of losing my hair is really scary."

"Okay, then, we'll do it and see if it helps. I'm just sorry I won't be here third summer term."

"I'll write and tell you how I'm doing."

Ruth Ellen smiled. "You'd better."

You are such a loser, Ashley thought, but then smiled brightly for Ruth Ellen's benefit.

The next morning, when Ashley got up, she found a note on the table.

Good morning, Sunshine!

I hope you have a great day. Be sure and have a good breakfast. I usually have Cream of Wheat, but I know that not everybody likes that. If you're in a hurry, a really good breakfast is peanut butter on toast. If you want, we can talk about breakfasts tonight.

Oh, I almost forgot. I made up a little bag of vegetables and wrapped up a couple of wedges of cheese for you to nibble on during the day. They're in the fridge. Have a great day!

Love,

Ruth Ellen.

Ashley skipped breakfast, but on her way out, she took a knife and stuck it into the jar of peanut butter, then set it on the counter for Ruth Ellen to see. On her way to class, she passed a garbage can. She tossed the vegetables and cheese into it and continued on her way.

Two weeks later, Ruth Ellen, full of hope and a secret pride in being able to change someone's life, left Ricks for good.

Ruth Ellen wrote several letters, which Ashley never even opened.

* * * * *

A week after third summer term began, Ashley sat up in bed in the middle of the night and looked over at her new roommate, who was sleeping. And then she stood up and walked slowly into the kitchen. Her mouth was dry, her stomach growling. She was surrounded with food, but she couldn't eat any of it because her body would reject it even against her will.

I've done this to myself, she thought. *Now I must undo it or I'll be in big trouble.*

She pulled the chair to the cupboards, stood up, opened the cupboards, sat down again, and looked at the food on the shelf. One by one, she rejected each item: pork and beans because of the pork, noodles because people who ate a lot of noodles were fat, tuna because it was packed in oil, peanut butter because it was mostly fat, soup because all the water would make her stomach look big.

By the time she was finished, she had rejected everything in the cupboard.

What am I going to do if there's nothing I can eat?

She opened the door of the refrigerator and looked in. There wasn't much to choose from. There were some leftovers from supper that before she would have eaten late at night and then thrown up. She hesitated to start for fear she'd do the same thing.

There's got to be something, she thought. *If there isn't, I'll have to drop out of school and go home and be told what a failure I am, and how could I have thrown away my only chance to go to college.*

She spotted the carton of eggs on a shelf in the door. At first she thought about fried eggs, swimming in bacon fat. She couldn't eat that because of the fat. But then she thought about boiled eggs: no fat, some protein, very little taste.

I could eat boiled eggs, she thought. *Well, not the yolk, because that's the fattiest part. And maybe some toast with no butter. And herb tea like Nathan gave us once, the kind that tasted like a musty closet.*

They weren't even her eggs, but this was an emergency. She filled a large pan with water, set it on the stove, and turned it on to high. She sat and waited for the water to boil, then set three eggs into the water, and waited.

I wish Jen were here, she thought, *and that things were the way they used to be, not like the way we left it. I wonder how Nathan is doing. He was the most fun of anyone. Or at least he was in the beginning, before he messed everything up between Jen and me.*

She closed her eyes and took herself back to one of their soccer games. She was on the sidelines arguing in Italian with Nathan, saying phrases that she only barely understood, putting on a show for the other team, so they'd think she was a hothead with a bad temper. She turned the bench over and stormed away. Nathan shouted at her. She turned around and began beating him on the arms and shoulders. He put the bench upright and ordered her to sit down. In protest, she waved her hands at him, then sat down. And then he turned to her and they both smiled at each other.

I wish I were like that now, she thought. *I wish I could yell at people and get mad and storm off. I wish I wasn't always quiet, always alone, feeling the calf of my leg or touching my stomach to see if I've lost any weight since the last time I checked.*

I've got to change what I've been doing or I'll have to go home. If I go home, my mother will keep piling more misery on me. And I can't take that anymore.

And what about my dad? Where does he fit into the picture? Other girls talk about their dads. Not that their dads were perfect but that they were involved. Mine never was.

The water was boiling vigorously. She turned down the heat to medium.

She caught herself touching her stomach again. When she breathed in, it went out, just like always.

I've lost two more pounds since I've been at Ricks. Just eighteen more to go. That's my new goal, but I don't think I'm going to reach it.

When the eggs were done, she took one out of the pan and ran cold water over it, then peeled it, cut out the yellow yolk and threw it away, shook some salt and pepper over what was left, and took a small bite.

She chewed slowly, trying very hard not to in any way trigger what had become her usual response to food, a retching rejection.

This will not make me fat, so it's all right to eat. Please, dear God, help me so I can keep this down.

She swallowed and waited.

Nothing happened.

That is very good. I'm doing great. Now if I can take another bite and keep it down. I don't have to eat the whole egg but even a part of it would be good. If I can keep eggs down, then I can get by here at college. If I can't, then I won't even make it to the end of the semester, and I'll have to go home and live with my parents, and I don't think I can stand that.

It took half an hour to eat the white from one egg and sip a little water. At one point she thought about having a piece of dry toast with it, but she didn't want to push her luck.

Eggs are good, she thought, as she brushed her teeth.

Just before she fell asleep, she put her hand on her stomach just to see how she was doing.

It wasn't good. Her stomach was still rising whenever she breathed.

* * * * *

When she woke up the next morning, she felt happy and hopeful. *Eggs and dry toast,* she thought. *That's what's going to keep me going.*

144

She took a quick shower, dried off, then worked on her hair. Instead of vigorously brushing it like she used to do, she tried to work it more with her hands, using a brush only at the last, and then very gently. After she used the brush, she refused to see how many hairs had come out. She didn't want to know because she knew it would depress her too much. *I had an egg last night. I've heard that's good for hair. So maybe I'll stop losing it.*

She took out one of the eggs she boiled the night before, and then settled down at the kitchen table to read an assignment for her next class.

She was embarrassed she didn't know whose eggs she had boiled the night before. When one of her roommates came into the room, she asked, "Are these your eggs?"

She said they weren't, and by then Ashley had to go to class, but not before having one of the eggs and a piece of dry toast.

As she left for class, she planned on going to the store at noon and buying a dozen eggs. It seemed like a reasonable thing at eight in the morning, but as the morning passed she began to be worried. For her to go to the store after classes without bingeing and purging might be a problem.

All I'm going to do is buy a dozen eggs. That's all.

You'll need some bread too.

All right, I'll buy a dozen eggs and a loaf of bread.

It wouldn't hurt to go by the bakery to see if they have any reduced prices on baked goods.

No, I'm not going to go by the bakery. I'm going to where they keep the eggs and then get some bread.

You have time to go out to the country.

No, I'm not going out to the country.

You mean you're never going to go out to the country again?

That's right.

You know you will. I mean, sometime you will.

Not today.

Today would be a perfect time to do it.

I can't do that anymore. It's not good for me.

You could still do it, though. I mean, there's no reason to completely stop, is there?

Yes, I'm afraid this is getting out of control.

You don't have to do it so many times in a day. Cut down to once a day. That'd be about right.

No, not even once a day.

What then? Once a week?

I don't want to do it anymore.

That's not reasonable. Once a week seems reasonable.

I'm not going to do it anymore.

What about buying one donut while you're at the store?

No, I can't do that.

Why can't you do it? One donut is not going to hurt you, is it?

One donut wouldn't be enough. Once I had one, I'd want a dozen. And you know where that would lead.

So, what are you saying, that you're never going to eat a donut your whole life?

Yes, that's what I'm saying.

That is totally unreasonable. You know that.

I don't care. I just know I can't keep this up.

Why not?

Because it's all I think about. I've been to school two months, and I don't even know the names of my roommates. I'm just barely getting by in my classes, and when I'm talking to a guy, all I can think about is the next time I can go into the country. That isn't right.

Guys don't want to have anything to do with you because you're fat.

I've lost a lot of weight.

It doesn't matter. You're still fat. Get your weight under control and then you'll have plenty of guys after you.

That's what you always say.

What if a guy sees your stomach popping out while you're breathing? He'll be grossed out and walk out and never come back.

I'll wear a baggy sweater. He won't see it.

Oh, he'll see it, all right, you can be sure of that.

I don't care then. I'll find some guy who doesn't care about things like that.

You'll never find anyone like that.

I'm not going to do it anymore.

Not ever?

Not ever.

Then you'll end up fat, just like your mother.

I am nothing like my mother, and I never will be.

You are, though. You'll be just like her if you don't do this anymore.

You're wrong. I won't ever be like her.

In class, Ashley hardly paid any attention to her teachers as she continued to argue with herself.

After her classes were over for the day, she drove to the store to pick up a dozen eggs and a loaf of bread. She walked directly to where the eggs were kept, picked up a carton, checked to make sure none of the

146

eggs were broken, then went to the bread section and picked up a loaf of bread. Then she started for the checkout counter, which would lead her past the baked goods.

She stopped in front of a large package of day-old raised donuts, marked down to half-price.

It's all right. It's no big deal.

She watched as she put the package in her cart. It was almost as if she'd given up control.

Five minutes later she was in the car with the package of donuts next to her on the seat.

I don't want to do this, she thought.

Secretly, though, you do.

No.

That's why you went to the store. Just like you always do after classes. This is no different. No different at all.

I can't go on this way.

Why not?

Because I'm doing it four, five, six times a day!

Cut down to three, then.

I can hardly walk up stairs now without feeling like I'm going to faint.

That's 'cause you're too fat. If you weren't so fat, you could run up the stairs.

I'm not going to do this today.

You already bought the donuts. What are you going to do, throw them away?

Yes.

You can't do that.

Why not?

It's a waste of money.

Doing what I've been doing is an even worse waste of money.

You can't go a day without doing this, so you might as well get it taken care of so you can forget about it.

I can't ever forget about it. It just keeps coming back at me, over and over again.

That's because you're trying to stop completely. Try cutting down first. Maybe three times a day at first and then after a while, maybe two times a day. And before you know it, it will be down to once a day.

I'll be dead by then.

You won't be dead. And you won't be fat. And you won't need to worry about getting fat.

She came to a stoplight. If she turned left, she'd head out into the country. If she turned right, she'd be on her way back to campus.

It'll just take twenty minutes, and then you'll be able to focus on your classes.

No, I'm not going to do it anymore.

You know you'll be thinking about this the whole day if you don't do it. You won't be able to study. If you want to pass your courses this semester, you'd better just turn left and go out in the country for a few minutes.

The light changed.

Ashley turned left.

That's better.

She was in tears.

I don't want to do this.

But you're going to do it anyway, aren't you?

Not necessarily. I can always turn around and head back to campus.

You're making too big a deal out of this. It's just a few donuts.

A few minutes later she parked at her usual place. She opened the bag of donuts.

I don't want to do this anymore, she thought.

Then why are you going to do it?

Because I can't stop myself anymore!

Don't think. You'll only make yourself miserable. Just enjoy the donuts while they last.

Afterwards she broke down and cried, then drove back to school.

She had no hope anymore.

13

Every Sunday after church during the fall semester, Jen cooked a big meal for Nathan. It was the one chance she had to have him by herself. The rest of the week they were seldom together, especially with him going to BYU and Jen to UVSC. To make matters worse, she worked four hours a day waiting tables at an upscale Italian restaurant in downtown Provo. If Nathan wanted to see her, he had to order spaghetti.

But each Sunday after church they were together for the entire afternoon.

They were not even in the same campus ward. At first she just went to his ward, but then her bishop called her in and encouraged her to attend her own ward. And so she did.

But not Relief Society. She went one time, and then quit.

Until Nathan found out and told her she should go.

And so she went the next time.

And when he asked her what she thought about it, she said, "I still don't like it."

"How come?"

"It's boring. Why can't I go to priesthood? I've always gotten along better with guys."

"That's what I've heard," he said.

She winced.

"I'm sorry. I didn't mean it like that," he said.

"Are you always going to throw my past up in my face?"

"I said I was sorry, didn't I?"

"You said that, but I'm not sure you meant it."

"I did mean it."

They sat in silence at the kitchen table, their plates empty except for the skin of the baked potato, which Nathan had, since childhood, refused to eat. The late afternoon sun streamed in through one window, delineating a line across the table with him in the sunshine and her in shadows. She dabbed at her eyes with her napkin, made out of paper but embossed and expensive, which she only used each Sunday with him.

He stood up, moved his chair next to hers, reached out to take her hand, and looked into her eyes. He said softly, "I really am sorry."

"It's all right. Maybe I'm just too sensitive about some things."

They sat that way for what seemed like an eternity. She knew he wanted to help but that he didn't know what to do or say. When he was like that, he reminded her of his father, standing there in his brown sweater buttoned to the top, looking very much like a little boy lost in a big city, so caught up in the ideas he gleaned from all the books he read that he could do very little to relate to simple everyday problems, like having a son being brought up to be an opera singer, even though such things were an embarrassment to his peers.

What if he turns out to be just like his dad, she thought.

"Please tell me about Relief Society," he said softly, reaching to touch her hand, which rested on the kitchen table.

"I don't belong there," she said, barely whispering.

"How come?"

She pursed her lips, trying not to cry. "Because they're all so pure," she whispered. "And I'm not."

She sat there, her eyes closed, tears rolling down her cheeks. She pulled her hand away from his, and placed both her hands on her lap.

She didn't know what she wanted him to do. This was her burden, and it weighed heavily upon her. She halfway expected him to walk out without a word and never come back. She would have understood and wouldn't have blamed him.

Nathan got up and went into the bathroom. He found a box of tissues, came back, sat down, plucked a tissue, and, with great patience, gently wiped away her tears.

"Do you want me to tell you everything I've done?" she asked.

He shook his head. "No. I will never want to know that."

"I'm ashamed of what I did. If the girls in Relief Society knew, they wouldn't want to have anything to do with me."

Nathan didn't tell her that wasn't so. He didn't say anything after that for the longest time.

And then he quietly got up and began putting the leftover food in the refrigerator.

She wanted to run away because she couldn't stand the awful silence, which to her meant he was trying to find a gracious way to walk out of her life for good.

But she didn't escape because she wanted this to run its course. If he was going to break up with her, she wanted it to be then and there, and not have their relationship die a slow death.

He put the dirty dishes in the sink, wiped off the table top, and then sat down next to her.

"Little girl, what church do you belong to?"

She looked up at him, startled that he would address her that way.

"What church do you belong to?" he asked again.

"The Church of Jesus Christ—"

He stopped her. "What does that mean?"

"It means it's the Church of Jesus Christ."

"It's His church, really? You believe that?"

"Yes."

"Is it his Relief Society?"

"Yes."

"It is?"

"Yes."

"Are you sure?"

Tears were running down her face. She grabbed another tissue. "Yes," she said, her voice barely audible.

"Would he tell you you're not wanted there?"

"I'm not sure."

"Maybe that's what you need to find out."

"How?"

"I think you know the answer to that, don't you?" He stood up. "I'm going to leave now, so you can do what you need to do."

"I don't know what you want me to do, Nathan."

He went into the living room and came back with his triple combination, looked up a scripture, pulled one of the expensive paper napkins from its box, and gently laid it on the page he'd chosen. He closed the book, placed it in front of her, then kissed her on the forehead.

"I'll call you tomorrow." And then he left.

She sat there without doing anything as the sunlight waned, afraid he had found a scripture that spoke of eternal damnation to sinners like she'd been.

It was seven o'clock when her roommate burst into the kitchen, and turned on the light. "What are you doing sitting here in the dark?"

"Nothing. Just thinking."

With her roommate home, she couldn't read what Nathan had left her, so she went up on campus and found an empty classroom.

She opened the book and carefully placed the napkin on the desk and started to read from Chapter 36 of Alma. It didn't seem to apply to her until she got to verse 17:

And it came to pass that as I was thus racked with torment, while I was harrowed up by the memory of my many sins, behold, I remembered also to have heard my father prophesy unto the people concerning the coming of one Jesus Christ, a Son of God, to atone for the sins of the world.

Now, as my mind caught hold upon this thought, I cried within my heart: O Jesus, thou Son of God, have mercy on me, who am in the gall of bitterness, and am encircled about by the everlasting chains of death.

And now, behold, when I thought this, I could remember my pains no more; yea, I was harrowed up by the memory of my sins no more.

And oh, what joy, and what marvelous light I did behold; yea, my soul was filled with joy as exceeding as was my pain!

Jen read the verses over and over again, at first not knowing if the same thing could happen to her, but then, gradually getting more courage and hope with each reading.

I've got to tell Nathan, she thought excitedly as she ran out of the room, down the stairs, and out of the building.

14

At least I'm managing it, Ashley often thought during fall semester as she drove back and forth between her apartment and places in the country where she could be alone to binge and purge.

For fall semester she had moved to an apartment of four girls in a housing complex just off campus. She shared a room with a perky brunette named Erin, who was majoring in elementary education. Because Erin was the only girl in a family with three brothers, two older than herself, she was very comfortable with boys. The boys in the ward appreciated her sense of humor and the way she teased them.

Ashley weighed herself every day, and would be happy or depressed depending on what the scales read. She wanted so badly to get below what she weighed in ninth grade, but no matter how hard she tried, she couldn't seem to do it. For that reason she was usually down on herself.

Every time she looked in the mirror, all she saw was fat. She thought her calves were still big because she couldn't seem to make them look like they did when she was twelve years old.

The foods she thought were safe for her to eat in the morning were either a boiled egg and toast or a protein drink. There was usually one binge between classes in the morning. Lunch would be a big apple, then two, three, four, or occasionally even five binges before she went to bed.

Dinner was usually a salad and some eggs. Her roommates would often compliment her on how much self-control she had.

She was spending so much money on food that she was often short of cash. When she would run out of money, she'd call her mother and make up a story that she needed additional books or lab supplies or rent money. It happened often enough that her parents finally sent her a credit card to use, but only, as they said, "for emergencies."

She vaguely realized that she was spending more on food than on books, tuition, and living expenses.

On the weekend of general conference, her roommates all decided to go home. By Friday afternoon they'd all left, so she had the apartment all to herself.

She spent the weekend bingeing. More than twenty times. At night she kept the lighting dim so anyone knocking on the door would think nobody was home.

On Sunday she didn't go to church but, instead, watched movies and binged and purged until her roommates came back that night.

"Did you have a good weekend?" Erin asked when she came back Sunday night.

"Couldn't have been better," Ashley said with a faint smile.

* * * * *

Ashley finished her exams on the first day of finals, but she stayed in her apartment until Thursday because her roommates were all gone by Wednesday at noon.

At two in the afternoon, she was bent over the toilet purging what had been a chocolate cream pie when she heard a knock on the door. Thinking that it might be their landlord, she jumped up and washed her mouth and face, and went to the door, not to open it, but to see who was there.

She peeked through a crack in the drapes and saw that it was Troy. He was holding a wrapped package in his hand.

He saw her looking through the window, so there was no choice but to open the door. But before she did that, she shoved the other three pies into the refrigerator and put the empty pie tin and fork in the sink.

She hurried to the door and opened it and smiled thinly. "Uh, hi, Troy."

"Merry Christmas," he said, handing her the neatly wrapped package.

"Thanks. But you didn't need to get me a present."

He ignored her remark. "Can we talk?" he asked.

"Well, I don't know. I'm trying to finish up a term paper. I missed the deadline, but the teacher said I could turn it in tomorrow morning at the latest, so I'm kind of rushed right now."

"It'll just be for a minute."

She let him in but didn't invite him to have a seat.

"Is it okay if we sit down?" he asked.

"Sure, I guess so."

He sat down on one end of the couch, and she took a seat at the other end. She looked at the clock. She had three more pies to go through, and she wanted to get on the road before it got too late. She didn't have time to waste.

"Can I ask you a question?" he asked.

"Uh, sure."

"How come you never return my calls?"

"It's probably because I don't get your messages."

"You must have gotten some of them."

"Well, I've been very busy."

Troy took a deep breath. He looked at Ashley, but she avoided his gaze. "I shouldn't even be saying this, but that first time we were together, when you were spouting those ridiculous Italian phrases, I thought that maybe there might be a chance that we . . . well . . . that we could be friends. And at the time I thought you felt it, too, but then you never returned any of my calls."

She felt sorry for him, that he needed people when she was so secure just by herself. *I'll have the banana cream pie next,* she thought. *As soon as he leaves.*

"Are you seeing someone else?" he asked.

"No, not really."

"Waiting for a missionary?"

She needed an excuse, and that seemed about as good as any. "Actually, I am."

He nodded. "I see. Well, that's great. He must be quite a guy."

"Yes, he is."

"That would explain why you keep to yourself so much."

"Yes, that's the reason."

He stood up. "Well, I'd better be going. Merry Christmas."

"Thank you. Merry Christmas to you."

She walked him to the door, said good-bye, then turned her attention to the banana cream pie.

And then to the pumpkin pie with ice cream.

And then to the apple pie with what was left of the ice cream.

And then she purged.

She started home. Halfway there, she stopped at a rest stop and finished off a loaf of French bread and a pound of butter.

And then she purged.

She had mixed feelings about going home. Thinking about her loss of privacy, she felt a sense of panic. She had gotten used to being independent, and now she was going to be back under her mother's watchful eye. It was going to take some doing to hide her bingeing. But she also looked forward to Christmas with all the cookies and sweets that would be around.

Four hours later, she parked her car at the curb in front of her house and began gathering up her things. In spite of all she had eaten, she hadn't kept anything down, and she felt weak. She dreaded going into the house. First of all her parents would give her a hug. She was wearing two sweatshirts to hide how thin she was, but she was afraid they would notice and make a big deal of it. She knew her mother would also insist on feeding her and that she would have to eat with her mother watching. Ashley knew she would have to be very careful to keep her mother from discovering her secret.

Just walking up the outside stairs to the house made her dizzy. She was afraid she might pass out in front of her parents, which would ruin everything because she knew they would insist on getting her medical attention, and who knew what might happen from that.

She entered the house and quietly closed the door. She wanted to catch her breath before she said hello because she didn't want them wondering why she was so winded just walking from the car to the house.

Finally she got her breathing back to normal.

She used all her energy to call out cheerfully, "I'm home!"

Her mother was the first to greet her. She hurried into the front hall and gave Ashley a big hug. "I was worried about you. I thought you'd be here earlier."

"It took a little longer than I thought it would."

"Well, no matter, we're thrilled you made it. Are you hungry?"

"Not really. I had something on the way."

"Well, I made a roast beef dinner for you."

"Maybe later."

"Whatever you say. You've lost a lot of weight, haven't you? What's going on?"

"To tell you the truth, finals week kind of did me in. I was studying so hard, and I had two papers due. I'm afraid I didn't get a chance to eat properly."

"Well, we'll take care of that."

"I'm sure you will. Is Alauna here yet?"

"Well, no, she called yesterday. Her boss is paying her double time if she'll work Christmas Eve day and the day after Christmas. She couldn't turn that down, but she sends her love. Oh, there's some messages for you on the machine."

A few minutes later Ashley played the first message. It was from Jen.

Her first words were, "Warrior Women of America! Be strong! Gosh, I sure hope this is the right number. If you're not Ashley Bailey, disregard this message. Ashley, are you home yet? I hope so. Did you hear? Nathan got his mission call. He's going to Kansas! Isn't that great? Maybe he'll baptize Dorothy from *The Wizard of Oz!* You think so? Hey, look, Nathan and I want to get together with you as soon as you get home. We don't have much time, you know. He goes into the MTC in February. Isn't that exciting? Call me, okay? I want to hear all about Ricks. I've missed you so much. So call me."

Ashley erased the message and went into the kitchen, where her mother was busy making Christmas cookies to give to the neighbors.

"It's so nice to have you home, Ashley."

"Thanks. It feels good to be here."

"Do you want to help me?"

"Do you mind if I don't? I'm a little tired from my trip."

"Of course."

Her father came in and gave her a big hug and told her he was glad to have her home.

"I'm glad, too," she said, but that wasn't the way she felt. She knew it wouldn't be as easy to carry on with her life-style while she was at home. She had no money of her own she could spend at grocery stores. At college it was easy to say there were extra expenses. But at home, what would be her excuse?

She could use food already in the house, but she would have to be careful so that her parents didn't suspect anything. The last thing she needed was to be diagnosed with an eating disorder and be sent away. She didn't need that.

I'm doing okay, she thought. *At least I'm getting by. And I'll get by here too. I'll just need to be careful, that's all.*

As soon as she could, she excused herself and said goodnight and went to her room. She pulled a tub of butter and some hard rolls out of her suitcase, then went into the bathroom, locked the door, and sat cross-legged on the floor.

She opened the tub of butter, broke off a big piece of hard roll and shoved it into the butter, then stuffed it in her mouth.

After she ran out of hard rolls, she dipped her finger in the butter and stuck it in her mouth until the butter was gone.

And from there it was only a short move to the toilet. And then it was all gone. Free, once again. She stood up, weak from hunger, and steadied herself so she wouldn't faint. *Well, that was fun. What's next?*

To clean up, she washed her face and mouth and brushed her teeth. She also ran a brush through her hair. She stared at the brush and the amount of hair that even a light brushing had pulled out. She hated that. *After I lose another ten pounds and start eating regularly, then I'll stop losing my hair. It's just because I'm on a diet, that's all. It's nothing to worry about.*

She heard the doorbell ring. And then there was silence. And then she heard her bedroom door open.

She turned on the shower so she'd have an excuse, opened the cabinet door and shoved the empty butter tub and plastic bread bag under the sink.

There was a knock on the door. "Ashley?"

It was Jen. Ashley didn't answer.

This time the knock was louder. "Ashley? Are you in there?"

Ashley turned off the shower. "What?"

"It's me, Jen. Nathan came with me. He's in the living room talking to your folks. We need to talk to you."

"I'm taking a shower."

"That's okay. We can wait. I'll go out and keep Nathan company. You come out when you're ready."

Ashley threw water on her face and hair to make it look like she'd taken a shower.

She was in no hurry to see Jen and Nathan. *What good is it going to do for me to see how happy they are together? If they're happy, well, then, fine, but I don't see what that's got to do with me. I'm happy, too. And I've made such good progress too. Just ten more pounds to go.*

She put on a shirt and then a large baggy sweatshirt hoping that Jen wouldn't notice her weight loss. Just before opening the door to go out, she hesitated.

I'd rather just stay in here by myself. It's easier that way.

Get it over with, she thought, walking down the hall to the living room.

Jen and Nathan were talking to her parents. Jen jumped up from the sofa and came over and hugged Ashley. "I missed you so much, Girl. How you doing?"

"Great," Ashley said, sitting down on the sofa away from the light. She was self-conscious to have Jen looking at her, fearful she would notice her hair and the weight loss.

"It's good to see you again," Nathan said, smiling hopefully at her.

"You, too, Nathan. How was BYU?"

"Great, but a lot more work than I ever expected," he said. "How's Ricks?"

"Real good."

"Great."

She studied Nathan's face. He seemed more relaxed and

self-confident. He still dressed like an intellectual. He still wore glasses—but now at least they were a little more fashionable—small wire frames that let people see his eyes more than the ones he used to wear. His hair had always been curly, but now was even more so. She couldn't tell if he'd had a perm or if he'd just had it cut long enough so it would be more noticeable. He was smiling at her warmly.

He never fit in when he was in high school, but I bet he does at BYU, especially among the intellectuals in his classes, where he can talk about opera and speak Italian. He really is a good-looking guy. If I'd have known he was going to turn out this good, I'd have kissed him back the first time he kissed me. And then I'd be where Jen is now, about to send him off on his mission.

She wanted to find something to criticize about Jen, but it wasn't easy to do. She looked so wholesome, like she'd been active in the church her whole life. And she seemed so energetic. Both her voice and her enthusiasm filled the room.

"I like UVSC too," Jen said. "And I see Nathan quite often, so that's good."

"I'm happy for you both."

Her parents excused themselves and left the room.

While Nathan and Jen jabbered about their first semester, Ashley tried to be a good listener, but at the same time, she was wondering what was in the refrigerator, and how long it would be before her parents would go to bed so she could go on another binge. She felt weak because she hadn't kept anything down all day. *I'm doing so good,* she thought.

"We were wondering if you'd like to go out with us tonight," Jen said. "You know, for old times' sake."

I don't want to do anything tonight except be in my room and go to the kitchen after everyone else is asleep.

"Tonight? Gosh, I just got back from a long drive. Maybe some other time, okay?"

"How about if we promise to get you back in an hour?" Jen asked.

"Well, I don't know."

"Please."

Just get it over with, she thought, *and then maybe they'll leave you alone for the rest of the vacation.*

"Well, okay, just for a little while."

Jen looked at Nathan. "Nathan, it's time now."

Nathan turned a bright red.

"Nathan has an apology to make."

159

He hesitated, then said, "I told Jen what happened . . . that one night."

"When Nathan kissed you," Jen said.

"And then later I lied to both of you when I said it never happened." His face was red. "So, I just wanted to apologize."

"For kissing me or for lying about it?" Ashley asked.

Nathan seemed stumped.

"For lying," Jen prompted.

Nathan nodded.

"I wasn't sure," Ashley said. "I mean, it could be for the other because I was never sure why you even did it."

"Me, either. It was a dumb thing to do."

"So, are you two going to get married?" Ashley asked.

Jen and Nathan exchanged an affectionate look. "Nathan needs to go on a mission first," Jen said. "After that, well, we'll see. The way it looks now, though, we probably will."

"I guess you could do a lot worse than Nathan," Ashley said.

"I've changed a lot this past year," Nathan said.

"You look the same to me," Ashley said cynically.

He seemed almost apologetic to say it. "I'm more spiritual."

Ashley scoffed, then turned to Jen. "Have you seen any difference in him?"

"I have."

"I don't believe it."

"I've changed, too."

"How?"

"The same way."

"So I'm surrounded by two spiritual giants, is that it?"

"People can change, Ashley."

"People can pretend things are different, too, but they never are. They're always the same."

"Have you changed?" Nathan asked Ashley.

She didn't want to talk about herself, especially to Nathan. "Yes, Nathan, I have."

"Have you been sick?" Jen asked.

"No, why do you ask?"

"No reason. You just look a little pale, that's all."

"I had a hard finals week."

Jen nodded. "Sure, that must be it."

"I'm real spiritual, too, Nathan, just like you."

There was an awkward silence. Finally Jen said, "Nathan and I feel bad that things aren't that great between you and us."

"Do you? You're the ones who paired up and excluded me from everything."

"We want for it to be the same, the way it was."

"It can't be that way again."

"Can't we start over?" Jen asked.

"No, we can't."

"Well, can we at least spend some time together over Christmas break?" Nathan asked.

"I'm going to be real busy."

Jen took a deep breath. She turned to Nathan. "Nathan, would you mind waiting in the car for a minute? Ashley and I have to talk."

"Sure, no problem."

Nathan went out to the car.

"Nathan really has changed for the better. He's grown up a lot and really is more spiritual."

"Whatever." Ashley paused, wanting to give some hope to Jen. "I met a guy at Ricks."

"No kidding? Tell me about him."

"His name is Troy. He's a returned missionary who served in Italy. He gets a kick out of all the messed-up Italian phrases I know."

"Is this going anywhere?"

"It could be. We get along real well."

"Where's he from?"

"Evanston, Wyoming."

"Any chance he'll come down over the holidays? I'd really like to meet him."

"Well, I don't know. We didn't talk about that."

"Oh, he'll be down, I'm sure of it."

"Well, ordinarily he would, but his grandmother is real sick, so he might need to stay close to home."

"Okay, but if he does come down, let us know. We can all do something."

"Sure, I'll do that."

"How much weight have you lost?" Jen asked.

"A couple of pounds maybe."

"Looks like a lot more to me. What's your secret?"

"Nothing special. I was just kept so busy with classes and everything. That's all."

"How much do you weigh now?"

"Gosh, I don't know. I don't even have a bathroom scale."

"Are you up to your old tricks?"

"What old tricks?"

"Being bulimic."

Ashley laughed. "No, I gave that up a long time ago."

"You're not lying to me, are you?"

"Why would you think that?"

"I can tell when you're lying, Ashley. Maybe others can't, but I can."

"I'm okay. In fact, I've never been better."

"You used to look at me when you talked, but now you turn your eyes away, so it's hard for me to believe you're telling the truth."

Ashley focused her gaze on Jen. "I've never been better," she said slowly.

Jen searched Ashley's expression. "You're sure?"

"Absolutely."

"Well, okay. Please spend a few minutes with us."

"All right, but just for like maybe half an hour."

Nathan was in the car listening to the radio.

"We've got her for an hour, Nathan. Isn't that great?" Jen asked.

"Great. What do you guys want to do?" he asked as the girls piled into the car.

"Let's go kick a soccer ball," Jen said.

Ashley panicked. She felt light-headed, even walking. She hadn't kept anything down all day.

"Just for a couple of minutes. For old times' sake."

"It's dark out."

"Nathan can keep his car running and the headlights on. It'll be fun. And then we'll take you home."

Ashley thought it wouldn't do any harm for a few minutes, but just getting out of the car made her dizzy.

They kicked the ball to each other. Ashley couldn't react, couldn't get to it. It felt as though she was running through molasses.

"You've gotten a little rusty there, Ashley," Nathan said.

"I haven't played since our last game."

"Me, either."

Jen kicked the ball wide. Ashley tried to get it, but it got past her. She ran after it, and then passed out.

15

Ashley came to with Jen and Nathan huddled over her. "I'm okay now," she said, trying to get up.

"Don't get up. Just rest," Jen said.

She sat up. "Really. I'm okay now. I don't know how that happened, but I'm okay now."

"You can tell us the truth, Ashley. We're your friends."

"There's nothing to tell."

"Do you want to go home now?" Jen asked.

"Yes."

"Okay. We'll get you home right away. Help her, Nathan."

Nathan helped her get up and would have helped her walk, except she shook free of him.

"I'm all right, Nathan, okay?"

"Whatever you say."

"I just tripped, that's all. It's no big deal. Anyone can trip on a rock."

"Sure, I do it all the time," Nathan joked.

On the ride home, Jen asked Ashley, "Do you want to talk about it?"

"Talk about what? There's nothing to talk about."

"You're not eating right, are you? How much do you weigh?"

"Too much."

"Is that what you think?"

"Yes."

"You should talk to your mom and dad about this."

"Yeah, right," Ashley scoffed. "They'd be the last ones I'd ever talk to."

"They could get you the help you need."

"I don't need any help. I just tripped on a rock, that's all."

"What have you eaten today?" Jen asked.

"I've eaten a lot."

"What have you kept down?"

"I don't see that's any of your business."

"I can't let you harm yourself. That's not what friends do."

"You've got Nathan now. That's all you care about."

"I'll always care about you," Jen said.

"Why?"

"Because you're the one who helped me get back in the Church. I'll always be grateful to you for that."

They pulled into her driveway. Ashley opened the car door.

"You want me to walk you to the door?" Nathan asked.

"No, just leave me alone," she snapped. She took three steps, felt bad for being so mean, then stopped, and turned around, "I'm okay now, really."

They said good-bye and waited until she entered the house before pulling out of the driveway.

Her parents were still up. She went into the living room where they were watching a movie on TV.

"I'm back."

"Did you have a nice time?"

"Yeah, sure. I'm going to bed now."

"Are you tired?"

"Yeah, a little, mostly from staying up too late for finals week. I thought I'd catch up on some sleep."

"Good idea. Are you hungry?"

"Not right now."

"The Sandvigs down the block brought us some caramel rolls," her father said. "They're very good."

"I'm not hungry right now. Maybe tomorrow, though."

"Sure, whatever you want."

Her father suggested they have family prayer. They knelt down. He asked Ashley to give the prayer. She said all the right things and then went to her room.

In the process of getting ready for bed, she weighed herself. She'd lost a pound over finals week. *Just ten more pounds to go,* she thought.

She felt weak from hunger, so she set her alarm for two in the morning so she could get up and eat some of the caramel rolls and whatever else she could find. And then she would get rid of it, so it wouldn't count against her.

I'm doing so good, she thought as she slipped between the cold sheets.

She was nearly asleep when she faintly heard people talking.

164

A short time later, the light in her room went on, and her mother and father stood in the door.

"What's wrong?" Ashley asked.

"Jen and Nathan are here," her mother said.

"What for?"

"They said you passed out tonight. They're very worried about you."

"There's nothing to worry about. I just tripped on a rock, that's all. And now I'm fine."

"We need to talk," her father said. "Jen and Nathan are in the living room. We'll talk there."

"This is so stupid," Ashley muttered, as she got out of bed. She put on a robe, went to the mirror to arrange her hair with her fingers to cover up the thinning spots.

Her mother stayed in her bedroom after Ashley started toward the living room.

When she entered the living room, Ashley glared at Jen but didn't say anything. She was certain it was Jen's idea to talk to her parents.

"Hi," Jen said.

"I don't even want to talk to you two."

"I understand," Jen said.

Coming from her bedroom, Ashley's mother joined them.

"I thought you two were my friends," Ashley said quietly to Jen.

"They are your friends," her mother chided. "I can see that now more than I ever could before. Jen, please tell me what you suspect is going on with my daughter."

Jen cleared her throat a couple of times. "Well . . . I'll try. Ashley, this is really tough for me. Nathan and I talked about it for a long time, you know, whether to say anything or not. I mean, you were my best friend in high school, and if it weren't for you I wouldn't even be active in the Church now. I don't know where I'd be, but I know I wouldn't be happy. So I'll always be grateful to you for helping me so much."

"Yes, I can see how grateful you are," Ashley snapped. "So what are you going to do, tell the world everything you know about me?"

Jen had tears in her eyes. Nathan went to put his arms around Jen but she shook him off. She started coughing. "Mrs. Bailey," she whispered.

"Yes?"

"Could I have a drink of water and maybe a box of tissues?"

"Yes, of course."

"I love you, Ashley. I'll always love you," Jen whispered.

Ashley wouldn't even look at her.

Her mother brought a glass of water and a box of tissues and put it on the end table next to where Jen was sitting.

Jen took a drink, then wiped her eyes, and blew her nose. "I think I'm coming down with a cold," she said.

"They say it's going around," Ashley's father said. "Everyone at the office has a cold."

More than anything Ashley wanted to humiliate Jen, to punish her for betraying a confidence. "Tell me, Jen, do all your friends at BYU and UVSC know that in high school you'd date any guy with enough money to buy you beer? I'm sure they'd be interested. Maybe I could come down and tell them everything I know about you. What would you think about a friend who would do that?"

"Ashley," her father said. "There's no reason to speak to her like that."

"It's all right," Jen said. She took a deep breath. "This is different, Ashley," Jen said with a quiet determination.

"How is it different?"

Jen reached over and touched Nathan's hand. "Nathan and I talked about it. This is different because it could kill you."

"What could kill me?"

"What you're doing to yourself."

"You don't know anything about what I do or don't do."

Her father cleared his throat. "Maybe we should start at the beginning. Jen, please tell us what's going on."

"Well, at girls camp, when we first starting hanging out with each other, Ashley was just starting to be bulimic. While the three of us were together, I'm pretty sure she quit. But now my guess is that she's back at it again."

Ashley shook her head vigorously. "Why do you think that, because I stumbled on a rock and fell down? Anyone could have done that."

"You're right," Jen said. "I don't have any proof."

"That's right. You don't," Ashley snapped at her.

On their way out, Jen turned to Ashley, "I really do love you, Ashley."

"You have a strange way of showing it."

"I love you, too," Nathan said.

"Come and give me a big slobbery kiss then, Nathan, just like before, okay? Jen won't mind, will you, Jen?"

"That is such a cheap shot," Jen said, more disappointed than angry.

Nathan and Jen left.

"We need to talk," her mother said.

"What for? Jen and Nathan don't know anything about me anymore."

"A few minutes ago I found an empty tub of butter in the waste paper basket in your bathroom," her mother said. "How did it get there?"

"I was using it to store some cosmetics."

"But it still had a little butter in it."

"That's right. It didn't work out very well. I had to rinse off all the bottles so it didn't work out very well. That's why I threw it away."

"There were some bread crumbs on the floor of the bathroom, too."

She remembered the trunk of her car had a garbage bag with discarded brownie containers. *If I keep denying this, they're going to keep playing detective until they find out the truth,* she thought. *So if all I do is lie then when they find out the truth, they'll never trust me again. And if they never trust me again, they won't let me go back to Ricks winter semester. I've got to go back there so I can keep working on getting down to my ideal weight.*

She suddenly came up with a strategy that would help her get back to Ricks after Christmas. She started to cry. "I'm so ashamed," she said. She held her head in her hands.

"Jen is right. I did have a slight problem with this in high school, and it's continued even up to now. I want to be done with it for good now, though. I'd like some counseling right away so I can stop this."

"Now we're getting somewhere," her father said.

"I've been thinking about stopping anyway, so in a way I'm glad this happened. I would just like to get over this as soon as possible, so I can get on with my life. This has taken up too much of my time. I'm ready to stop this as soon as I can, and I think I can if I just have someone to talk to who's dealt with people like me."

"We can certainly arrange that," her mother said. "I'll start calling around."

"Is there any chance I could talk to someone tomorrow?" Ashley asked. "I'd like to get started on my recovery as soon as possible."

"We'll see."

"Thank you, Mother, for looking out for me."

"You're my baby."

"Yes, I know. Well, I think I'll go get some sleep. I feel so much better now that this is out in the open."

She hugged her mother and father. She didn't like it because she didn't like being in close contact with anyone. But she did it anyway because she knew it was necessary.

She went to her room and turned off the lights and sat in the dark until she heard her mother shut the door to her parents' bedroom.

She waited half an hour longer, and then, with the lights still off, she quietly opened a suitcase and took out a box of chocolates she had bought as a Christmas present for the family. She sat cross-legged on her bed in the dark and ate the entire two pounds of rich candy, then went to her bathroom and threw it all up. Before crawling into bed, she hid the empty box in her suitcase. She would throw it away in the outside garbage sometime when her parents were out of the house.

Merry Christmas, Mommy Dearest.

16

Christine Bailey spent most of the next morning phoning around, trying to find a counselor who worked with girls with eating disorders.

"Do you think your daughter is willing to change?" the counselor asked.

"Yes, I think so. She was the one who suggested she needs help."

"I see. Well, that's a good sign."

And it was true. Ashley was willing to show rapid progress, so she'd be able to get away from her parents, go back to college, and continue on just like before.

For her part, Ashley spent the morning at the computer in her father's downstairs office.. She searched the Internet, reading about eating disorders so she could be knowledgeable enough to give the right answers, so her parents would let her return to Ricks.

As she examined each website, she disregarded any warnings she read about eating disorders, deciding they were put there just to scare people. *I'll worry about that later, after I get thin. Right now any risk is worth achieving my goal.*

All I want to do is lose ten more pounds and then I'll stop for good.

With her mother now aware of what was going on, there was little chance to binge and purge. To compensate, Ashley went as long as she could without eating. She ate very little breakfast, saying she wasn't hungry.

Her mother made her eat lunch, though. Ashley ate everything put in front of her then stayed at the table for as long as she could, then told her mother she was going to take a walk.

She walked a block to a ballpark, went into a Little League dugout and threw everything up. She was relieved. *I'm glad I can still find a way to do this, even with my family knowing about it,* she thought.

On the way back, she worked out a game plan for the visit with the counselor. She must show a willingness to change. She must appear to change her thinking. She must ask for another time with the counselor as soon as possible. She must check to make sure they have counselors at Ricks College who work with girls with eating disorders.

And then I'll go back and everything will be just the same, and I'll be free to do what I want.

Later that day when Ashley walked into the counselor's office with her parents and met the counselor, Elaine Hardvigsen, Ashley was encouraged. *She doesn't look all that smart. It shouldn't be that hard to fool her.*

Elaine was in her mid-thirties. She wore wire-rim glasses, slightly tinted. She was wearing a creamy-white blouse buttoned to the top, and navy blue dress slacks. She had a round face and wore very little makeup.

She's fat. Too bad. I could help her. Not that she's going to ask for my advice, though. Too bad. If she lost ten pounds, she'd be a lot better. Like I'm going to be when I get down to my ideal weight.

"What time do you want us to pick her up?" Mr. Bailey asked.

"Oh, I'm sorry. Didn't I make that clear?" Elaine said. "I'll need to talk to the entire family. Your daughter is not like some broken-down lawn mower you can leave and pick up when it's fixed. If someone in the family is hurting, the entire family has to be involved."

"David, I very specifically told you she wanted to talk to the whole family," her mother said.

"When did you tell me that?"

"We'll talk about this later," her mother said.

"I need to go move the car. I parked in a fifteen-minute parking spot."

"I'll go with you," her mother said. "We can talk on the way."

"When you come back in, give Ashley and me a few minutes. Then I'd like both of you to join us."

Ashley smiled as her parents left.

"You're amused about something?" Elaine asked.

"Right now my mother is complaining to my dad what a bad first impression they're making."

"Why does that amuse you?"

"Because they're under the gun here. I thought it would just be me you'd be interested in."

Elaine ushered Ashley into her inner office. "Please sit down and make yourself comfortable."

Ashley sat down. *The way she's got the room arranged is supposed to make me feel at ease, but it doesn't. Too much clutter.*

"What can you tell me about your parents?"

170

"There's nothing to tell."

Elaine smiled.

"What are you smiling at?" Ashley asked.

"I was just thinking. I probably would have said the same thing when I was your age."

She's trying to get me to relax and feel at ease with her, Ashley thought. *So be careful.*

"Let me ask a couple of questions while it's just us girls. How long has it been since you had your last period?"

What is wrong with this woman anyway! Ashley thought. *I don't know how to answer that. I don't know what she's after.*

"I can't remember."

"You can't remember because it's been such a long time or because you just don't pay attention to things like that?"

What is she trying to find out? I should've spent more time on the Internet reading about eating disorders. I'm not sure where this is going. Maybe I should just tell her the truth.

"It's been a few months."

"I think I know the answer to this, but I need to ask it anyway. You're not pregnant, are you?"

"No!" Ashley was offended at the suggestion. "There's no chance of that."

"Why do you think it's been a while?"

"I don't know."

"It's because your body is just trying to survive."

"Oh," she said, not being able to come up with a better response.

"Ashley, describe your father for me."

"Why? You've seen him."

"Not a physical description. What kind of a person is he?"

"How much do you get paid by the hour?" Ashley asked.

"Why do you ask?"

"I would have thought you would address *my* problem."

"And what *is* your problem?"

"I have a slight eating disorder."

"Do you want to get over it?"

"Yes, of course, as soon as possible."

"Really? Why?"

"So I can get on with my life."

"Really?"

"Yes."

"And you're being totally honest with me?"

"Yes, why wouldn't I be?"

"Because my experience is that for the typical young woman with an eating disorder, her life is usually one gigantic lie. I mean, think about it, they have a colossal secret about themselves that nobody knows, and they'll do anything they can to protect that secret."

"I'm not like that. I came to you for help, remember?"

"Yes you did. Good point." She paused to write herself a note, then looked up.

"I believe you were about to describe your father to me."

"He's a very important man, and he's very busy. He probably wishes he were some place else right now."

"Do you wish he would spend more time with you?"

"Not really."

"Why not?"

"Because he's very busy. He wouldn't enjoy it. Not really. He'd be thinking of all the things he has to do."

"Would you enjoy it?"

"I don't know. Probably not."

"Why's that?"

"I'm not a little girl anymore."

"Did you use to enjoy spending time with him?"

"I suppose I did. I can't remember. It's been a long time."

"What do you remember doing with your father that was fun?"

Ashley thought for a moment. "He took me to *The Nutcracker* ballet one Christmastime. Just the two of us."

"Was that fun?"

"It was so long ago, but, yes, I think I had a good time."

"What else?"

"Not much else. Like I said, he's very busy."

"Any other memories?"

"He used to call me his 'little princess.'"

Elaine's eyebrows raised. "Really?"

Ashley felt she'd made a huge blunder. *She'll think I'm living the way I am to stay little. That is so stupid, but that's the way these people are. I really don't need her pursuing that.*

"But that was a long time ago."

"Do you wish he'd say it now?"

"No, not at all. I'm nearly a woman now, so I can't be his little princess. No woman can be anyone's little princess."

"That's very insightful, Ashley. Do you think of yourself as a woman?"

"Sometimes I do."

"What is the difference between being a woman and being a girl?"

172

"Why don't you ask my mother?"

"All right, I will. Let me go see if they're back yet."

When her mother and father entered the room, Ashley noticed her father's neck was red. It got that way when he was angry. She wondered what her mother had said to him while they were gone.

"Mrs. Bailey, we were talking about what it means to be a woman as compared to being a girl. Ashley thought you might be able to tell her."

"I'm not sure I can put it in so many words."

"Well, please give it a try."

"I think many women have a sense of satisfaction of who they are, whereas girls often are not sure who they are."

"That's very good. And very true. Thank you. Ashley, what about body shape? How does that differ between a girl and a woman?"

Ashley felt a sudden panic but she tried not to let it show. "Well, women look like women, and girls look like girls."

"What differences do you notice about your mother's appearance and yours?"

"Well, I think that's obvious, isn't it?"

"I'm not sure it is, so just tell me what you're thinking."

"Women are, well, more filled out than girls."

Elaine nodded. "That's fairly accurate I'd say. When were you the most comfortable with your body?"

Ashley thought about it and then said, "Probably in third grade."

"Third grade?"

"Yes."

"Why?"

"Nobody made fun of me then."

"Did they make fun of you later on?"

"No, not me, but they made fun of some girls."

"Why?"

"Because they were fat."

"How old were you when you became aware that some girls were being made fun of?"

"I can't remember."

"When was it the worst?"

"Junior high."

"Did boys make fun of other boys because of their body shape?"

"I don't know. Probably not as much."

"Let's go back to third grade. What did you like about your body in third grade?"

"I'd rather not say."

"Why not?"

"It was a long time ago. I can't remember."

"Well, is there anything you can remember about being in the third grade?"

I remember the calves of my legs, she thought. *They weren't fat. And my stomach was flat.*

"Not really," she said.

"Were you skinny then?"

"She was. Very," her father said.

"How much do you weigh now, Ashley?"

"I don't know."

"Did you weigh yourself this morning?"

Ashley saw a way of ending this. *All I have to do is to have a moment where I say, Now I understand why I've been doing this. I've seen the light and now I know where I went wrong. But is this that moment? If I do it too soon, she'll know what I'm up to.*

"Yes."

"How often in a day do you weigh yourself?"

"Three or four times."

"Have you set goals about how much you want to weigh?"

"Well, yes, I have."

"What is your goal?"

"To lose ten pounds. I'm almost there."

"What will you do when you reach your goal?"

"Quit doing . . . you know . . . what I've been doing."

"Really? You'll quit?"

"Yes."

"Some girls like to get to a few pounds lighter than their goal, so they can stand to gain a little weight."

"No, I'd just be happy if I reached my goal."

"Some girls set a new goal of another five or ten pounds. Are you saying you wouldn't do that?"

"Oh, no, I'd never do that. It's not like I'm out of control or anything. I just went on a diet and it got a little out of hand. Now I can see that what I was doing to myself wasn't good. So I've learned my lesson. I guess I'm going to be the easiest patient you ever had."

Elaine pursed her lips. "I'm afraid this is much more complicated than you think it is."

"Of course you think that. After all, you do get paid by the hour, so it's to your advantage to drag this out as long as possible."

Her father smiled.

"Ashley," her mother warned.

By his smile, Ashley knew her father agreed with her assessment of Elaine's efforts—that it was basically a waste of time and money.

"I promise I won't weigh myself anymore. I think that will pretty much take care of it. And maybe if I don't have to fix my meals, then I'll eat more regular. That's been most of the problem. I get so busy that when I get back to my apartment, I'm too tired to cook anything, but if I had a meal ticket, then I could go eat a normal meal. I think that would help a lot."

"We can get you a meal ticket," her father said. "That's no problem."

There, I've given everybody a quick out. Father, you'll take it, won't you? You don't believe in counseling anyway. I can tell. And what about you, Mother? Do you really want your church friends to know everything isn't just wonderful in your perfect little family?

"What do you think, Mr. Bailey?"

"Well, I don't know. It seems like Ashley has given us some good ideas about what she could do to get out of . . . whatever it is that she's doing. So maybe we ought to let her try those things and see how it goes . . ."

Good job, Father. I knew I could count on you to take the easy way out.

"My experience is that this is much more deeply rooted than that," Elaine said.

"For some people I'm sure it is," Ashley said.

Elaine continued. "It usually begins in an effort to try to lose just a few pounds but then it becomes much more complicated, and much more devious, and much harder to pull yourself away from it."

"So, in other words, you spend months, maybe years with some of your clients?" Ashley asked.

Her father suppressed a grin.

Daddy is on my side, she thought.

"Yes, I do. I'm sure you don't believe me, Ashley, when I say this is much more difficult than you think it is. Let me ask you a series of questions, and you tell me where you are in the spectrum of those who exhibit eating disorders of one kind or another."

I'm at least as smart as you are, Elaine, so you don't scare me.

"All right."

"How much time in a typical day do you spend thinking about food?"

"Not much. Just before I eat, I guess, or when I'm hungry," she lied.

"When you get up in the morning, do you ever try to see how long you can go without eating?"

Of course, who doesn't do that? That's just natural. But I can't say that.

I've got to make this appear as not a big problem, something that can be fixed easily.

"I usually have breakfast," she said.

"What do you usually have for breakfast?"

"A boiled egg, a piece of toast, and orange juice."

Her father nodded his head. "That sounds pretty healthy to me."

"Do you enjoy eating with others, or do you prefer to eat by yourself?"

"I guess it varies from day to day. Sometimes I'm in a hurry to get to class, so I'd rather just eat by myself and get going."

"That's like me in the morning," her father said.

Elaine turned to Ashley's father. "Please let me ask Ashley these questions without any input from you. Afterwards, you can say whatever you'd like. Is that acceptable to you?

"Yes, of course."

Elaine continued. "Have you ever passed up an opportunity to be with others so you could be by yourself and binge and purge?"

Ashley wasn't sure how to answer the question. She hesitated. "Once in a while I've done that I guess, but it was more like I didn't really want to be with those particular people more than anything else."

The questions continued, but with each one Ashley carefully tried to present the image of someone who was willing to make changes, so this wouldn't be a problem anymore.

Her father bought it. She wasn't so sure about her mother.

"What would you like me to work on until we meet again?" Ashley asked. "I could read some books on the subject or whatever you'd like. I just want to get this all behind me."

"I appreciate that attitude, Ashley, but are you saying it just so you can return to college and continue living the way you have been?"

"No, not at all. I can see the way I was going wasn't in my best interest."

"I'm glad you can see that. I guess this calls for a celebration. Before you go, I'd like to share with you some of my birthday cake. I've got some ice cream, too."

Ashley's smile disappeared. *If I have any cake, I'll throw it up, and then they'll know.*

She looked at her dad, who was looking at his watch. *Daddy is late.*

"Well, that sounds great, but I don't know if we have the time. Daddy, do you have an extra forty-five minutes so we can have cake and ice cream?"

"Well, of course I'd like to, but . . ."

Three minutes later they were in the family car heading home.

176

"I think that went really quite well," her father said.

"Me, too," Ashley said with a smile. "She's nice."

Ashley's mother said nothing but sat staring out of the car window.

Once they got home, Ashley went to her room and shut the door, trying to figure out how she was going to get by during the holidays with her mother watching her every move.

She'll be looking for me to mess up so she can send me away to a clinic. So I'll have to be very careful. She's probably not going to leave me alone. And even late at night, she might stay awake to try to catch me. So what do I do?

If I can get away with Jen and Nathan, maybe I can find a time to do it. That's my only hope until I get back to school.

17

Ashley, Jen, and Nathan spent the first part of the evening watching a movie, and then, bored, they drove to the park and kept the car running with the lights on the soccer field. In the cold night air, they kicked the ball to each other.

"*Mi scusi, per favore*," Nathan said. "*Si puo ballare qui?*"

"What does that mean, Nathan?" Jen asked.

"It means, 'Excuse me, please. Can one dance here?'"

"Did you speak Italian at BYU?" Ashley asked.

"Sometimes," Nathan said, kicking the ball to Jen.

"What for?"

"It makes me happy. To be in a crowd and yell something out in Italian. It really brings people together."

"You're really strange, Nathan," Ashley said.

"*Grazie*," he said.

"Can we go get something to eat?" Ashley asked.

"Like what?"

"I don't know. Maybe a pizza."

"Sure, whatever you want. Let's get one and come back here and eat it on the fifty-yard line."

Ashley scowled. *No, that won't work. I need a bathroom I can go to after I eat,* she thought. "It's too cold. Let's just go to Pizza Hut," she said. "That'd be nicer."

"Are you going to eat and hurl?" Jen asked.

"No," Ashley said, trying to sound as though she were insulted.

"Be honest," Jen said.

"I don't want to talk about it, okay?"

"We're your friends, and we want to help you."

"You two have already ratted on me, so I'm sure you'll understand if I don't confide in you anytime soon."

"We don't mind if you're mad at us as long as you quit messing up your life," Nathan said.

"What about you, Nathan? You're not perfect, either, you know."

"I never said I was."

"So why don't you face the truth about yourself? You don't really speak Italian. You go around putting on this big act like you're the world's expert on practically anything, but the truth is you're not that smart, not that good-looking, and not that much fun to be with."

Nathan took it in, and then, with a slight smile, asked, "*Può riparare il guasto?*"

"What does that mean?" Ashley asked wearily.

"Can you repair the fault?"

"Meaning what?"

"Can you help me?"

"No, I can't. Ask Jen for that. I'm out of the picture."

"Can I help you?" Nathan asked.

"How?"

"By telling you what I see when I look at you."

"What do you see?"

"You probably think that what you've done to yourself is making you look better. But it doesn't. The truth is, Ashley, you don't look very good."

"Well, thanks a lot, Nathan. With that kind of tact, you'll for sure be a great missionary."

"No, it's true. You look like a toothpick."

"At least I have some control over my life. That's more than most people can say."

"And you walk like an old lady. You never laugh anymore. And what do you do instead? You keep to yourself and pig out then throw it all up. And one other thing, why do you keep feeling the calf of your leg all the time?"

Ashley removed her hand from her leg. She hadn't noticed she was doing it.

"Look, a lot of people have things they have to overcome," Nathan said. He paused. "I had something like that in high school. I know what it's like to be carrying a secret about yourself that nobody else knows. At first you think it's going to solve all your problems and then, before you know it, you find out it's the cause of all your problems." He paused. "So don't go saying I don't understand, because I do."

"What was your problem?" Ashley asked.

"I'd rather not say."

"Did you have to go to your bishop about it?"

179

Nathan glanced guiltily at Jen, for whom all this was news, then said quietly, "Yes. He helped me a lot."

Even though Ashley wasn't sure what the problem had been, she was impressed Nathan would admit to having once had a problem that, for him, had been hard enough to overcome and serious enough to get his bishop involved.

"Thanks, Nathan, for telling me," she said.

His face was red. "Sure."

"Everybody has problems from time to time," Jen said. "I did, too. You both know that. But the thing is, Nathan and I faced our problems and worked through them. And we think you need to do the same, too."

"Sometimes," Ashley said, barely audibly, "I guess I am a little out of control."

"Do you ever wish you could stop?" Nathan asked.

"Sometimes."

"There's counselors at Ricks who can help, right?" Jen asked.

"Yeah, there are."

"So maybe you should start going to see one of 'em," Jen said.

"Maybe so."

'You want us to go up there and help you set it up?" Nathan asked.

"No, that's okay. I can do that."

"But will you?" Jen asked.

"I will."

"All right, and then you can tell us how it's going."

"Sure, no problem."

"Well, we all know each other a lot better now, don't we?" Nathan said, standing up, his face still red.

"Yeah, I guess we do."

"And now we're back together again," Jen said, inviting both Nathan and Ashley in for a group hug.

It was a good feeling.

* * * * *

Two days after Christmas, Jen called. She sounded frantic. "I need your help, Ashley."

"What's up?"

"My mom just told me she and Billy James Dean have decided to get married tomorrow. Please, you have to come to the wedding. It's going to be at the courthouse, and a justice of the peace is going to do it. I can't believe she's actually going to go through with this. Nathan is still at his grandparents' place in St. George. I need you to be there with me. Oh, this is so stupid! I don't think I can make it without help."

The next day, Ashley picked Jen up, and they drove to the courthouse.

The ceremony was to be held in an office. Billy James Dean was wearing a plaid shirt with a turquoise bolo tie. His hair was slicked down so much it glistened like freshly waxed mahogany. Jen's mother was wearing a simple blue dress. She seemed more bewildered than happy.

Besides Jen and Ashley, there were two friends of Billy James Dean to witness the event. One owned a secondhand store located next to Billy James's pawn shop, and the other was a man of sideways glances, always checking the door as if he halfway expected the place to be raided.

Everything seemed drab compared to Billy James Dean. It almost seemed that he sucked the vitality from everyone else in the room, so they looked nearly lifeless compared to him.

As soon as Jen and Ashley entered the room, he hurried over to greet them. "Thanks a bunch for coming to our festivities, Sweeties." He took Ashley's hand and kissed it. "As a token of my appreciation for you taking a part in this here wedding, I would like to present you with a timepiece. This one once belonged to Winston Churchill." He ceremoniously handed Ashley a corroded old pocket watch.

"And this one, for my new daughter, once belonged to Eleanor Roosevelt. There you go, Sugar. Enjoy. Think of it as a gift from your new daddy." He kissed Jen on the cheek and shook Ashley's hand, pumping it for what seemed an eternity. "Look around, take a look at all the flowers I got for these festivities."

It was true. There was a vase of flowers on a secretary's desk and another sitting on a counter.

"These must have cost a fortune," Ashley said, trying to be positive.

"Not if you got connections, Sweetie." He leaned close to her and said confidentially. "I'm in tight with a certain funeral director."

He then collared the justice of the peace and gave him a watch that he explained had once belonged to Albert Einstein.

The justice of the peace wasn't impressed. "If this goes past five, I'll have to charge you double."

Billy James leaned into the justice of the peace. "No problem, Your Honor. Once you start, skip all the 'dearly beloved' garbage and just get to the point, okay?"

While the couple were signing some documents, Jen said quietly to Ashley, "I don't think I can stand to stay here."

"It'll be over fast."

"How can she go through with this?"

"I don't know. Have you talked to her about it?"

"Yes. You know what she said? 'Billy James isn't that bad.' Is that any reason to get married?"

"Maybe she loves him."

"How could she? Look at him."

"He's very enthusiastic."

"So is a con artist."

True to his word, the justice of the peace, near retirement with bad legs and anxious to get home to put his feet up, raced through the ceremony. In two minutes it was a done deal.

Billy James gave a slobbery kiss to his bride, then turned around and smiled at the four witnesses.

"When I was getting my hair cut this afternoon, my barber asked me what I thought about this being my wedding day. You want to know what I told him?"

Apparently nobody did, but that didn't stop Billy James. "'Hot time in the old town tonight!' That's what I said. Doesn't that just kill you?" He gave a raucous laugh that ended with him coughing up phlegm, then depositing it in a tissue he swiped from a secretary's desk. That was bad enough, but what was even worse was that he stopped talking to visually inspect what he'd coughed up, and then continued on where he'd left off. "You get it? Hot time in the old town tonight, right?"

"Oh, my gosh," Jen moaned. "I think I'm going to be sick. Where's the bathroom?"

Ashley slipped her arm around Jen's waist and whispered in her ear. "That's my line."

"This has got to be the cheesiest wedding of the century," Jen said quietly.

Billy James, with one eye on the clock, which now read five minutes to five, went to the corner of the room and grabbed a grocery sack, then set out a six-pack of Sprite and a package of powdered donuts and some napkins on a secretary's desk.

"Well, folks, let's celebrate this happy occasion!" He glanced at the clock. "You know what? It might be better if we congregated in the hall and talked. You can stay as long as you want and eat up all the snacks, but me and the Mrs. need to get heading off for our honeymoon. So thank you all for coming." He took his bride's hand and pulled her toward the door.

"Billy James?" the bride said.

"What, Sweetie?"

"I need to say good-bye to Jen."

"Good-bye, Jen!" Billy James called out, and then said to his bride, "There, I did it for you." He started walking fast. "Race you to the car!"

Ashley and Jen watched them hurry to the car and drive away.

"You want any donuts?" Jen asked.

"No, let's just get out of here."

"Thanks for helping me get through this," Jen said as they walked to the car.

"That's what friends are for."

"We are good friends, aren't we?"

"Yes, I think we are."

Jen unlocked the car. "One thing I've learned tonight."

"What?"

"When I get married, it's going to be in the temple," Jen said.

* * * * *

Three weeks later, Ashley was back at Ricks for winter semester. Her parents had agreed to let her return only if she promised to continue getting help at the counseling center on campus. But she had managed to put off seeing anyone by calling before or after hours and hanging up without giving her name or phone number.

She was back to bingeing and purging several times a day, just like she'd been doing before fall semester ended.

Jen's phone call came on a bleak Monday night in mid-January.

"Something awful has happened, Ashley."

"What?"

"Nathan's older sister, Alexis, was killed in a car accident. She was married and had two children. Nathan is really devastated. The funeral is Thursday. I know it'd mean a lot to Nathan if you could make it."

"That is so awful. How did it happen?"

"She'd been grocery shopping and had just turned onto the street when she was hit by a pickup going over seventy miles an hour in a thirty-five-mile-an-hour speed zone. Nathan says she probably didn't even know what hit her. At least her two kids were at their grandmother's place and not with her, so they're okay."

"Oh, Jen. That's horrible. Please tell Nathan I'm really sorry."

"Can you come to the funeral?"

"Yes, of course. I'll be there."

The next morning Ashley went to all her teachers and told them about the accident. They were very understanding and made arrangements for her to turn in assignments late.

Ashley had planned to drive to Utah Wednesday afternoon after classes, but as the day progressed, the weather deteriorated. It got colder, and it looked as though it would begin to snow. Not only that but there was a winter storm watch for the area.

When Ashley returned to her apartment to get ready to leave, she found a voice-mail message from her mother: "Ashley, your father and I have been watching the weather reports, and it doesn't look very good. Maybe you shouldn't even try to make it down. I'm sure Nathan and his family will understand."

Ashley looked outside. It was beginning to snow, but it didn't seem that bad. *I should start out and see how far I can make it,* she thought.

Before she left the apartment, though, another plan was beginning to form in her mind. She packed into her car, along with her suitcase, her electric frying pan and a box of groceries. *Just in case,* she thought, trying to keep a positive note to her preparations.

The further south she went, the better the weather became, until, just beyond Pocatello, it stopped snowing.

She began to look carefully at the signs for motels along the way. Finally she found what she was looking for—a small, run-down motel that advertised rooms with kitchenettes.

A short time later she pulled into the motel parking lot, went inside, paid for a room, drove to the room she'd been given, and moved her things inside.

There was a strange mixture of smells in the dingy room—cigarette smoke from twenty years of use and the pungent smell of some kind of deodorizer. The faucet had a steady leak, the bed creaked, and the TV remote didn't even work.

This isn't right, my being here, she thought.

It's perfect, though, she answered.

I'm not going to stay here very long, she thought. *Just long enough to have a few pancakes, and then I'll be on my way.*

There was no need to rush, the way she had to when she did pancakes in her apartment, when any moment a roommate could barge in and catch her. She turned on the TV and made up a dozen pancakes, then sat in front of the TV and leisurely ate them.

And then made a trip to the bathroom.

And then made up a dozen more delicious pancakes, dripping with butter, and covered in syrup.

And made a trip to the bathroom.

And then she slowed the pace a little. She got interested in an old movie and watched it all the way through.

When the movie was over, she made a dozen more pancakes.

And then made a trip to the bathroom.

I should leave now, she thought. *I could make it home in a couple of hours and then get some sleep and go to the funeral tomorrow.*

But she stood up too fast and nearly fainted. *Maybe I'll get some sleep and leave early in the morning. The funeral isn't until two o'clock tomorrow, so if I leave at eight, I'll still be able to make it in time . . . if it isn't snowing.*

Her alarm went off at six-thirty the next morning. She took a shower and put on the clothes she'd worn the day before.

Before I leave, I should have breakfast, she thought.

No, I can't do that.

Why not? It doesn't make sense to stop for something to eat when I can cook my own breakfast. It'll be faster this way.

No, I need to get out of here, she thought.

There's nothing wrong with having breakfast, is there? Go ahead.

She made up a batch of pancakes.

And then made a trip to the bathroom.

And then she made up another batch of pancakes.

And made another trip to the bathroom.

At noon, she realized it was too late to make it to the funeral, so she made another batch of pancakes.

And made another trip to the bathroom.

At one o'clock, there was a knock on the door.

Ashley went to the door.

It was the girl who cleaned the rooms. "I was just wondering . . ."

"When is checkout time?" Ashley asked.

"Noon."

"Oh, I see."

I should just go now.

Where can you go? You've missed the funeral. And your roommates don't expect you home until Sunday. Besides that, you've got Mommy's MasterCard. So stay another day.

No, I can't stay another day.

Why not? This has been perfect.

What I've been doing isn't right.

Maybe this will get it out of your system, and you'll never do it again.

"Do you want me to come back?" the cleaning girl asked.

"I'll be staying another day," Ashley said. "And you don't need to bother cleaning the room."

"Are you sure?"

"Yes, the room is fine just the way it is."

185

"Do you want me to tell the manager you'll be staying another day?"

"Yes, please."

The girl started to leave.

"What are they saying about the snowstorm?" Ashley asked.

The girl looked confused. "What snowstorm?"

Ashley closed the door.

And made another batch of pancakes.

A little while later she watched the weather channel. The winter storm watch had been canceled, although there were scattered flurries on the Malad pass between Idaho and Utah.

She called her parents and told them she'd had to stop because of the storm. That it was still snowing and the wind was blowing, and that the weather report said that it would clear up by the next day, at which time she'd drive back to Rexburg. She asked them to phone Jen and explain why she hadn't been able to make it to the funeral. Then she went to a store and bought more pancake mix, cooking oil, and syrup.

And then she made herself another batch of pancakes.

* * * * *

She stayed all weekend at the motel, making it back to her apartment at seven Sunday night. She was exhausted and went straight to bed.

At nine o'clock her roommate woke her up. "There's a phone call for you. It's long distance."

Ashley sat up and took the phone. "Hello?"

"What happened to you?" It was Jen, and she sounded angry.

"I got as far as just past Pocatello, and then it started to snow real bad, so I couldn't make it. Sorry."

"When exactly was it snowing that hard, Ashley?"

"Thursday afternoon."

"Really," Jen, tight-lipped, said.

"I would've come if I could. You know that."

"I was talking to a friend today at church. He drove down from Idaho on Friday morning. When I asked him if he'd had any trouble getting through the snow, he said, 'What snow?'"

Ashley felt a pain in her stomach.

"Well, I guess he went through the area before it started to snow."

"Why didn't you come?"

"I didn't even know Nathan's sister."

186

"But you knew Nathan, and he was hurting. You didn't even care, did you?"

"I tried to come down. What more did you want me to do?"

"Was it really too much to ask of you as Nathan's friend to get your head out of the toilet?" With that, Jen hung up.

Ashley sat on the bed. *So that's it then,* she thought. *I've betrayed the only friends I've ever had. It's just as well, I guess. I only dragged them down anyway. They'll be better off without me. I don't have time for friends. I'm too busy just trying to keep up.*

She left the apartment with the intention of studying but an hour later she found herself in her car parked on the side of a gravel road just outside of town. She had several boxes of Twinkies next to her on the seat.

This will make me feel better, she thought. *It always does.*

I wonder if Nathan even cared that I didn't come down? Could I have helped him? I should have gone to the funeral and at least shown that much support.

She tore the cellophane off one of the packages of Twinkies and stared at the little cakes. *How many of these have I gone through this school year? A thousand? I am so messed up. No friends. Nobody I can talk to. Just one binge after another. It just goes on and on, day after day.*

I'd be better off dead.

I wish I were dead.

But could I do it?

Maybe I could just veer into the bridge on my way home. But what if I didn't die? That would be even worse.

Nathan, I'm so sorry. You won't ever want to talk to me again, will you? I don't blame you after what I did.

Slowly, she brought her first Twinkie to her mouth.

And then she broke down, crying.

She sat there sobbing, unheard, alone, isolated.

She cried for half an hour, but then, before leaving, she took care of business. She finished off the Twinkies, then opened the car door and vomited the yellow mass onto the ground. And then started back to her apartment.

I don't want to die this way, she thought, *but I have nothing to live for.*

18

On Wednesday of the next week, Melissa, one of Ashley's room-mates, approached Ashley to ask a favor. She wanted Ashley to go out with her cousin Brandon, who would be visiting for the weekend.

"So, can you come with us Friday night?" Melissa asked.

"I'll think about it."

"What could possibly be the problem?"

"Well, for one thing, I don't know him."

"I know, but he's my cousin, and he's really a great guy. Returned missionary, fun to talk to, good dancer, great sense of humor. I mean everyone likes Brandon. And it's not like you'd be all alone with him. I mean, Shane and I will be there with you. Everyone in the apartment will be gone Friday night, so if you don't go with us you'll be all alone."

"Let me think about it, okay?"

She didn't really need to think about it. She knew what her answer would be. She'd stay in her apartment Friday night. With her room-mates gone, it would give her time to be alone.

Although she did regret missing Nathan's sister's funeral, she had to admit that being in the motel all alone had made the bingeing good because she hadn't been rushed. She was tired of making trips into the country, having to eat quickly, then purge, and drive back to town.

She needed more of that kind of time to herself.

I'm supposed to want to spend time with guys. And I do think about it once in a while, but not that much. Because guys are trouble, and it's just too hard to even talk to them, and I keep hoping they don't notice how fat I am, and I keep wanting to excuse myself, and not come back, until I get down to what I weighed in ninth grade. And I'm afraid they'll put their arms around me or give me a hug, and I don't like that because they'll know how fat I still am. Or how cold my hands and arms are, or that I'm losing my hair. It's much better to be alone.

Once I get to my goal, then I'll be outgoing, and I won't mind being with a guy. Except I still won't know what to say. And I'll still be afraid of saying the wrong thing. And I still won't want to be hugged or kissed.

Sometimes I think I'm going backwards in time. My weight is dropping to what it was when I was much younger and my reproductive system has shut down and I've lost whatever interest I ever had in boys. It's like being in fourth grade all over again.

Well, I'll figure this out sometime. Right now, though, I need to plan my weekend. I'm sick of pancakes. This weekend maybe I'll go with ice cream on hot apple pie, or ice cream with chocolate topping.

This will be great. I'll be all by myself. I'll get me a couple of movies and some frozen pies and a couple of gallons of ice cream, and I'll have a real good time.

I just wish my throat would quit bleeding though. It's starting to worry me. But it's just temporary, so I guess I can stand it.

She told Melissa she wouldn't be able to go out with her cousin on Friday because she had to write a term paper that was due Monday and she hadn't even started.

On Friday afternoon she went shopping, buying four frozen apple pies, three half gallons of ice cream, and two bottles of chocolate topping. And, just in case she ran out, she got some more pancake mix and some blueberry syrup. She was all set.

After supper, which she skipped, she put several books on the kitchen table to give the impression she was studying, in case anyone dropped in.

She was in her room reading when Melissa's cousin showed up.

Ashley opened the door a crack to get a look at him. He was tall, maybe six-foot-two, and had sandy hair and an easy smile. One thing she liked about him was how much he delighted in teasing Melissa.

I could be the one going out with him tonight, she thought. Maybe we'd have a good time. Maybe he would even make me laugh with his sense of humor.

But maybe not. I never know what to say around a guy. So most of the time I don't say anything. I just clam up and hope he doesn't notice the fat on my calves or that my stomach goes in and out when I breathe.

And then, also, if we went out, we'd probably eat. I gag so easily now that if the food is rich and full of calories, then I can't eat it without having to purge, and that's always awkward and even embarrassing when I'm in a rest room stall and someone comes in and hears me throwing up.

And I'd be afraid he'd try to hold my hand, or put his arm around my waist, or that we'd dance close, or that he'd try to kiss me. I don't like that. I can hardly stand my body the way it is now, and I don't like the idea of being physically close to a guy because I'm afraid that when he gets with his friends, he'll make fun of me, like I've heard guys do about other girls.

And even if he liked me and we got along together, that wouldn't be any good either because if he liked me then I'd have to try even harder to lose weight. But I can't work any harder than I am now. I can hardly climb stairs as it is, and I don't want to even think what I'd do if I had a boyfriend to try to lose weight for so he'd keep liking me.

It's much better this way, to be all alone by myself with my treats.

Finally everyone left, and she was by herself alone in her apartment with the whole evening in front of her.

She went down to her car and opened the trunk and hauled her groceries back to the apartment. She had to stop three times to catch her breath, but nobody saw her.

An hour later, after finishing her first apple pie with ice cream, she was on her way to the bathroom when she heard a knock on the door. She couldn't turn around to answer it because the food was already about to come up and so she ran into the bathroom and closed the door.

She purged the food then got up and wiped her face, then swirled baking soda in her mouth to neutralize the stomach acid, which was starting to take the enamel off her teeth. She couldn't even chew gum now because the sugar in the gum gave her a mouthful of pain.

Whoever was at the door was still knocking.

It's probably just the paperboy wanting to collect. Well, that's just too bad. I'm not the one who decided to take the newspaper, anyway. That was Erin's idea, and I'm not paying for it. The boy will just have to come back when Erin is here.

She hurried to the door, all set to tell the paperboy to come back. She opened the door and there, amazingly, stood her parents.

"Mom . . . Dad, what are you doing here?" she stammered.

"We came to visit you," her mother said.

"Oh," she said, still stunned.

"Can we come in?" her mother asked.

"Yes, of course."

They walked in and looked into the kitchen area.

"Smells good in here," her father said.

"Oh, that. One of my roommates baked a frozen apple pie and took it over to some guys in the ward."

Her dad went into the kitchen. "They left the oven on," he said.

"Oh, really? I'm glad you caught that. I'll be sure and talk to her when they get home tonight."

Her mother went into the bathroom and then came back. "You forgot to flush after you threw up."

"Oh, that wasn't me. That was one of my roommates. She's had the flu all week."

"Is she here? I'd like to see what I can do to make her feel better," her mother said.

"It got so bad they had to take her home. That's where my roommates are now. And it happened so fast they didn't have a chance to turn off the stove."

"Ashley, can I ask you a question?" her mother asked, turning to look Ashley in the face, "Do you ever tell the truth anymore?"

"I don't know what you're talking about."

"Jen and Nathan came over to talk to us last night," her father said.

"So?"

"There wasn't a snowstorm on your way to Nathan's funeral, was there?"

"There was, but it didn't last too long, but I didn't know how long it was going to last."

"What did you do?"

"I stayed in a motel until the storm passed."

"There wasn't a storm though, was there?" her mother asked.

"There was."

"Ashley, let me just tell you what I've found out," her mother said. "Since the credit card is in my name too, I phoned and asked what purchases you've made recently." They gave me the name of the motel you stayed at. I called and talked to the manager. He told me you stayed Thursday, Friday, and Saturday nights, and that you stayed in your room the whole time. He told me there was no snowstorm. Yet you stayed there three nights. Why?"

"You always tell me to exercise caution, so that's what I was doing, exercising caution."

"I could see you staying one night for that reason but not three nights." As she spoke she went into the kitchen and looked in the refrigerator, and saw three pies still in their boxes. "And I found out you also used your card to make some purchases at a grocery store. I phoned and talked to the man who runs it. He remembers you buying enough pancake mix, butter, and syrup to feed the whole town." She opened the freezer and saw the half-gallon containers of ice cream.

"I had to eat, didn't I?"

"Jen thinks you holed up and binged during Nathan's sister's funeral."

"I would never do that. Nathan is my friend."

191

"Ashley, for your own sake, tell us the truth," her father said. His voice was flat, and he sounded tired.

Why should I? You've never wanted to know the truth about me before, so why start now?

But she didn't say it. She couldn't remember the last time she'd been completely open with her parents. "I don't know what you're talking about."

"I thought we had an agreement that you would get counseling when you came back here," her mother said. "How many times have you gone for counseling?"

"You tell me, Mother. You seem to have all the answers tonight."

"That's right. I do. The counseling center has no record of you."

"I talked with someone on the phone, though."

"Who?"

"I can't remember. A secretary."

"We sent you up here with the idea that you'd start seeing a counselor, but you haven't done that, have you?" her father said.

"Not yet, but I'm going to set something up first thing on Monday."

"It doesn't matter now," her father said. "We're here to take you to a clinic in Orem where they treat eating disorders."

"I won't go."

"You will do whatever we say," her father said.

"You don't have any authority over me anymore."

"We're paying for your education."

"I don't need your money. I can always get a job."

"Who would hire you, Ashley?" her father challenged "You have no skills, except for lying, and there are very few companies who want a liar on their payroll."

"David," her mother said as a reprimand, "we didn't come here to argue. We came here to rescue our daughter."

Ashley sat down at the kitchen table and grabbed a book and opened it as if she were studying. "I don't need to be rescued," Ashley said. "I'm doing fine."

"You're not doing fine if you're still throwing up," her father said.

"It's my body, isn't it? I should be able to do with it what I want."

"We will not stand idly by and let you engage in self-destructive behavior," her mother said. She began to cry. "Look at you, Ashley. You're nothing but skin and bones. Can't you see what this is doing to you?" She sat down and put her hand on Ashley's arm, gasped at how cold it felt, and then broke down completely.

Ashley watched numbly as tears rolled down her mother's cheek.

It was like coming into a movie in the middle, watching characters on the screen you don't care about anyway.

Her father, likewise, at first just stood there and watched. And then, wanting to do something but not knowing what it should be, he went in the bathroom and brought out some tissues and put them in front of his wife. "It's okay," he said feebly. "We're going to take care of this like we should have when we first found out."

"I don't see how you can stop me from doing what I choose to do," Ashley said coldly. "Oh, I suppose you can get me admitted into a treatment center, but it won't do any good, because some day they'll release me, and when they do I'll go on doing what I want. This is my life now. I'm not hurting anyone else, so I don't see that it's any business of yours."

"You're only hurting yourself by this," her father said.

"What does that matter? I don't count. I never have."

"You're our daughter, and we love you," her father said.

"If you love me, then leave me alone and let me live my life the way I want to live it."

Her mother had regained her composure and now was all business again.

"That's not an option when it comes to self-destructive behavior. Pack up what you want to take to the treatment center. You'll be there two months."

"I'm not packing anything."

"Then let's go," her mother said.

"I'm not going."

Her father approached her. "You are, Ashley, one way or the other. Now get in the car and let's go. We have a long drive ahead of us."

"What about my classes?"

Her mother had thought about the answer to that question on the drive up from Utah. "I'll call the dean of students on Monday and tell him you've dropped out of school due to medical problems. Your college days at Ricks are over. Even after you're released from the treatment center, we'll need you home where we can keep an eye on you, and where we can monitor your eating."

She thought of running away, but she could no longer run, at least not more than a few feet.

This is insane. It can't be happening now. Things were going so well for me.

"We need to go," her mother said.

"What about all my clothes and things? I just can't leave them here."

"I'll call your roommates tomorrow and ask them to pack everything up," her mother said. "I'll come up and pick it up sometime next week."

"Why are you doing this? Why can't you just leave me alone?"

"Because we love you, that's why," her mother said.

You don't love me. You love what you hoped I would be, but never me, the way I really was.

"Let's go," her father said.

They walked her out to the car, opened the back door while she got in and closed it.

In a few minutes they were on the highway, traveling south.

They're actually going through with this, Ashley thought. *What have I done that's so awful? I just went on a diet, that's all. People go on diets all the time. It's just that my diet worked, and I lost weight. Why do I have to go to a treatment center for that? What have I done that's so terrible that I have to be put away?*

She reached down and felt the calf of her right leg. There wasn't much there but bone, but if she pointed her toe down and relaxed the muscles, she could still feel flab. *I still could stand to lose another ten pounds,* she thought.

"I have a term paper due Monday," she called out to her parents in the front seat.

"You're not a student at Ricks anymore," her mother said.

"It's a waste of money to just drop me out of school."

"When it comes to your health, money is no consideration," her mother answered.

No matter what I say, it won't make any difference.

It was then, with all hope gone, that she started to cry.

*   *   *   *   *

She gave into despair and cried for half an hour.

And then once she was spent emotionally, her mind took over. *They're united against me. That's not a good thing. I need to split them apart. But how?*

She studied her mother and dad in the front seat, trying to come up with a way to exploit their differences.

They're not even talking to each other. That's not good. It's like their only goal now is to get rid of me at some hospital, and then they'll relax and talk to each other.

In some ways I'm like my dad. He likes to reason out his moves. What can I do to change his mind? What would be the one thing that would bother him about putting me in a treatment center? That's easy enough to answer. It's the money. I wonder if this is going to cost them some money or if the insurance will pay all of it. That's important to find out.

Ashley leaned forward. "How expensive is it going to be for me to be at the place you're taking me?"

"That is entirely none of your concern," her mother said tersely, looking straight ahead as if that would make the car go faster.

"Will our insurance cover it?"

"Some of it will be covered by insurance," her father said.

"But not all?"

"No, not all," her father answered.

This is just what I need, she thought. "So where is the money coming from to pay for the rest?" she asked.

Her mother turned around. "That is absolutely of no concern to you. We are going to do what's best for you, regardless of the cost."

"Why can't I know how much it costs? Am I a part of this family or not?"

"Yes, of course you're in this family," her father answered.

Yes, all right! I always know how to get to my dad, she thought proudly.

"Will my being in this program make it harder for Alauna to have the money she needs to finish college? If it does, then I think that going to a treatment center should only be done after everything else has been tried. Like more counseling."

"It's too late for that. We've already made up our minds," her mother answered.

"Couldn't we at least stop somewhere and talk about it?" Ashley asked.

"We're done talking," her mother snapped.

There was a long, uncomfortable silence.

"Well," her father began, "if Ashley wants to talk, then I think we should honor her request."

"What on earth is there to talk about?" her mother asked.

"We won't know until we do it, will we?"

"Fine, whatever you say," her mother grumbled, "You do know she's manipulating you, though, don't you? Just like she always does when she wants something. Like she manipulated my mother when she wanted a car to take to college. Why we ever agreed to that is beyond me."

"She needed a car," her father said.

"Why do you always give in to her?"

They ended up at a McDonald's in Pocatello. It was near closing

195

time and most of the business was take-out. They sat in a booth in the far corner of the place. Her parents ordered hot chocolate; Ashley decided on ice water because it had no calories.

"You wanted to talk. Well, go ahead, but it's not going to change anything," her mother said bitterly.

Ashley started in. "I know you'd do anything you could for me, even go into debt so I can go to a treatment center. But the thing is, we haven't really tried counseling. What if you let me finish out the semester? You can check each week with my counselor and make sure I'm showing up for counseling and working hard to overcome my problem. And then, at least, I'd be able to finish up my classes this semester."

"Anybody can go to counseling and put up a good front, and not try to change," her mother said. "The way I look at it, we need results, and we need them now."

Ashley fought the impulse to get into an argument. "If you find out that I'm not making any progress, then you can always send me to the clinic. It won't cost you any more money to do it that way, and it might save you a lot of money and me an entire semester of college."

Her mother shook her head. "The truth is, Ashley, I don't trust you anymore."

She tried to look full of remorse. "I know. I brought that on myself. I'm really sorry."

"I think she has a point," her father said.

"I want this taken care of before she ends up dead."

"That's what I want, too," Ashley said, "but I don't want to throw away an entire semester, either."

Her mother sat fuming and her father looked pained. After a few silent moments he said, "Let's at least go back and see what's available at Ricks in the way of counseling."

Her mother threw an old conflict between them back in his face. "You told me you have a very important meeting on Monday. We might not be able to talk to people at Ricks until Monday."

"I guess I'll have to miss the meeting then, won't I?" He stood up. "Let's go. It'll be late by the time we get to Rexburg. We'll be lucky to get a room tonight."

"It's Rexburg, Daddy," Ashley said with a grateful smile. "They'll have plenty of rooms."

When they reached Rexburg, they stopped at Ashley's apartment while she packed a suitcase. Then they drove to a motel, got a room, and prepared for bed. There were two beds in the room. It had been a long time since the three of them had shared a motel room. It seemed crowded. Ashley didn't like being that close to her parents.

At two-thirty in the morning, Ashley woke up hungry. She hadn't kept anything down all day except for the ice water in Pocatello. She remembered seeing some vending machines in the lobby. She listened to the slow, even breathing of her parents and quietly slipped out of bed, put on some clothes, grabbed the room key, and stepped out of the room.

Five minutes later she was shoving money into the vending machine until finally she had a small pile worth her while.

She sat at a dimly lit table near the pool, and, one by one, finished off the candy. She had to eat fast because the gagging reflex now came almost immediately after swallowing, and she wanted to get through everything before she purged.

Just before she was ready to make a run for the rest room just off the lobby, her father showed up at the registration desk. She dropped down and hid in the dim lighting of the pool area. He looked ridiculous because he was wearing pajama bottoms under his winter coat and shoes with no socks. He stood at the desk, impatiently punching the bell. A minute later, the room clerk, who had been sleeping in a back room, came out.

The gagging reflex, over which she now had no control, began rising in her throat, and her stomach was convulsing. She panicked. *No, not now! If I do it now, it'll make too much noise. And if Daddy finds me like this, he'll change his mind, and they'll drive me to the treatment center right away.*

"I'm looking for my daughter," she heard her father say. "She's staying with us tonight, but when I got up a few minutes ago, she wasn't in the room. Have you seen her?"

"No, I haven't. Sorry. How old is your daughter?"

"She's a student at Ricks."

"I haven't seen anyone. Sorry."

"I'll check outside. Thank you." He left through the front door.

Still out of sight, Ashley crawled to the pool.

The sleepy room clerk waited until her father left and then returned to the back room.

Ashley didn't have time to make it to the rest room. She threw up into the pool as quietly as she could.

She stared at the mass of undigested food floating on the top of the water.

They probably have filters to take care of that, she thought.

Keeping down, she made her way to a side entrance, let herself out, and walked through side lots and back alleys until she was a block away from the motel, then turned around and started back. She didn't have a coat on, and it was cold out, so she walked as fast as she could.

She could feel her heart fluttering. She panicked. *What is going on? This is new. Am I going to have a heart attack? Will I even make it back to the motel before I die? What have I done to myself?*

Her breathing was labored, and she couldn't seem to get enough air in her lungs, but she didn't dare stop to catch her breath because it was so cold.

Her father, standing in front of the motel, saw her coming.

She slowed down to try to catch her breath before she got to him.

"Where have you been?"

"I couldn't sleep, so I decided to take a walk."

"You should have told us what you were going to do. I woke up and found you gone. I was worried."

"I was okay. I just needed a walk, that's all."

"Did you walk to some place where you could buy food?"

"No, I wouldn't do that now. I'm trying to get better. You know that."

"I don't know anything anymore."

"I know that if I don't shape up, you'll put me in a treatment center. I don't want that to happen."

"I'm glad you realize that, because it's the truth."

"That's why I'm going to try to get my life back the way it should be."

"Where did you walk?" her father asked.

"Oh, you know, just around."

"Without a coat?"

"It's not that cold out if you walk fast."

"Well, let's go see if we can get some sleep."

"Whatever you say, Daddy."

"It's been a long time since you called me daddy."

"Yeah, it has." She paused. "You used to call me your little princess."

"I remember that. You were my little princess, too."

"Yes, I was. I remember. Daddy, don't worry. I won't let you down on this. I'll do whatever it takes."

"That's my good girl."

Just before returning to her bed, she thought with a smile, *This is going to be easy. Almost too easy. All I have to do is say the right things until they think I'm cured. And then they'll go away, and I'll continue on the same way. No matter how much I look like I'm cooperating, I'll never give this up because I'm doing so good right now.*

She thought back proudly on her day. She hadn't kept anything down except for the ice water, and that didn't count.

I'm doing so good, she thought, just before falling asleep.

* * * * *

She was awakened as her father, wearing swimming trunks he'd bought at the check-in desk, opened the door, let light in, and came into the room.

Ashley sat up, looked at her dad with his paunch stomach protruding over his wet swimming suit. "Did you go swimming, Daddy?" she asked.

"Yes, I did."

"How was it?" she asked.

"It was fine. Do you want to go? They have suits you can buy."

"Oh, no. That's fine. I'm just glad you went, that's all."

She hurried to the bathroom and a short time later was in the shower, with the fan on, quietly laughing that her father had gone swimming in her vomit.

Oh, that's just too funny, she thought. *I just wish there was someone I could tell about this, but there isn't. Nobody else would think that was very funny. Except me. And I think it's funny because that's what he deserves for trying to change me when I'm doing so good by myself. Who does he think he is, anyway? He has no business getting in my way. I'm perfectly able to take care of myself.*

What she envisioned happening was that she would go to counseling for the rest of the semester. But none of the counseling would make any difference. And every time she met with the counselor, she'd tell him she was doing a lot better. She didn't mind lying if it would keep her out of a treatment center.

I can be so sincere when I'm lying, she thought with a smile. *It's one of the things I do best.*

As she dried herself off, she looked in the mirror. She didn't like what she saw.

Her stomach still moved in and out when she breathed. And she could still pinch her sides and come up with some loose skin. The same with her upper legs and her calves.

I need to lose at least another ten pounds, she thought. *But that's going to be hard if I'm visiting a counselor each week. Especially if she asks me to weigh myself. Of course I could put quarters in my pockets. Or weights in my shoes. I'll think of something. I can't turn my back on all the progress I've made so far.*

I wonder what it'd be like to get down to what I weighed in sixth grade. That'd probably be just about right.

An hour later they went to eat breakfast at the restaurant next to the motel. Ashley ordered a boiled egg and a cup of herb tea. She carved out the yolk and set it aside, then ate the white part slowly, being very aware of the almost morbid interest her parents were paying to her eating habits.

I've got to keep this down, she thought. *If I don't, they still might end up taking me to the treatment center.*

She had also ordered toast with no butter, but when the waitress brought it, it had butter on it. That meant she couldn't eat it because butter was fat and fat was bad. She only ate butter when she was planning on purging.

"Don't you want your toast?" her mother asked.

"No, I'm full."

"You hardly ate a thing," her father said.

"Eggs are good protein," she said.

"You should eat your toast, too," her mother said.

"I'm full."

"Just take a bite."

She felt like she was walking across a mine field. She looked carefully at the toast. *There's no butter around the edges,* she thought. *If I can just take a few bites, then they'll be happy. But if I even taste the butter, then I know I'll throw up, so I'll have to be careful.*

She took a tiny bite of the toast near the crust. It didn't taste of butter. She smiled at her parents, proud of the accomplishment.

She took two more bites. "Now I really am full," she said.

After breakfast they returned to the room. Her mother phoned the counseling center, but they were closed for the weekend. She called the college operator to get the home phone of the director of the counseling center. She called and talked to the man for a while and then hung up.

"We have an appointment first thing on Monday," she said.

"There's no need for you to wait around here all weekend," Ashley said. "I can go see the counselor Monday morning and then call you after and tell you what he said. I'm sure you need to get to work Monday, don't you, Daddy?"

Before her father could answer, her mother said, "We will stay here and talk to him together on Monday."

"You don't have to tell me that, Christine," he challenged. "I am perfectly aware that we'll be here Monday."

"Well, I wasn't sure if you have actually resigned yourself to that fact," she shot back.

Sitting in a chair watching TV, Ashley laid her head back and stared at the ceiling. "One, two, three, four."

"What are you doing?" her mother asked.

"Counting the holes," she said.

"It won't kill us to be together as a family for the weekend, will it?" her mother said.

"What are we going to do all weekend?" Ashley asked, irritably.

After a long pause, her mother smiled. "Let's go to Yellowstone Park!"

* * * * *

By the time they reached West Yellowstone, it was snowing heavily. Thick, low-lying clouds hid the peaks of the nearby mountains. The park rangers advised no travel into the park. And so they were stuck at West Yellowstone. They got a motel room across from a city park, then, for lack of anything else to do, took a walk along the snow-covered walks past the stores that were boarded up for the winter. And then they returned to their room.

Ashley, bored and depressed, turned on the TV to see what was on. They only had ten channels. And one was the history channel. And the other was public television. So that only left eight channels. One channel was the shopping channel. Another was CNN. And then there was another CNN channel. One channel was showing a movie in black and white.

Five minutes later she had exhausted all the possible channels. She looked at her watch. It was one o'clock on a Saturday afternoon, and she was stuck in a dingy motel room with her parents for the entire weekend.

This is going to be the low-point of my life, she thought. *But I'm not going to complain because if I do, then they might just put me in the treatment center. Even this is better than that. Anything is better than that.*

Her father turned to the history channel and watched as each battle, or so it seemed to Ashley, of World War II took place.

After forty-five minutes of that, Ashley's mother grabbed the remote and turned the TV off. "We're not going to sit here all day and watch this," she said.

"What else is there to do?'

Her mother paused. "We'll make a snowman."

Ashley and her father looked at each other and both scowled at the same time.

"C'mon, get up, it'll be fun," her mother said.

201

"We don't have boots," Ashley complained.

"Or gloves," her father chimed in.

"We'll borrow them from the motel manager. C'mon, c'mon, let's go!"

Ten minutes later the three of them were standing in the middle of the park in over-sized parkas and rubber overshoes, wearing heavy-duty winter gloves.

"Okay, you two, get going, start with a snowball and roll it around until it gets big," her mother called out.

"This is so stupid," Ashley muttered under her breath.

"We're staying out here until it's done, so you might as well get started."

"We'd better do what she says," her father said.

It was easy at first, but then as the snowball got bigger, it got progressively harder to roll it. Her dad stopped working on his and came over to help Ashley, who was struggling.

"Can I give you a hand?" he asked.

"Thanks."

"It's been a long time since we've done this together, hasn't it?"

"We never did this together," Ashley said.

"Oh, I'm sure we did."

"Maybe you did it with Alauna, but you never did it with me."

"Really? I thought we had."

"It's not that important."

"Of course it is. That's probably big enough. Let's go work on the other one."

They rolled the other snowball around until it was almost as big as the first one.

"The hard part will be getting one on top of the other."

They packed it down and then struggled together to lift it up and place it on the other one.

"Now we need a smaller one for the head," her father said.

"I'm going to go find a store that's open and see if I can get something we can use for the eyes and nose and mouth," Ashley's mother said, then disappeared into the snowstorm.

Ashley started another snowball and let her dad lift it up and place it on the top of the emerging snowman.

"I think it's going to be okay," she said.

"It's going to be the best snowman in West Yellowstone," he announced.

"That's because there aren't any others yet."

"So this one is the best, just like I predicted," he said with a smile.

202

They stood there admiring their work.

"Ashley, I'm sorry for not being the kind of father I should have been."

She was shocked to hear her father admit any failing on his part.

"Life has a way of turning sour on you if you're not careful," he said. "The one quality that people admire about you, if you push it too far, it turns out to be the thing that will end up causing you the most problems." He paused. "Like with me, it was working hard for my family. I kept it up and I kept it up and then all of a sudden I realized I don't even know my family anymore." He put his hand on her shoulder. "I don't know you very well, do I?"

"No, not very."

"Maybe we can change that," he said.

"It's all right the way it is, I guess."

"It isn't, though. Not at all. I've missed out." It was painful for him to say it. "It's probably my fault you're bulimic."

"No, that's not it. This is my problem. The truth is, I don't even think about you much." As soon as she said it, she felt bad that she might have hurt his feelings. "I didn't mean it that way. What I meant is that I didn't start this because of being mad at you or anything."

"Why did you start?"

"I don't know. It started out I just wanted to lose a few pounds and then it kind of got out of control."

"What you're doing. It's not good. It scares me."

"I try not to think about it."

"I do that, too, sometimes."

"Let's make another snowman," Ashley said. "It could be the wife to the first one."

"All right, we might as well. Your mother must be hiking to Utah to get the eyes and nose and mouth for our snow people."

"Maybe so."

The snow was coming down hard enough it almost seemed they were the only ones on the planet. There was hardly any traffic on the highway next to the park.

"I should have spent more time with you when you were growing up. We could have done more things like this."

"Why didn't you?"

"Good question." He paused, then continued rolling a large snowball. "I was just thinking the other day. I've worked twenty-five years at the same place. When I first started working there, it was just the boss and me, working part-time after school. And then after my mission, I dropped out of college and started working there full-time. Because of our hard work, we turned it into a profitable company. All the time you were growing up, I'd always say, 'After we finish this job, I'll have more time to spend with the family.' But there was always another job, just as important, just as demanding, making it impossible for me to be with my family as much as I should have been."

"And then somebody else bought the company, right?" Ashley asked.

"That's right. Mergers—that's the big thing these days. They buy a profitable company, downsize it, get rid of the people who've worked there for years, hire cheaper labor, break the company into smaller pieces, sell each piece, and move on."

"You're still working there."

"Yes, but they've already hired my replacement. He's twenty-two years old. When he came, he didn't know anything about landscaping. They made him my assistant. As soon as I teach him everything I know, they'll fire me, and he'll take over."

"That's not fair."

"That's the way it is these days."

"I'm sorry, Daddy."

"It's okay. I'll survive. But right now I'm thinking 'What good has all my work accomplished?' If I hadn't worked as hard, then the company wouldn't have been as successful, and I wouldn't be wondering when they're going to fire me. And I'd have been the kind of father you and Alauna should have had." He sighed. "I was thinking on the drive up here of all the times I missed seeing your concerts when you were growing up."

"We weren't very good."

"That's not the point. The point is you're my daughter, and I should have been there."

"It's okay, Daddy."

"Did I ever take you to the zoo?"

"We went as a family, but not just you and me."

"I should've done that. I always meant to."

"It's okay."

"Let's finish up this snow woman," her dad said.

It ended up the same size as the snow man.

"It looks the same," her father said. "How is anyone going to know this is a snow *woman*?"

"We could put a sign on her that says she feels apologetic about the way she turned out," Ashley said.

"We'd have to put the same sign on the snow man, too," her father said.

"Let's make a snow child to go with them," Ashley said.

"Good idea. Children bring hope to a couple."

"Well, at least at first they do," Ashley said. "And then they grow up and turn out to be big disappointments."

"Sometimes it's hard to tell who's the biggest disappointment—the parents or the children," her father said.

She didn't say anything for a long time, trying to take in all her dad had told her. And then finally, she said softly, "We've never talked like this before, have we?"

"No. I was always trying to be strong."

"And I was always trying to be invisible."

He seemed surprised. "Why did you want to be invisible?"

"So you'd be proud of me that I hadn't given you a bit of trouble."

"You mean like what Alauna put us through," he said.

"Yes."

"What does Alauna think about our family?" he asked.

Ashley hesitated before answering. Then she said, "When she left, she told me the sooner I left home, the better off I'd be."

"I see," he said.

"It's not your fault, Daddy."

They made two snow children.

"The family looks cold and lonely," her dad said.

"That's the way it is with snow people," Ashley said.

"That's the way it's been between you and me, isn't it?"

"I guess so."

"Maybe we can change that."

"Wouldn't that be something if we could?"

"It would be. I think we should try to get closer." He took off his hat and put it on the snowman's head. "You know, it's painful for me to realize how much you and I are alike."

"There're good things about that, too, you know."

"Maybe so, but one thing is for sure. If we're going to fix you, we're going to have to fix me as well. I will be with you on this for as long as it takes."

She felt an emotion she hadn't felt for a long while. "Daddy, I love you." She threw her arms around him, and he held her tight, and, together, they both shed tears.

And then they heard someone coming. Embarrassed, they pulled apart, and dabbed at their eyes.

"I got a package of carrots and some charcoal briquettes," her mother said.

"That will be perfect to bring this snow family to life," Ashley said, hopeful for the first time in a long time.

19

On Sunday Ashley and her parents went to church in West Yellowstone, and then drove back to Rexburg.

"Do you want me to stay with you in the motel tonight, too?" Ashley asked her father as they pulled into Rexburg.

"I definitely think that would be for the best," her mother said.

"What would you like to do?" her dad asked, looking at her in the rearview mirror.

"Well, if I stayed in my room, I could catch up on a few things."

"Can you stay out of trouble there?" her father asked.

"I'm pretty sure I can."

"Well, okay then, that's what we'll do," her father said.

Her mother glared with disapproval at her dad but didn't say anything.

A few minutes later Ashley waved at her parents as they drove away. *I'm not going to do it tonight because I promised I wouldn't and they may ask me tomorrow and I don't want to lie.*

She walked in the apartment, went to the freezer, and saw the ice cream she'd put there the night she was busted by her folks. She had planned to put it on her next batch of pancakes.

Not now. I need to see who's here first.

Not that I'm going to do it.

But I could do it.

If nobody's here, I should do it. Who knows when the next time is when I'll have a chance.

But I promised Daddy I wouldn't do it. He's trusting me not to.

It doesn't matter what you promised. You're going to do it, so you might as well do it now and then it'll be taken care of and you won't have it hanging over your head any longer.

She did a quick search through all the bedrooms. One of her roommates was taking a nap.

She'll sleep through it. It's all right. Do it now.
I promised Daddy I wouldn't do this.
Go to the freezer, take out the ice cream, have a taste, then decide.
No, I won't go to the freezer.
You have no choice in this.
I do have a choice.
No, you gave up your right to make choices about this long ago.

She put on her coat and went outside. The wind was howling, and it looked like it was about to snow.

She walked to the John Taylor building on campus and went into the chapel and sat down and tried to pray. It had been so long since she'd prayed for anything that doing it now seemed like a futile gesture.

A student came in. "Is it okay if I practice?"

"Yeah, sure, go ahead."

"Thanks." he said, then moved toward the organ. He had a high-pitched voice and pronounced each syllable with annoying precision. "You're just sitting here?"

"Yes."

"It's a nice place to come when you have a problem," he said.

"I guess so." She didn't want to admit she had a problem.

"That's why I come," he said, sitting down at the organ.

She relaxed. "Me too, actually."

"The music helps me. Maybe it will help you, too."

"I bet it will."

He was taking off his shoes. "I'll say a prayer for you while I'm playing."

"I'll say one for you, too."

He clasped his hands and stretched. "Thank you. Well, here goes."

The music soothed her and made her feel better for a while, but after a few minutes, the organist stopped playing and asked her where she was from.

She was seated about halfway back in the chapel, in the center section, and they had to speak up to hear each other.

"Salt Lake City," she answered.

"No kidding? I'm from Draper."

"How about that?"

He was leafing through a large book of organ music, trying to find his next piece. "I just got back from a mission to Russia. Do you speak Russian?"

"No."

He found the piece and placed it on the organ. "That's part of my problem."

"What?"

"My life has no purpose now that I'm off my mission."

"My life has no purpose, either, and I haven't even served a mission."

"We should talk."

"Play another song first," she said.

It was very difficult to play. She didn't know the name of the piece, but she thought it had been written by Bach.

Once he was a minute into the music, he had to concentrate so hard he lost track of her. And that's when she quickly left the building because she was afraid he'd come down and talk to her and, maybe, offer to walk her home.

I don't need that kind of stress in my life right now, she thought.

On the way back, she had to stop a couple of times to catch her breath, and her heart started its erratic fluttering, but other than that, she had no problem.

When she got to the apartment, her roommates were all there along with some guys from the ward. She said hello and then retreated to her room.

She got ready for bed, but when she crawled in she found she couldn't sleep. She could hear the sounds of laughter. Everyone sounded happy. Even Melissa, her roommate, who was at least twenty pounds overweight. *How can she be happy when she weighs so much? I weigh a lot less than her, and I'm still not happy yet.*

She began to fantasize about the half-gallon of chocolate ice cream in the freezer. She thought about how good it would taste, but of course she'd have to wait until everyone was asleep, and she wasn't sure how long that would take. Her roommates and the boys with them were keeping her from her ice cream.

Maybe in the morning when I wake up, I'll have a little taste, she thought. Then she fell asleep.

She woke up at four in the morning, got up and went into the kitchen, opened the freezer, and took out the ice cream.

This will help me feel better, she thought. *I'm worried about having to go through counseling, afraid of what the counselor is going to tell me. Maybe he'll recommend they put me in the treatment center. If that happened, I'd lose all control over my life, and I like to be in control.*

I promised Daddy I wouldn't do it. So I shouldn't. But it will make me feel better if I do.

I don't think I can give this up for good. It's like my best friend. It's always there for me, no matter what. I don't have any friends here or anyone I'm really close to. I need something to help me get through each day. For me this is it.

If I do it, though, when I promised I wouldn't, then I'll have to lie. But it's all right if I lie because I can't give this up, no matter how many times I say that I can. So I'll have to lie all the time from now on. I might as well get used to the idea of never telling the truth.

The most important thing is to do whatever I need to do to stay out of the treatment center where they'd watch my every move.

No matter what happens, I have to make sure I can keep doing this. That's the most important thing. It's more important than telling a lie once in a while. Everyone tells a lie once in a while, and I certainly can because I'm no good anyway.

When I'm doing it, then I'm in control. And I have to be in control or else things will make me feel bad. And I don't like to feel bad. And I don't like it when I'm with people because I'm afraid I'll say something stupid and everyone will laugh at me.

So that's the reason I'm going to eat all this ice cream and then puke my guts out.

She opened the carton. And then she started crying.

Daddy, I'm so sorry. I'm so sorry you have me for your daughter. You deserve so much better. Life would be so much better for you and Mom if I were dead. I'd like to do it but I don't know how. Maybe someday I will. There's nothing for me to live for anyway. Just more of this for the rest of my life.

She opened a drawer and grabbed a large spoon.

How can I do this when Daddy and I made snowmen and we cried together and hugged in the snow.

I hate this so much. This battle goes on and on, day after day.

"I'm not going to do this," she said quietly to herself. "Maybe tomorrow after my parents are gone, but not today while they're here."

She could not stand to let the ice cream continue to tempt her by its very presence. She grabbed a serving spoon and the ice cream and ran into the bathroom and locked the door and went to her knees in front of the toilet and plunged the spoon into the ice cream, lifted out a large scoop and dropped it in the toilet. And then another scoop, and another until it was all gone, then she slid the carton into the toilet and rinsed it out, pulled it out, dumped it in the garbage, and flushed.

And then, in tears, she took a long shower.

For just a few minutes she thought of it as a small victory, which it was, until she started to fantasize about what else there might be in the refrigerator that she could devour.

* * * * *

She managed to hold out until seven o'clock when her parents picked her up to go to breakfast.

"How did you do last night?" her father asked when she got in the car.

"I did real good," she said.

"Great! I'm proud of you."

"It wasn't easy, though, and I'm not sure I can stop for good right away."

"I understand. It'll probably take a while."

"I'm sure it will."

"I still think it would be better to have you in an inpatient facility," her mother said.

"It may be that we'll end up there, but I think we need to try this first," her dad answered.

"But why wait? If the company lets you go, you'll lose your medical benefits, won't you?"

"They'll probably give me a couple of months of medical coverage after that," her father said.

"But you don't know that. We won't be able to afford inpatient care without medical insurance."

"I know that."

"Have you even looked into what they'll offer when they let you go?" her mother asked.

"It's not for sure when they'll let me go."

"They've given you every indication you're not valuable to them. I think it's just a matter of time," her mother said.

"Ashley wants to finish the semester, and so I think we should pursue that first."

Her mother turned to look at Ashley in the back seat. "Ashley, if you're not going to work hard with the counselor they have here, then I think you should tell us, so we don't end up having to sell the house just to pay for your in-patient care if your father is let go."

"I'll try. That's all I can say. I'll do my best."

"And what if your best isn't good enough? Then where does that leave us?" her mother asked. "Living in some tiny apartment on welfare?"

"I'll get another job," her dad said, impatiently.

"Who's going to hire you at your age?"

"Something will turn up."

After they were seated in the restaurant, Ashley glanced over at a large woman with metallic red hair at the next table. She was working on a large stack of pancakes, drenched in syrup.

Ashley felt like grabbing the pancakes and running into a corner where nobody could find her and devouring them.

I can't do that, though. At least not today. Maybe tomorrow after they leave and I'm all by myself once again.

Although she'd only ordered one boiled egg and toast with no butter, and there was still half the egg left, she couldn't eat any more because her stomach ached due to all the tension she felt at the table. She wrapped her arms around her stomach and lowered her head and rocked back and forth.

"What are you doing?" her mother asked.

"Nothing."

"Stop rocking back and forth then," her mother said.

It was too much for her. She felt like she might throw up. "I need to go to the bathroom."

"No, you can't go right after you eat," her mother said. "Don't think I don't know what you're up to."

"What if she really has to go to the bathroom?" her father asked.

"Then I'll go with her. Ashley, do you still want to go to the bathroom?"

She didn't have time enough to explain. She ran into the bathroom and threw up what she'd eaten of her egg and toast and orange juice.

Her mother stayed outside the stall, listening to the last of her vomiting.

Ashley stood up, wiped the perspiration from her forehead, opened the stall, saw her mother glaring at her, brushed past her and went to the sink and rinsed her mouth.

"Your father and I are very disappointed in you."

"Welcome to the club," she said on her way out of the rest room. Her mother stayed behind.

"Did you throw up?" her father asked when she sat down at the table.

"Yes."

"How come?"

"I don't know."

"Was it because there was too much tension between your mother and me?"

"I don't know. Maybe so."

Her mother returned to the table. "You forgot to flush the toilet. I did it for you."

Ashley, with tears in her eyes, closed her eyes and whispered,

211

"Please, Mother, just leave me alone. Whenever I'm with you, even for a few minutes, I start feeling sick to my stomach."

Her mother's lip quivered. "That is so unfair, after all I've done for you."

Ashley had her arms wrapped around her stomach and she was rocking back and forth again. "I've got to get out of here. I'll be in our room."

She walked back to their motel room, turned the TV on, and sat on the end of the bed, numbly watching a home decorating show.

She heard a key in the lock, and then her mother came in the room.

"Ashley, we need to talk," her mother said.

Without even being aware of it, Ashley folded her arms and wrapped her arms around herself and lowered her head.

Her mother didn't say anything.

Ashley looked up. "Go ahead," she said softly.

"Go ahead with what?"

"Tell me how much I've let the family down."

"This is not that kind of a talk," her mother said.

"What kind is it?"

"The kind where we get to know each other a little better. Let's go sit in the hot tub."

"What about Dad?"

"He's on his cell phone, tying up some loose ends wearing some of his customers. He'll be a couple of hours."

A few minutes later, Ashley and her mother, wearing swimsuits they'd bought at the check-in counter, settled down in the hot tub. To hide her body, Ashley kept a towel wrapped around her shoulders. They were the only ones in the hot tub, although there was a young family with children in the swimming pool.

"These suits are pretty bad, aren't they?" Ashley said.

"I think they're the same kind they give to prison inmates," her mother said with a smile.

"I can't believe they can make a swimming suit out of paper," Ashley said.

"I hope there's no time limit to how long you can be in the water before they fall apart."

"That would be a problem, all right. What would we do?" Ashley asked.

"I'd yell fire and point that way, while you got up and ran the other way to our room to get us some clothes," her mother said.

"How about if I yell and you run?" Ashley asked with a grin.

"No, you can run faster than I can."

Ashley nodded. "If there'd ever be an incentive for me to run fast, that'd be it, all right."

"I agree."

After a long, awkward pause, her mother said, "This is strange, isn't it, for us to be to be in a hot tub with nothing to do."

"I keep waiting for you to tell me to clean the pool area."

"Let's pretend we're strangers and we're guests at the motel and we just happen to show up here at the hot tub at the same time. How would that go?"

"I don't know."

"What's your name?" her mother asked.

"Ashley."

"Where are you from?"

"Salt Lake City."

"That's in Utah, right?"

Ashley smiled. "Why, yes, it is."

"Are you a Mormon?"

"Yes, I am. My whole family is."

"What's it like growing up in a Mormon home in Utah?"

"I don't know how it is for others, but I know how it was for me," Ashley said.

"How was it for you?"

"Hard."

"Really? In what way?"

"So much was expected of me."

"In what way?"

"Every way."

"Could you be more specific?"

"Taking piano lessons . . . getting good grades . . . being at the top of my class . . . being popular . . . keeping my room clean . . . going to church . . . always doing the right thing . . ." Ashley's voice became more troubled with each item on her mental list. "Looking good so people will like me . . ."

"Excuse me. All these things you mentioned, are they part of the teachings of your church?"

Ashley shielded her face with her hand. "They might as well be."

"Why do you say that?" her mother asked.

"It's what's expected of us when we're growing up. We have to be the best at everything."

"Why?"

"I don't know why. We just do."

"Who checks up on you to make sure you're doing it?"

"Our parents. They're always after us to do better. They call it 'developing our talents.'"

"That doesn't sound too bad."

"Maybe not, but it never ends. As soon as you do what they ask on one thing, then they start up on something else."

"Like what?"

"Like writing in my journal . . . and going to seminary . . . and being polite when the home teachers come and . . ." She paused. "Do you want me to go on? There's a lot more I could name."

"I get the point," her mother said.

There was a galvanized bucket and a dipper next to Ashley. She picked it up and looked inside. It was nearly empty. Still clutching the towel around her upper body, she went over to a spigot on the wall, filled the bucket with cold water, brought it back, then settled back into the hot tub. "It got so I hated to come home because you'd be on me about something I hadn't done. It was like being caught between the jaws of a vise that keeps getting tighter and tighter."

"Oh, Baby, I never meant it that way. Don't you know how much I love you?"

"No, not really," Ashley said, picking up the dipper and filling it full of water, and then slowly pouring it back in the bucket. "I might have known that when I was just a little kid, but not anymore."

"Ashley, I'm sorry. I adore you. I thought you knew that."

"You do?"

"Yes, I do. I didn't say it enough, did I? I should have."

Her mother reached out to her and held her while they shed tears that dripped down their faces and into the hot tub.

A man and his two grandchildren came into the pool. Ashley pulled away. She hoped they wouldn't come in the hot tub.

They didn't. They went in the shallow end of the swimming pool.

After sitting quietly for a minute or two, Ashley's mother said softly, "I've got a confession to make. I've gone through most of my life feeling inadequate."

"Why?"

"I dropped out of college my freshman year. Most of the wives of our friends finished college."

"They're not any smarter than you," Ashley said.

"No, probably not, but they are more confident. I've thought about going back, but there's always been something in the way–family responsibilities and church callings. I never went back. I signed up for a correspondence course once, but I only did the first lesson. And then I quit. . . . You know the thing that worries me the most about your

214

father losing his job? That I'll have to go back to work. Not as a teacher . . . not as a secretary . . . because I don't have the training or education I'd need for those jobs. I have this horrible image of me working at a fast-food place and having one of the wives of our friends coming in and seeing me there. That would be bad enough . . . but if it happens, I'll probably mess up her order. 'Was that five fries and four Big Macs or four fries and five Big Macs?' And then she'll have to speak to the manager about me."

Ashley laughed. "Oh, Mom, that won't happen."

"How can you be so sure?"

"None of your friends go to McDonald's."

Her mother smiled through her tears. "That's very comforting to hear." She splashed Ashley.

"Don't."

Her mother splashed her again.

"I'm warning you, Mom. Don't mess with the tiger."

"Tiger?" her mother said with a big smile.

"You heard me right." Ashley thought about having a water fight with her mother, but she just couldn't bring herself to start it. It would be like writing on the Mona Lisa with crayons—it just wasn't done. And so the moment passed.

"I think I tried too hard to make sure you didn't make the same mistake I made—that you and Alauna would get to BYU, that you'd graduate first, before you even thought about getting married—that you'd know how special you were and wouldn't let anything stand in your way."

"Mom, are you saying you wish you hadn't married Dad?"

"No, that's not it. I love him. It's just that I wish I'd been a little older before I met him."

Ashley pulled the dipper out of the bucket and dumped it over her head. The coldness of the water made her let out a little yelp, but then it felt good to be cooled off again.

"That's not something you had control over, is it?"

"No, of course not. After we met, things progressed very fast. If we'd waited any longer to get married, well, . . . it would have been difficult."

"In what way?"

"We were so much in love that to have to say goodnight at the end of each day was almost more than either one of us could stand."

Ashley was still puzzled. "Why?"

"We both very much wanted to be physically intimate. Would you hand me the dipper please?"

Ashley had never been more embarrassed in her life. She felt her face turn warm. She poured some more cold water over her head, then filled the dipper again and handed it to her mother, who did the same thing.

"I'm sorry. Did that embarrass you? How about if I put it this way? We were very much in love, but, at the same time, we wanted to be worthy to be married in the temple. So we didn't have a long engagement."

"It's hard to think of you and Daddy being . . . you know . . . that way."

"I was your age when we got married."

"Well, okay, I guess that explains it." She paused. "Except . . ."

"Except what?"

"I can hardly imagine wanting to . . . you know . . . be intimate."

"I understand. I was the same way, until I fell in love with your dad."

"Can we move on to something else?" Ashley asked. "Because if we keep on this topic, I'll have to go fill the bucket again."

"Yes, of course." Her mother touched Ashley's shoulder and began to massage it lightly. "After we were married, we didn't have much money, so I quit school and went to work so your father could finish up. It was fine, really. I'm basically very happy." She paused. "It's just that when I was in high school, I always thought I'd finish college. That's all I'm saying."

"Okay, that makes sense," Ashley said.

"So maybe that's why I'm so intent on having you and Alauna finish college. But not only that. I'd like both of you to graduate from BYU."

"Why BYU? Are you trying to live your life over again through Alauna and me?"

Her mother thought about it. "I suppose that's a possibility."

"I'm not sure that's such a great idea."

"You're right. It isn't. I'll need to be careful from here on in. Turn around and I'll do your shoulders and neck."

Ashley turned her back to her mother, who massaged her shoulders through the wet towel. "That feels good, Mom."

"Your dad likes me to do it when he's had a hard day."

Ashley lowered her head and relaxed. "I can see why."

"It makes me want to cry, seeing how much weight you've lost."

"I'm still fat though."

"Do you know that some girls die from this, and on their death bed they still think they're too fat?"

"I've read that."

"I think you should realize that your perception of yourself is warped."

"Is it?"

"It is."

"Maybe so."

"What can I do to help you?" her mother asked.

"I'm not sure. To tell you the truth, I haven't really liked you very much the past year or so."

"Really?"

"I've thought of you as my enemy."

"Why?"

"Because nothing I did was ever good enough for you."

"And what about your father?"

"I hardly ever thought about him. He was totally clueless about me and my life. I wasn't sure he even cared about me. The only time he showed any interest in me was when you dragged him in to be some kind of token father. Whenever we had a family council, you coached him what to say beforehand, didn't you?"

"No."

"You did, Mom. I could hear you sometimes."

"I was just filling him in."

"He is my father, isn't he? So why did he need to be filled in? I mean it's not like he'd been away for a year. He and I lived in the same house. He should have known what was going on."

Ashley turned around to face her mother. "Do you want me to do you now?"

"That would be very nice."

Ashley tried to give the same kind of massage her mother had given her. The only problem was she didn't have as much strength in her hands. "Sorry. That's not very good, is it?"

"No, it's fine," she said, lowering her head. "It's very easy to be critical of your father, but . . . you don't know what it's been like for him at work."

"Why don't I know?"

"Because we didn't tell you."

"Why didn't you tell me?"

"We didn't want to worry you."

"I can't believe what we've become. We're living together in this big house, and each one of us is hurting, but nobody is talking to anyone else. I mean, why do we even call ourselves a family? I could get the same response living with strangers in a big apartment building where nobody ever speaks to anyone else."

Her mother had tears in her eyes. "Looks like I've pretty much made a mess of things."

217

"It's not you, Mom. It's all of us. We're all to blame."

"Yes, I suppose we are." Her mother grabbed a towel and dried her face. "Let's start over. From now on, let's be totally honest with each other. Agreed?"

"All right."

"Okay. How did your problem with eating start?"

"It started with a diet. I didn't want to be fat."

"But you were never fat."

"It didn't matter. If you hear someone being made fun of, it still affects you."

"How?"

"It makes you want to never be in the position to be made fun of." She paused. "And so I decided to go on a diet."

"What happened?"

"I lost a few pounds, and then I set a new goal. And then . . . it became an obsession." It was embarrassing to describe it, but Ashley went ahead.

"I discovered how good it felt to eat and then throw up. I could eat anything I wanted and as much as I wanted without any consequences. Then it got out of control. At first it gave me such a feeling of being in control . . . that this was something I had complete control over . . . but then it was the one in control. That's where I am now."

They might have talked longer but a salesman, bald, loud, and twenty decibels too cheerful, plopped himself down in the hot tub with them. "Plenty warm in here, isn't it?" he asked in a big friendly way. His hairy stomach protruded out into the hot tub.

Ashley and her mother soon escaped to their room to get ready for what lay ahead.

* * * * *

When Ashley and her parents arrived at the counseling center at Ricks College, there were already three students in the waiting room.

I wonder what they're here for, Ashley thought as she glanced quickly at the others. *The blonde looks like she could be anorexic. I'm not sure about the other girl though. And the boy? I have no clue about boys. Just as well, I suppose. When it comes to boys, it's better not to know.*

They're looking at me, wondering why I'm here. We're all so embarrassed to even be here. If you come here, it means you're totally messed up. Everybody knows that. At least I don't know any of them, so it's not going to get back to my roommates.

218

They're probably wondering why my parents are here with me. They're probably thinking this must really be serious.

A large man came out of his office with a folder from his previous client. He handed the folder to the secretary. "Ashley?" he asked.

Ashley and her parents stood up and followed him to his office. Once inside, he stuck out his hand. "I'm Dr. St. James."

They all shook hands then sat down in a semicircle.

"Well, what seems to be the trouble?" Dr. St. James asked.

"Ashley here has an eating disorder," her mother said.

"Is that true, Ashley?"

They were all staring at her. It wasn't the question that bothered her as much as the way it was asked. As if someone were to ask her if she was left- or right-handed. For some reason, she had always thought of her problem as something apart from who she was. Maybe because, at least at first, it was just going to continue until she lost ten more pounds. But that was twenty pounds ago.

"Ashley, did you hear the question?" Dr. St. James asked.

"Yes."

"Is it true that you have an eating disorder?"

After a long pause, she said, "Yes, it's true."

"So tell me why you came today."

"To get help."

"Would you likely have come here on your own?"

"You mean if my Mom and Dad hadn't come up here this weekend?"

"That's right."

"No."

"How come?"

"Because I didn't think it was that serious."

"What do you think now?"

"I think it's probably not a very good thing to do."

"You don't sound totally convinced."

"At first I thought it was a good way to lose weight."

"Now what do you think?"

Ashley pursed her lips. "I think that . . . maybe . . . it can get out of control, if you let it."

"Before we get together, then," Dr. St. James said, "I'd like you to have a complete medical examination, and then I'd like you to see a dietitian so you can know from an expert what exactly this can do to your body. And then come back and see me and we'll talk some more."

As they were leaving, Ashley looked to see if the three other students were still there. The girls were not, but the boy was still there.

A short time later, they pulled out of the parking lot.

"Where are you going now?" her mother asked.

"Back to the motel. We need to try to get a doctor's appointment and see about getting a dietitian to talk to Ashley."

They returned to the motel and informed the desk clerk they would be staying another day.

"First of all, I should probably phone my office and let them know I won't be in tomorrow," her dad said.

Ashley was sitting on the edge of the bed watching TV, more as a way to escape than anything else. Even though she could hear her dad on the phone, she pretended to be totally immersed in the program she was watching.

"Colleen, this is David. Look, we've got a situation in our family I need to work on, so I won't be in at all today, and maybe not tomorrow either . . . No, nothing serious . . . just something I have to take care of . . . well, all right, put him on."

There was a short pause and then, her father, his voice much more respectful, began to speak. "Yes, hello, Roger. That's right. I won't be in today for certain and probably not tomorrow either . . . Yes, well, I'm sorry you're disappointed . . . no, it's a family-related situation . . . I don't think I'd like to divulge any details to you, Roger, but it is very important. Why don't you have McPherson just take charge of my responsibilities? . . . Well, I'm sorry he's not ready for that . . . but this would be a good chance for him to show what he can do . . . No. I'm in Rexburg now, Roger, and even if we left now, I wouldn't make it back by the end of business today. I guess McPherson will just have to take care of it. Here, let me give you our number at the motel."

He gave their phone number and then listened a good long while. "Well, I'm sorry, too, Roger. I know how important the contract could be for us, but I've got a family emergency here, and, as a matter of fact, this is the first time I've missed work in over twenty years . . . Yes, I know you haven't been in the company for that long. I guess you'll just have to take my word for it, won't you? . . . No, I'm not coming in today. I thought I made that perfectly clear. No, not tomorrow either . . . Roger? . . . Roger?"

Her father looked in disbelief at the phone.

"What happened?" Christine asked.

"He hung up on me." He stood up. "I need to take a walk for a minute. Christine, while I'm gone, why don't you call around and see if you can get us an appointment with a doctor and with a dietitian." He put on his coat and walked out of the room.

Ashley stayed there for a minute but then got up and put on a coat and went out to find her father.

It was snowing hard and so taking a walk was all but impossible. Her dad was in front of the motel, standing under an arch, looking at the snow that was accumulating on the cars in the parking lot.

She came and stood next to him.

"You're mad, aren't you?" she asked.

"Not mad . . . I'm furious."

"How come?"

"After all I've done for them, this is the thanks I get. After I get their pea-brained adolescent replacement fully trained, they'll fire me. And that'll save them a lot of money. Probably all the extra money will go into a bonus for the one who fires me. And then they'll move on to another company. It's so unfair, sometimes I get so mad I could spit."

Ashley collected some saliva in her mouth and spit. "There, I did it for you."

He smiled and spit, too.

"Is that better?" she asked.

"Some, but it's not enough."

"We could throw snowballs at the cars in the parking lot," she suggested.

"The people who own the cars might not appreciate us doing that."

"It's new snow. We wouldn't actually hurt any of the cars."

He bent over and picked up some snow. "I'm not even sure I could hit a car with a snowball."

"There's only one way to find out," she said.

He made a snowball and threw it. And missed.

"You get three tries," she said. "I'll try, too."

It took them eleven throws before they improved their accuracy, just in time for Ashley's mother to see the snowball hit a windshield.

"What on earth are you two doing?"

"Throwing snowballs at cars," her dad said.

"You'll put out a windshield," she warned.

"We haven't yet," her dad said. "Actually, we've only hit one so far."

"It's fun. Want to try it?" Ashley said with a smile.

"This is so unfair," her mother said angrily.

"What's unfair?" Ashley asked.

"David, for years everything relating to the family was my responsibility. You were never around. I made all the decisions. I was the one who had to deal with everything. It wasn't easy, but I did it because I knew how busy you were. And now, after all these years, you finally decide you want to be a part of the family. So where does that leave me?

I end up the villain and you the hero. Well, it isn't fair. Where were you when I needed you? I could have used your help then. With you, your family is for fun and games. And that leaves me to do all the hard work and make all the hard decisions. Well, I think this whole thing stinks." In tears, she turned and walked quickly back inside.

"I'd better go talk to her," her father said.

"What do you want me to do?"

"Nothing. I just need to talk to her, that's all. Everything's changing so fast."

Ashley waited another five minutes and then went inside and sat at a table near the swimming pool, pretending to be interested in the play of children in the pool.

She waited for half an hour and then her dad came out to find her. "We'd like to have family council," he said.

She followed him back to their room. Her mother was sitting at a chair, her makeup streaked, her eyes bloodshot, with a box of tissues on the table, and a waste paper basket one-third full of used tissues nearby.

"I am not the villain, Ashley," her mother said. "I'm not the reason you're bulimic. So don't go around blaming me for that."

"I won't," Ashley said.

"You will, though. It's just human nature to blame someone else. So you'll blame me. But we all share in this. Your father, too."

"That goes without saying," her dad said. "Christine, you're right. I should have been a better father, and a better husband, but I wasn't, and I'm sorry for that."

He stood up and placed his hand on Christine's shoulders. "But we can change. We can all change, and I think we need to. Not just you, Ashley, but all of us."

The phone rang and her father answered it. "Hello . . . Roger? I'm sorry but I just can't get back tomorrow. Like I said, it's a family emergency . . . No, I'm not going to let my wife take care of it, Roger. That's what I've been doing all my life. This is something the two of us need to face together. Well, I guess that's up to you, Roger . . . I–." He listened for a moment longer, then quietly hung up the phone.

He sat, gazing numbly at the carpet for several long moments without speaking.

"What?" her mother asked.

"I've just been fired."

"Oh, no!" her mother said, bringing her hand to her mouth.

He ran the fingers of both hands through his hair. It may have made him feel better, but it also showed Ashley how little hair he had left on top.

"What do we do now?" her mother whispered.

Her dad took a deep breath, lifted his head, and, quite uncharacteristically, winked at Ashley and said, "I guess it could be worse."

"How?" Christine asked.

He smiled faintly. "Well, Ashley and I could've broken a windshield with a snowball."

20

Later that day, after several phone calls, they made appointments with a dietitian and a physician, and an appointment for the next day with Dr. St. James.

It was going to be two hours before the doctor's appointment, so they had a light lunch at the motel restaurant and then returned to their room. Ashley ate only a boiled egg and two crackers.

Back in their motel room, Ashley turned the TV on just to break the silence but kept the volume down so she could hear what her parents were saying.

"Are they going to keep you on payroll for a week or two?" Ashley's mother asked.

"No, I wouldn't think Roger would do that. I don't see him going out of his way for me."

"So we won't have any money coming in at all?"

"They'll have to pay me for some vacation time I didn't use."

"I can't believe he fired you. That is so unfair."

He shrugged his shoulders. "That's life. It may not be so bad. It might even be fun. It'll be like starting over again."

"We're too old to start over."

"We don't have a lot of choice, do we?"

"We may lose our home over this."

"That's true. Maybe we'll end up in a small apartment like we had when we first got married."

"I'd hate that."

"I'm not sure I would. Sometimes I feel like our possessions own us instead of the other way around. We'll get by one way or the other. We'll just have to work together to face our problems, whatever they are, whenever they come."

"This is a lot to cope with all at once."

"Yes, it is."

"You don't seem that stressed-out about it," her mother said.

Her father nodded. "The truth is, since the takeover, I've hated my job. They've put so many restrictions on the way we did business it just wasn't fun anymore. Maybe I'll start my own company and run things for once the way I want."

"If you do that, we won't have any money coming in, but plenty of money going out."

"I'll get a business loan."

"But what will we live on?"

"We have some savings," her father said.

"That won't last very long."

"It might not need to. I've got customers who I've done business with for years. They might switch over to me once they know I've started out on my own."

At least they're facing their problems, Ashley thought. *Maybe I should do the same thing with mine.*

An hour later Ashley was sitting in a patient examination room waiting with her mother for the doctor to show up. While her father stepped out of the room, she had changed into a hospital gown. With the two slits down the sides it covered her but was immodest enough for her to ask her father not to come in. He went to the waiting room.

The doctor came into the room, glanced at the chart, and said, "Ashley?"

"Yes."

"I'm Dr. Carruthers. What seems to be the problem?"

Ashley swallowed. "My parents think I have an eating disorder." She paused, then added, "Maybe I do."

"How long has this been going on?"

"About a year and a half."

"Why are you coming to get help now?"

"My mom and dad found out how bad it was, so they came up here to get me some help."

"And how do you feel about them doing that?"

She glanced at her mom. "At first I was mad at them for butting into my life . . ." She pursed her lips. "But now . . . I can see they're . . ." She let out a long, troubled sigh, "concerned . . . because it's taken over my life."

"I see."

"I've decided I want to stop."

"Why? To please your parents?"

"I suppose that's a part of it. I'm closer to my mom and dad now

225

than I've been for a long time." Again, a long pause. "But that's not the only reason . . ."

"Go on."

"It's all I think about anymore."

"And what do you want me to do today?"

"Make sure I'm okay . . . physically. Dr. St. James at Ricks College said it was something we needed to do."

"Do you have any idea why he might have suggested that?"

Tears started rolling down Ashley's cheeks. Her mother fumbled in her purse for a tissue and handed it to her.

"Ashley, did you hear the question?" Dr. Carruthers asked.

"To find out how much damage I've done to myself," she said quietly.

"That's right," the doctor said. "To find out how much damage you've done to yourself. Are you aware of some changes in your body because of what you've been doing?"

"I try not to think about it."

"But you're aware of some things, aren't you?"

"Yes."

"Like what?"

"I've lost some of my hair," she said quietly, her head down, her right hand over her face to avoid making eye contact with him.

"Anything else?"

"My teeth hurt whenever I eat something sweet."

"Why do you suppose that is?"

"I read once that stomach acids can dissolve tooth enamel."

"Anything else you've noticed about your physical condition?"

"I'm cold all the time, and I don't have any energy. Even walking is hard to do."

"Anything else?"

She barely whispered, "I haven't had a period for a long time."

"Anything else?"

"My heart is doing some kind of fluttering thing. I can't describe it, but it scares me whenever it happens."

The doctor nodded. "Well, we'll do a thorough examination, and I'll order some tests and some lab work, and then I'll send you over to a dentist, so he can assess what damage has been done to your teeth. So let's get started. Can you stand on this scale so I can weigh you?"

She looked at the scale as if it were a frightening monster. She didn't want her mother to know how much she weighed because she knew it would upset her. At the same time, she was afraid that if she stepped on the scales, she might have gained weight, and she knew that would depress her.

When she stepped on the scale and saw the reading, her immediate reaction was *I'm doing so good,* followed almost immediately by a feeling of guilt. By letting her mother and the doctor know how much she weighed, she felt as though she was betraying what had become the primary focus of her life.

"Good heavens, Ashley," her mother said, "it's a wonder you're still alive."

The doctor listened to her heart and lungs with his stethoscope, and then measured her blood pressure. And then he asked a long series of questions while making notes on a chart.

"Do you ever have chest pains?"

"Just the fluttering. And that's only when I push myself."

He wrote a long, detailed note, then continued the questioning.

"Weakness?"

"Yes."

"Fatigue?"

"Yes."

"Dizziness?"

"Yes."

"Let me have a look in your mouth."

He used a wooden tongue depressor and a light to look into her open mouth.

"The back of your throat is raw. Does it hurt?"

"Yes. It bleeds sometimes."

Her mother gasped.

"When did that start?"

"Just recently."

"Do you ever have headaches?"

"Yes."

"How often?"

"Almost every day."

"What about abdominal pain?"

"Yes, almost every day, but especially when I'm under a lot of tension."

"What's the most times you've binged and purged in a day?"

She looked at her mother, ashamed to answer the question.

Her mother touched her arm. "It's okay. We're all in this together. We're a team now."

She sighed. "Twelve times."

"In a day?" the doctor asked, trying to be objective and nonjudgmental, but still his eyebrows raised a tiny bit, reflecting his surprise.

"Yes."

"I see. Well, it's good you want to turn this around. Very good indeed."

Fifteen minutes later the doctor turned her over to a nurse for lab work.

An hour later Ashley felt she'd given a sample of every liquid in her body.

Next they drove to the hospital to see a dietitian.

Shannon Baker seemed much too cheerful and too young to be a dietitian. Ashley expected a dietitian would be a no-nonsense, middle-aged woman with her hair in a bun who spent her professional life saying, "You shouldn't eat that." But Shannon, not much over twenty-five, had a quick, easy smile and a confident manner. She shook hands with Ashley's parents then turned to Ashley. "So, Ashley, how you doing today?"

"Okay, I guess."

"That's great." She sat down next to Ashley, looked her in the eye and smiled. "What can I do for you?"

"I'm not sure. Dr. St. James at the counseling center at Ricks suggested I meet with a dietitian."

"Why?"

This time she experimented with saying it right away. "Because . . . because I have an eating disorder." Each time she said it, it got easier.

"I see. What do you think I'm going to tell you?"

"I don't know."

She laughed. "When you go to a doctor, you sort of know what's going to happen. Or if you go to a lawyer, you can almost guess what they'll say. But nobody knows what a dietitian does."

"What do you do?"

"What I'll try to do for you is to blow apart all the wrong ideas you have about food. You spend a great deal of time thinking about food, just like me. The only trouble is you've probably got some false notions about food. It's my job to educate you." She smiled, "Don't worry. I'm not going to tell you to eat your green beans. Let's get started, okay?"

Ashley liked Shannon's casual friendliness combined with her obvious expertise.

She began to fill out a questionnaire. "Let's go through this. Do you consider yourself fat?"

She looked at her mom and dad trying to decide what their reaction would be if she told the truth.

Shannon caught the glance. "Mom, Dad, do you think I could go through this with just Ashley? There's a waiting room just down the hall. I'll come and get you when we're done."

Her parents left.

"Now, it's just you and me. It will speed things up tremendously if you're honest with me as we go through this."

Ashley nodded.

"Do you think of yourself as fat?"

"Yes."

"Thank you. Answer this honestly, too, please. Is it ever okay to eat foods containing fat?"

"No."

"So, basically no fat, right?"

"Yes."

"Is it true that fat in food makes a person fat?"

"Yes."

"If you got on the scale tomorrow and found that you'd gained two pounds, would you panic?"

"Yes!" She said emphatically.

"Do you think that certain foods are bad?"

"Yes."

"Do you keep a lot of your fears about food and eating to yourself because you're afraid no one would understand?"

"Yes."

Shannon went through a long list of questions, recording Ashley's answers along the way.

"Thank you. You know what? I think you were honest. That's very good. Okay, the next thing is I want to try out some new software. In order to do that, I need you to first change into these leotards, so I can take a picture of you. Then I'll download it into the computer. And then you can see how you'd look at different weights. We have a dressing room where you can change."

A few minutes later Ashley emerged from the dressing room, wearing the leotard. She felt self-conscious and folded her arms in an effort to cover her chest and stomach.

"Okay, stand on the white line there, look at me, and I'll take your picture. Just let your hands hang down normally."

Shannon took two photos with her digital camera and then downloaded them.

They sat next to each other in front of the computer. And a short time later a picture of Ashley appeared on the screen, along with her height and weight.

"Okay, here's how you look now. If you do a right-click, like this, it shows what you can and cannot do at your current weight."

Ashley right-clicked the mouse. The screen listed:

Ashley:

Cannot engage in physical activity without feeling faint.

Often has headaches.

Cannot concentrate for more than short periods of time.

"Okay, now you can use the arrow key to go up or down in weight, whichever way you'd like to go."

Ashley scrolled down five pounds and then pushed Enter.

A new picture of her appeared on the screen. She didn't look much different.

"I'll leave you to play the game. I've got some paperwork to catch up on."

Shannon left Ashley alone with the software.

Ashley was excited at first that she could see what she'd look like at any weight she chose. She went down in weight five pounds at a time not bothering to notice what the limitations on her lifestyle would be at each weight.

At fifteen pounds less than her current weight, an alarm sounded. Shannon came out of her office.

"Did I do something wrong?" Ashley asked.

"Oh that. Don't worry about that. It just means you've died, that's all. Oh, one other thing, be sure to right-click the mouse on each weight."

Ashley chose five pounds above the weight she would die at. She looked carefully at the image on the screen and was disappointed to see her thighs still looked fat. She right-clicked the mouse.

There was only one line to the limitations. "Bedridden. Life expectancy: one year."

It's just trying to scare me, she thought.

She scrolled up to her present weight. Even at her present weight, her life expectancy was listed as limited. And one of the notations was that she might not be able to conceive or have a baby. She hadn't thought about that, and seeing it stated on the screen shocked her. It had always been her expectation that she would get married someday and have children.

She continued going up in weight by five pounds each time. It wasn't until she reached twenty pounds above her current weight that there were no abnormalities listed or limitations on how long she might live.

She went up and down in weight, seeing her future change back and forth.

After half an hour, Shannon came back. "How you doing?"

"Okay."

"Well, what do you think?"

"It was interesting."

"Did you learn anything from all this?"

"Yeah, I did."

"What did you learn?"

"That if you keep losing weight, eventually it will kill you."

"That's right. What else?"

"That if you lose a lot of weight, you give up things you can do, like sports, or even having enough energy to get through the day."

"So, in other words, there's a price to be paid."

"Yes."

"Have you ever thought about that before?" Shannon asked.

"No, not really. I thought I just needed to keep losing weight."

"Until?"

"I don't know. It was always . . . lose more weight."

"So, where would that have ended?"

Ashley stared numbly at the keyboard. "Eventually it would have killed me."

"That's right. And even if you'd stopped short of that, what would it have done to the quality of your life?"

"I don't understand."

"Would you be able to live an active life weighing twenty pounds less than you weigh now?"

"No."

"Are you able to live the kind of active life you'd like to live at the weight you're at now?"

"I do okay."

"Can you run up a flight of stairs?"

Ashley thought about it. "No. I can hardly walk up stairs without stopping to catch my breath."

"How much time do you suppose most people spend thinking about food?"

"A lot."

"That's not true, Ashley. Most people think about food only before they sit down to a meal, and, also, while they're eating. The rest of the time they think about other things."

That was a revelation to Ashley.

"How much time do you spend thinking about food?"

Ashley pursed her lips, turned her gaze to the floor, and wiped a tear from her eye. It was painful to admit. "All the time—from the minute I get up to when I fall asleep at night."

"Isn't that interesting? If you eat normally, you don't give much thought to food. If you have an eating disorder, that's all you think about."

Ashley nodded her head.

"Isn't there anything else you'd like to think about other than food?"

"Yes."

"What?"

"My life."

"Like what?"

"My mom and dad . . . school . . . my friends . . . my religion . . . things like that."

With her parents back in the room, Shannon explained about the food pyramid, about basic nutrition, and about intuitive eating. She spent considerable time talking about fat—explaining how unsaturated fats like those found in olive oil are necessary to give hair a natural sheen and improve the texture of skin and hair and fingernails and to lower cholesterol.

"The last thing in the world I want you to do is to focus on dieting, watching fat grams, or counting calories. Basically, if you eat the way your mom has taught you, you'll be in pretty good shape. I'd like to see you at least once a week, just to see how you're doing, and to answer any questions you might have. If you'd like, we can set up a time now."

After they left the hospital, Ashley's folks took her to lunch. Even after all Shannon had taught her about nutrition, Ashley still found it nearly impossible to find something to order. She couldn't bring herself to eat any food she had come to think of as fatty, such as chicken or any kind of meat. Anything with carbohydrates in it, like spaghetti, was also out of the question. She knew, too, that if she were to eat something like fries or cornbread with butter and honey that she wouldn't be able to keep it down. Even with her parents there, she'd end up in the bathroom, having to purge.

"Have you folks decided?" the waitress asked.

Her dad looked at Ashley. "You ready yet?"

"Maybe I'll do the salad bar."

She fully expected her mother to say, "Oh, you need something more substantial than that." But she didn't.

While they were waiting for their food, her mother said, "Your father talked to Roger on the phone while you were in with Shannon."

232

Ashley turned to her dad. "What'd he say?"

"He said they needed me to come into work and straighten out the mess McPherson has made with me gone."

"What did you tell him?"

"I told him he should have thought about that before he fired me."

Ashley smiled. "What'd he say to that?"

"He said he wanted me to work there another month to do some training."

"What did you say?"

Her dad smiled. "I said I have more important things to do than that. He got mad and threatened a lawsuit. I told him, after you fire a person and tell him to clear out his desk, he has no more obligation to work for you. That made him mad, so he hung up on me."

"So?"

"So we'll stay here with you for as long as we need to."

"That's good. Thanks."

After lunch they went to a dentist, who examined Ashley's teeth. He confirmed what Ashley already suspected. She'd lost some tooth enamel. It would cost a lot of money to fix, but with her father out of work, and their insurance situation unclear, they would have to postpone doing anything about it.

She felt guilty for being such a burden on her family.

And then they returned to the counseling office at Ricks to talk to Dr. St. James. "What have you got for me, Ashley?" he asked.

"I want to change."

"You're sure?"

"Yes."

"How come?"

"Because . . . it's not good for me to do. And I'm scared." She paused. "And also . . . because my mom and dad are helping me."

"That's important to you, isn't it?"

"Yeah, it is."

"That's really good."

"My dad . . . got fired from his job because he wouldn't leave here and go back to work today."

"Well, there's more to the story than that," her dad said.

"But when it came to choosing your family or keeping your job, you chose your family," Ashley said.

"So you're out of a job?" Dr. St. James asked.

"Temporarily. It's no problem. The company was going to downsize in a few months anyway. This is just a little earlier than I expected, that's all."

"My folks and I have had some good times since they've been here," Ashley said. "We made a snow family during a snowstorm in West Yellowstone on Saturday." She knew that sounded kind of trivial, and she quickly added, "That was good because we got to talk."

"Sounds great," Dr. St. James said.

"It was," Ashley said.

"What else has happened?"

"I'm trying to be more a part of the family," her dad said.

"And how's that working?"

"It's going to take some getting used to," Christine said. "When you've gone so long being the one who made all the decisions, it's hard to change."

"Brother Bailey, you might try having every family decision go through you for a week. And then tell me how it turns out." He paused. "Oh, I guess I'd better find out. Will you be able to meet with Ashley and me next week?"

"Yes, of course," her dad said.

"Excellent," Dr. St. James said.

"Well, Ashley, I think you're off to a good start."

"I think so, too."

"I'd like to talk to Ashley alone for a few minutes, if I may," Dr. St. James said.

"Yes, of course," her mother said. And then her parents left.

"How are you feeling right now?"

"I'm not sure . . . scared, I guess."

"And that's because?"

"I'm not sure I can quit." She sighed. "I'm not sure I even want to change. I do, but then, when I think about it, I'm not so sure."

"I understand. Any change is hard to do. It's up to you, really, isn't it?"

"Yes, I guess it is."

Ashley had never been with anyone who seemed so willing to listen.

"I do want to change, though."

"Okay."

"Do you want me to promise I won't ever binge and purge again?"

"No, I'll never ask that of you."

She'd been staring at the floor. His answer surprised her enough that she looked up at him. "Why not?"

"It's too much to ask, especially now."

"What do you want me to do then?"

"Let's just see if we can find out what's happening. Keep track of

234

the times you throw up between now and our next visit. When you threw up, how was your day? What feelings were you experiencing just before then? Maybe you could write it down, and then we'll talk about it when you come in. The reason for doing this is to see if we can understand the relationship between your eating disorder and your emotions."

"That's all?"

"That's all for now."

"I thought you'd tell me what a disgusting habit this is."

He shook his head. "You're not an eating disorder, and you're not disgusting."

A few minutes later Dr. St. James asked her parents to come in. And they talked some more.

The arrangement they made was that Ashley would visit with Dr. St. James twice a week, once alone and once with her parents. That was in addition to her weekly visits with Shannon at the hospital, and once every two weeks with the doctor, so he could monitor her physical condition.

They left the counseling office.

"We can stay here in Rexburg for as long as you'd like," her dad said.

"I think I'll be okay here by myself until you come back," Ashley said.

"You sure?"

"Yeah, I think so."

"Well, all right, I do need to take care of some things—clean out my desk and make some inquiries about starting up on my own. If you think you'll be all right, maybe we'll head back home."

"Thank you for everything," Ashley said.

"Hey, no problem," her dad said. He looked at her, then took her into his arms. He held her for a long moment, then reached to draw her mom into their embrace. The three of them stood together, holding each other, saying nothing.

After a time, he said, "I think we'll go down to Provo and see how Alauna is doing. What do you say, Mother?"

Christine smiled. "That might be good."

Although she had agreed that her parents should go home, Ashley felt vulnerable watching them drive off, knowing that what happened from then on was up to her.

It was all good to have great expectations about how her life was going to change, but the fact was she couldn't escape her feelings about food. From the moment she walked into her apartment, there were decisions to be made. What would she eat, and when would she eat it? How much?

Also, she couldn't suddenly throw out the fear she had about certain foods.

She made it through supper by resorting to a boiled egg and dry toast, eaten alone, after everyone else had finished and left the apartment for the library.

She felt like she was walking a tightrope blindfolded—one small slip, and she'd be back to where she'd been, with no one to talk to, and nobody she could ask for help.

She was, once again, isolated and alone, slowly eating one hard-boiled egg and one dry piece of toast, wondering if she could get it down without involuntarily throwing it all up again.

She thought about praying, but she wasn't sure if her words would even get out of the room.

God must hate me, she thought. *Or at least not want to have anything to do with me. I don't blame him. I won't even ask him for help. I got into this by myself. I'll have to get out of it by myself.*

I remember at girls camp being told that God loved us. I could believe he loved the other girls, but I couldn't believe he loved me. And I still can't believe that. But even if he doesn't care for me that much, maybe he wouldn't mind giving me someone who could help me get better. I don't expect any miracle or anything like that, but if he could just help me a little, so I don't end up dying.

She threw up once that night. She had been able to keep her egg and toast down, but when her roommates came home with a cake and ice cream to celebrate one of their birthdays, she had eaten a little with them. Then, feeling guilty and afraid she was going to get fat, she went in the bathroom and turned on the shower, threw up, then took a shower.

Afterward she felt depressed and discouraged. *Nothing has changed, nothing at all. Everything is the same as before.*

She sat down at her desk and grabbed an old notebook and found the first empty page and wrote the date, then stared at the page as she tried to remember how she'd felt just before throwing up.

I felt fat.

That's all that would come.

* * * * *

She and her parents met with Dr. St. James the next week, on a Friday afternoon.

"How did you do this week?" her father asked hopefully.

"Real good," she said with a cheery smile, but it was a lie because she knew that what her father meant was *Did you throw up during the week?* And she had. Several times. In spite of meeting with Dr. St. James.

Dr. St. James raised his eyebrows at her answer, but he didn't say anything.

"I'm so proud of you," her father said.

She couldn't let it stand. "Actually, I had a few problems," she said softly.

"You threw up?" her mother asked. "How many times?"

"Don't ask me how many times I puked during the week!"

Her parents were shocked at her outburst.

Her mother thought they had solved the problem. "Ashley. We had an agreement," her mother said. She turned to Dr. St. James. "I really think it would be better if she were at home with us. Don't you agree?"

"Actually, I don't agree," he said.

"So you're just going to let her keep on doing this, is that right?" her mother asked.

"We're making progress."

"Well, that's all fine and good," her father said, "but what if she dies first?"

Dr. St. James paused, then said, "Ashley, maybe it would help if I talked to your mom and dad alone. Can you give us a few minutes? I'll come and get you when we're done."

Ashley left.

"You want to make her stop doing this, don't you?" Dr. St. James asked.

"Yes, of course."

"Well, the truth is, you can't stop her. So don't even try."

Ashley's mother gaped at him. "What do you want us to do, just sit around and do nothing?" she asked.

"No, you just be the mom and dad, and let me worry about the eating disorder."

"But I can't see that she's making any progress."

"This is a long process. Throwing up is just the tip of the iceberg. If we only concentrate on what she eats and whether or not she keeps it down, we'll overlook the underlying reasons why she's doing it, and she's doomed to fail."

"So why is she doing this to herself?" her father asked.

"That's what she and I have to find out, but it will take time."

"Well, all right, we'll give it time, but will you tell us if she gets to the point where it's time to put her in an inpatient facility?" her father asked.

"Yes, of course."

Ashley's mother slowly nodded her head. "All right, we'll give it time."

"I'm glad you're concerned enough to ask Ashley how she's doing, but you might think about asking questions like, Are you making progress? Are you feeling okay? Are you angry with us? Are we giving you the kind of support you need? I think she might be willing to answer those kinds of questions."

"All right, we'll try to do that from now on," her father said.

Dr. St. James stood up. "I'd like to talk to Ashley alone for a few minutes, and then I'll bring you in and we'll talk some more."

They left and Ashley came back in.

"What did you tell my mom and dad?"

"I told them to be patient."

"Oh," she said softly, nodding her head. "I was wondering what you'd say."

"That's what I told them."

"Are they disappointed in me?"

"I don't know. I guess you'll have to ask them."

"They are. I know they are."

"Why?"

"Because I didn't stop—you know, doing it."

"Did you keep track of the times you binged and purged?"

"Yes, I did. I wrote it all down."

"May I look at it?"

She handed him her notebook. "It's in here. I put a paper clip where I started keeping track."

He turned to the page that had a paper clip on it and read what she'd written.

She waited for him to finish. The afternoon sun was making its way across the floor of his office. She wondered why she felt so comfortable and at ease in his presence. *It's because he listens.*

Time seems to slow to a crawl when I'm here. It's almost like time doesn't exist and that he has as much time as he needs to talk to me. And yet I know that's not true. He has other people coming, and yet he never makes me feel like I have to hurry up for him.

After carefully reading everything she'd written, he looked up. "Were there any more times that you purged that you didn't write down?"

"No."

"So this is all?"

"Yes."

"Was it hard to write it down after each time?"

"Yes, it was."

"Why?"

"I was embarrassed that you'd know that I'd messed up. I thought about not telling you all the times I did it."

"So I'd be proud of you?"

"Yes."

"And, also, so your folks would be proud of you?"

"Yes."

"What would have happened if you had misrepresented what really happened?"

"It wouldn't have done me any good," she said softly. She folded her arms tight to her chest and rested her head on the back of the chair and looked up at the ceiling. A section of acoustical tile, four feet across, had been water damaged. She wondered when it had happened.

"That's right. It wouldn't have done you any good. Nice insight." Dr. St. James glanced down again at what she had written.

"Let's see. The first time it happened, you wrote you'd had some ice cream and cake, and that you felt fat. Is that right?"

"Yes."

"Fat like Santa Claus? That doesn't sound so bad. I mean, he's fat, and he's jolly."

Ashley laughed. "No, not like that."

"What is it like to feel like you're fat?"

"I feel disgusted at myself."

"Why?"

"I don't know. I just know it's a terrible feeling."

"Maybe this week you can try to expand on your feelings. Be more specific. How about that?"

"I'll try."

That evening Ashley and her parents drove to Jackson Hole, Wyoming, and checked into a motel. The next day they toured the shops in town and then went out to watch the skiers.

"We should all go skiing," Ashley said.

"Oh, no, I'd fall and break my leg," her mother said.

"You could take lessons."

"That would be fun," her dad said with a look of sadness in his eyes.

Ashley knew what it was. "We don't have very much money now, do we?"

"We're fine," her dad said. "It's just that we have to watch things a little more carefully than we used to, that's all."

"Sure, that's fine, it was just a thought," Ashley said. She felt bad being such a burden on her family.

Her dad hugged her. "We can have plenty of fun without spending a lot of money."

"Sure, we can."

They tried. But surrounded by skiers, the contrast between what they could afford to do and what everyone else was doing was almost too much.

"Let's go back to the motel and sit in the hot tub," Ashley suggested. "That doesn't cost any money."

And that's what they did.

"Ashley, are you going to let Jen know what's going on in your life?" her mother asked.

"I don't think so."

"Why not?"

"I'm sure she doesn't want to have anything to do with me."

"Of course she does."

"Not after I missed Nathan's sister's funeral," Ashley said.

"Why don't you let me talk to Jen," her mother said.

"Well, you can talk to her, but I know it won't do any good."

They went to church in Jackson Hole and then drove back to Ricks. After lunch, her parents left for home.

On Monday, Jen called Ashley from Orem. It was awkward at first, but they gradually got going and talked for nearly an hour. It seemed just like old times.

21

One week later, at two o'clock on a Friday afternoon, Ashley stood at the window and looked out at another dreary winter day. Her bag was packed and standing by the door, as well as a plastic bag of celery, carrots and cherry tomatoes for snacking on.

She felt nervous, but at the same time, excited because Nathan and Jen were picking her up and driving her back to Utah for Nathan's farewell on Sunday.

This could be really good for me. We'll be together again, she thought, *and it will be like it was in the beginning, because Nathan is going on a mission, so Jen and Nathan will have to pull away a little because they're going to be away for such a long time.*

Nathan and Jen are the only ones I can really open up to, the only ones who really understand me. They know the worst about me and yet they're still my friends. That means a lot to me.

She looked at her watch. *They should've been here a half hour ago. There's no telling when they'll get here.*

Maybe they won't come. Maybe all this was just some cruel joke they decided to play on me.

No, they'll be here.

But even if they come, it won't be the same. Nathan must hate me because of not going to his sister's funeral.

There's some ice cream in the fridge. I saw it there last night. It's not mine but it's been there for a long time. I have time to eat a little of it. Not all of it. Just a little.

She shook her head. It was back again. No matter how hard she tried, it always came back—the inner voice that tried to get her to binge. She wasn't sure how she'd created it, but it talked to her, as if it were a separate individual, apart from her. And yet she knew it came from her mind. And because it came from her mind, she hoped she could gain control over it.

When have I ever eaten a tiny bit of ice cream? she asked in her mind. *Never. Or at least not recently. No, I'll leave the ice cream in the fridge.*

This will be your last chance to binge all weekend. You'd better take advantage of it.

No.

At least just go to the freezer and see if the ice cream is still there.

No.

It may be so old it has freezer burn. If that's the case, it might as well be thrown out. You should take it out and take a taste to see if it's still any good.

No.

Nathan hates you. Jen is only doing this because your mother asked her to do it. That's the only reason. You're going to have a rotten weekend.

No.

If you want to prove you're over this, then just take a taste of the ice cream and then put it back, and then you'll know you don't have a problem anymore.

No. I won't do it. Not now and not later today. And not tomorrow.

You're going to do it. It's just a matter of time. So you might as well do it now.

She stood up, grabbed her things and left the apartment, deciding to wait outside on the first floor by the entrance.

This is a mistake. I never should have agreed to do this. I just want to be alone, to be by myself, and not have to talk to people.

She closed her eyes. *The truth is I miss bingeing. I miss being all by myself and not having to talk to people. It's harder this way. I'll probably make a complete fool of myself this weekend. I'll say the wrong thing, and people will make fun of me. Or else I'll totally alienate both Nathan and Jen. There's so many things that could go wrong. I'd be better off in the apartment by myself making pancakes and watching movies.*

I might be able to quit doing it, but I'll never quit thinking about it. Whatever bad things you can say about it, it did fill some of my needs.

I hope I don't say anything stupid this weekend.

I wish I were back in my room eating ice cream. I'm not doing that anymore though. Because it's not good for me. I know now how bad it was for me. So I'm moving on and leaving that behind me.

Besides, if I did it, then I'd have to write it down, and talk about my feelings just before doing it. I'm tired of doing that all the time.

Even so, though, I miss it. Like now. When I'm not sure what's going to happen. When I have to talk with people and don't know what to say. Like Nathan's family. Do they know why I didn't come to the funeral? Will they be talking about me behind my back?

242

How is Nathan going to treat me, knowing what I did instead of going to his sister's funeral?

Why did I ever agree to do this when I could have spent the weekend by myself, not worried about saying the wrong thing.

Just then a car pulled up to the curb and Nathan and Jen got out, ran to her and gave her a group hug.

"*Buon giorno! Buon giorno, la mia ragazza!*" Nathan boomed out in his Italian voice.

"*Buon giorno, il mio ragazzo!*" Ashley, in tears of happiness, answered back.

"*Buon giorno, Ashley!*" Jen called out, throwing her arms around Ashley.

"How do you say . . . ?" Nathan said in English with an Italian accent . . . "it's so good to be together again?"

"All right!" Jen said, pumping her fist. "The terrific threesome is back!" She looked at Ashley's suitcase. "You ready to go?"

"I am."

"Before we go, let's do 'Oh Antonio!' on campus," Nathan suggested.

"I brought the dresses, just in case," Jen said.

"And I have the topcoat and the mustache in the car too," Nathan said.

"Let's do it, Babe!" Jen said, breaking out with a mischievous laugh.

"Well, I guess we could," Ashley said.

"Yes!" Jen shouted. "Look out, Ricks College, 'cause here we come!"

They hauled their costumes to an out-of-the-way set of rest rooms in the basement of one of the classroom buildings. Only one girl came in while Jen and Ashley were making themselves up, and she didn't stay long.

Twenty minutes later they left the building on their way to do *Oh, Antonio* at the Manwaring Center, the social hub for students at Ricks College.

"Okay, girls, crank it up," Nathan said softly.

"Oh, Antonio!" Jen cried out, giving Nathan a big kiss on his cheek.

"*Grazie, grazie,*" Nathan said.

"Oh, Antonio!" Ashley cried out, giving Nathan a kiss on the other cheek.

Nathan put his arms around the two girls and pulled them close to him as they continued on their way. "*Non ho un elenco dei campeggi!*" he called out. ("I don't have a list of campsites.")

They sauntered through the Manwaring Center with the two girls clinging to Nathan, Ashley on his left, Jen on his right. They paused

243

every few feet so Nathan could shout out something in Italian, which would cause the girls to laugh hilariously, and cry out, "Oh, Antonio, Antonio!" And then they each leaned to kiss him on the cheek.

Students ignored them from the front and only stared at them after they passed.

Five minutes later they were done. They hurried back to the car and drove away.

"That was great," Nathan said, pulling off his mustache. "Just like it used to be."

"I think one of the girls recognized me," Ashley said.

"So what?" Jen asked.

"Right, so what?" Ashley said.

"You know what? Sometimes I wish I really was Antonio, and that girls clung to me and thought everything I said was really clever and funny."

"Well, you are pretty funny sometimes," Ashley said.

"Girls don't cling to me though," he complained.

"I cling to you," Jen said.

"Yeah, that's true. But . . . it's not universal."

"How many do you want clinging?" Jen asked.

"I'd just like to be thought of as terribly talented and witty. But the older I get, the less outstanding I am. I had such high hopes for me when I was in high school. But now after a year in college, I've decided I'm about average."

"You mean about average at BYU, don't you?" Jen asked.

"Yeah, I guess so."

"When they were in high school, everyone at BYU was considered to be smart or gifted in some way," Jen said. "So when you all get together, you might be average in that group, but you're still outstanding."

Nathan thought about it and then nodded his head. "You're right. I shouldn't feel so bad. But I'll never be an Antonio."

"And we'll never be mindless bimbos clinging to a fool," Jen said.

"In a way, you know, it's too bad," Nathan said with a slight smile.

"Too bad for you. Not for us," Ashley said.

"You're right. Actually, I wouldn't even want that. But, you know what, having you two in my life in high school was the best thing that ever happened to me." ✳

"We did have a fun time together, didn't we?" Jen said.

"Until . . . well . . . until . . . ." Nathan said.

"Until you two fell in love," Ashley said. "I'm okay with that now.

244

Really, I am. It was too much to hope for that we could stay friends, the three of us, all the way through high school."

"I think it would have been better for you if we had," Jen said to Ashley.

Ashley felt a deep sense of loss for what she'd been through, but she knew full well that she couldn't change the past. She sighed and said, "Well, probably so, but I've learned and grown. I'm doing better now."

"That's really good," Jen said.

"You bet, that's great, Ashley," Nathan said. "Way to go."

They stopped at a gas station to change. There was hardly enough room for two people in the women's rest room, so Ashley changed first. When she came out, Jen went in to change. Nathan was standing next to the car, waiting.

"I really like the way you look now, Nathan." Ashley said.

"Really? Thanks. I was kind of weird-looking in high school wasn't I?"

She sighed. "Everyone is."

"I guess so."

A short time later they were on the road heading south, with Nathan at the wheel. After a few miles, he began to yawn.

"Want me to drive?" Ashley asked.

"I'm okay."

"I'm not tired. Really."

"Well, okay." He pulled over.

A minute later Nathan and Jen were in the backseat.

"I promise not to look," Ashley teased, adjusting the rearview mirror and smiling at her friends.

"You can look all you want," Jen said. "Nothing's going to be happening. The truth is, we're kind of shifting gears right now."

A few minutes later Ashley did look in the rearview mirror. Nathan and Jen were both asleep, sitting close together, their heads laid back on the seat.

They really do look good together, Ashley thought. Nathan had grown a couple of inches and put on a few pounds, and he was starting to look more like a man instead of a boy.

Jen had always been attractive but, at UVSC, had learned to show off the beauty in her face to good advantage.

She's using makeup now, Ashley thought. *I wonder who taught her that. Her eyes almost jump out at you. And she doesn't go in for extremes in clothes like she used to, so that's good.*

They both seem older than me somehow. I wonder why that is. They seem more accepting of themselves than I am. I feel like I'm still back in ninth grade socially. She sighed. *It's the eating disorder that's done it. I just quit maturing socially. I have so much to catch up on.*

After leaving Pocatello, Ashley knew they'd soon pass the motel where she'd stayed during the time of Nathan's sister's funeral.

I need to let Nathan know how bad I feel.

Forty minutes later she took the exit, and, a few minutes later, pulled in front of the cabin she'd stayed in.

Nathan and Jen woke up. "Why did we stop?"

"Get out of the car, you two. I need to show you something."

Still groggy from their nap, they got out of the car.

"This is where I was when I should have been at the funeral," Ashley said.

"Oh," Nathan said.

"Nathan, I'm ashamed of what I did. I wish I could live that part of my life over."

"I know. It's okay. Really."

"I hope someday you'll forgive me."

He reached for her hand and looked into her eyes with kindness. "I forgive you now."

"I . . . wasn't myself . . . for a while . . . but I'm better now."

"I can see that."

Ashley let out a big sigh of relief. "Every time I pass this place, I'll remember what happened here."

"When you do, remember what happened here today, too," Jen said. "That you apologized, and that we told you we still love you."

"I will. That will soften it." She touched Jen on the shoulder and then Nathan.

"You know what? I feel like I can talk to you guys about anything. I've never felt comfortable revealing my thoughts. I keep everything inside. That's part of my problem."

"We'll always be here for you," Jen said.

"I hope you'll write me on my mission," Nathan said.

"Are you kidding? Of course I will. You know that."

"And if I can help, please let me know how you're doing. I'll do anything I can for you," Jen said.

"You've already done a lot for me by still being friends, even after not being at your sister's funeral."

"Don't worry about it." He put his arms around her and pulled her close to him, and then, so there'd be no misunderstanding, did the same with Jen.

Jen looked up at him with a mischievous grin and said softly, "Oh, Antonio."

Nathan was embarrassed. "Are we ready to go?" Nathan asked.

"Yeah, let's go," Ashley said.

With Nathan driving, Ashley sat in the backseat, looking out at the shades of dull brown and white passing by as they continued on their way.

Nathan looked at Ashley in the rearview mirror. "How's your family doing these days?"

"My dad's out of work."

"That's hard to believe," Jen said. "I mean, he always worked so hard."

"Yeah, he did." Ashley paused. "My folks might have to sell our house."

"That's awful," Jen said.

"I know. It is. It's a nice place, and everything, but . . . I don't know . . . it brings back memories."

"From when you were . . . ?" Nathan asked.

"Yeah."

"What's your dad going to do?"

"I don't know."

"That must be hard on him."

"Yeah, I guess so. He doesn't talk about it much."

"Just like you, right?" Nathan asked.

"I guess so . . . but I'm getting better. Jen, how are Billy James Dean and your mom getting along?"

"Okay, I guess," Jen said. "To tell you the truth, I don't see them much anymore."

"How come?"

"I can't live in the same house with him being married to my mom."

"Why not?"

"It's just too weird. He wears these gaudy bright red silk pajamas that he swears were given him by the emperor of Japan. And he has my mom wearing a kimono. After one night in the house after their honeymoon, I decided I was never going back there to live. And I still can't see why my mom married him. I mean, doesn't the church mean anything to her? She just goes along with whatever man comes into her life. What is wrong with her anyway?"

"She's married to him though," Ashley said.

"So?"

"So marriage is honorable, isn't it?"

"Not to him it isn't."

247

"So do you even call to see how your mom is doing?" Ashley asked.

"Not really. She doesn't need me anymore. She's got Billy James Dean."

"I really think you should keep in touch with your mom."

"You're probably right. I think I will . . . sometime."

Two hours later they pulled into Ashley's driveway. Nathan helped her carry her things to the doorstep, and then left.

Ashley stepped in and called out, "I'm home! Anybody here?"

There was no answer. She checked in the garage. The family car was gone. Her parents might be shopping. She expected them to come home any minute.

The first thing she did was go into the kitchen and look in the refrigerator. It was nearly empty.

She walked through the house. In nearly every room there were boxes, some full and taped shut, others partially full, and some still empty. The house was still for sale, but a visiting professor from Ireland had informally agreed to rent it for a year while he taught at the University of Utah. He and his family would be arriving in a month.

Everything will be different from now on, she thought. *In some ways that's a good thing. I won't ever binge and then retreat to my room and to my own bathroom. That was almost too convenient.*

The family is changing. I never felt so close to Daddy as I did at West Yellowstone. We could talk to each other so easily then, maybe because, after being fired, he had nothing left but his family. And for me, I knew I had to change too, so we were both in a new situation. It was good for me. So maybe whatever happens will be good for him too.

There won't be as much money as before, so I'll probably have to get a job from here on in while I'm in school. But that's okay because it'll keep me busy, and that's good because it'll keep me from thinking about food.

She went to her room and pulled out her bathroom scale from where she kept it in the bathroom.

I wonder how much I weigh, she thought. *I should find out. It wouldn't hurt to find out. I haven't weighed myself for a long time. I used to weigh myself several times a day just to see how I was doing.*

No, I won't do it. That's how this all started. I won't get into this again. I feel good. I've got energy now. People tell me I look good. Of course what they mean is I don't look like I'm going to die anytime soon.

I'm not going to backslide. I'm not going to go back to the way I was. And I'm not going to weigh myself.

She grabbed the bathroom scale and took it to a box in the living room that was nearly full. She put the scale in the box and found some packaging tape and sealed the box shut.

That's it, she thought. *I'm free of that temptation. With any luck that box will remain sealed for years. And by the time it's opened, it won't matter anymore because I'll be over this hurdle.*

A few minutes later her parents pulled into the driveway and hurried into the house.

"Ashley?" her mother called out.

Ashley came out of her room and started down the hall.

"I'm so sorry we weren't here when you came home," her mother said, giving her a big hug. "We weren't sure when you'd be here, and your father and I had to meet with our attorney."

"What for?"

"Your father will tell you."

"How's my princess?" he asked, giving her a big hug and a kiss on the cheek.

"Doing good, Daddy," she said.

"You look real good," he said. "Are you really doing okay?"

"Yeah, I am. Pretty much."

"That's great. Well, let's eat. We got Chinese. It's in the car. I'll go get it."

A few minutes later they were eating out of boxes in the dining room. "So, you're packing up, huh?" Ashley asked. "Must take a lot of boxes for a house this big. I can help while I'm here. Especially with my things."

Her parents quit eating.

"Well, as a matter of fact, we need to talk to you about that," her mother said.

"What about?"

"You tell her," her mother said.

"Well, from what I can gather, since I left the company, business has really dropped off."

"I always said that if it wasn't for your dad, they never would have made a dime. And now everybody knows that's true."

"So, are they going to hire you back?" Ashley asked.

"Not exactly. And I wouldn't have wanted that either, because, you never know, I could get things moving again, and they could sell it again from under me."

He cleared his throat. "So, last week, they called and asked me what I'd think about buying the company."

"Is that possible?"

"Well, that's why we've been meeting with a lawyer. Of course we don't have enough money to do that, but with some creative financing, it is possible, but just barely."

"I see."

"We haven't decided what to do because we wanted to find out how you felt about it first," her father said.

"I'm not sure what to say," she said.

"What it means is, if your father continues with the company, we won't have to sell the house."

"So everything would be the same?" Ashley asked.

"That's right."

Including me? Ashley thought.

"Well, that's what you should do then," Ashley said.

"Are you sure?" her dad asked.

"Absolutely. I know how hard you've worked. It's not right to just walk away from what's taken you so long to build up." As she said it, without even realizing she was doing it, she reached down to touch the calf of her right leg.

"Well, that's what we'll do then. I'll sign the contract tomorrow morning," her father said.

"Aren't you proud of your father?" her mother asked.

"Of course I am," Ashley said, feeling a strange loss in her life but trying to be upbeat and positive.

"It'll be a lot of work, especially in the beginning, to get things back to the way they used to be, but I'm really quite hopeful this is going to work out for everyone concerned."

"Oh, I'm sure it will work out great."

Ashley wasn't hungry anymore, and, in fact, had a dull pain in her stomach. She dabbled at her food, eating tiny pieces, trying not to show her feelings of betrayal.

Ten minutes later she was done eating. She went to the box she'd just sealed up, and retrieved her bathroom scale and took it to her room and closed the door.

She placed the bathroom scale on the floor in her bathroom but didn't get on because she was afraid of the consequences if she did.

Nothing ever changes. Not really. Not with me and not with my father and not with my mother and not with this house. Here I am, once again, in the bathroom about to weigh myself, ready to pay whatever price necessary to get to some magic number.

What good has the counseling done, and all the talking about nutrition, and all I've done to try to get out of this prison that I find myself in. None of it has made a bit of difference. Here I am, just like always. Why did I ever think I could change, that things were going to be different? What ever led me to believe that?

It wasn't that I was glad Daddy had been fired and that we would have to sell the house. But if things could change that much for him, maybe they could change for me as well.

All I have to do is step on the scales. Who knows what will come from that?

She went out of her bathroom and closed the door and went to her bed and knelt down and closed her eyes. She mouthed the words but didn't let any sound come out. "Father in Heaven, I need you to help me. I know I've been bad and you probably hate me, but I don't want to start again. Please, Father in Heaven, please help me."

There was a knock at the door. She stood up. "What is it?"

"Guess what, it's snowing," her dad said excitedly. "You want to make a snow family?"

She wiped her eyes. "Just give me a minute, okay?"

"Sure. I'll be rounding everything up while you get ready."

"Sure, Daddy."

She hurried as she got dressed, grabbed a knitted cap in the closet, put on her coat and hurried into the garage.

And soon they were in the front yard. "What do you want to start on?" he asked.

"The father."

"Right," he said. "That's the hardest to get right. I will try to get it right this time, though, Ashley. No matter what happens with the company, I'll save time for you. I promise you that."

"Thank you. I was worried about that."

They made an outstanding snowman and then a snow mother, and finally they worked on the snow child.

There was something she had to say but she didn't know how to say it.

Her father had called her princess for as long as she could remember. One time, when she told a counselor that, she'd wondered if because of not feeling closer to her dad, she'd tried to stay a princess by not allowing herself to become a woman. At the time Ashley scoffed at the suggestion, but later, she wasn't sure if it had any validity or not.

If I never say anything, he might be calling me princess when I'm forty years old. So he's got to stop sometime. Maybe now would be a good time.

"Daddy, I don't want you to call me your little princess anymore. Is that all right with you?"

"Of course. I'll call you anything you want me to call you."

"Call me Ashley."

He laughed. "All right, I can do that. That should be easy enough to remember."

They had a wonderful time outside in the snow and when they

were finished, her father got out some Christmas lights and wrapped them in a circle around the snow family so people driving by could see their creation.

Late that night, after her parents had gone to sleep, Ashley slipped out of the house and went into the backyard. It was still snowing. She hadn't bothered to put on her boots or her coat. With each step, she sunk to her knees in snow.

She was carrying the bathroom scale with her under her arm. She walked to the edge of the backyard to where snow had drifted up to her waist. She made her way to the top part of the snow and pushed the bathroom scale deep into the snow drift, then walked back, following the same footsteps she'd taken to get there.

Just before going inside, she turned to look. It was snowing hard and soon the snow would cover her tracks and nobody would know she'd been there. The bathroom scale wouldn't be found for a long time. It was buried and gone.

Ashley smiled. *Things don't always have to be the same,* she thought just before going inside again.

22

As Ashley continued meeting with Dr. St. James throughout the semester, she became curious about him. She learned from looking at the pictures on his wall, and by asking questions each time she visited his office, that he'd played basketball for the University of Utah. He still had a fierce devotion to the school. On the days that Utah played BYU, he told her he always hung a Utes flag on his house. His vanity Idaho license plate read "GO-UTES."

She also noticed that on Tuesdays, when many faculty wore white shirts because of the Ricks College devotional, Dr. St. James wore a colored shirt. It wasn't exactly rebellion, but it was interesting to Ashley.

He was six-feet-four-inches tall and weighed two hundred and thirty pounds. He didn't seem like a person who'd even be happy sitting at a desk most of the day.

"How come you went into this?" she asked him once as she was leaving.

He smiled. "What I really wanted to do was to play in the NBA, but near the end of my junior year, I messed up my knee. I chose psychology because I thought it would be easy."

"Was it?"

"At first. But then, once I started actually doing counseling, it got harder. Dealing with someone's life is always a challenge. I never take that for granted. Never."

Each time she went she was never quite sure what to expect. Sometimes, it was very comforting to talk to him, especially when he pointed out signs of the progress she was making. But at other times, he challenged her, and that always brought anxiety.

Such was the case, early in March, when she reported that while talking to her parents on the phone, she had told them she hadn't thrown up at all for the past three days, when in fact she had done it four times.

253

"Ashley, let me ask you a question. What is it like for you, someone who's basically honest, to find yourself lying and being deceitful?"

"You said I didn't have to stop right away."

"We're not talking about stopping. We're talking about basic honesty. I just want to know if it's hard for you to realize you've become a person who lies and deceives the people who love you the most. Is that hard to deal with?"

"I'm not a liar," she said quickly.

"But you do lie, though. Don't you?"

"No."

"You lied to your parents on the phone just a couple of days ago, didn't you?"

"Yes."

"People who lie are called liars. People who misrepresent themselves are called cheats. Maybe it's time that you faced the truth about yourself."

She was near tears. "Why are you doing this to me?"

"I just want you to face up to what you've become, that's all. As long as you're in an addiction, you're going to be dishonest. You know that and I know that."

She broke down and cried, but he made no effort to comfort her.

After several minutes, he looked at the clock. "I have someone else coming in."

"Why are you being so mean to me?"

"I just want you to face what you've become, that's all. I care enough about you to tell you the truth about yourself."

"What do you want me to do?"

"Try being truthful for as long as you can. Even if it's only for a few hours. To be perfectly honest, I'm not sure you can do it for even a day."

"You don't know anything about me!" she shot back. "I'll show you."

He shook his head. "Talk is cheap, Ashley."

She stormed out of his office, furious at being accused of being a liar, dead set to prove him wrong.

The next time she met with him she was brutally honest. "You know that snowstorm we had two days ago? Well, I walked to the store in the snow and bought cereal and milk, then went back to my apartment. But my roommate was there, so I went on campus and found an open custodian's closet and went in there and closed the door and ate all the cereal and then threw it all up where they clean out their mops."

He nodded. "That kind of behavior isn't who you are. An eating disorder is an illness. In order to get better, you need to separate who you are from your illness."

"I don't understand."

"You are not an eating disorder, are you?"

"No."

"What are you?"

"A person . . . with an eating disorder."

"Exactly. That's two entities then, right? You, on the one hand, and your eating disorder on the other. It's like a war between the two of you. Sometimes you have the upper hand, sometimes your eating disorder is calling the shots."

At first it didn't seem to make any difference in the way she thought about herself, but in time it did help her to believe that she was basically a good person, but that some other entity sometimes took control of her actions.

As Dr. St. James suggested, she never again reported to her parents if or how many times she threw up in a week. And they, to their credit, stopped asking. But she did tell them how she was feeling, and what support she needed from them.

From then on when they met she reported on how her week had gone and what feelings she had experienced each day. When she told him she had thrown up, she would say, "That wasn't me. That was my eating disorder." And during session after session, Dr. St. James accepted that assessment from her.

* * * * *

One day in early April, he stopped her in mid-sentence with, "Ashley, you have a choice now. You understand things you didn't understand before. It's time to move from separating the illness to accepting responsibility for the choices you make."

Once again, she felt confusion and anxiety. She rested her head on the back of her chair and stared up at the water-damaged acoustical tiles on the ceiling. She felt depressed.

Dr. St. James continued. "Part of the progress you've made has come from making a separation between you and your eating disorder. But I'm afraid that you're starting to use that more as an excuse."

"What do you want me to do now?" she asked wearily.

"You have the power to choose what you do, don't you?"

"Not always."

"Don't give me that. You always have the power to decide what you're going to do."

"You're the one who told me that when I threw up it was my eating disorder."

"Yes, and look what you've done with it. Now you use it to justify your every foul-up, don't you? Well, fine, you can continue to do that for the rest of your life if you choose. But, on the other hand, maybe it's about time you grew up and started taking responsibility for your actions. Are you going to go the rest of your life thinking of yourself as some weak-willed wimp, who has no control over her actions? Aren't you tired of not being in charge of your life? Why don't you take control for once? Are you going to live your life acting out the part of some helpless victim?"

"You have no right to talk to me like that!"

"I can talk to you anyway I want. You want to know why I can? Because it doesn't matter what I say or what you say in these sessions, because the simple fact of the matter is that I have seen very little willingness on your part to risk anxiety and make a different choice. We talk, and we talk, but you keep on doing what you've always done."

She swore at him. "I'll show you what I can do!" As she stormed out of his office, she saw a pile of papers on his desk. With one swipe, she knocked them onto the floor.

"You be back here on Wednesday, Ashley! You hear me?"

"Oh, I'll be back, you can bet on that! I want to see the expression on your face when I prove you wrong!" She slammed his door shut on her way out.

The next morning she was still furious at Dr. St. James when she went in the bathroom to take a shower and found someone had used her shampoo again. It had been happening, off and on, all semester.

She put on a robe and wrapped it around her and stormed into the next bedroom. "All right, which one of you has been using my shampoo!"

There were two girls still asleep. Ashley grabbed one of the girl's blanket and yanked it off the bed.

"What did you do that for?"

She thrust the shampoo in the girl's face. "This is my shampoo! Have you been using it?"

"No. Can I have my covers back?"

Ashley turned in her fury to the next girl, who by this time was awake and holding onto her blankets.

"What about you?" Ashley snapped.

"I haven't been using it because I have some of my own, just like it."

"I don't think so! For your information, there's no other shampoo in the bathroom just like this."

"I always bring mine back with me so nobody will use it."

"Oh, yeah? Well, let me see it then," Ashley demanded.

The girl showed her the shampoo. It was a nearly full bottle.

"That's mine!" Ashley said triumphantly. "This is yours." She handed the girl a nearly empty bottle. "Thought you could get away with it, didn't you?"

"Sorry. I didn't do it on purpose."

Ashley shot a withering glance toward the girl. "Maybe that's true, maybe it isn't."

It wasn't until two hours later that Ashley realized how harsh she'd been to the girl.

And it made her smile.

When she next met with Dr. St. James, she told him she hadn't thrown up since their last meeting.

"How did you do it?" he asked.

"By being mad at you."

He smiled. "So you took control then, didn't you?"

"I did."

"Good. That's what needs to happen."

That made her even more angry. "You tricked me, didn't you?"

"I don't know what you're talking about."

She slammed the desk with her hand. "Don't give me that! You always know what you're doing. Sometimes I really hate you."

"If it helps you to hate me, that's fine. I can handle that. The point is you took charge of your life. That's very significant. Congratulations." He wrote something on a piece of paper and handed it to her.

It read, *You have the power.*

She posted it on the mirror in the bathroom and told everyone in the apartment to leave it there.

And every morning she looked at it and smiled.

*   *   *   *   *

She was, once again, looking up at the water damage on the acoustical tile of Dr. St. James's office.

"My roommates hate me," she said sullenly.

"How come?"

"I've become such a grouch lately. Any little thing goes wrong, and I'm on the warpath. One of the girls was supposed to empty the garbage this week, but she didn't, so I took the garbage and dumped it on her bed and yelled at her and told her I didn't appreciate living in a pigsty."

His eyebrows raised. "Really?"

257

"Really."

"Sounds to me like you're standing up for yourself, is that right?"

"I am. Big-time. But they liked me better when I was nice."

"Do you like yourself more now?"

She smiled. "I do."

"You can go through life being a people pleaser, but hating yourself, and always feeling like you don't measure up. Or you can go through life feeling basically okay about yourself because you always stand up for yourself, no matter what. Which of those two options is better?"

"Well, I'm with myself a lot more than I'm with anyone else."

"That's true."

"So I guess I'd rather be true to myself."

"Good for you. Also, you'll get better at being self-assertive as time goes on. I mean, you don't always have to yell at the top of your voice to stand up for yourself."

She started laughing. "Now you tell me."

That even made Dr. St. James laugh.

"Can I ask a question?" Ashley asked.

"Of course."

"What happened to your ceiling?"

"The bathroom on the next floor had a toilet that overflowed during the night. They're going to fix it."

"If they do, can I have the acoustical tiles they replace?" she asked.

"Why would you want that?"

"It will remind me of all the times I've come here this semester."

Dr. St. James laughed. "I'll find out when they're going to make the change, and request they save 'em for you."

"That'd be great."

He looked at his calendar. "We don't have much time left before the end of the semester."

"No, not much."

"There is one more thing I'd like to discuss with you," he said.

"What's that?"

"There has to be a spiritual component in your recovery."

"I suppose."

"Do you ever pray?"

"Are you serious? This is Ricks. We pray all the time."

"Do *you* ever pray?"

"Whenever I'm asked."

"Do you ever pray—just by yourself?"

"Sure, once in a while."

"Do you ever pray for yourself?"

"Of course."

"What else do you pray for?"

"My family."

"Do you ever pray for help in your recovery?"

"I have in the past."

"Do you read the scriptures?"

"I'm taking a Doctrine and Covenants class, so I keep up on the reading assignments."

"Let's read about someone who prayed for help." He opened his scriptures.

"This is in Enos in the Book of Mormon, starting with verse 3." He began to read.

Behold, I went to hunt beasts in the forests; and the words which I had often heard my father speak concerning eternal life, and the joy of the saints, sunk deep into my heart.

And my soul hungered; and I kneeled down before my Maker, and I cried unto him in mighty prayer and supplication for mine own soul; and all the day long did I cry unto him; yea, and when the night came I did still raise my voice high that it reached the heavens.

And there came a voice unto me, saying: Enos, thy sins are forgiven thee, and thou shalt be blessed.

And I, Enos, knew that God could not lie; wherefore, my guilt was swept away.

And I said: Lord, how is it done?

And he said unto me: Because of thy faith in Christ, whom thou hast never before heard nor seen.

Dr. St. James set the book on his desk. "Do you ever pray in mighty prayer and supplication for your own soul?"

"You mean now?"

"Yes."

"I usually pray for others, but not for myself."

"Why's that?"

"I'm not sure."

"Do you ever pray that you can learn to accept your body just the way it is now?"

She shook her head. "No, I never do that."

"How come?"

She sighed. "Because I don't like my body."

"Why's that?"

"Because it's ugly."

"Even if that were true, it's the only one you've got. I think you should show it some respect."

"Why?"

"Because God gave it to you."

She smiled. "Can I turn it in for another model?"

"Nope, sorry. What would you think about asking God to help you accept your body just the way it is now?"

"I'm not sure he'd pay much attention to anything I'd say to him."

"Why's that?"

"Because God doesn't want to have anything to do with me now."

"What makes you think that?"

"Because I've made such a mess of my life. I'm not worthy to ask God for anything."

"Is that the way you really feel?"

"Yes."

"Why don't you ask your home teacher for a blessing?"

"What good would that do?"

"It might help you to realize that God loves you."

"I'm not going to pour out all my secrets to my home teacher."

"You don't have to. All you have to say is 'I'm going through a difficult time now, and I think I'd like to have a blessing.'"

"If I do that, he won't have any idea what it's about."

"He doesn't need to know. Heavenly Father will bless him to know what to say."

She shook her head. "I don't think that would do any good."

"Try it and then report back. If I'm wrong, then I'll never ask you to do that again."

She nodded. "Nothing is going to happen."

The next Sunday after church, she asked Brett and Christopher, her home teachers, for a priesthood blessing.

They gave it to her in the bishop's office on campus because she didn't want her roommates wondering why she was asking for a blessing. The bishop and his counselors stepped across the hall to another room so it would be just her home teachers giving the blessing.

She sat down in a chair they pulled into the center of the room.

"What is this blessing for?" Brett asked.

"I just need a blessing, that's all. To help me get through a difficult time in my life."

Brett seemed puzzled, but asked for her full name, then he and Christopher placed their hands on her head.

She wasn't prepared for what happened. It wasn't so much what they said as how she felt when they said it. It was a feeling that she was loved by Father in Heaven.

Tears began to run down her face.

It was not a long blessing, but one sentence hit home: "Before you were born, you were really happy that you were going to get a physical body and that you'd be able to use it to bless others."

She began to sob.

Brett, not even knowing the reason for her reaction, paused, trying to divert his attention from her reaction to whatever else the Spirit would have him say.

He went on. "I bless you to learn to be good to yourself. You are one of Father in Heaven's greatest miracles, and He loves you."

He continued. "You have been given a wonderful . . ."

Ashley could tell he was having a tough time.

He cleared his throat and then, in nearly a whisper, said . . . "body."

Through the pressure of their hands on her head, she felt their discomfort.

Christopher coughed.

As an afterthought, Brett added, " . . . and mind."

Apparently embarrassed, he ended the blessing shortly after that.

When she stood up and turned to them, both young men avoided looking her in the eye. She wiped the tears from her cheeks and hugged each one. "Thank you so much. That was just what I needed."

Sensing their embarrassment, she didn't linger to talk. She thanked them again and started to leave. But before opening the door, she turned back to them.

"Guys, it's okay. It's what God wanted me to hear."

They both gave a sigh of relief.

She smiled and walked away, feeling very strongly now that her body and her mind and her spirit were from God, and, thus, were good.

*　*　*　*　*

Winter semester was fast drawing to a close. Her plans were to spend the summer at home, working for her dad to earn enough money to come back in the fall.

She had made progress because of counseling with Dr. St. James, and yet there was never one dramatic moment when she quit bingeing and purging for good, but, with time, it happened less. She began to gain greater understanding about what triggered the binges. For the most part, she found that it often had less to do with food and more to

261

do with the way she felt about herself as a person, and whether she faced a bad feeling head-on or tried to numb it with food.

"Where did you begin to feel that you were somehow not acceptable the way you were?" Dr. St. James asked in mid-April, just a week before finals week.

"I don't know. I was okay with myself when I was little. My mom says I used to run around the house with no clothes on when I was three." She smiled. "So I guess that shows I was pretty comfortable with myself then."

"That's probably true."

Ashley's head was resting on the chair and she was, once again, staring at the water damage to the acoustical tile. On one tile there was a mark that resembled a letter V or even a mountain peak.

"Sometimes girls who have an eating disorder were either emotionally or physically abused while growing up," Dr. St. James said.

Ashley sat up and looked at him. "Does that sometimes trigger it?"

"Not necessarily, but some young women with an eating disorder have had that problem." He paused for a moment, then asked, "Has anything ever happened to you in a sexual way that caused turmoil in your life?"

She rested her head on the back of the chair and continued staring at the water damage on the ceiling. After a long period of silence, she said, "I can't remember anything like that ever happening to me."

"I'm glad you've never been hurt in that way. In the future, if there's anything you do remember, just know that I'm always willing to talk to you about it."

"Okay, I'll remember that."

"Let's go on to something else then." He stood up, stretched, and walked over to the window, then turned and came and sat on the edge of his desk. "Over the years, we've found that eating-disorder families often, but not always, fall into one of three types of families. The first type is the chaotic family. Children in such a family are often the victims of physical or sexual abuse. And then there's the family where the parents are abnormally overprotective. The third type is the perfect family. They place inordinate importance on externals like appearance and achievements."

"Do I have to pick one of the three?" Ashley asked.

"No. Of course not. Most families don't fit neatly into one or the other category. Sometimes there's a mixture. But is there anything you remember about your family that reminds you of any of these categories?"

Ashley thought back to a night when her mother and father waited for Alauna to come home. Alauna had been drinking, and they found out and there was an argument with yelling and threats. Ashley, in bed with the lights out, heard it all.

That was about as chaotic as it's possible to get. And yet I felt pressure to be perfect too, to get good grades, to always look my best, to get into BYU, to develop my talents. So maybe I come from the so-called perfect family.

Dr. St. James seemed content to remain silent while she sorted through her thoughts. When she lowered her gaze from the ceiling to him, he asked, "Have you figured it out? Where do you think this feeling that you were somehow not good enough began?"

"Have I ever told you about my sister Alauna?"

She told him about Alauna's rebellious attitude when she was in high school.

"I remember one day my mom saying, 'Well, at least Ashley isn't giving us any trouble.' I remember thinking, 'I'll try to be as good as I can so they won't have to worry about me.'" She shook her head. "That was a dumb idea, wasn't it?"

"Not necessarily, but sometimes even a noble thought, if it's carried to the extreme, can cause problems."

"Well, I'm not perfect now, that's for sure," she said with a slight smile. "Just ask my roommates."

Dr. St. James smiled. "You go, Girl." He glanced at the clock. "We ran over today."

"Sorry."

"Don't be. I think it was a productive session. See you next time."

* * * * *

Two days later, even though it was to be their last meeting together, Dr. St. James started out as usual. "What feelings have you experienced since the last time we met?"

Ashley sighed. "Mostly stress because of exams and term papers coming due."

"How did you handle it?"

"On Saturday, I went on a picnic with my home evening group. That was fun. We played softball."

"Sounds fun."

"It was."

"Anything else?"

She thought back. "No, that's about it, pretty much." She hesitated. "Well, actually, there is something else that's been worrying me."

"What's that?"

She hesitated, then said, "I'm not sure what I'm going to do when I'm home and can't come talk to you."

"If you want, I can make a few recommendations of counselors you could meet with when you're home."

"All right. Thank you."

"No problem."

She shook her head. "So this is it? I just walk out of here?"

"You'll be back in the fall, right? We can meet then, if you think it would be productive."

She shook her head. "That's not what I'm feeling."

"Okay."

She felt almost overcome with the sense of loss. "I'm going to miss you."

He nodded. "It is hard to say good-bye when two people have experienced what we've gone through. I'll miss you, too. We've had a good relationship."

There was more she needed to say. "I haven't really thanked you for all you've done for me."

"Whatever progress you've made, you're the one who did it."

"But I couldn't have done it without you."

"I'm not sure about that, but one thing I can tell you. I feel honored to have had even a small part in what you've accomplished since we've been meeting. You've done well."

She rummaged through her backpack, then handed him a small box. "I'd like you to have this."

"What is it?"

"A box of candy."

He smiled. "Really?"

"Yes. I know you like candy."

"I do." He opened the wrapping and lifted the lid off the box. "It smells wonderful."

He held the open box out to her. "Will you join me?"

She smiled back. "I knew you'd do that."

"Why did you know that?"

"It's your one last test, right?"

"How's it a test?"

"To see if I still think of some food as bad."

"Do you?"

"A little. It's hard not to."

"It's just a little chocolate, that's all."

She met his gaze boldly. "I know that. One piece of chocolate can't hurt anyone."

Together, slowly, they savored the taste of the chocolate in their mouths.

"Delicious," he said.

"I agree."

"Would you like another piece?" he asked.

"No, thanks. One is plenty for me," she said with a triumphant smile on her face. "I'm not eating another piece just to please you. I'm not into pleasing people anymore, not even you. One piece of candy is all I want, and that's all I'm going to have."

"Me, too. I'll probably have one tomorrow about this time."

"I hope you do." She stood up. "Well, thanks for everything."

"Have a good summer," he said, extending his hand.

"I will. I'll be with my best friend. We always do well together."

"What's her name?"

"Jen. Her name is Jen, and I love her."

"Ashley and Jen. Sounds like a good combination."

Ashley broke out into a big grin. "You have no idea."

23

The end of April, at the end of winter semester, Ashley came home for the summer. She found her mother in the backyard working in the garden.

"Mom, I'm home!"

"Ashley, my darling! I'm so glad you're home." They gave each other a big hug.

"How was your trip?"

"It was good."

"Sit down and tell me how your week went."

They talked for an hour, mostly about the details of their everyday experiences.

It felt good to Ashley.

When her dad came home, he hugged Ashley and gave her a kiss on the cheek.

"It's great to have you home."

"It's great to be home."

"Your father has something he wants to ask you," her mom said.

"What?"

He cleared his throat. "I was wondering, before you start working, that is, tomorrow, if you'd . . . well . . . if you'd like to go to the zoo with me."

"The zoo?" Ashley asked.

"That's right. I was hoping we could play catch-up."

"Can you get the day off?"

"Of course. I'm the boss."

She thought about it for a moment, then laughed. "That'd be great, Dad. I'd really like to do that with you."

The next day at the zoo, they stopped at every exhibit they came across. For some reason her dad insisted on reading out loud the information about each animal or bird they came to. Ashley couldn't decide if she should pretend she couldn't read yet or not. *Is this as awkward for him as it is for me?* Ashley thought.

All around them, or at least it seemed to them, were fathers and daughters—the dads still young, the daughters varying in age from four or five up through ten or eleven, enjoying their day at the zoo.

She wasn't sure if her dad was aware of the sense of loss she was feeling, but once, near the end of their time together, while reading the nesting habits of some obscure South American bird, his voice wavered, and he stopped reading.

"I'm sorry," he said quietly. "I should have done this when you were little, when this would have meant something to you."

She patted his arm. "It means something to me, now, Daddy."

"I don't know what happened when you were growing up. I was just too busy."

She put her arm on his back and rested her head on his shoulder. They didn't say anything, but some of the other visitors at the zoo were left to wonder why a man and his grown-up daughter were standing there crying while looking at a toucan bird.

Finally, a small boy approached them. "Did one of the birds die? Is that why you're so sad?"

"Tommy . . . it's none of our business," his mother called out harshly.

"No, it's just us," Ashley said to the boy. "We're just so happy to be here at the zoo together."

The boy and his embarrassed family moved on.

Ashley gave her dad one of her tissues and they tried to fix themselves up again.

"I think we've seen everything," her dad said.

"I think so."

"So, you want to go home?"

"Sure, that'd be fine."

Arm in arm, they walked slowly toward the exit. There was a man there, selling helium-filled balloons.

"I don't suppose you'd want a balloon, would you?" her dad asked.

Ashley considered. "Yeah, I would. Thanks."

"What color?"

"Red?"

He nodded. "One red balloon coming up."

She watched him as he got in the line for balloons, standing there with a mother of a five-year-old and a father of a whiny eight-year-old boy, who didn't want to wait his turn in line. One boy took the money from his father and ran excitedly in front of everyone, thrust out his money, and asked for a red balloon. It was the last one, and he was given it because he was so excited and, also, a very cute little boy.

Her dad looked back at her with a defeated expression.

There were three green balloons left. *People must not like green balloons,* Ashley thought.

"Green would be great, too!" she called to him.

He nodded, and when his turn came bought a green one and brought it back to her.

"Do you want me to tie it on your hand?"

She smiled. "Sure."

He knotted the string around her wrist, then in an impulse put his arms around her.

"I am sorry, you know," he whispered.

"I know. Me, too."

Then they walked together to their car.

* * * * *

Ashley was working for her dad in the office, and when a secretary quit, Ashley asked her dad if she could try to get Jen working there, too. He agreed, and after a few phone calls, Jen moved back from Provo. Because she refused to live with her mom and Billy James Dean, she rented a small basement apartment.

Jen and Ashley enjoyed being together again, but, even so, there was still some tension between them whenever Ashley suggested Jen visit her mother and Billy James Dean.

"They have their life, and I have mine."

"She's still your mom."

"No, she's *his wife.*"

"You act like she's committed some really bad sin. All she did was get married."

"Yes, that's all."

"What's wrong with that?"

Jen snorted. "You were there."

"Have you been back at all to see them since they got married?"

"After they came back from their honeymoon, I stayed there. One night was enough for me."

"What happened?"

"I could hear them laughing in their bedroom."

"They can't laugh in their bedroom?"

"It was just too weird, that's all. I can't understand what she sees in him."

268

"You don't have to, do you? As long as she's happy, right? But one thing you have to do."

"What?"

"She's your mom. You've got to try to patch things up between you."

"Forget it. Not as long as she's married to him."

After that, Ashley backed off, but she didn't give up the hope she could do something to bring Jen and her mother closer together again.

A week later, they were on their way to downtown Salt Lake City to shop. Ashley was driving and took a sudden detour.

"This isn't the way."

"I have to stop by to get something."

Ten minutes later she pulled up in front of Billy James Dean's pawn shop.

"Let's go in here for a minute and look around."

"I'm not going in," Jen said.

"Yes, you are. We're both going in. We're going to give Billy James a copy of the Book of Mormon, and then we're going to bear our testimony."

"That is the dumbest idea you've ever come up with," Jen complained.

"Maybe so, but you're coming in with me."

"I am not," Jen said.

"Don't make me beat you up," Ashley said with a slight grin.

Jen looked over at her. "Excuse me?"

"You heard me."

"Forget it."

"Jen. Please do it. If not for you, then, for me."

Jen pouted but then, finally, shrugged her shoulders. "Fine, but it won't make any difference."

"We'll never know until we try."

There were no customers inside the store. Billy James was busy polishing some of his gaudiest jewelry.

Ashley glanced around the shop. It was filled with what could only be described as unique junk, some of it in such bad taste that it almost took on an appeal of its own—a bronze spittoon, an old push lawn-mower painted a bright red, a two-foot-high hula dancer lamp, whose hips jiggled when you turned on the light.

"Well, look what the cat drug in," Billy James said with a big smile.

Jen slid the copy of the Book of Mormon toward him.

He glanced down at it, then up at her, then shook his head. "I can't give you nothing for this."

Jen cleared her throat. "It's priceless to me," she said softly, barely above a whisper.

"Then you should keep it. The most I could give you for it would be maybe a quarter."

"I want you to have it."

"What am I going to do with it?"

"Read it."

"You want me to read it?"

"Yes."

Billy James Dean picked it up and flipped through its pages. "No pictures."

"No."

"I like books with pictures."

"Oh."

"But I'll tell you what I'll do."

"What?"

"I'll read it . . . if you'll do one thing for me."

"What?" Jen asked.

"Go visit your mom. She misses you not coming around anymore. You don't even call her. See, to me, that's not right, so is it a deal?"

Jen stared at him for a moment, then said, "It's a deal."

He picked up two bronze medallions and handed one to each of the girls. "These came from ancient Inca ruins."

"No, they didn't," Jen said.

His enthusiasm gave away to an uncharacteristic seriousness. "You're right. I don't know why I say things like that. Nobody believes me anyway."

Jen looked at her watch. "Well, we need to get going."

Billy James grinned. "Thanks for stopping in. You'll be dropping by the house, then, to talk to your mom, right?"

"Right."

"That's all I needed to hear. Have a nice day."

Before they got to the door, Billy James said, with all seriousness, "I really do love your mom."

Jen turned around to face him. He had a strange smile on his face, almost a kind of sadness.

"I know."

"I wasn't sure if you did or not."

Jen sat without saying anything during the rest of the ride to town.

When Ashley finished parking the car and turned off the key, Jen put her hand on Ashley's arm and said, "Thanks."

"No problem."

270

Should I knock or just walk in? Jen debated with herself as she approached the home she'd spent her high school years in.

She knocked.

When her mother opened the door, she seemed surprised to see Jen. Her first reaction was joy, but then, having spent a lifetime being disappointed by others, it occurred to her that Jen had come by for something she'd left when she moved out.

"Hi, Mom. I was in the area and thought I'd drop by and see how you are getting along."

"Please come in."

"Thank you."

Jen stepped inside and looked around. Everything had changed: a couch covered in a garish Scottish plaid, a player piano painted blue, and a six-foot totem pole standing in the corner, gave the living room a distinctive, Billy James Dean look.

"You've made some changes since I've been gone," Jen said.

"Yes. Billy James doesn't like things to be boring."

"Well, this certainly isn't."

"I agree."

"And how are things working out between you and Billy James?"

"It's never boring, either."

Jen blushed. "I . . . uh . . . guess that must be true."

"You were disappointed that I married him, weren't you?"

"Well, yes, I was, not because of him so much."

"What then?" Jen's mother asked.

"I was disappointed that the Church means so little to you."

"It means a great deal to you now, doesn't it?"

"Yes, it does."

Jen didn't even know how to explain how much the teachings of the Church had helped her straighten out her life, but she knew she had to say something.

"If it weren't for the Church, I'd have kept on making the same mistakes over and over again."

"You're disappointed I've never been strong enough to live the way the Church teaches, aren't you?"

Jen didn't know how to answer the question without hurting her mother's feelings.

"It's all right," her mother said. "We need to say what's on our minds."

Jen started in. "After girls camp that one year, when I started going to church with Ashley, I wished I hadn't done some of the things I did.

271

I wished I could have had a mom and a dad, and that I'd have been taught how to live, and that I could have avoided some of the mistakes I made."

"Wishing don't change things," her mother said.

"I know that, but you asked me, and I told you."

They sat in silence for what seemed an eternity. Only a few feet separated them. Jen was sitting on the Scottish Pride couch made by a company that began with great hopes of capturing the market of people whose ancestors came from Scotland. They made twenty couches and then went out of business. Billy James Dean bought their entire inventory, and, over the years, had managed to sell five. The other fifteen were kept in a rental storage facility in Draper.

Jen's mother sat on an old all-wood kitchen chair, which Billy James Dean claimed had been built personally by Brigham Young.

"You don't know what it was like for me after your father left. There was no money coming in. I had to work to keep food on the table. Waitressing isn't easy work, but it was all I could find. I'm sorry I wasn't around all the time, but I really didn't see what else I could do."

Jen sighed. "I know it was hard for you, and I'm grateful for all you did to provide for me, but . . ."

"What?"

"Nothing."

"No, say it."

Jen took a deep breath. "When I started going back to church, I remember thinking I have to keep active in the Church because . . . because I didn't want to turn out just like my mother." As soon as she said it, she wished she hadn't.

Her mother stood up as a signal that it was time for Jen to leave. "And you've succeeded at that, for which I congratulate you." Her face was expressionless, though her chin was trembling.

Jen stood up, too, but didn't move toward the door. "Mom, I'm learning other things from the Church. I haven't mastered it yet, but I'm getting better."

"What kind of things?"

"I'm beginning to understand how much the Savior loves me, and that helps me learn to love others."

Her mother's face softened a bit, and she looked as though she were going to cry.

"Mom, what I'm trying to say is, can we start over again?" Jen asked.

"I don't know. Can we?"

"I think we should."

They came together in a long tearful embrace.

And then when they were both too messy with tears, her mother grabbed them some tissues from a dispenser that had the seal of the United States Navy on its front, which, according to Billy James, had once belonged to President John F. Kennedy.

24

The phone call came a week later, on a Saturday around noon. It was Sister Ross, the stake girls camp director, and she sounded desperate.

"Ashley, I need your help. Girls camp is scheduled to start Tuesday morning. I fully intended on being the director this year, but yesterday I hurt my back trying to move some things in the garage to get to our camping gear. I just got home from the chiropractor, and he has absolutely forbidden me from going to camp."

"I thought you had given up going to girls camp," Ashley said.

"Oh, I say that every year, but when it comes right down to it, I can't say no. I know this is a terrible imposition, but can you and Jen possibly help me out?"

Before Ashley could respond, Sister Ross went on.

"My assistant is Sister Hunsaker. She's very organized, and she can run the program, but she's very pregnant and unable to get around much. She doesn't think she can do this all by herself. So I'm calling to see if you and Jen could help her out. Sister Hunsaker can't even get to camp until Tuesday anyway. And I need somebody on Monday to get the camp ready. I'm sorry to have to even ask, but I can't think of anyone else. Is there *any* chance you and Jen would be available to help?"

Ashley took a deep breath. Because she was working in the office for her dad, she was pretty sure she could get some time off. "Have you talked to Jen?"

"No, I thought I'd talk to you first."

"I'll do it, if she will."

"Oh, thank you so much! I knew I could count on you."

At first, Jen said no, but Ashley talked her into it.

On Monday morning, Ashley and her dad, in a company pickup filled with groceries and supplies that had been stored in Sister Ross's garage, drove up to girls camp. Jen followed behind in her car.

The first thing they did was unload the food into the cement block commissary. Ashley's dad would have done all the work, but Jen and Ashley told him they needed to help, too. And so, a few minutes later, he got ready to leave.

"Thanks, Dad, for all your help." Ashley reached out for a hug.

"Glad to do it. If you need me to stay, I can."

"No, that's okay, we'll be fine."

"All right. I'll be heading out then."

He honked and waved as he pulled away and drove off.

Jen and Ashley spent the next few hours organizing, going over the menus, separating the food in the commissary into what would be required for each day of the camp, making sure they had everything they needed.

"Well, I guess we'd better set up our tent and cook ourselves some dinner," Ashley said.

"I've got an idea," Jen said. "Let's camp tonight at the Lone Wolf campsite."

"We'd have to haul everything up there."

"We did it before, we can do it again."

"It might rain, so we'd need to set up the tent, too," Ashley said.

"I'll help this time. Please. For old time's sake?"

"Of course. We should definitely do that."

They returned to the commissary and got two cans of pork and beans, not because it was their favorite food, but because of sentimental reasons.

They worked well together, not talking much except for mundane details of how to set up the tent.

An hour later they were sitting next to a fire, eating pork and beans and saltine crackers, and drinking hot chocolate.

Ashley got up and moved into the woods. "This is the stump where we arm wrestled," she said.

"I won, didn't I?" Jen asked.

"No, you lost."

"Really? I thought I won."

"You won the leg wrestling, but I won the arm wrestling."

Jen nodded. "I knew I'd won in the end."

Ashley came back to the fire. "We both won . . . in the end."

"Looks like we did, all right."

As she passed Jen, Ashley bent to kiss Jen on the cheek, then sat down on a log on the opposite side of the fire. "You are and always will be my very best friend."

"Mine too."

They both had tears in their eyes.

"This is so stupid," Jen muttered, wiping her eyes with the sleeve of her sweatshirt.

"I totally agree."

Jen's nose got involved in this, too, but that was too much. She found a tissue in a pocket and blew her nose. It broke the silence of the forest.

"Good grief, you sound like a moose," Ashley complained with a slight grin.

"Excuse me?" Jen asked, pretending to be insulted.

"I said you sound like a moose when you blow your nose."

"That is so rude," Jen protested.

"Maybe so, but it's the truth. I just said it for your own protection. I mean, we don't want some love-sick moose coming around looking for you, do we?"

"Hmmm," Jen said as if she was trying to make a decision. "Does this moose have a good personality?"

"Not that good, actually."

"Then the answer is definitely no."

Like air out of a leaky balloon, their lighthearted mood escaped, and they were left with their thoughts, staring at the fire.

"We've come a long way since we were first here," Jen said.

"We have. That's for sure."

"What's your greatest regret?" Jen asked.

Ashley shrugged her shoulders. "That's hard to say. There's so many."

"I know. For me, too."

Ashley tossed a stick in the fire and watched it catch fire. Each waited for the other to talk about the past.

But much of their past was very painful, and so the moment came and passed and then was gone.

Ashley looked at her watch and then stood up. "Well, we've got a lot to do in the morning. What do you say we get some sleep?"

"Sure, might as well." Jen looked up at the night sky. "The clouds have pretty much gone. How about if we sleep under the stars tonight?"

Ashley thought about it. "I guess we could. If it starts raining, we can still get in the tent."

Five minutes later they lay in their sleeping bags looking up at the stars.

"It's so beautiful," Jen said quietly.

"I know. It is."

A minute passed with neither of them saying anything.

"Oh, look, a shooting star!" Jen called out.

"That was great! Maybe there will be some more."

They watched but none came.

"Jen?" Ashley said.

"Yes."

"There's one thing I've never told anyone. When it was the worst, I used to slip the sacrament bread out of my mouth into a tissue because I was afraid it would ruin my record for the day."

"You did?"

"Yes. I never even thought about what the sacrament is for. Hardly ever."

Jen considered that, then said, "When I was at my worst, I gave up all hope that I could ever come back. Or that Jesus even cared what happened to me."

"Look, another shooting star!" Ashley cried out.

"This must be the best time to see 'em."

"I guess so."

"We were both wrong, weren't we?" Jen asked. "I mean, about Jesus."

Ashley nodded. "He never gave up on us."

"That fact means more to me now than it ever has in my life."

"I know. Me, too."

Jen yawned. "Well, I'd like to keep talking, but I'm kind of tired. So, good night."

"Good night, Jen."

Two minutes passed, and Jen was nearly asleep.

"Wow, look at that! Two at a time," Ashley called out.

Jen sat up. "Excuse me, but are you going to give me a running commentary on every shooting star you see for the rest of the night?"

"Yeah, pretty much, why do you ask?" Ashley asked.

"That's it. I'm going to sleep in the tent." Jen crawled out of her sleeping bag, stood up, and dragged it into the tent.

"There's another one!" Ashley called out.

"Get in here!" Jen demanded.

"You are so hard to live with late at night. I'm going to write Nathan and warn him what he's getting himself into if he comes back and marries you."

"In the tent now! You hear me, Girl?"

"I'm definitely writing Nathan tomorrow."

"I don't care—as long as I get some sleep tonight."

Ashley dragged her sleeping bag into the tent. "I'm not going to say another word for the rest of the night."

"Good."

"I mean it."

Jen giggled. "That was three words."

"Oh, so that's how you're going to be, is it? Well fine, I'm going to sleep now."

"Good."

When Jen woke up the next morning, Ashley was gone. Jen got dressed and went out to find her. The sun had not yet reached where they were camped but was lighting up the hillside about half a mile away.

She found Ashley sitting on a ridge overlooking girls camp, drinking a cup of hot chocolate.

Ashley turned to greet her. "Good morning, Sunshine."

"It will be a good morning in about another hour," Jen grumbled, sitting down next to Ashley on a fallen tree that made a good chair.

"Life is good, isn't it?" Ashley said.

"It can be."

Ashley took a sip of her hot chocolate. "One thing I've learned to do is to slow down and not to go running at full-speed all the time. That's what I'm doing now. Relaxing. Just looking around and thinking what a beautiful world we live in. It's good to do that, you know."

"I know."

"What I did took away my feelings, so now I have to ask myself, How do I feel? That's what I learned in counseling—to honor my feelings and not try to numb them. That's why it's important for me to slow down and relax, like I'm doing now."

They sat sharing the hot chocolate and watching as the line between the sunshine and the shadows advanced toward them.

A few minutes later they were also bathed in sunlight.

"That was beautiful," Ashley said.

"I agree. And it was great sharing it with you."

Ashley stood up and stretched. "I guess we'd better get going. We've got a lot to do before all the girls and their advisers show up."

They turned their attention to the list Sister Ross had given them, and they worked hard for the next two hours getting the camp ready.

The last thing on their list was to clean up the shower and restroom area.

Ashley was hosing out the shower area while Jen, who lost the toss of the coin, was cleaning the toilets with a brush.

Spraying one of the walls, Ashley accidentally splashed the stream from the hose off a supporting post, sending a spray of water over in the area where Jen was working.

278

"Hey, watch it!" Jen called out.

"Oh, did I get you wet?" Ashley asked innocently.

"Yes, you got me wet. Be careful."

"Right," Ashley said, flicking her wrist, sending another spray of water in Jen's direction. "Oh, sorry, my hand slipped again."

Jen came out of the stall. "Are we going to have an episode now?"

"No, of course not. My only interest is to accomplish the work I was assigned to do, that's all."

"Good." As Jen turned to return to her work, Ashley nailed her in the back with a narrow stream of water.

"Oh, I'm so sorry! I guess I slipped again."

Jen forced a smile. "Don't worry about it. She went to the sink and held her bucket under the nozzle. As it finished filling up, she said, "Anyone can slip with a hose, . . . or a bucket!" With that, she charged at Ashley and drenched her, then turned to run away. Ashley followed her outside the building, sending a stream of hose water after her. When Jen was out of range, she turned to look back, and Ashley dropped the hose on the ground.

"You giving up so soon?" Jen taunted.

Ashley tilted her head. "Turn around."

Jen turned around and saw a group of twenty girls, their advisers, and a few fathers who'd come to help set up.

"We were just cleaning out the shower area," Ashley said as officially as she could.

Jen tried her best to sound like a drill sergeant. "Start setting up the tents. We'll be by for an inspection in fifteen minutes, and we want every tent set up by then. So get moving."

Jen and Ashley took the hose back to the boiler area on the other side of the shower building and then went back to their tent to change out of their wet clothing.

They walked through camp, urging the fathers to let their daughters set up their own tents. They also confiscated boom boxes, cell phones, Internet access ports, and hair dryers. Then they went up on a small hill that overlooked the camp and watched the activity below them.

"It's our turn now, isn't it? I mean, to be responsible," Ashley said.

"I guess so."

"I hope we do okay."

"Me, too."

"Looks like those first-year girls are having some trouble with their tent. Maybe we ought to go give them a hand."

Jen scoffed. "Yeah, like we're world experts, right?"

"We may not know much, but we know more than they do, okay?"

"Sure, let's go."

By eight that night, all the tents had been set up, everyone had eaten their supper cooked over the fire, and Sister Hunsaker had given a "Welcome-to-Camp" talk. She introduced Ashley and Jen as her assistants.

They sang camp songs, had a few skits, closed with a group prayer and then everyone was sent to their tents for the night.

Ashley and Jen weren't tired. They sat next to the fire to talk—and to discourage any late-night mischief.

"You hungry?" Jen asked.

"Yeah, kind of."

"Let's go check out the commissary, see if there's any Oreo cookies that might have spilled out of one of the bags," Jen said.

"You think there might be such a bag?" Ashley asked.

"Oh, yeah, I can almost guarantee it. Those bags break open so easily."

Ashley nodded and they started down the gentle slope to the commissary.

Once they got there, Jen opened the door with her key. Instead of turning on the light, she turned on her flashlight, then set a box over it to dim the light.

They opened the large box of Oreo cookies and pulled out an individual bag.

They were about to open it when they heard voices. Jen quickly turned off the flashlight.

"You think we've been busted?" Jen whispered.

"If it's Sister Hunsaker, let's tell her we were doing an inventory of all our food," Ashley said.

"Shush, they're coming."

They stood quietly.

The intruders were close enough for Jen and Ashley to make out what they were saying.

"What if we get caught?" a girl asked.

"We're not going to get caught. All the leaders are asleep. We need someone to crawl through the window and open the door. Chelsea, you go."

"Why me?"

"Because you're the littlest. It'll be easier for you."

"We should've brought a flashlight."

"If we start shining a flashlight around, then we'll get caught for sure," the ringleader said.

"What if there's nothing good in there to eat?" another girl complained.

"Don't be so negative all the time. There'll be cookies. There's always cookies. Chelsea, get going. The sooner you're in, the sooner we'll be back to our tent. I'll boost you up."

The window, which someone had left unlocked, was slid up by two of the girls, and then a girl was boosted up. She rested her hands on a box of canned beans and crawled inside, and then slowly she lowered herself down to the floor. In the dark she didn't see Jen and Ashley standing there, not more than a foot from her.

Jen leaned toward the girl and whispered in her ear. "We were expecting you."

The girl screamed.

Jen shone the flashlight in her eyes. "Thought you could break in here and steal food, did you? Well, maybe we should show you what we do to girls who try that stunt." Jen flung open the door and shouted after the two girls who were running up the path. "We know who you are!"

Chelsea made a run for it.

"You try that one more time and you'll all have to write a note of apology to Sister Hunsaker!" Ashley shouted after the girls.

Jen turned to Ashley in disbelief. "A letter of apology? Is that the best you can do?"

Ashley shouted back. "Forget what I said about a letter of apology. It'll be much worse than that! It'll be really awful! You won't like it, that's for sure!"

Jen sighed and shrugged her shoulders. "Must I do everything around here?"

She shouted to the fleeing girls. "We'll make you stay all alone by yourselves at the Lone Wolf Mountain campsite!" She turned back to Ashley and smiled. "There, *that's* how it's done."

* * * * *

It was, by all accounts, a successful girls camp, with very few problems.

On the night of the traditional talent show, the stake president brought Sister Ross to camp, who said a few words of encouragement to the girls, and then told in way too much detail about Jen and Ashley's famous camp prank.

"That's not fair!" one of the first-year girls complained. "You didn't let us get away with anything this week."

"That's because we never sleep," Ashley said.

That wasn't entirely true, but they did stay awake that night, as wave after wave of girls tried to trick the tricksters. All to no avail.

The next day they broke camp. Jen and Ashley offered to stay behind to take care of the numerous details associated with closing up the site.

They worked until two in the afternoon. Then, just before leaving, they took one last tour of the camp.

"They want us back next year," Ashley said.

"Really?"

"That's what Sister Hunsaker said."

"The only problem is you might be married by then, once Nathan gets back from his mission."

"Me? What about you? You could be married by then, too."

"I suppose, not as likely, though," Ashley said.

"Oh, you never know. When you find the right guy, you'll go fast."

"Not me."

"Don't give me that. You will. The guy you marry probably won't even get unpacked from his mission before you'll have him at the altar."

"That is so not true!" Ashley protested.

"I know you, Girl."

They were at the car. Ashley took one last look at the campsite, then glanced at Jen, and said simply, "We've both come a long way, haven't we?"

"I think so."

They got into the car. "Except I'm starving!" Jen complained. "What do you say we get something to eat? I'm so sick of official girls camp food. How about a pizza?"

Ashley smiled. "A pizza sounds good."

The car made a small cloud of dust that followed them down the dirt road as they left the camp.

Until next year.

Ten Facts about Eating Disorders

1. An eating disorder can give a false sense of control.

Many who suffer from an eating disorder fear "not being in control." They may have suffered painful experiences in childhood, which they could not control or stop. They mistakenly believe that by denying themselves food or getting rid of food, they are in control of their circumstances and can avoid the very things they fear, such as pain, disapproval, criticism, abandonment, etc. They do not believe that another being, whether a person or God, will see more in them than what they see in themselves. As a result, this false sense of control is substituted for meaningful and loving relationships. Experiencing vulnerability and trust in a safe relationship is a beginning step in changing this pattern.

2. Eating disorders are a false form of communication about pain and suffering.

Those with eating disorders are often unwilling or feel unable to be direct and honest with God or others about their pain, suffering, and feelings of unacceptability. Instead of sharing how lonely, inadequate, or empty they feel, they express to God and others what a bad person they are or how undeserving they are of love and acceptance. Part of spiritual healing comes out of directness and honesty in relationships with other people and with God.

3. An eating disorder can give a false sense of being unworthy.

Those suffering often feel that there is something wrong with them, that "other people deserve kindness and love but I don't." They have usually stopped praying because they feel that they are unforgivable, unacceptable, or undeserving of a relationship with God. They feel too unworthy to ever be forgiven. Healing can start when a person is willing to be no better or no worse than any other person and is willing to share their similarities with others.

4. An eating disorder can be false evidence against self.

A person with an eating disorder can use the eating disorder as her evidence that she is bad, unacceptable, and deserving of punishment. Whenever she feels happy, hopeful, or peaceful, she may chase these positive feelings away with a long list of personal negatives. The truth is that the eating disorder is not who they are. As they begin to separate who they are from what they do, they can begin to give up this painful attack against themselves.

5. An eating disorder can be a false pursuit of perfection.

Those with eating disorders have been deceived into thinking that if they obtain perfection in their bodies, in self-control over their bodies, or in body image, that somehow this perfection will make up for other perceived inadequacies and failures. Women with eating disorders often talk about the need to be perfect "for everyone else," but this is really a false perfection. Seeking perfection becomes a substitute for love because they assume that if they can do something very well, people will love them. Instead of understanding that self-improvement is an ongoing and unfolding process, they become perfectionistic and adopt an "all or nothing" approach, often leaving God out of their self-improvement pursuits. In order to change this pursuit for perfection, they can begin to learn that it is okay to make mistakes, and that by learning from those mistakes, they can make improvements in their lives.

6. An eating disorder can be a false form of comfort and safety.

For many, eating disorders relieve anxiety and help them avoid painful emotions. This false sense of security is a temporary absence of pain rather than a true form of comfort. Almost before finishing one binge-and-purge episode, they begin to plan another. In this false sense of comfort, relief, and safety, the eating disorder becomes their refuge from the storm, often instead of God. Seeking divine help again is important in finding real comfort and peace.

7. An eating disorder can give a false identity and perception of self.

Those with eating disorders can lose their sense of self and become frightened at the thought of giving up the eating disorder. They ask, "What will I be without it? This is me. This is my life." Anyone who focuses the majority of their mind, body, and soul on the demands of an eating disorder soon has little room for anything else. Understanding that God and others can accept you with your strengths, weaknesses, "pluses and minuses," is a spiritual experience that can help in the recovery process.

8. An eating disorder can be false compensation for the past.

Sometimes an eating disorder is an attempt to make up for past childhood abuse or trauma, family problems, or personal mistakes. Women sometimes can punish themselves in an attempt to resolve the guilt of the past. In the eating disorder, they often overlook God as a source of the comfort, inspiration, and guidance that they need. Letting go of the past is a spiritual process in which they can give to God what they cannot correct from the past and ask for help to do things differently in the present and future.

9. An eating disorder can be a false attempt to avoid personal responsibility for life.

An eating disorder can become a sufferer's excuse for everything that is missing in their life. Blaming life's troubles, relationship problems, feelings of inadequacy, and inability to function in life on their eating disorder dismisses them from being accountable for their life, as if it is beyond their control. It is painful to be that frightened of life ahead. Taking responsibility is very different from blame, judgment, or fault. It is an acceptance of the fact that, "I have learned it, I have choices about it, it is mine to change, and I have the ability to change."

10. An eating disorder can be a false pursuit of approval.

Many people with eating disorders have substituted approval for true acceptance and love. Gaining approval from others becomes their primary purpose in life. The problem is that approval does not last. Seeking the temporary approval of other people rather than the more healing acceptance that comes from God leaves a person feeling empty and starved emotionally. God's approval can bring peace, comfort, and hope rather than worry, anxiety, and pressure to please others; real love can greatly diminish one's need for approval from others.

How an Eating Disorder Can Harm One's Spiritual Life

"The eating disorder consumed every aspect of my life. My life was centered entirely around food and weight. I felt unworthy and undeserving of having a relationship with God. I hated myself and did not think it was possible for anybody, including God, to love me. I did not feel that I was good enough to merit a relationship with God." (20-year-old woman)

* * * * *

"My eating disorder destroyed my relationship with God. It blocked me from him and I lost all faith and trust in God. I became very angry with him because I felt like he had abandoned me. Eventually I just stopped thinking about him. My eating disorder became my God, and my body became the Devil." (25-year-old woman)

How Prayer and Spirituality Can Help in Healing

"I believe that God answered my prayers and my family's prayers for making a way for me to get better. He helped me feel loved and not alone in my most difficult days away from home. He gives me answers and instructions that help me, makes me hopeful in the scriptures, and I know that he is there to support me and help me recover." (18-year-old-woman)

* * * * *

"I believe spirituality is a pivotal aspect of recovery. I don't think it is possible to get through this without having faith in God or a higher power. When I am in my eating disorder, I feel alone and tend to isolate myself from the world. I feel lonely and disconnected. It is easy to give up on life if you don't have a belief that there is something greater than yourself to live for." (19-year-old-woman)

* * * * *

"It is only through the grace of God that I was able to pull through my eating disorder. Because of his unconditional love and the Atonement, I am able to be whole once again. Never in my life have I felt so much peace and comfort. I rely in him in all I do. Praying for strength daily, I am able to win this battle." (28-year-old woman)

* * * * *

"Once I came to the realization that the only way I was going to recover was through God, a huge weight was lifted off my shoulders. I was humbled in his presence. I pray every time I feel anxious, depressed, or not myself. I ask him to help me to work things out and to listen to what is going on around me. Once I put my recovery in God's hands, things started to fall into place." (19-year-old woman)

Prepared by Center for Change (www.centerforchange.com)